A VIOLENT LIFE

CONTENTS

PIER PAOLO PASOLINI

A Violent Life

TRANSLATED FROM THE ITALIAN
BY WILLIAM WEAVER

CARCANET

First published in Italy with the title
Una Vita Violenta
by Aldo Garzanti Editore in 1959

This translation first published in Great Britain
in 1968 by Jonathan Cape Limited
and reprinted by Carcanet Press in 1985 and in paperback in 1996

This edition published in 2007 by
Carcanet Press Limited
Alliance House
Cross Street
Manchester M2 7AQ

A CIP catalogue record for this book is available from the British Library
ISBN 978 1 85754 963 8

The publisher acknowledges financial assistance from Arts Council England

Printed and bound in England by SRP Ltd, Exeter

To
Carlo Bo and Giuseppe Ungaretti,
my witnesses in the trial of
RAGAZZI DI VITA

NOTE

References to individuals, events and real places described in this book are the fruit of invention. At the same time, I would like to make it quite clear to the reader that everything he reads in this novel really happened, substantially, and continues really to happen.

I thank the 'ragazzi di vita' who, directly or indirectly, helped me write this book, and especially, with true gratitude, Sergio Citti.

PART ONE

1

Who Tommaso Was

Tommaso, Lello, Zucabbo, and the other boys who lived in the little shanty-village in Via dei Monti di Pietralata, were, as usual after lunch, in front of the school at least half an hour early.

But some other little snotnoses from the neighbourhood were already there, playing with a penknife in the mud. Tommaso, Lello and their bunch crouched around the players to watch, satchels dragging on the ground. Two or three more boys showed up, with a ball, and they all threw their books on a mound and ran behind the school, to the open lot that counted as the main square of the slum.

Lello and another kid who lived near by, in Block B, tossed up to divide the teams. Tommasino didn't feel like playing; he squatted down on the ground with a couple of others, to watch the game.

'Hey, Carletto, has the teacher come?' he asked a squirt sitting beside him.

'How should I know?' the kid answered, with a shrug.

'Who's staying in today, to clean up?' Tommasino asked, after a while. He'd been at home the last few days, with a fever.

'Lello, I think,' Carletto said.

'Aòh, how about a drag?' He turned abruptly, angrily, to another kid who was sitting on a stone, smoking.

Tommasino stood up and went towards the goal, on the other side of the field. Lello, legs apart, arms outstretched, was bent over, his face grim, all intent on the game, ready to make a dash for the ball.

'Hey, Lello!' Tommasino called.

'Whaddya want? Fuckoff,' Lello said, not even looking at him.

'You doing the cleaning up today, after school?'

'That's right,' Lello answered curtly.

Tommasino sat down near a little pile of stones that served as a goalpost. After a while Lello looked round at him.

'Getcha ass outta the way ... Whaddya want anyway?' he said, turning back at once and staring at the centre of the field, where the others were chasing the ball, with a steady stream of curses. Tommasino shut up: calmly, keeping his legs crossed over the dried mud, he took a butt from his pocket and lit it.

Lello soon gave him another glance and saw he was smoking. With one eye still on the field, he was quiet for a while, then, in a lower, hoarse voice, he said: 'Tomà, how about a smoke?'

Tommaso took another couple of drags quickly, then stood up to give the cigarette to Lello, who accepted it without losing track of the ball. He began to smoke, narrowing his eyes, still prepared to hurl himself into the game.

Tommaso stood there, his hands in the pockets of his shorts, which were held up by a length of string. They were so big they looked like a skirt.

Just then the kids in the game rushed the goal in a bunch, and a boy on the other team, exhausted, managed to give the ball a kick. It rolled gently towards the pile of stones. Lello made a big dive, though it wasn't necessary: he could have caught the ball just by bending down a bit. Then he flung it back into the centre of the field. He picked up the butt he had dropped and took a few drags, pleased with himself.

'Terrific, Lello,' Tommaso said, knowingly.

Lello made no reply, but you could tell he was feeling big, smoking with a smart look on his face.

'Aòh, Lè, how about asking the teacher to let me help clean up today?' Tommaso asked after a moment, trying to seem casual about it.

'We'll see,' Lello conceded, now following the game with less passion, almost fed up with it. Tommasino sat down near him again, but not for long: a minute or two later the boys back near the school began to yell and wave. The teacher had arrived: it was time to go inside. The players gave the ball a few more kicks, then ran off, pushing and fighting, as they collected their books from the pile. They went through the broken gate into the little courtyard of the school.

By two, or two thirty, life stopped again in Pietralata. All you could see were bunches of little kids outside the blocks of houses, maybe a woman or two working. Nothing but sun and garbage, garbage and sun. But it was only March, and the sun set early, over there, behind Rome. The air turned dark, almost icy. When the boys came out of school again, the sun had begun to go down. The slum was still deserted, because the working men came home later, the movie-house had just opened its doors, and the two or three bars hadn't yet filled up with the usual bums.

The kids came running from the school and scattered over the dirty yards, all through the neighbourhood: walls of cheap housing, a row of lines for washing like so many gallows, a few washtubs with two feet of black mud around them, and maybe a little more light than inside the school.

Lello had stayed behind with the teacher because it was his turn to clean up: his turn came several times in a week because the teacher picked a boy at random, neither as punishment nor reward. In any case the work never took more than half an hour, a couple of swipes with the broom among the desks, dusting the teacher's desk a bit and the pictures. Lello got it over with fast because he was used to it by now; when he had finished, he ran off alone, towards his house.

He was a little scared, going through the fields now in darkness or almost. He ran the whole way, hair flapping in his eyes, black and shiny as two mussels, his American T-shirt, printed with a flower-pattern, flapping over his pants. The peasants had stopped working in the fields, and Via delle Messi d'oro, its cherry trees and almonds just budding, was deserted. From beyond the farmhouses you could hear some older boys singing, imitating Claudio Villa, and still far-ther on, the bugles at the Fort were giving the soldiers the signal to go out on their five-hour passes for the evening.

There, under the pier of the aqueduct bridge, was Tommasino.

He still hadn't gone home and was waiting, his satchel hanging over
his shoulder.

'Tomà. What's up?' Lello asked, walking past him and climbing
up the iron ladder of the pier.

Tommasino followed him up the ladder without saying anything, his little round, freckled face looking greasy as usual.

Lello went off along the bridge, a chief, not even turning to look
at the slave trotting after him.

'You in a hurry, Lello?' Tommaso said, behind him, a sly look on
his face, 'fa crissake!'

Lello was already busy climbing down the pier on the other side.
He jumped into the clover field and began to run along the path,
among the canes. Tommaso, worn out, ran after him, panting.

'Wait for me, goddammit!' he yelled.

But Lello, not giving him a thought, kept on running, and it was
only when he had left Tommaso well behind that he slowed down,
playing among the canes and the willow-shoots as he walked. When
Tommaso was at his heels again, he started racing down the sloping
fields, then up again, among the rows of broccoli, already showing,
with a tree here and there.

He left Tommaso behind once more, but when he reached the
level ground at the top of the hill, he slowed again to a walk. This
time he chose to let Tommasino overtake him. The kid was sweating like a running tap. Together, they went down over the little
mounds to the cluster of hovels below, where they lived, on the
road between Pietralata and Montesacro, just before the place
where the sewage from the City Hospital empties into the Aniene
river.

In the shanty village some lights had already been turned on,
reflected in the mud. The other kids were playing outside their doors
while inside, in those one-room houses where families of ten or
eleven lived, you could hear women yelling and arguing or babies
crying.

When they saw Lello and Tommasino, their friends stopped playing and came over to them.

'You eaten yet?' Zucabbo asked, flushed and dishevelled.

'Eaten, my ass,' Lello shouted at him.

'Fuckoff,' Tommasino added solemnly. 'We just got home from school. You blind or something?'

'Aòh, hurry it up,' Zucabbo said, not taking offence, 'we're going.'

'Go ahead,' Tommasino said, nasty. 'You think we don't know the way? You're not going to carry us, are you? What a dope!'

'Listen, you can go screw yourself ... ' Zucabbo said, angry all of a sudden. 'If you want to snap it up, okay. If not, we're leaving you behind.' And he struck his left hand three or four times against his right palm, pointed in the direction of Montesacro.

Lello meanwhile had run inside his shanty; less than a minute later he was outside again with two slabs of bread filled with roast peppers in his hand. He nodded towards the others and said 'Let's go', his mouth stuffed.

Seeing Lello, Tommasino had also run into his house. But his mother hadn't fixed supper yet. He could have cried with rage, but he didn't waste time complaining. He came straight out and, his stomach empty, set off after the others, already on their way.

The road to Montesacro, its asphalt reduced to a slab or two in a bed of dusty rubble strewn with filth and garbage, followed the Aniene.

The river flowed past the stinking slopes, especially smelly at the emptying-point of the hospital sewer. On the far side there were more embankments, where you could see blocks of flats, little houses, some construction sites, and more villages of hovels. Beyond the Aniene, fields stretched away towards the Tivoli hills, indistinct in the cold air.

After a few curves, the buildings, some finished, some not, became more crowded together; they rose up everywhere, against the sky on little hills, or down below in the valleys, amid the remnants of gardens, cultivated fields, along the rivulet of the Aniene.

Beyond that circle of excavations and scaffoldings, the rough, narrow road turned into the Via Nomentana, just above the Battery, a little before the new bridge. Below, at the crossroads, there was a flat space full of pine trees with some carousels: a little

amusement park. A few people were strolling about, especially
in the vicinity of the table-football games.

'How about a game, Lè?' Zucabbo shouted, when they were near
this tent, crammed with little snotnosed kids.

Lello nodded and hurried towards the tables, but they were all
engaged.

Two against two, some kids slammed at the ball, legs wide, sweating, flushed, while others, the spectators, leaned against the fence
with a bored, sarcastic attitude. They had turned up the collars of
their jackets, standing there chilled, hands in their pockets, because
the March cold, after sunset, was no joke.

Tommaso and his pals plunged into the already thick crowd of
impatient customers waiting for a table to become free. And, meanwhile, to keep in fighting trim, they were all yelling, smartass:
'Keep it up, Ace!' 'That's showing them, Trigger!!', shouting more
out of boredom than anything else, their mouths working from
habit.

Some of them, like Tommaso and his crowd, were poor kids
who lived in the shacks along the Aniene; but most of them were
boys of good family, students, who lived in Montesacro or in the
new buildings on the Nomentana Battery. When four players left
one of the tables, Lello, Tommasino, Zucabbo, Sergio, and Carletto
grabbed it by main force, pressing their dirty bellies against the edge
of the table, ignoring the protests of the four or five characters who
had been waiting.

'It's our turn, we've been here an hour!' one student protested
loudly, sticking his chest out. The four from Little Shanghai didn't
deign to glance at him, their sly eyes on the manager, a poor bastard
like themselves, thin as a sardine, who stretched out his hand, took
their money without a word, and collected the little balls from the
drawer.

Only Tommasino, with a world-weary manner, said to the
student: 'Clear out', as he prepared to play.

But the other four, as if by silent agreement, had already grabbed
the handles, Lello and Carletto playing against Zucabbo and Sergio.
Tommasino moved forward, his little belly also pressed against a

corner of the table, his angry eyes glistening among the freckles on his greasy face. 'Hey,' he said blackly, menacingly, towards the others, 'What about me?'

'Fuckoff,' Lello said, curt and annoyed.

'No, no, we gotta take turns,' Tommaso said, with deep conviction.

'Get your ass away from the table!' Zucabbo gave him a shove, pushing him from the edge of the table.

'Some friends!' Tommaso shouted, disgusted, filled with anger and tears, wanting to start a fight then and there. But the others were already playing, not looking at him.

He stood off to one side, grim, muttering to himself, his throat tight with rage. 'Lousy bastards. Shits. Whodda they think they are?' Then little by little his rage subsided; he watched the game with a glum, critical eye, charged with contempt.

'Where did you guys learn to play?' he shouted, sarcastic, when one of them missed.

The others paid no attention, didn't even hear him; they flicked the handles so hard they almost split the ball.

'Look at him! What a dog!' Tommasino shouted, when Carletto missed. 'He ought to be on the Lazio team!' And he burst out laughing, his mouth wide, loud enough for everybody standing round to hear him.

'Haw, haw, haw,' he laughed, pressing his stomach with his hands thrust into the pockets of his shorts, writhing like a cockroach that's been stamped on.

'You guys make me throw up ... ' he said when he had calmed down a bit, with a grimace of even greater disgust.

'I'm leaving. What's the use staying here to watch these punks!' Again laughing loudly, to irritate the others, he left the tent and started wandering among the attractions of the park.

There were a few people in the illuminated grounds, some older boys with motorbikes, a bunch of soldiers, and even more sailors. They walked in little groups, assuming an idle, menacing air, humming or trying to pick up the girls behind the counters of the shooting-galleries. Tommasino imitated them, strolling among the pines, stopping to watch the Dodgems, almost all empty, and the little airplanes with two or three customers riding around in them, huddled in the seats, white-faced with cold.

In this way, gradually, he came to the end of the pine grove, just under the Aniene bridge, where the embankment began, covered with streams of refuse.

There he began to observe the situation. At the corner of the bridge, above him, under a kind of white column like a tombstone, two whores were standing, crossly, one in a red topcoat, the other, testy and rumpled, wearing a black sweater. Both were squat, with bellies that made them look pregnant, short, fat legs, black, hairy faces, low foreheads like monkeys. They were swinging their purses.

They stood motionless up there, or else they took a few steps back and forth. Meanwhile four or five sailors, at a loose end, were climbing up among the trees from the amusement park. They struggled up the little path of the embankment and approached the two whores on the bridge. They parleyed for a while, the girls answering back, bad as a couple of bum cheques, and the sailors enjoyed themselves, watching the girls get mad and pretend they didn't need the men's money.

In the end they made a deal and started to climb back down the slope, the whores and two of the sailors. The others stayed up on the bridge, smoking, waiting their turn. The sailors had already reached the clearing when the whores had taken only a few steps: they were coming down on all fours, peering below them with outraged expressions, placing first one foot, then the other on the slippery, steep embankment, their feet slipping out of their shoes. Finally the girls also reached the bottom and, clutching their purses tightly, they passed Tommasino with the two sailors, heading for the next slope which, thick with bushes, went down to the Aniene.

When they had disappeared into the darkness, Tommasino went after them to see whether they were staying there in the bushes, in the rubbish and used condoms and dirty paper, or whether they were heading for the little cave, still filthier, under the old bridge.

After following them and discovering they were going to the cave, he ran back, whistling and snickering loudly for his own bene-

fit, slipping between the carousel and the Dodgems until he was in
the lighted area in the centre of the park. But he couldn't find his
friends, not in the table-football tent or anywhere around. 'Fuckemall!' he thought angrily. And he began to go back down again
quietly, alone, towards the bushes by the Aniene, stopping every
now and then. As he was walking along slowly, he ran into Lello,
leaning against the railing of the Dodgems, watching the only two
cars moving around, each with a pair of sailors in it.

Pleased with himself, Tommasino tiptoed up behind him and
covered Lello's eyes with his hands. Lello was pissed off and gave
him a shove backwards that sent him rolling on the ground. Tommasino burst out laughing. But Lello, still in a fury, looked at him
and grumbled: 'Go fuck yourself.'

'Hey,' Tommasino said, 'there're some whores around — did
you know that?' He was silent for a moment, then added: 'How
about going to watch, eh, Lè?'

Lello shrugged. Tommasino suddenly forced another laugh. 'I'm
going,' he said, rubbing his belly against the railing and stretching.
'They're with some sailors,' he added, his eyes shining. He balanced
himself with his hands on the railing, body tilting forward, tugging
at the bar now and then.

All at once he let go, leaping back on the ground, and started off
towards the river, glancing at Lello and nodding at him to come
too.

When he had gone maybe ten or twelve yards, there under the
last pines, Lello ran and caught up with him. All excited, but with a
serious expression, Tommasino led the way towards the first
withered bushes, and they plunged down among the little paths
along the slope, scattered with scraps of paper and filth. They wandered about for a while, then came to the foot of the little cave. The
two whores and the sailors had stayed just inside the entrance because there was at least six inches of shit inside, and in the dim moonlight that penetrated down there, you could see them standing, the
whores against the slimy wall, the two sailors over them, like two
lizards hit on the back with a stone.

Tommasino and Lello sat down behind a big bush, watching the

two couples through the tattered branches. Tommasino sat sideways, his legs outstretched on the few blades of dirty grass.

'Go ahead, Lè,' he said after a while, looking at the other boy, as
if he couldn't stand it any longer. Lello, on his knees, started doing
the same. 'Sure, you really don't feel like it, eh?' Tommasino said
slyly.

'Don't feel like it?' Lello said, 'Why not?'

'Didn't you do it in school today?'

'Fuck you,' Lello said, annoyed, 'I've had about enough out of
you.'

'Come on. You did it, all right,' Tommasino insisted, stubbornly
trying to joke about it.

'You wouldn't want any of that, would you?' Lello said.

Tommasino rolled on the ground, choking with laughter. 'Why
should I give a shit?' he said, so loud that the two couples in the cave
looked around, alarmed. Then he calmed down and went back to
work, beside Lello, who was all hunched over, his forelock dancing
over his eyes. 'All the same,' Tommasino said after a while, 'I'd like
to try it once.' He said this in a tone of indifference, as if he wanted
to gratify a whim, an insignificant trifle. 'If I give you a hundred
lire tomorrow,' he added, 'will you let me take your place?'

'What can I do with a hundred?' Lello said scornfully.

'I'll make it two hundred,' Tommasino said, 'okay?'

*

The next morning Tommasino got up at six, when it was still
dark; it was raining a little, with an occasional gust of wind. The
sun came out and it cleared up, then rained some more, then the sun
reappeared.

By noon Pietralata was soaked through, glistening. On the old,
dried mud of the central lot there was a thin crust of new mud,
chocolate, where the little kids rolled like piglets, playing ball.

In one hand Tommasino was carrying the empty sack which had
contained old iron; the other hand was in his pocket, where he had
crumpled the two hundred-lire notes earned collecting scraps of

metal from the rubbish piles along the enbankments of the Via
Tiburtina.

'Hey, kid,' he shouted to one of them, mouth wide, legs apart,
'I'll play too — how about it?'

'No, you won't,' the kids all yelled, 'we're even!'

'Screw you all,' Tommaso shouted, 'What difference does that
make? You think you're the National squad?'

'Fuck off and leave us alone,' shouted one of the snotnoses, with
a voice like a broken gramophone.

Tommaso's only reply was to move with slow, dragging steps
towards the goal, where he threw his sack on one of the two piles of
stones and moved into the field, among the bunch of kids.

One of them, a kid who looked like an apple, rushed at him, half-
crying, yelling as if his gullet would burst: 'Are you gonna fuck off
or not? Goddammit!'

But at that moment the ball came in their direction and Tommaso gave the kid a shove, knocking him on his ass in the mud.
Laughing, red-faced, he ran after the ball with those little legs of
his that looked like a spaniel's.

'Here comes the big star!' an older kid yelled then, his hands
funnelled at his mouth. He was lounging with two or three pals at
the edge of the little field, sprawled in a bit of shadow against the
crumbling wall of a garden full of dirty paper and pieces of old
urinals.

Tommasino pretended he hadn't heard that crack.

'Hey, Stinkfeet!' the same kid shouted, standing up and calling
Tommaso by the nickname of his elder brother, another freckle-
faced redhead, who always stank like a sewer. 'You think you're
somebody, eh?'

Tommasino kept on running, throwing his legs here and there on
the mud, a pair of boats on his feet, tied with cord and string, still not
giving a thought to this other guy who was about to confront him.

The other character was beginning to enjoy himself. He stood up,
his face bold, a blissful smile creeping into his narrow eyes, staring
forward, absorbed in his pleasure, in profound spiritual ecstasy.
He thrust his hands into the pockets of his pants that hung on him so

loosely you could see his bellybutton below his T-shirt. He came
closer to the edge of the field, wetting his lips with his tongue.

'Hey, Stinkfeet,' he started in again. 'You better keep your legs
spread. You're dripping like a duck, Cancha see that?'

This time Tommasino, running and sweating, with an inch of
tomato sauce on his face, turned and laughed, watery-eyed, a little
wrinkle cutting his forehead in two: 'Cut it out, Zimmì,' he yelled.
'Look at me! I'm just like Pandolfini!' And he hurled himself after
the ball, head down, into the tangle of kids.

'Go ahead and yell,' the other guy answered, grumbling, his face
more and more lit up by his own idea of himself. 'Enjoy yourself.
This is your big day.' Then he added, in an aside: 'Take a look at
him,' inspired, 'looks like an ad for piss.'

'Fuck you,' Tommaso shouted, more resentful now, his big head
floating above the bunch of chickens running after the ball. His eyes
were almost crying, his flat mouth stretched in a venomous smile,
revealing a row of little brown teeth.

The first wiseguy was now joined by another. He was a big
bastard, maybe twenty-five or more, with curly hair over his neck
and a flashy scarf, a yellow face like a hungry fox. The two of them
stood side by side, on a level with the goal.

Their foreheads were thrust forward; so were their mouths, their
forelocks, the crutch of their pants. Their hands were in their pockets.
'Jesus,' shouted the one old enough to be a father, looking like a kid
trying to act smart for the first time. 'You even have the nerve to
talk? With ten years of activity behind you?'

'Yeah, ten years!' Tommaso shouted mockingly, his little face
stung with rage, 'I'm not even thirteen yet!'

'So what?' Zimmìo said, fierce, but as if he were saying something
big, and therefore allowing himself to laugh, 'you were taking it
already when you were ten, weren't you, down at Little Shanghai?
A member of the Stinkfeet tribe?'

'Bring me your sister!' Tommaso yelled, smartass, his voice
coming out of his nose.

The older guy became benevolent, hypocritically sharpening his
big nose and his chin against his scarf. 'You hear that, Zimmì?' He

said: 'We'll have to watch out for this little bastard. I tell you: starting tomorrow I'm locking my sister in the house. I'll buy her some iron pants, all right!'

'What?' yelled Zimmìo, in a suddenly caressing tone, 'Then they were lying when they told me it was your Ma who taught you how to blow a whistle?'

'You leave my Ma out of this,' Tommaso blurted, taking a couple of steps towards the pair, 'bastard!'

'Gonna beat us up, eh?' the younger one said, with a look that would have made a Chinaman mad. 'Who're you? Tinea the bandit?'

But at that point another band of wiseguys was passing in the distance. 'Hey, Shitter,' one of these yelled at the older one, in a voice that could barely be heard, 'whaddya wasting your time there for? Come over here with the grown-ups!'

'What?!' Shitter yelled gaily, 'Can't you see we're operating?'

'You going into Rome?' Zimmìo shouted, promptly forgetting about little Stinkfeet.

'We're going to collect some cash!' one of the distant group shouted.

'How about us going too, Shitter?' Zimmìo said to his friend.

'Okay, let's go,' he answered.

'Hey, wait for us!' Zimmìo yelled at the gang that was drifting off among the blocks of houses.

'We're the Terror of Pietralata!' one of them shouted happily. 'You said it!' another yelled, 'the Californians!'

'The bus! The bus!' said Zimmìo, who with Shitter following him had started after the others, with the walk of a man born tired. Now he began to run like a cripple, the other guy at his heels, towards the stop of the Number 211, arriving from Montesacro loaded with poor bastards and soldiers from the Fort. The others also ran, whistling, a pack of jackals.

Here and there, hoarsely, the noon sirens blew.

Tommasino, already covered with sweat, was racing around the field among the little kids who came up to his chin, all red and tattered. Heads lowered, tongues hanging out, their hair — uncut for at least a year—in their eyes, they flung themselves on the ball, all of them on the defensive, or all attacking at once.

Tommasino moved above those dirt-encrusted heads, the ball always between his feet, or almost always; the more he kept it, the more he was determined to hang on to it, dribbling, kicking the other kids in the shins. Sometimes he even pulled the little snotnoses off him, grabbing them by their rags. They got mad and howled, but Tommasino ignored them. He went on playing dirty, snickering loud, pleased with himself both because of his successful business deal that morning and because of his fancy playing. 'I'm a big shot around here!' he shouted, opened wide his little, lipless mouth with its brown, chipped teeth.

Finally one kid, small as an unweaned puppy, faced him and yelled at him: 'Hey, shithead!' Tommaso broke off his running and forgot about the ball. He pulled down his lips, nauseated, his face even redder, and said to the snotnose: 'What did you say?'

The kid, wrapped in a pair of pants without a button, a shirt that had more holes than a colander, stood fast where he was, swelling his chest out, his eyes hooded.

'Fuckoff,' he muttered, loud enough, 'shithead.'

'You go fuck yourself—you hear me?' Tommasino said, menacing, the veins in his neck taut, as he moved in. Maybe if he had said no more the kid would have taken it and would have run off after the ball, but Tommasino repeated: 'You hear me?' and flicked the kid's nose with his finger.

The kid turned bright red, his face swelling as if somebody behind him were blowing him up with a pump: 'Bastard, cocksucker, who let you in here? Fuckoff, goddamm you!'

White-faced, without a word, Tommaso gave him a slap that made his head spin. Then he said, his eyes owl-like: 'Watch out, or I'll give you another that'll snap your head right off!'

It took the kid a minute to realize what had hit him, that his head was suddenly facing the other way. Once he caught on, he started screaming his guts out.

He cried, standing still, his body thrust forward, his mouth open scattering tears all around like crumbs.

Tommasino, infuriated at the kid's loud crying, put a finger to his nose grimly and shouted: 'If you don't cut that out, I'll give you the rest of what's coming to you.' And since the kid didn't stop, in a fit of anger, Tommasino gave him another couple of slaps and, as an extra touch, a push that knocked him down. And when the kid was on the ground, his little body stretched out in the mud and his legs in the air, Tommaso added a couple of kicks in the ribs.

The kid, rolling in the mud, started yelling as if they were cutting his gut open. Then he stood up and, without looking around, ran straight off home.

'Now he's gonna get his brother. You're in the shit,' said another snotnose who had hypocritically looked on, like the others. Tommasino, with his smartass walk, muttering further threats in an important tone, went towards the goal, collected his sack and, pretending he wasn't in the slightest hurry, cut across the field towards the bus stop.

His eyes still glassy with righteous wrath, he cast indignant, offended glances in every direction, peering also, however, in the direction of the kid's filthy house, to see if by any chance the big brother was coming out. Once out of danger, at Sora Anita's stand, he even started singing, wearily, as he walked along, giving an occasional owl-eyed look behind him, as if to say: 'Watch out, or you've had it!' Or to say: 'I'm a big shot, all right. Compared to me, Pandolfini's a punk.' While his wide mouth, through the rows of brown teeth, was singing: 'What apples, what apples ... ', croaking among the sparse cherry trees of the dirty little gardens along the Aniene.

*

A thick cloudbank meanwhile had spread over the sky, beginning beyond the river, from the houses of Montesacro, in the far distance. It blacked out all the light that had earlier filled the sky, still damp with rain, now reflected in the stinking fields.

Tommasino, who hadn't heard the sirens blow a little while before, thought it was late, that dusk was falling.

He began to run, mud spattering from his shoes, already caked with it, down the little paths, half-buried among the gardens and the slopes. He passed the aqueduct bridge, trotted over the hillocks, muddy and green, until he reached Little Shanghai. 'They've probably left already, the bastards!' he was thinking angrily, going down among the hovels, across the little, water-soaked lot in the middle of them.

He went straight to Lello's house. Nobody was home, except the old mangy black dog, too weak to bark, starved as he was, barely able to stand up, look around, and move from the rickety door, made of planks so rotten they stank, to a little mouldy wall where he lay down in the mud, mixed with piss and remains of soup.

'Shit,' Tommaso said, grim. He swerved and went towards his own house, a little farther up.

'Hey, Ma,' he said, entering and dropping the sack, 'are we ready to eat?'

But the pot on the little stove hadn't started boiling. His mother was in the next room: room, that is, after a manner of speaking, because the shanty was all one, divided only by a grey, rotting curtain and a cardboard partition over an armature of bits of planks of every description, nailed together haphazardly.

Tommasino knelt down and looked under a box which, with a battered little dresser, the stove and two chairs, comprised all the room's furniture, barely able to fit into it at that. From this box he took out some ragged comic books and started reading.

The other two kids were also home, Tito and Toto, Tommaso's two younger brothers, who had been staring at him in silence from the moment he came in.

Seeing him reading, one of them crawled over on all fours and looked up at him, staring, with his little swollen face where the snot, dripping, had divided the dirt into patches, greyish in the centre, black at the edges. His eyes, pale blue, almost white, looked blind under his curls, also plastered with dust and snot.

Staring up, on all fours, he began a kind of grumbling, a sound that came from his stomach, barely passing through his gullet. He was laughing. Seeing that Tommasino paid no attention, he moved a bit closer and put his head on his brother's knee, his chin on his thigh. Annoyed, Tommaso brought his knee up sharply, and his brother did a somersault on the floor, banging his head against the dresser.

He was about to cry, belly in the air, as he lay, but at that moment his attention was attracted by a little hunk of bread he had dropped behind the dresser that morning. Rolling over on his belly, after two or three tries, he managed to snatch the piece of bread and began to suck on it again.

The other kid, Toto, meanwhile had been playing with the bowl of water placed in the centre of the room to collect the drops of rain that filtered through the ceiling—two or three pieces of tarred canvas—then he started hopping here and there, God knows why, the way a dog does when he sees a fly buzzing round his nose.

When lunch was ready, Tommasino ate a few spoonfuls of soup in a hurry, took his bread with some greens in it, and went outside again, chewing.

Zucabbo and Sergetto were playing with a penknife on the drier end of the lot.

'You seen Lello, Sergè?' Tommaso asked, as polite as he was capable of being.

'No,' Sergetto answered curtly, not even looking at him. Zucabbo missed at that moment, and Sergetto fell on the knife.

'I'm going off to school,' Tommaso shouted, smartass again.

'Go ahead,' Zucabbo muttered, 'what the fuck's holding you up?'

Tommaso started singing in a forced voice, clutching the two hundred-lire notes in his pocket, as he walked all the way back to Pietralata.

Lello's mother was Sora Anita, the woman who sold peanuts and candy by the bus stop. Tommasino arrived there and went up to her.

'You seen Lello, Signora?' he asked her.

'He went into Rome to buy some liquorice for me; he should be back any minute,' she said.

Tommasino then squatted near the stand, at Sora Anita's feet, on a scrap of pavement. It seemed evening already, and was cold. In that chill, dark air, against Pietralata, the stand seemed even smaller, on its tripod, with a kind of tarpaulin over it for when it rained.

There were lots of boxes of mouldy, eroded cardboard, and Tommaso gave them a look, gulping: in one, a handful of sweets; in another, roasted seeds; in another, some dirty sticks of liquorice; in a little sack hanging from one corner, a few lupins. Sora Anita sat on a little chair, guarding her merchandise, crossly, so fat she couldn't close her legs.

Maybe half an hour later Lello came along with a package of suckers. He argued a moment with his mother, handed over her change, and had a fight because he tried to keep fifty lire for himself. He won. Not looking at Tommasino, as he hadn't looked at him on arriving, he went off.

Tommasino stood up, with a bored manner, stretching slightly, then overtook Lello.

'Lello,' he said. Lello half turned, a mean look on his Arab's face, his flowered American shirt flapping over his narrow hips and torn shorts.

'Whaddya want?' he said.

'Like we said ... ' Tommaso reminded him, slyly.

Lello pressed his fingertips together and waved them, in a suspicious and interrogatory gesture, before Tommaso's eyes.

'I've got the two hundred,' Tommaso said, allusive.

'Aaaah,' Lello remembered and opened his fingers, to scratch himself carefully and pensively, inside his pants.

'Here,' Tommaso said, holding out the cash.

Lello didn't accept it at once. He raised his hand half-way and looked, bitter and contemptuous, at the two bills Tommaso was giving him.

'Two hundred?' he said, disgusted, pissed off. 'What can I do with two hundred?'

'Crissake,' Tommasino said, 'Whaddya mean? That's what we said.'

'Well,' Lello said, 'I can't help it. If you cough up some more, okay; if not, the deal's off.'

He looked Tommasino in the eye, profoundly, for a moment, rubbing thumb and forefinger together; then he began walking away again, towards the school.

'All I've got's another fifty,' Tommasino said. 'Let me have a
smoke at least, okay?'

Lello was silent. Tommasino turned black, then dug out the other
fifty and held it towards Lello: 'Here, goddamm you,' he said.

Lello quickly grabbed the two hundred and fifty, slipping the
money into his pocket and narrowing his eyes, bored, hiding his
satisfaction.

It was almost time to go to school now: a bit of sunshine had
come out, making Pietralata's mud gleam; the kids were scattered
here and there, waiting. Then the bell rang and they all went inside,
pushing one another, shouting. The slum was half-deserted, silent,
under the sun.

When school was over and they all came out again, making even
more racket than when they went in, Tommaso remained alone in
the classroom on the ground floor.

Dozens of little bastards, since the day the slum had been founded,
had carved their names and their friends' on the desk, with *viva* or
abbasso in front of them, and a lot of other words, too; there wasn't
a square inch of smooth wood left.

Tommasino, holding a rag, had started dusting those desks,
slowly; in five minutes he had done no more than two of them,
pushing the rag back and forth at random, stopping to rub at that
mass of holes and gaps filled with dirt. He was intent on watching
the teacher: this was why he was there, why he had gone to all that
trouble with Lello. He stared hard at the man, his little face white
because of the cold in the room, with its bare, cracked walls, the
two windows that admitted the dying light.

Then, since the teacher didn't even notice him, Tommasino
stopped dusting altogether; when the teacher saw him idle, he'd
bawl him out at least.

Instead the teacher was bent over his desk, writing in his ledger,
his head plastered with brilliantine, four or five hairs erect behind,
like spaghetti, where the parting ended.

When Tommaso had slowly finished the first two desks, he took
a rest, sitting at the third, playing with the rag and slamming the lid
of the inkwell.

This was his way of cleaning up, sitting there sprawled in the seat. The teacher, unaware, went on writing in his ledger. Tommasino dropped the rag on the bench and, very slowly, slid along the back until he had stretched out his legs and was lying there, his head down, his hands between his thighs, which, as he rubbed along the bench, half-emerged from those ragged shorts that looked like a skirt.

In that position Tommasino looked up at the teacher again, as if expecting him, now, to say something. Not a word. Screw you ... Tommaso thought, his face frozen, growing gradually more taut with anger.

He stayed like that for a little while, watching the teacher and widening his legs still farther, one under the desk and the other against the desk-top, changing his angry expression into a grimace of boredom, almost of merriment. 'Hey, you nut,' he went on, almost aloud, 'wake up!'

He took the rag again and gave the rest of the desks along the wall with the windows a hasty lick. He did the other two rows almost at a run. Then he went out for the broom and started sweeping haphazardly here and there.

While he swept, he whistled softly, making all sorts of faces; he noticed the teacher had looked up at him for a moment.

Then he stopped sweeping and went up to the teacher's platform, standing there, waiting for the man to look at him again. When the teacher raised his eyes, Tommasino said to him: 'Can I go to the toilet?'

'Go ahead,' the teacher said, muttering as if he were also thinking: Why ask me? Do as you like!

But Tommaso didn't go to the bathroom, and he didn't pick up the broom again either. He set it against the wall and came back to a bench, where he sat down, busying himself with his pants once more.

He wore a filthy shirt, whose sleeves his mother had had to cut off because they were so tattered they weren't even good for rags; and so, under it, he wore an undershirt which had fairly good sleeves, though the rest—which couldn't be seen—was in shreds.

But Tommasino could feel it all the same. And with the excuse of
arranging that ball of rags, he loosened the string that held up his
pants and, passing one hand over his stomach, he pulled up the
lumps of cloth that had formed around his waist. With the other
hand he held up the pants and the string.

The teacher raised his head, with a serious, worried expression,
then asked, so softly he was almost inaudible: 'What's wrong with
Lello's mother?'

'Don't know, sir. She's sick,' Tommasino said, still arranging his
pants over his guts. The teacher let it go at that and looked down at
his desk again. It was dark now, but what little light came through
the windows, filling the room, seemed almost blinding in the
frozen air.

Tommaso was still there, motionless on the bench, his face half-
sly, half-bewildered, furious.

'Whaddya waiting for, shithead?' he was thinking. 'What's
wrong with me? I'm as good as Lello. I'm better than anybody in
this class. You think I don't know my way around? I was the first
one to catch on to you, you dope. I told Lello, even before you
started in on him. But he's stupid. I know a lot more about it than
he does!'

While Tommaso was thinking in this way, becoming more and
more angry, the teacher blotted the ledger, closed it, and stood up.
'Let's be going,' he said, 'it's late.'

Stretching, a bit awkward, he took his raincoat from a hook
behind the desk and put it on. Tommasino looked at him, filled
with amazement and fury. What's the big hurry tonight? he was
thinking.

But the teacher nodded to him again, with a serious expression, and after locking the ledger in the desk, went towards the
door.

Tommasino ran to put the stub of a broom and the rag in a corner
of the lavatory, then caught up with the teacher, who was going out,
already among the houses and the patches of beaten earth, the
tatters of asphalt.

'Good night, Puzzilli,' the teacher said, in a soft voice, still serious,

thinner and weaker than his boys. He started walking towards the
bus stop.

' 'Night, teacher,' Tommasino said, at his distance, 'and fuck you.'

He watched the man from the end of the road, but he couldn't
get over his fury. Then he followed him as far as Sora Anita's stand.

Won't have anything to do with me, eh? he was thinking,
crossly. Afraid? Lousy faggot. What's Lello got, that bastard, without even a father? A nothing. You oughtta try with me. I'm a good
kid, not full of lies like him. You faggot!

He crouched down on the edge of the pavement near Sora Anita,
and stayed there, watching the teacher all the time he stood waiting
for the 211. Tommasino's eyes were glazed, as if an idea were
coming to him, as if he were grimly considering it.

The 211 came along, the teacher got in line to board it. Tommaso
was still watching. When the teacher had climbed in and the bus
was moving, all of a sudden Tommaso stood up: Aha? So that's the
way it goes, eh? he thought. I'll show you, you smart bastard. I'll
take a tuck in your cock, all right. You'll see ... Ten years ... Jesus
Christ himself wouldn't be able to get you off this rap.

Then and there, without even saying good-bye to Lello's mother,
he ran off in the same direction as the bus, along the Via Tiburtina.

Lello, in the meanwhile, with a couple of other kids, was wandering around the neighbourhood. He had covered the whole area,
puffing the butts collected in the streets. Then they had gone on the
warpath and had climbed up on Monte del Pecoraro, to make bon-
fires with piles of packing boxes along the scraggy slope. They
chased one another down, and the first to reach the bottom started
yelling at the others: 'Come on, come on!' At the foot of the hill,
there was somebody looking for the church, a lady with a car big as
a building. It was all full of stuff to hand out to the poor. They
gathered around her, all making a racket, to be given something:
'Hey, Signora, here I am! Me! Me!'

The chauffeur gave them two or three packages of powdered
milk. They started tearing the packages open, cramming the powder
into their mouths; but they soon tired of that, and they took to
blowing it at one another, spilling it down their backs. They came

to the movie-house, white as plasterers, and started milling around, trying to sneak inside.

There, from the door of the Cinema Lux, Lello saw Tommaso running past. He didn't look at anybody, already exhausted, his tattered shorts flapping around his legs, his frozen arms hanging limply along his sides.

Lello narrowed his eyes, taking in the kid's peculiar behaviour. He took a few steps along the road.

'Where the fuck's that bastard going?' he muttered, concentrating.

Just to make sure, after a moment's reflection he followed him. Lello ran after Tommaso all along Via di Pietralata from the Cinema Lux to the Fort on the Tiburtina. There was no danger of Tommaso's looking back: he ran straight on, bent over, as if he had just had a beating, as if they had given it to him good.

Then, since the soldiers had already come out for their free evening, there was a bunch of them at the bar on the corner. So Lello had to gallop, to keep Tommaso in sight, and he was just in time to see him turn, still at a trot, down towards Tiburtino Terzo.

'Where the fuck's he going?' Lello repeated to himself, more and more worried, moving to the other side of the street, along the embankment.

Tommasino was running along the pavement, the Monte del Pecoraro side. When he came to the end of it, at the square, he stopped for a moment to look around, then, cutting through the traffic, he crossed the street.

Lello flattened against the low wall, crouching in the mud among the weeds; then he started running again, to get to the square before Tommaso had disappeared.

He hid again behind a crumbling old tower, where there was an electricity station on top, with a family living below. From behind the tower he could see the whole square, its street-lamps already lighted. Just opposite him there was a little clump of houses, the Bar Duemila, and behind, the inner part of the square, closed off like a courtyard.

Tommasino was heading straight there: in the midst of a little group of pines, in the background, there was a building with a lot of

2

square columns in front of it: an old Fascist gymnasium, the plaster peeling, now used as a barracks.

Lello turned pale with rage, his forelock shaking over his eyes: 'Lousy spy,' he whispered, his eyes trained on Tommaso, almost in tears.

Tommasino went up the two steps to the building, beneath the brown colonnade, where he presented himself, tiny as a little pile of rags, before a carabiniere who was standing guard, armed, at the door.

2

Night in the City of God

'Hey, Al, you seen Lello?' Tommasino asked a certain Aldo, who was passing by. 'Who'd of noticed him?' the latter said with a gesture filled with such disgust he couldn't help spitting. Then he repented having acted so smartass about it, and added: 'He's probably dancing.'

'Thanks for nothing,' Tommasino said, and went on his way: it was the street where the school was and Communist Party headquarters, where there was dancing on Sundays. And in fact, the pavements, if you could call pavements those two tracks of mud and stones on either side of the road, were full of guys all dressed up and soldiers from the Fort. It was winter, December: but it was so hot you sweated, and the mist covering Pietralata and the fields along the Aniene looked like the steam of a bath. Tommasino walked along the middle of the road in his leather jacket, his hands in the pockets, which were at the level of his elbows; one foot after the other, as if they were hurting him, bent slightly forward and very weary.

'Say, you seen Lello, Cazzitini?' he repeated to another boy, dressed as if this were August, with his ringlets of hair falling over his nostrils because of the humidity.

'No,' he answered curtly, but Tommasino wasn't even listening; he kept asking the question just to be asking it, to stir up a bit of dust: he knew that sonofabitch Lello was on the dance-floor.

The hall was in a little one-storey house, painted pink, with three tiny windows in a line, and a door opening from a little yard along the road. A house like all the others around there, in rows of ten or twelve, identical, with their filthy yards in front. They were the

houses of the dispossessed, there in the middle of the blocks of the
housing development, Here and there, a twisted tree, with never a
leaf, and a latrine or two made of planks.

The door and the windows were open: and the light fell into the
yard. Inside and out there was a swarm of kids, youngsters, of stacked
little girls and old drunks; it was like being in a village square.

'Goddamm you, Lello,' Tommaso shouted at the top of his voice,
his face nasty, as he went in and saw Lello propped against a piece of
wall as full of holes as a sieve. 'Leave me alone!' Lello answered, and
left him there at once, because the orchestra, three kids and a thin
old man, had struck up a samba. Lello flung himself through the
mob at top speed and, before all the others, without bowing or asking leave, presented himself to a girl in black velvet. A moment
later there he was dancing the samba, flinging her first to the left
then to the right like a woodpecker with a worm. While she spun
around, Lello chomped chewing-gum and, with a twist of his ass,
threw back his thighs tightly sheathed in American jeans, and his
feet with their pointed, buckled shoes, first one, then the other.

The little orchestra seemed to be doing piece-work, especially the
kid who played the accordion, black as an African, and with a row
of teeth, displayed like a dead cat's, glistening gaily.

Beyond a partition about a yard high, there was the bar-room, or
rather, a barrel, a table, and a werewolf who waited on it, already
drunk as a skunk.

At the table there was Shitter, with Buddha, Nazzareno, and
another two or three bums: not novices either, about twenty-four
or maybe twenty-five.

'Hey,' Tomasso said to Shitter, 'when's he gonna get a move on?
What's he waiting for? Holy Year?'

Shitter didn't answer him; he and the others were busy examining
photographs. 'Aòh, Shitter,' Tommaso began again, almost chanting, 'Why doncha go and call that bastard? It's late.'

But Shitter was too absorbed to move. He looked at Tommaso
sweetly, his eyebrows raised and replied, spitting: 'It's not even four
yet.'

'Four!' Tommaso said, 'it's night already.'

'Fuckoff,' Shitter said in a low voice, and went back to looking at the picture one of his friends was passing him.

He peered at it, barely lowering his eyelids, and then he made a face that no one would ever have imagined: the slack jowls already with a few wrinkles, the mouth that looked like a razor-cut, with lips of pale, almost white flesh, the eyes watery and without brows, the head going bald, with filthy curls over the neck: everything seemed to swell in a laugh that forced him to bend down till his chin was almost touching the barrel.

'You mean you're an athlete, too, eh?' he said, his jaws breaking with laughter.

The other one, Nazzareno, ripped the snapshot from his hands, looking him in the eye.

'Shithead,' he grumbled, his lower lip so bent in disgust that it reached below his chin.

'Shithead!' he repeated, not finding another word. And then he looked at him, shaking his chicken-head briefly, as if to say: 'You're making a big mistake. You've got things all wrong.'

Though still racked with laughter, Shitter gave him a bitter look: 'Why don't you go off to the Old Folks' Home?' he shouted, 'Get going!'

'You think you're better?' Buddha snapped, the third of the company. With this, he took his wallet from his pocket, and began to dip delicately in its compartments until he finally produced a photograph where he could be seen with other friends, including Shitter.

They were in bathing suits, in a row; the ones behind standing, those in front, crouched down; and they were all looking straight at the camera, showing off. They all swelled out, to seem tougher: there was Nazzareno who looked about to explode from the effort of extending his pectorals and forcing his shoulders forward, his hands on his hips. Shitter looked like an old woman, thin as a cod. Observing him now, both Buddha and Nazzareno began to laugh, too; but their laughter was more like yelling, which sandpapered their throats and was such an effort they had to bend double, almost rolling under the table.

Shitter looked at them with detachment, his brows drawn up, his

eyes cloudy, his lips thrust out: obviously he could hardly keep
from laughing himself.

Tommasino looked on, laughing, red in the face, waiting for the
others to stop. When they had calmed down a little, he took his
wallet from the inside pocket of his jacket.

'You dopes,' he said, in a pitying tone: 'Here are some real tough
guys,' he added then, patiently, almost screaming, because there
was a terrible racket, what with the orchestra and the scraping of
feet of those bastards dancing the samba.

In the first picture there he was with Lello, Zucabbo, and Carletto
on the beach at Ostia. Zucabbo and Carletto were sitting on the
step of the cabin, each with a pair of fingers making horns behind
the other's wet head; Tommasino was half-sitting, half-leaning
against the little wooden railing; in the centre, against the door,
apart, with a tight little bathing-slip on, handsome, serious, erect,
well-made, there was Lello.

Tommaso slapped the photograph under the nose of the others,
without letting them even get a look at it. He stuck it back into his
wallet and took out another. In this one, there was only himself,
Lello and Zucabbo, all dolled up, walking side by side across Ponte
Garibaldi: it had been taken the previous summer, and behind them
a band of pilgrims could be seen, turning obliquely. All three were
walking with their hands in their pockets: the weather was fine, they
were in shirtsleeves, and you could see their chest muscles. The
others managed only to glimpse this picture, too, because Tommaso merely whisked it under their noses, as if they were to sniff it.
'Turds!' he said finally, triumphant. And, to conclude, he dug out a
last photograph, winking at Shitter.

It was a little snapshot, even smaller than passport size, and Tommaso took it by one corner between thumb and index finger: holding it high, he turned it towards Buddha and Nazzareno. It was a
photograph of Mussolini, black in the face, under a cap with an
eagle insignia on it.

Buddha and Nazzareno acted dumb, rather than afford Tommaso
any satisfaction; they gave the photo only a sidelong glance, enough
to be slightly surprised, seeing what it was.

'Aw, fuck you ... ' Buddha grumbled, 'what's he supposed to represent? That shithead. Eh, Spy?' Spy, after Stinkfeet, was the new nickname they had given Tommaso. Then Buddha yawned, stretched, preparing to concern himself with other things, so he didn't even hear Tommaso, who looked at Mussolini and said: 'There he is, he was a real man, awright!' and sat looking at him, smartass, with admiration.

With a sudden burst of rage, as if he had only then been reminded of him, Shitter said: 'Well, what's that bastard Lello doing anyhow?'

'So you've finally caught on?' Tommaso said, slow and bitter, carefully replacing the photograph in his wallet. The samba was over, but since the orchestra played numbers in groups of three, the couples were still standing on the floor, while the guys without women slipped along the wall, giving the girls who were dancing a look, to sign them up for the next round.

Shitter started yelling, in the midst of the room, spattering saliva: 'Lello, goddammit!'

But Lello was in the centre of the crowd of couples and couldn't hear him, or if he did, he was playing smart. Shitter, followed by Tommasino, started hunting, moving around the room, against the patches of plaster. At that moment the orchestra broke into a Charleston. As if somebody had stuck a finger up their ass, all the dancers gave a leap: they bent their knees slightly, standing on their toes, and began to fling their bottoms from side to side, wildly.

Shitter and Puzzilli quickly glimpsed Lello, who, since he was Pietralata's number one dancer, had been waiting only for this Charleston to display his skill. His girl, though she was all frowning and serious, was a better twirler than he, and with one hand holding her dress against her thigh, she let herself go with a vengeance. 'Sonofabitch,' Shitter yelled at Lello, who was spinning near him. He didn't even answer. And the two friends had to wait patiently while Lello vanished where and how he pleased.

Outside, the heat was suffocating: the sun had gone down, and in the mist over Pietralata and the surrounding countryside only the last light remained.

They went down along the street, which became more and more crowded now that it was evening, all full of young people shouting and singing, and little kids making a racket.

The three friends arrived at the bus stop at the end, passing Lello's mother, still seated at her stand, with a barricade of kids around her.

Lello didn't even look at her, and as they were leaning against the columns of the shed, he muttered, smartass, still chewing his gum: 'I was born tired, I was,' and he began a yawn, without finishing it.

The bus seemed never to come. Tommaso's bright eyes darted around; he was content, thinking of the big programme that lay ahead of them.

Shitter was leaning against the column beside Lello, a sack of rags, with the little collar of his topcoat turned up, and over it his filthy curls, damp from the fog. His light coat was shiny, wrinkled, and greasy, falling to his shins, so he looked like a priest, and he exploited it to act even more comical and to pretend he was that much smarter.

He was the son of a whore and a crook and he had three other brothers, scattered around Rome. His father spent two years in stir, and then a month on the outside, and you might say Shitter had never seen him. His mother had gone on the streets before he could walk. At Ponte Garibaldi, where she worked, because her pimp lived at Campo Buozzi, they called her Granny, because her hair was all white.

When Shitter was maybe thirteen or fourteen and found out his mother was a whore, he decided to wait till he was a bit bigger; then two or three years later, he turned up where she was on the job, grabbed her by the throat, and yelled at her: 'Now you're going to give me five hundred a day, or I'll kill you.' She was scared and she promised, because Shitter wasn't kidding. And so, without letting the pimp know about it, she gave Shitter fifteen thousand a month. The other jobs he got mixed up in were more for the hell of it than for the money.

*

Rome was all dripping. Especially around the Tiber, from Testaccio to Porta Portese, to the Lungaretta. Rain fell, so dense and so fine that it dissolved before it hit the pavement. The avenues and the narrow side-streets were full of that hot steam, with the Aventine floating on one side and Monteverde on the other.

It was six or seven in the evening, so when Tommaso, Lello and Shitter got off the number 13 at the little garden opposite Ponte Quattro Capi, the place was deserted, or almost; there were only the first whores beginning to stroll around and some motorbikes cruising from Ponte Garibaldi to Caracalla. But once the boys had crossed the bridge, to the Lungaretta, there was all the usual Sunday-night confusion. The kids went by in bunches, coming out of the Cinema Reale, the Esperia, the Fontana, or from some of the cheap parish movies run by the priests, wandering around for a breath of air before going home to supper.

All of them were wearing coats or scarves, but only for show; and Lello had been right to come out without overcoat or leather jacket—apart from the fact that he didn't have any—all handsome and smart in his red-and-blue-striped jersey, and, around his neck, a tightly-rolled kerchief of grey silk with little red flowers.

The M.S.I. party headquarters was in Vicolo della Luce. But Tommaso and the others didn't have to go all the way there; they ran into Ugo at the corner of the alley.

He was lighting a butt: that's why he had stopped there at the corner, and he made a grimace that wrinkled his whole face, under the waves and curls as hard as cobblestones.

'Well?' Tommaso said to him, holding his hand out, uncertainly. Ugo threw away the match and took a long drag.

Then, his tongue between his taut lips, he spat out a bit of tobacco which irked him and wouldn't drop off his wet mouth.

'Hi there, kids,' he said, giving the three of them his hand. Tommasino returned to the subject at once, crossly, his nose curled as if something stank: 'Whatcha doing out here?' he asked, starting along the alley towards the party headquarters.

'There's nobody there now,' Ugo said.

'What?' Tommaso answered, with the other two looking at him, curious.

'Coletta said to wait for him here, at Piazza dei Ponziani; come on,' Ugo added, and without waiting for an answer, he started down the Lungaretta.

'Why?' Tommasino asked, following him, displeased.

Ugo faced him; he put his hands together like he was going to say an Our Father. Then with a rapid gesture he turned them, still joined, but towards his knees, the tips of the fingers against his chest: when they were in that position, he pressed the finger-tips together, and waved his hands rapidly against his chest and under his chin, five or six times, interrogatively, then translated the gesture: "Whadda you care?"

He spat and walked on, along the Lungaretta glistening with warm rain.

At Piazza dei Ponziani there were Enrico, the Loon, and Salvatore. The newcomers saw them at once because, since the square was a bit out of the way, it was half-empty, and the three were standing at the corner of Via dei Vascellari, outside the bar.

Tommasino and the others went towards them, and all shook hands. The other three didn't even move: they stayed there, leaning against the wall, one leg outstretched and the other foot also against the wall, or crossed over the first. They were half yawning, as they waited, because this was the agreed meeting-place. Very weakly they did raise their right hands, without changing the blissful, mocking expression on their faces. Perhaps to pass the time, they were watching the olive-seller on the other side of the street, his wooden bucket of olives on the pavement. 'Coletta?' Ugo asked, just to be asking.

'He'll be along soon,' one of the three said, his eyes like two lighted matches.

'You mean there's just us?' Tommaso said, disgusted.

'So what? We know our business, don't we?' the other guy answered.

Tommaso, frowning and looking around angrily, let out a bitter little laugh at that, his flat mouth opening to reveal his brown, ragged teeth.

Meanwhile, the one with the neon eyes, the Loon, weary but determined, walked towards the olive-seller, as his friends followed him with their eyes.

'Give me fifty lire's worth of olives, chief,' the Loon said.

The chief, who was an old shepherd drifted into the city from some God-forsaken village in the Abbruzzo, looked at the Loon's hand holding the cash and held out his own, to collect it. The Loon gave it to him, and the man was about to dip his ladle into the brine, pocketing the coin, when he realized it was fake: he looked at it, and saw that it was a fifty centesimi piece, from pre-war days. He flashed a foolish smile. 'It's no good,' he said, his eyes brightening.

The Loon didn't laugh. 'No good?' he said gravely, burning with indignation. 'You've got it all wrong,' he added at once, conciliatory, as if to close the argument. But the old man went on smiling foolishly, casting wise looks to left and right. The others had also come over, in the meanwhile.

'Well, are you gonna give me those olives, or not?' the Loon said, losing his patience again.

'When you give me real money,' the man said, his cheekbones pulled up to his eyes.

The Loon hung his head, looking up from below, smacking his tongue against his palate as if it were bitter; and he began, in a low, calm voice: 'How dare you suspect my money, you lousy beggar? This money's historic, you know that? Go on, take it. And watch out next time, about refusing good money. The very idea! I gotta mind to punch you a coupla times in the mouth.' The seller went on laughing, embarrassed. 'This is the only real money Italy's ever had,' Salvatore added from a distance, shouting, 'you dope! And give us our change. Snap it up!'

At that moment, from the other end of Via dei Vascellari, Coletta appeared with five or six guys. Coletta was tall, thin, dark, with a long head and too much hair, which stuck up behind, and with a greenish face sliced by a twisted mouth. His eyes were always serious like those of a little boy somebody's insulted, and staring, full of brooding grief and anger.

The others were almost all rich kids, some wearing duffle coats,

some wearing glasses, faces puffed and purple, bags under their
eyes, and black fuzz over their badly shaved throats. In the bunch
there was also a friend of Tommaso's, who lived in his neighbourhood, on the Tiburtina, a certain Alberto Proietti, who looked like
Alberto Sordi; but he was already an accountant, and he lived in a
little villa before you got to the Fiorentini factory, with some tattered festoons of grapes under the cornice, and a lawn in the courtyard. Tommaso swelled at seeing him, and went over to give him
his hand solemnly.

Shitter meanwhile felt like eating a few olives. He addressed the
hick curtly: 'Give me a hundred lire's worth,' he said, putting his
hand in the pocket of his overcoat. The hick pretended he hadn't
heard. Shitter grimaced at him: 'A hundred lire's worth,' he repeated.

Then the seller said, 'Gimme the money first.' Shitter stared
at him again, patiently. 'Now look ... ' he said, affably, 'a hundred
lire's worth.' 'Money first,' the man repeated stubbornly, since God
only knows how many times he'd been cheated, poor bastard.

A kind of charge seemed to run through Shitter, who raised one
foot, grinding his teeth, preparing to give the bucket a kick. 'Now
I'm gonna give this bucket a kick, right into the middle of the
square, so go fuck yasself!' he shouted. 'Come on, gimme those
olives!' The man, resigned by now, ready even to be hanged perhaps, still held out stubbornly: 'No, no, I wanna see the money,' he
said.

Shitter was silent, looking at him. Slowly his face swelled, his
mouth tightened, rose towards his nostrils, his eyes popped. All the
muscles of his face were trembling, as if he were changing skin. He
seemed uncertain whether to abandon himself to convulsions of
rage and kick that stupid face in front of him, or else to burst out
laughing.

'Hey, what is this?' he said in the end, almost in a low voice. 'Did
you take a good look at me? I'll smash the hundred lire in your
mouth!'

With this, he took two or three hundred-lire notes from his
pocket, selected one, plunged it suddenly into the water, and with a

slap that could be heard in all the surrounding streets, plastered it
against the man's face. Then, without even looking at him, still
trembling, he went to his friends, who were in a circle, watching
and laughing. Coletta patted him on the shoulder, then said to them
all: 'Let's go!' moving at the head of the band, his face looking like
it was painted on a banner, towards Ponte Rotto.

They all went off, swaggering, some this way, some that.

Coletta walked along with his hands in his pockets, always in the
lead, looking ahead with his eyes narrowed, white as asparagus.

Since he assumed complete responsibility for their seriousness,
the others were a bit nonchalant, following him like parrots. Ugo,
the one whose father and brother had been killed by the partisans,
who now lived alone with his mother, doing a bit of thieving,
walked with Enrico and Salvatore, accosting all the cunts they passed.

The others, students more or less, came after them, in pairs like
geese, and Tommasino stuck to them, at the side of this Alberto
Proietti, his friend, because they weren't bums, like the other kids,
back at Pietralata. 'If I run around with this bunch, it's all to the
good for me,' Tommaso thought, flushed. 'More presteedge!
There's a big difference between having a coffee or going to the
movies with these guys and with those other nuts. The lousiest of
this bunch has a doctor or a lawyer or an engineer for his father:
people who aren't scared of anything!'

They covered the whole distance from Ponte Rotto to Largo
Argentina. Here they met other groups, walking along with
assumed indifference, like them, from the sections around there,
from Borgo Pio to Ponte or Panìco; and even from zones farther
away, Monteverde or Alberone, because there were plenty of
buses from those places. But, among themselves, they all played
dumb, pretending not to know one another, and they went about
their business, each on his own. Only Coletta said: 'Wait,' and went
towards a florist's below the tower, where the bunch from Monteverde was going by, led by a short kid, shady-looking, laughing like
a baby. With this guy, Coletta went down a side street towards a
half-deserted dairy. A little later he came back, holding a package in
his hand.

The others were leaning against the low wall along the Largo Argentina, below the tower, staring at the cunt.

When Coletta came back Ugo was heading for one going by in a red dress, and was yammering behind her, ecstatically: 'Where you going? Gonna take a shit, eh, cutie?'

But Coletta, with his package under his arm, cut him short, turned briskly and said: 'Come on, let's go.'

Still acting casual, they started off again. It was Sunday, and they really looked like a bunch of guys going to the Teatro Altieri, which was around there, laughing a bit or maybe singing a song. They passed Masetti, cut over towards Piazza della Minerva, and there, in an alley in sight of the Pantheon, they made another stop.

Coletta called Lello, consigned the package to him, and went off again, this time towards Piazza della Rotonda, beyond the rows of taxis and carriages, while from all the side streets other groups continued arriving. When he came back, after another ten minutes or so, his expression had changed: he looked like a dead man restored to life, his eyes shining. The moment had come.

From the wall Ugo, Salvatore, the Loon, and the others were spitting down at the cats lying on the stones around the Pantheon. But already the other groups coming from the side-streets were beginning to form one big crowd, and now they were greeting one another, making a racket, joining up, mingling, calling to friends. With Shitter at his side, Coletta started down towards the little square in front of the Pantheon. Among the rows of hacks and cars, in front of the bars that were beginning to pull down their iron shutters, about a hundred of them had gathered, the Fascists.

Lined up here and there, on the narrow sidewalks, at the corners of the streets, on the steps of the fountain, they began to whistle, to organize the uproar. When other squads arrived and the square was almost full, the piercing whistles became louder, more constant. The taxi drivers and the hackies had drawn back to the kiosk, and there, slumping, white-faced, they muttered curses.

All the lines of Fascists headed towards a corner of the square, the beginning of Via del Seminario where there was a little hotel called the Albergo del Sole. The waiters had already run off, having hastily barred all the windows, and only the door was half open, with the proprietor peeping out every now and then, shitting his pants with fear. 'Throw out the Czechoslovaks!' the missini shouted mockingly in the meanwhile, and then more whistles, still louder. 'You're nothing but shit!' they shouted. 'Go back where you came from!' 'Did they bring you, or did you come on your own?' 'Go back to your curtain!' 'Hey, you Czechs!' one shouted, and five or six buddies around him let out a chorus of Bronx cheers. 'Take it easy,' the hotel owner said. 'It's not my fault, if they sent me these Czechs!'

In the meanwhile, from two or three groups, that were spreading the word, you could hear: 'Bring on the shit! The shit!' And, in fact, five or six bastards, assigned that operation, which promised to be sweet all right, advanced from the side streets. Bent over, laughing and shouting a bit, they came forward, with quick steps, buckets in their hands: buckets, washtubs, dishpans. All were filled with a dark-yellow liquid, nice and thick. They took it and began throwing it against the door and the wall of the hotel. It required a special technique, to prevent the shit, once thrown, from spattering back on those who had thrown it and on the others standing near by. Deftly, they took the bucket by the handle and by the bottom, and then, with a sharp movement, they emptied it, one here, one there. There was a stink that took your breath away, and they all laughed and laughed, almost coughing their guts up.

As they were used, the empty buckets disappeared again. In no time a dozen had been emptied against the wall. The mess dripped down the façade, which had turned all brown. Everybody was about ready to go away, when, suddenly, announced by new yells, Coletta — face white, hair in the wind — was seen passing by, package in hand, followed by the group of friends.

He took up his position facing the little door of the hotel, before the owner had time to close it: the man tried to stop him, but the others held him fast. With the butt of his cigarette, Coletta lit the fuse, ran a few more steps, and threw the package inside the mouldy corridor. An explosion was heard, and they saw a burst of flame. At that moment the police siren began to scream. 'The turds! The

cops!' the guys farthest away began to yell. There was a mad dash,
some went on whistling and making rude sounds, others started
shoving, to clear out. The police arrived from two directions, from
Via del Seminario and from Piazza della Minerva; so the missini
who were caught in the middle began to run off along the little
side streets. Some were caught, about ten, others got bopped on the
head, and the majority retreated, disappearing at full speed through
the neighbourhood.

Tommasino, Shitter, Lello, still with Coletta, Salvatore, Alberto,
Ugo, and the Loon loped wearily, like old hyenas, up Via dei
Crescenzi. Their legs worked hard, while the faces above them
laughed as if they were out for a stroll. 'Keep at it, Lello!' Tommaso shouted, with a snigger. 'Go on, or the cops will fuck us for
good!' They reached a corner. Via Oberdan and Via del Teatro
Valle: they started down one street at random, and reached another
crossroads. 'This way.' 'No, that way.' Finally, they stopped, sweating so hard they spouted like stripped taps. 'Aòh, I'm fed up with
running,' Ugo said fiercely. He was all decked out, flannel trousers,
a salt-and-pepper jacket with martingale, gold chain, ring and
wrist watch. 'I'm so hungry,' he said, 'I'm about to shit myself.'
'Me, too,' Tommaso said, 'I haven't eaten since last night!' 'Aòh!'
Ugo said, angry again, 'If we don't get a move on, I'm gonna drop
out!' 'Let's go eat a pizza at Fileni's,' Salvatore said. Ugo reacted
abruptly: 'Let's go,' he said, 'whadda we waiting for?'

They didn't go straight to Trastevere by the route they had taken
before, but made a broad circle. They caught the tram at Ponte
Vittorio, after walking the length of Via del Governo Vecchio.
They got off at Ponte Garibaldi and took Viale del Re where, a bit
beyond the Cinema Esperia, there was the pizzeria they were talking
about.

It was full; there happened to be just one table free, in a corner
near the oven. They flung themselves on it, pushing each other and
making a racket, among the other people eating their pizzas at the
tables. 'Grab it,' they yelled, 'there!' as if they were in a square
instead of a pizzeria. They fell on the chairs, laughing like bums, and
promptly called the waiter. 'Six pizzas!' they shouted. 'And two

litres of sweet wine.' 'I want mine with mushrooms,' Ugo ordered.
'Us, too, then,' the others shouted, 'we're not fasting, are we?'

Near by there was another table filled with Trasteverini, older
guys. They knew one another, and exchanged greetings, barely
moving their fingers as if they were gummed with glue. 'Hi, Fats,'
Ugo said to a young man, broad and white as a fresh bunch of
lettuce. The boy looked at him, then, slowly taking the glass in his
hand, began to observe Ugo, staring, his eye mocking. When he
took a gulp, he set down the glass, still looking at Ugo and said:
'It's not New Year's Eve yet, ya know? Wait a while, before you
start throwing confetti around!'

Ugo's face turned sly and, shouting, because everybody was
shouting in the pizzeria under the neon tubes, the tongues of fire
from the oven, he answered serenely: 'We're still plenty tough, and
we can do what we like!'

'Oh, sure,' the young man said benevolently, nodding his head,
'but the tyranny's over, for your bunch!'

Ugo replied, sharp and triumphant: 'We were able to run a
tyranny, but you guys can't make it.'

'Because we aren't killers like you!' the Communist answered.
Ugo looked at him, still acting calm, but prepared to lash out; his
other friends, too, were beginning to get mad, especially Tommaso,
who looked at the guys at the next table with a rage in his eyes as if
he could tear them limb from limb and eat them raw, hair and all.

Ugo changed his voice and his expression, as if he were speaking
not to the big blond guy but to the wind: 'We're killers, eh? You
comrades are the killers, like all the bums with your ideas, who
killed my father and my brother!'

The other man waited a moment before answering, smiling
vaguely, also at the wind, then he picked up his glass again, swayed
it a moment, then said: 'Let's skip it. Drink another glass of wine,
and I'll drink mine, and the argument's over.'

The waiter arrived with the pizzas and two litre carafes, and all
exhausted and breathless, he began to set the table, while some other
people called him from another corner. 'I'm eating my heart out,'
Salvatore said, who had his back to the comrades. 'I'd like to eat

their hearts,' Tommaso said, in a low voice, his face yellow with
hatred. 'If they let me have my way, I'd line them all up with their
faces to the wall.'

Shitter had already begun to eat his pizza. He had cut it into four
sections, taken one in his hands, folded it, and was eating it in bites
like a sandwich. The others did the same; laughing and making a
noise, they began to stuff themselves, trying to cheat each other on
the wine. After a while, when things seemed calm again, the fat guy
said in a serene tone, 'Aòh,' to Ugo, provocatively: 'I'll buy you
half a litre, if you'll come over to my side.'

Ugo gave him a venomous look, beginning to speak, saliva
spurting from the corners of his mouth: 'What? You wanna push
me around, too? You think you're better than me? You don't know
fuck-all about politics! Listen: I believed in that man. You can think
what you want, but he did everything he could for all of us. In his
time there weren't all the scandals your bunch is making now. Look
at the Foro Mussolini, look at all the plans that were made, that
really existed—we know that today. But your party betrayed him!
I'd bring him back to life ... So he could spit in your face!'

One of the blond's comrades nudged his elbow, but he was controlling himself anyway; in fact, he had an affable smile, though
Tommaso's voice could clearly be heard as he said, his eyes dripping
venom: 'To hell with those murderers!'

Two litres is a lot of wine, but they finished it off in no time. So
the Loon ordered another litre. They drained that one, too. Little
by little, they all became happy again, and they were so excited
they couldn't sit still. One was singing on his own, another put his
feet on the table. Finally Shitter opened his mouth and said: 'Aòh,
tonight I really feel on the ball. I feel up to committing the crime of
the century.'

Although they laughed, the others pricked up their ears, because
Shitter wasn't exactly joking.

'Well then,' the Loon said, 'if you feel so hot, let's go out for a
few thrills.'

'Let's go, let's go!' Lello shouted, 'I'm fed up with sitting around
here.'

They were all high. Their eyes shone like coals in their little brown faces. 'Aòh,' Salvatore yelled, enthusiastically, 'how about pulling something at Alduccio's bakery? We could sell the flour after?'

'What good's that!' the Loon said, holding up his hand. 'How about knocking off these two rolls of copper wire, down by the railway at La Magliana?'

'Are you nuts?' Ugo said, 'the railway wire is guarded now. There's a tobacconist's I know about, though. Are the rest of you game?'

'We've got to pick up a car then,' Salvatore said, ready to get started.

'What's hard about that?' Lello said then, cool, his smile blissful below his slightly rumpled hair. 'In a couple minutes we can open it, grab it, and get started.'

With this, he stood up and went straight towards the door of the pizzeria, opposite the oven, without looking back.

Quickly, Shitter stood up, ready to go and act as lookout, and, like an old dog, he followed Lello into the street.

Outside, the air was hotter than ever. Along Viale del Re the bars had moved tables outside, and many people were sitting at them. The plane trees were full of little birds: there were thousands and thousands of them on the boughs still full of half-dead leaves and their chirping made an almost deafening din. Some little kids, in undershirts, were roaming around beneath them, with slingshots.

Happily, Shitter at his heels, Lello headed for Ponte Garibaldi, crossed it, and went up Via Arenula back to Largo Argentina.

Here the two of them stopped and observed the movement. They caught on immediately that this was a good place. They took a turn around the square, then glanced up Via Botteghe Oscure. Since there was a concert at the Teatro Argentina, the area was full of cars, you could hardly move. Near one row of cars, in a little space at the beginning of Via Botteghe Oscure, there was a Fiat millecento sports model, off to one side, its muzzle sticking out.

Lello moved over to it, looked around, aimed his knee hard at the door, grabbed the handle with both hands, and gave it a sharp

yank. The door opened, and Lello slipped behind the wheel, opening the other door. Shitter got in on that side and promptly ripped
out the wires: tying them together, and bending down a bit, he
held them in his left hand, while in his right he held the wire of the
headlights. Lello started the engine, turned down Via Botteghe
Oscure and, after crossing Ponte Rotto, in two minutes he was
back in front of the pizzeria in Viale del Re.

'Grrranadaaa ... ' they were singing inside, in the heat and the
smoke: against the mouth of the oven there were two musicians,
green as jailers, and all of them, over the music, were eating and
talking still louder.

'Hey, you shitheads!' Lello said, when he reached his friends'
table, where they all seemed plastered, having finished off the third
litre. And he immediately retraced his steps to the door, without
waiting for them.

The others, who had already paid, stood up and fell in behind.

Outside, all of them high, they looked at the car, piled into it, and
sped off at once towards the Trastevere station.

'Grrranadaaa ... ' hick-faced Salvatore began to sing happily when
he was sprawled on the seat, ' "tierra soñada por mi!" '

All of them, some lying back, some looking out of the window,
were pointing like dogs, with laughing eyes. Ugo stuck his head
out and yelled at the quail they were passing: 'Hey, you fearless
cunt! Hey, golden hole! Cozy coozy!' 'Where're we going?' Salvatore asked, with enthusiasm, interrupting his song. 'Aòh, where're
we going!' Tommaso repeated, equally happy.

Shitter half-turned, holding the wires, opened his mouth and
said: 'We're gonna live it up!'

Meanwhile they were driving along a dark street between Porta
Portese and the Slaughterhouse; there they fixed up the wires,
twisting them together, then they set off, full tilt, towards Testaccio.
They cruised along the Tiber a while, then headed for San Giovanni,
singing and enjoying themselves. Suddenly the Loon yelled: 'Look,
look, a foreign car!'

'Lello, Lello, follow it,' Ugo shouted at once, 'we'll see where it
stops, and where it stops we'll knock it off.'

This foreign car was an old, shiny dark Käpitan, driving along calmly, with bags, suitcases, and a pram in the luggage rack on top. Inside there was a man, a woman, and a couple of little kids.

Lello began to follow it, and in this way they crossed the square before San Giovanni, and on and on, they reached the Via Casilina, at the turning for Torpignattara, opposite the hotel for German pilgrims. There was nobody around, only an occasional car and a few empty trams. The people in the Kapitan got out, rang a bell, a watchman came to open a gate, and they went inside.

It all had to be done in a minute, before the porter came out to collect their things. 'Aòh, who's got a knife?' Shitter hissed. 'Me!' Tommaso said, producing one of those American knives complete with corkscrew, screwdriver, and can-opener. Shitter and Tommaso got out and went under the car: Tommaso began to cut the ropes with the knife: Shitter took the pram, which was in the way, and hurled it on the ground, against the pavement. In less than a minute they were back at the Fiat, whose doors were open and motor running, with the tool kit and the luggage in their hands. They loaded the stuff in and made off, at the very moment that the porter's lodge and the garden came alight.

It started raining again, from the red clouds that shrouded the city: the Fiat sped through all that water like a motorboat, taking the curves on two wheels. 'I really like being in a car when it rains,' Salvatore said joyfully. 'There're two things I like,' he added, as the car slipped among the puddles, 'riding in a car when it rains, and shitting in a field, watching the people go by on the road!'

They reached the railway bridge, went through the arches of Piazzi Lodi, and were back at San Giovanni. They cut through Porta Metronia and the Passeggiata Archeologica, and two minutes later they were in Trastevere again, under the rain that was pouring down, gaily playing 'La Cumparsita' on the cobblestones.

They went along Piazza Santa Maria, took a narrow street, and stopped at another alleyway, all dark, near Piazza Renzi.

Ugo got out and, running under the warm rain, grazing the walls, reached Piazza Renzi and suddenly turned into a tavern that was the only lighted place in the whole square. He stuck his nose inside, saw

a friend, went to him and muttered: 'I gotta talk to you!' Then, at
a look from the other man, he went out again and waited for him,
standing under the cornice.

A moment later the friend was there. 'I just got some tools,' Ugo
said, 'I don't know what's in the bags. You wanna make a deal?'

'Well,' the old man said, 'if it's stuff I can place, bring it up. I'll
go ahead to my house.'

'Look,' Ugo said, 'there're four jacks. I can't carry the stuff by
myself. I'm bringing a friend along.' 'He can keep his mouth shut!'
he added, to reassure the man, then ran back towards the car.

'Okay,' the man agreed, 'but make it snappy,' and he went off in
the other direction, towards his own alley.

In less than a minute Ugo and Shitter were behind him with the
stuff. They turned into the alley, full of garbage floating on the
water, went into a narrow doorway, climbed the stairs, where a
single electric bulb was dancing in the wind. They stopped on a
dark landing: the door was ajar, and they went inside.

The man was waiting for them, and he led them into an empty
room with only a little table and two or three chairs. Ugo and Shitter set down the stuff, four suitcases and two handbags, and immediately all three began to open them, ripping off the locks. They
glanced at what was inside, mostly suits, linen, and books, and began
to bargain. 'Spit out some lousy offer,' Shitter said menacingly, 'go
ahead.' The old man offered twenty-five thousand; the two friends
wanted at least fifty. No yes, yes no, and the old guy had the usual
bright idea of dragging out the money and showing it to them,
because he knew the type: they got greedy, seeing the cash, and in
their anxiety to get it quickly, they agreed to his price.

He went to a little sofa where a big baby-doll was propped up,
the kind they raffle off for charity; he took off its head and brought
out a nice handful of cash, along with a revolver that was there
among the wads of money. Shitter couldn't take his eyes off it.
'Lemme have a look at it,' he said. He grabbed it and got the feel of
it. 'Is it loaded?' he asked, observing it. 'No,' the old man said, who
was standing there stupidly, playing dumb too, with the doll in his
hand.

Shitter looked at the gun, then at the pile of cash, eating it up with his eyes. 'Okay, twenty-five, goddammit ... ' he said, trembling, 'but you gotta throw in this.' The man began to groan, saying it was dangerous, he didn't want to get into trouble, and this and that: but in the end he said yes, and they bought it.

'Just don't tell where it came from!' the man insisted; but the other two weren't even listening to him, slipping off, loaded with cash, snappy and elegant. The car was there in the darkness, with the others inside, quiet as corpses: they divided up the cash, a little more than four thousand a head, then they set off again.

'Where we going?' Salvatore asked, his heart full of joy.

'To drink!' Shitter said, his eyes dripping like a dog's.

'Let's goooo!' Tommaso yelled. Lello turned here and there, at random, into some alleys, then over Ponte Sisto and along the Lungotevere, speeding. The rain had stopped, there were patches of clear sky, brightening now. In three seconds they were at Ponte Rotto, in another three at Ponte Sublicio, and in three more at the Ostia Station; they spun along with smoking tyres, grazing the pyramid, whistling at two or three whores who worked those parts, then along Via Marmorata and into Testaccio. They were so drunk their eyes were popping. In Via Zabaglia a truck was parked, and the whole street was blocked off. It was a truck full of Christmas trees: the tailgate had come off, and the trees had all fallen in a heap, into the middle of the street. The driver was hard at work, putting a beam in place of the bar. But meanwhile you couldn't pass that pile of wet trees, with some little kids yelling all around them.

'Aòh, I'm hungry,' Tommaso shouted, resentfully, seeing a restaurant near by.

'Hey, don't turn back,' Salvatore said to Lello, immediately making himself Tommaso's ally.

Lello, since he didn't feel like going into reverse, got out, laughing, and slammed the door, heading straight for the restaurant. 'Let's go eat, come on!' he shouted.

They were all alone in the place, and they started acting tough: Lello ordered mussels; Tommaso, lamb's head; Shitter, chicken and a pizza; and the Loon, a pizza with the works on it. Ugo wanted cod fillet, and Salvatore, rice balls. Then they all ordered some fried potatoes for first, then some sheep-milk cheese, and finally raw fennel with oil and pepper.

They got back into the car, drunk to the bone, and drove along the river, under the soaked trees that the wind shook, blowing handfuls of leaves to the ground.

'Aòh, we're broke,' Ugo said to Lello, as they were speeding along again. 'We gotta try again,' he added angrily, with a face as if he wanted an argument.

'Okay,' Lello said not putting up a fuss. 'It's just a matter of moving around.'

Ugo was fighting mad, with both fists clenched, held against his chest at the level of his chin. 'So where we going?' he said.

'Let's try downtown,' Salvatore said, with his usual enthusiasm, 'maybe we'll run into something along the way.'

'Forward, young Fascists!' the Loon yelled, agreeing, 'The world is watching us!' and Tommaso, with a nasal voice and his mouth twisted, added: 'We're still the same: we shall conquer!'

They went back along Via Marmorata and turned back on to the Lungotevere. 'Hey,' Lello said, determined, before starting the car again, 'You feel like trying for a lot of cash, or a lot of years in the clink?'

'What? What?' the others asked. 'Armed robbery,' Shitter said, and after a bit of hesitation, he pulled the revolver from his pocket.

'Yeah!' Lello confirmed, as his friend had understood him at once.

'How much money and off who?' Ugo wanted to know.

'If we knock off a gas station,' Lello said calmly, already driving the car at a hundred an hour down the Portuense.

'Where?' Ugo asked.

'A good spot, one we can handle, on the Cristoforo Colombo, the Appia, the Ardeatina. Where do we wanna go?'

They were all for it, and they argued a bit about what place, then they went towards Ponte Milvio, and took the Via Cassia for a place Ugo knew. Cutting across the Janiculum and Monte Mario, they were soon in open country, all hilly. After a few miles through meadows and woods, with pieces of Rome shining here and there in the distance, Salvatore, the Loon, and Tommasino, who argued a while before giving in, got out and prepared to wait, leaning against a mound of dirt, with dogs barking all around from the farms.

The other three pulled up at the gas station just before La Storta, Lello at the wheel, Shitter beside him, and Ugo on the back seat.

They drove in. It was all dark and deserted with only the Shell conch shining like the moon.

'Fifteen litres, kid,' Lello said to the attendant, a man about twenty-five, thirty, swollen with sleepiness. He began to wait on them, bending over to put the nozzle in the tank. Meanwhile, Lello yawned and said to Shitter: 'Take a look at the tyres.'

With that excuse, Shitter quietly got out and looked at the tyres. 'The tyres are okay!' he said. As soon as he had finished saying this he turned the pistol on the man, who was hanging the hose up again. He held the weapon an inch from the man's chest and made his hand tremble to show he was afraid, because when a man's afraid that's when he's most likely to shoot. But he didn't have to put on much of a show, because he was really trembling, not with fear but with rage. 'Give me the cash,' he said.

'Sure, only don't kill me. I gotta family,' the attendant said, white as a candle, quickly taking off his bag and handing it to Shitter. With the pistol still in the man's back, Shitter glanced inside it, and saw there wasn't much cash.

He gritted his teeth, looked the man in the face again, his lips twisted in anger. 'Go inside,' he ordered him.

The man obeyed at once. With the pistol behind him, he went into the little cabin. 'Open all the drawers,' Shitter ordered him again. Again the man obeyed, and in one drawer Shitter found some more money: he grabbed it and stuffed it in his pocket. Then he locked the man inside and shouted through the glass. 'Don't move, or I'll fry you.'

He dived into the car, keeping the pistol aimed sideways, as the car screamed off.

'How much did we pick up? How much?' Ugo said. But Shitter kept quiet, counting the cash. They collected Tommaso and the others, stiff from the dampness, with two or three dogs from a farm barking at them, running back and forth beyond a cane fence.

'How much did you get?' Tommaso said, with a grimace. Shitter showed the wad.

'Come closer,' the Loon shouted, at the sight of the little pile of bills. It was about thirty thousand.

Tommaso exaggerated his grimace, and said to Ugo: 'So this is the kind of place you know about?'

'Shithead,' Ugo answered. 'Go knock off your own then, instead of talking all the time!'

Tommaso shut up, his nose on his mouth, and then his only answer was to start singing the old Fascist song:

> ' "We never gave a damn about the threat of jail,
>   We don't give a damn about the risk of death ... " '

Singing like this, under the starry sky, they went back to Ponte Milvio, drove along the river, turned on to Ponte Duca d'Aosta, opposite the obelisk, and when they were in the middle of the bridge, Shitter, with a burst of anger, got out the revolver and threw it in the river, yelling: 'We don't need you any more!'

'Why not?' Tommaso said, still liverish, 'you shithead!'

Shitter turned towards him and belched in his face.

Arguing, they took a broad avenue towards the Via Flaminia, then Lello drove around all those streets, avenues, and squares at random, until he found a darker street, and there they parked the car. They walked for a while, casing the set-up. There were plenty of cars around, lined up along the pavements, but almost all of them with safety devices. Finally they found another Fiat, easy, made for them. They grabbed it and went off again. Tommaso was dissatisfied.

'Aòh, why don't we put a scare into another gas station,' he said, 'this time I'll show you a really good place.'

'Where?' Ugo asked.

'The road to Fiumicino,' Tommaso said curtly. 'Go on,' he then ordered Lello who, heedless of fate, happy and carefree, was driving wildly with one elbow out of the window.

They crossed half of Rome again and were back on the Via
Portuense. The Permolio plant's flame fluttered, high as a throne
in the night's peacefulness.

All around, in the humidity that had thickened again, in fumes,
in steam as black as smoke, the neighbourhoods with their dying
lights seemed to be sleeping in the silence there along the Via Portuense, behind the Forlanini Hospital. The moon had risen and was
also smearing yellow over the clouds, swollen and vague in the fine,
spring-like warmth.

'We're okay,' Salvatore said, swaggering, 'who's gonna have a
better Christmas than us, this year?'

'Stop, stop!' Ugo shouted, all of a sudden.

'Stop!' he repeated, furiously. Lello put on the brakes abruptly,
and the car skidded a bit on the wet asphalt. They were going
through a broad part of the Portuense, wide as a square, with lots of
sleeping little houses and blocks of apartments and beyond a high
wall the last pavilions of the Forlanini. On their left there was a
deserted avenue and, on their right, opposite a urinal, a gas station
with its lights on. As they passed, Ugo had seen that, inside the glass
cabin, the attendant had fallen asleep.

'Pull in,' he muttered to Lello.

'Cut it out, let's go on, for Chrissake!' Tommaso said, angrily.

'Shut up, baby, and let us work,' Ugo said.

'Ya gonna stop here?' Tommaso insisted, raising his hand and
arm to their full length. 'You wanna go to jail, eh? Let's go to my
place!'

Ugo paid no attention to him. 'Go on, get out,' he said to the
Loon, his face like his ass, but with a mouth that was beginning to
laugh nervously. The Loon followed him, after Lello had pulled
up to the gravel pavement, and Ugo quickly went to the glass
cabin, shining in that crummy silence.

'Come on, we'll knock off Number Two,' he whispered.

'Isn't he cute in there?' the Loon said in a breathless voice, looking
at the attendant asleep inside the cabin.

He must have fallen asleep suddenly where he sat, knocked out by
fatigue, in a deckchair, his head against a corner of the glass wall,

and his bag on his thigh. He was wearing a light blue overall and a
peaked cap with a vizor twisted over his clump of black hair. The
Loon slowly opened the glass door, while behind him, Ugo grabbed
the metal strip below it ready to bash his head in if he woke up.
When the door was open the Loon, light as a cat, slipped slowly inside and began to put his hand on the bag over the man's stomach.
As he worked with his hands, he stared at the man's face, not taking
his eyes off him for a minute. He must have been a peasant who had
come to Rome not long ago, from Abruzzo or from Puglia; you
could tell by his broad, sun-baked face, by his mouth that had a
dumb expression even in sleep, and also by the strength you could
sense within the folds of the unbuttoned overall.

With his left hand the Loon raised the bag just a little, with his
right he opened it and grabbed the money inside, taking even the
coins. Then he drew back again, his eyes still on the man's face, and
shut the door. Ugo set the metal strip against it, and they ran backwards towards the car. But they had hardly turned when they saw
Shitter, who had come after them. Yellow as a corpse, he had bent
over the compressed air pump and, grinding his teeth, he was ripping it from its place, with an effort that threatened to kill him. He
was gasping, and a kind of death-rattle came from his throat.

'Whaddya doing, Shitter?' the Loon asked, breathless. But there
was no answer. It was nothing to joke about, and Ugo was suddenly
afraid. 'Let it go,' he said, 'it's probably got a serial number anyhow!' But Shitter wouldn't listen, so to hurry things up, Ugo lent
him a hand. They unscrewed the pump and carried it together to
the car. They managed to stick it inside, and Shitter sat on it, as the
car rocketed off towards Fiumicino.

Tommaso was sitting erect, like a snail when it comes out of its
shell and points its horns. He looked forward, observing the road,
towards the place he knew. His face had turned almost brown,
like he had put it on the stove, while the others divided up the take.
Venomously, he glanced at the piles of buildings, all alike, which
flew past them in the darkness, then the stupid little houses of the
Fort, then Parocchietta on top of a hill, then all the fields swollen
with water like sponges, filthy, and finally Trullo, with the yellow

lots in rows and four lamps burning, illuminating that landscape of hunger and death.

'This way?' Lello shouted, as the speedometer clocked them towards Magliana.

'Yeah,' Tommaso said, his mouth twisted. But Shitter, all of a sudden, yelled: 'Stop a minute!'

'Whaddya mean stop?' Tommaso said, acidly, 'Go faster, Lello!'

Shitter turned towards him, his face drooling, and he shouted in a broken voice: 'Fuck you!' Then he wheeled around to Lello: 'Stop,' he repeated furiously, 'Stop!' Lello jammed down the brake and stopped in a little street near the Magliana railroad.

Shitter got out: there was a pine tree, and, behind it, a little wall: four sheds around, crushed by the silence, among the muddy garden patches, and over it all, a little mound of black muck. Shitter went against the wall, behind the remains of a couple of bushes, and pulled down his pants. They heard him sighing and moaning, like he was being tortured, stripped naked, bound and gagged; and he could only make a kind of cat-like moan. Finally he came back, buttoning himself up and pulling his belt; he was soaked to the bone, and the windows of the car were white too, with breath inside, dampness outside; all of them were dripping. Tommaso said to him angrily: 'You did it, eh? Let's get going then!' Shitter turned his face to him and let out another belch.

The sky was again covered with clouds, all grey and dark. Below, the rows of lights of the railway seemed to filter up from underground. They began to pick up speed: but Shitter felt sick again. All that dampness had given him the shits, and he writhed, biting his knuckles. Every now and then he let out a fart, with a stink that strangled the others, who held their noses and rolled down the windows.

Suddenly Shitter said again: 'Stop! Stop!'

Tommaso went wild: 'Aòh!' he yelled, 'aren't you tired of shitting yet?'

'Stop, goddammit,' Shitter yelled, desperate.

Lello, calm, stopped again. They had passed La Magliana, and

there were no more houses; only, to the left, all those godforsaken
lights along the track. Shitter ran off wildly, pulling his pants down
again. He squatted at the edge of the road, against a kind of valley
full of burrs, which rose up towards the sky, between two cut-away
hills of tufa, also covered with burrs. Shitter stayed here, moaning
through clenched teeth, his neck taut in pain. Then he slowly stood
up, drew up his pants, buttoning himself; the peace was so complete
you could hear a dog barking three or four miles away, beyond all
that damp earth and those filthy mounds, towards Rome, or towards the sea, you couldn't tell which: and it sounded like a lost
soul, crying.

They passed Ponte Galeria at full speed; and meanwhile the first
raindrops began to fall again. Everything was dark and deserted.
Then, at the end of a curve, they saw some lights: a few houses and a
tavern. Farther on was the gas station, in a space that had just been
cleared beside the road, full of gleaming white gravel, all lighted up.
The attendant was busy cleaning a motorbike with a rag, a butt
stuck in his lips, the smoke burning his eyes.

When he saw the customers, he raised his head and flicked the
butt away, examining them. He let them know right off he didn't
like their looks. He was a peasant, too, with a mass of hair that stood
up on his head like a crouched bird, some dark and some blond: and
a thin face, long, nasty, with high cheekbones. He looked at the
friends, asked how much, and went to the pump slowly, with
studied calm, prepared for any false move. He must have kept a
revolver in one of his overall pockets, one of those deep pockets
that reach almost to the knee. Meanwhile, Lello yawned, at the
wheel, and played his role again: 'Hey, Spy, take a look at the tyres
and see how they are.'

Tommaso had got up, and Ugo had slipped out, too. Tommaso
gave a couple of kicks at the tyres and said: 'They're okay,' and
meanwhile looked at the attendant, his mouth trembling. The
moment the man took the pump in his hand, Tommaso fell on him,
twisting his arm behind his back: Ugo sprang from behind, and put
an arm around the man's throat, pressing so hard that his eyes
popped. Shitter had come out of the car, too: he promptly put his

hands on the bag, and began to work, moaning as if he were about to cry, and trembling so hard with rage he couldn't open it.

At that point, from the cabin on the edge of the railway embankment, the attendant's helper emerged. He stood still for a moment, between the light and the darkness, as if frozen stiff. He was a short, squat blond, with pale, nasty little eyes. He promptly put his hand in his pocket and pulled out his pistol: a snub little Mauser, and he aimed it, ready to shoot the three thieves. The other man, with Ugo's arm holding him, managed to yell: 'Don't shoot!' In fact, Tommaso and Shitter had immediately taken refuge behind the attendant, shielding themselves with his body. Tommaso pulled out his knife and held it against the man's side, shouting fiercely to the helper: 'If you shoot, we'll cut his guts out!' Lello, from the wheel yelled: 'Let's put him inside!' The little blond was still standing there under the light, his pistol aimed, not shooting.

'Come on, let's load him in,' Tommaso shouted. At that moment they saw a band of light from Fiumicino, at a curve under the hills, and a moment later a car appeared, moving fast with another behind it. They whipped past the gas pump, flooding the place with light. Without noticing them, already at work, Ugo, Tommaso and Shitter got into the car, dragging the man after them. They stretched him over their legs, half-smothered. Lello started the motor, turned around, and they darted off towards Rome. They were just in time to hear the two or three shots the blond fired into the air. When they were a few miles from the pump, they took the man's gun away from him, made him get out, after tearing off his bag, and then beat him up: Tommaso held him with one arm behind his back, and Ugo began to slaughter him, first in the stomach, then the face. A bit of blood spurted from his teeth at once, and from an eyelid, and he threw up. Then Shitter got out too, and with a kind of moan, began to hit him in the face, the belly, adding a few kicks. When Tommaso let go and the man fell to the pavement, Shitter gave him a couple more kicks in the back and all over, wherever they happened to land. Then they rolled him swollen and bleeding down the railway embankment, into a clump of bushes.

It was still drizzling, and the fields were covered with strips of

white fog, and above, in the sky, the moon was shining like a blood-
stain. Shitter, after all that work, began to feel bad again: he writhed,
his hands pressed against his belly, huddled over, his head almost
between his knees. He stank up the whole car: they could hardly
breathe. But the others didn't even notice; they were too busy
dividing up the takings.

After they passed the railway at La Magliana and plunged down
a narrow road among the canebrakes, they came out at the new
bridge towards the E.U.R. and Shitter started yelling for them to stop.

Laughing, Lello put on the brakes, and Shitter rolled down the
slope at the end of the bridge, among the bushes swollen with rain;
slipping in the soft mud two feet deep. And he couldn't stop himself
until he had slid down below the arch of the bridge, in the tall grass.
Then, he started letting fly for the third time. Afterwards, clinging
to the bushes, he pulled himself up, almost vomiting from the
effort, white as a corpse. But as soon as he got to the car, he didn't
get in, and without a word, he grasped the pump he had been holding under his legs.

'Now whaddya doing?' Tommaso snapped, baring his teeth like
a dog. 'Fa chrissake!' the others said, all holding out their hands,
disapproving his conduct. Ugo grabbed him by the shoulders, trying to pull him into the car. But Shitter, still not saying a word,
freed himself from Ugo, and holding the pump in his hands till his
bladder was about to burst from the effort, went down again below
the bridge, getting all wet as if he had dived in the river. He hid the
pump in a hole in the mud among the bushes. Then he came back
up, and still not talking, sat down again in his place, his teeth chattering.

'So you made it,' Salvatore said to him, as the car crossed the
bridge and sped towards San Paolo. 'You don't have enough breath
left to fart!' he went on, mocking.

'Don't say that to him!' Tommaso said bitingly, 'or else, just to
prove he can, he'll kill us all with poison gas!'

Shitter was silent, because he really didn't have enough breath to
answer.

'Now where're we going?' the Loon asked, full of enterprise, as if they had just started running around. They had more than ten thousand apiece in their pockets, and life was about to begin.

The last shower of rain fell: then everything cleared up, wet and shining through the warm mist. 'How about going dancing?' Lello said gaily, looking ahead, with a smile that illuminated his face like a beacon.

'Dancing?' Ugo said, who had syphilis in the brain. 'It's midnight! Let's go eat and drink!'

But Tommaso snapped, the corners of his mouth reaching his chin in disgust: 'Who gives a shit about food! You nuts! Let's get laid, for Godssake!'

'He's right!' the Loon yelled.

Lello brightened still more: 'How about dipping it, Ugo?' he asked.

'Let's go,' Ugo said, immediately in agreement.

'We're a smart bunch, all right: we can dance and we can steal and we can fuck good, too!' Salvatore yelled.

Shitter returned to life and farted with his lips.

They stuck the car in a sure place, next to the Basilica of San Paolo, and started walking towards the bar at the beginning of the tramline, twinkling under the pines.

'Let's go to Big-nose Marianna!' Ugo said.

'There're six of us!' the Loon said, 'she won't let us all in!'

'I'll talk to her!' Ugo said. 'And besides, we got the cash! We show her a couple bills, and she'll drop her pants, too!'

'Let's take the 18 then,' Salvatore shouted, running towards the stop.

Not a sign of a tram. Then they went into the little bar, which was about to close, and shouting like grackles, they ordered a miniature bottle apiece, some stuff they had seen outside in the window. One wanted Strega, another whisky, another, mistrà: and they went off to drink it under the pines, yelling in the deserted square, full of puddles.

All of a sudden Ugo started running like crazy, towards the deserted avenue of the basilica. 'Let's go, dopes!' he shouted. The others, not understanding, ran after him, gulping their drinks.

They dashed into the avenue just in time for Ugo to flag down the taxi he had seen from the distance.

'Come on, you bums,' he yelled, 'I'll pay the fare!'

Laughing and shoving, now completely, blindly drunk, they climbed in.

First of all, as they got out of the taxi at Santa Maria Maggiore, they ran into a dog, coming straight towards them, on the wet cobbles of the steep street.

'Let's take him with us!' Salvatore shouted, in a sudden burst of affection, forgetting Big Nose, with eyes you could only see the whites of because he was so drunk.

Staggering, he began to undo his belt.

'Let it go!' Tommaso shouted instead, looking poisonously out of the corner of his eye at the old dog making a big fuss over the company.

Moving as if he were swimming, Salvatore, his pants falling off him, had begun to fasten the belt around the dog's neck. Patiently, the dog let him do it, looking around.

Ugo was peeing, swaying, his legs apart and the bottle in his hand, facing the Basilica, with the steps and the domes that rose all the way to the clouds. Then he turned and came over to the dog, too. 'If we see a night-watchman,' he said, 'we'll turn him on it!' 'Old Bobby,' he said then, patting the dog's neck.

'What is it? This dog queer?' Tommaso said, scornfully.

'Show him your ass!' Shitter growled at him.

'Come on, sponger,' Salvatore shouted happily at the dog.

All of a sudden the Loon was also seized by an access of affection: he knelt on the cobblestones, glistening with water, and began grabbing the dog by the neck, pulling him around: and with this he ground his teeth and bit his lips, rubbing his face against the animal's muzzle and saying to him: 'you lousy bastard, you!'

Slowly they reached the neighbourhood where Big Nose Marianna lived, somewhere around Via Merulana.

'This way!' Ugo said, turning into an ascending street.

'No, it's over here,' the Loon yelled, starting to take another street, full of shut doors and façades with little columns.

'No, no,' Ugo answered, infuriated, 'it's up above.'

'Doncha remember? There was the traffic light,' the Loon said.

'No, no, there, there's that little park!' Ugo yelled. 'You remember the time we went through the park!'

'Aw, come with me,' Lello shouted, 'you're all pissed, you don't know your ass from a hole in the ground.'

He went straight up the hill, the others after him, still quarrelling, shouting with lungs full of drink, and the dog barking too, without the breath to assert himself.

They wandered around and around, up and down the street two or three times, passing the garden in front of the Cinema Brancaccio, turning back, along all those streets full of little columns and wrought-iron gates, with all the doors in a row, shut: but they couldn't find the door of Big Nose Marianna.

Instead, as luck would have it, they came to the Gatto Rosso. They found themselves outside it all of a sudden, because, thanks to the alcohol they had drunk, they had come running down Via dei Santi Quattro, all with cock in hand, pissing on the run, zig-zagging, for the third or fourth time, yelling: 'Look at the nice penmanship!'

Forgetting to button himself up in his surprise, Lello took a running leap towards the lighted entrance, with a row of Vespas outside, motorbikes, cycles, Guzzis, Gileras, and Benedettis: he jumped on a cycle, shouting: 'Let's go dancing, kids!', and the others after him, with the dog. Salvatore quickly tied the dog to the handlebars of a motorcycle and followed the others, who were already in the corridor, arguing with the manager.

'Nothing doing, fellas,' he said, almost gaily, 'we're closing up in five minutes!'

Ugo stared at him, as if he hadn't understood.

'You won't let us in?' he said, 'Why? Is our money the wrong colour?'

'But this is the last dance!' the manager said; the man from the checkroom had come over, and so had the cashier.

Lello, meanwhile, had gone forward to take a look at the situation. In the little hall the last couples were dancing: the orchestra was hammering out a tango, and the lights were a dark red. Sticking his head inside the room, Lello yelled at the maestro at the other end of the hall, in one corner, 'Play for me, oh, Johnny Guitar!'

Then he came back, shouting: 'Well, aren't we going in?'

'Fellas, it's all over now!' the manager said, his moustache drooping. Lello was seized with a fit of nervousness. He took out two thousand-notes and flung them on the counter of the checkroom. 'We'll pay extra,' he said, 'all right?' and without waiting for the man to answer him, he went into the hall, the others after him, soaked to the gills. The manager followed them, at their heels. Lello went over to a blonde to ask her to dance, a little tramp huddled in one corner. She was about to say no, but the tango ended: a girl friend of hers came up, with her partner, and all three left.

The lights changed: the normal illumination came on, with only a few red lamps here and there, and everybody got ready to go. Those who had overcoats went to get them, then put them on a chair for the last dance.

The friends wandered around here and there, through the long, narrow room. Shitter was sitting on the edge of the floor; he had taken off a shoe that was hurting him. Ugo had gone towards the orchestra at the back. They really began to play the last dance. It was a rumba that started normally, then got hotter and hotter, going so fast that you couldn't follow it: a lot of the couples stopped dancing and pressed around the exit: only two or three maniacs were left on the floor, twirling to the end, like they had St Vitus dance. The rumba ended, and then they went off, too, towards the door.

Ugo had taken his stand in front of the orchestra, and when it stopped, he said, gaily: 'Come on, play us "La Cumparsita"!'

The musicians looked at him, their necks swelling, and a knowing smile in their wise eyes, saying sure, sure, as they began to put their instruments away.

Ugo turned mean right away: 'Aòh!' he yelled, tautening his mouth as if to break it, 'I'm not kidding, eh!'

'Hey, kid,' the leader said, calm and peaceful, 'skip it, we're all sleepy.'

Ugo turned towards his friends, stuck his fingers in his mouth, whistled: they came over quickly, followed by the manager.

'Now then,' Ugo said, pointing his index finger and raised thumb towards the orchestra and moving his hand rapidly as if he were saying no: 'aren't you gonna play for us?'

'Hey, kid,' the leader said again, 'we're on salary!'

Ugo turned towards the manager, winking like a one-eyed man: 'How much do you give this bum?' he yelled.

'We're Union inspectors!' the Loon yelled with a laugh.

'Let's cut the talk. You gonna play for us?' Ugo yelled.

The leader looked at him, seriously, into the balls of his eyes. 'Fellaa ... ' he said, as if to say: 'Behave yourself: can't you see it's no good?'

Lello intervened: 'Why doncha wanna play?'

But Ugo shoved him aside with one hand and stepped forward, shouting: 'We'll pay you, you creeps!'

'Okay,' the leader said, 'but we can't play here in the hall; they've got to shut up.'

'Then you can play outside!' Ugo shouted, as if he were singing.

'Here, have a drink!' Shitter muttered, digging the half-full little bottle of Strega from his pocket: the maestro looked at it and, as Shitter watched happily, drank a gulp. Then the others took out the bottles they had left and offered them to the whole orchestra.

'Isn't your Mamma calling you?' the moustached manager said, 'Isn't it your bedtime?'

'Listen, Hairy,' Ugo said, 'I can buy your whole damn orchestra!'

No sooner said than done. He dug out the money, a nice wad of hundreds and thousands, with some ten-thousands in the midst. The leader gave it an inquiring look.

'Here,' Ugo shouted at him, 'if you play for me, I'll keep you happy for a month.'

'Aòh!' the leader said, 'we might play something. But it has to be outside.'

'Any place you say!' Lello said.

They immediately started for the exit, all of them dancing and singing.

Ugo, at the door, turned to the manager, his hands funnelled at his mouth and yelled: 'Find yasself another band; this one's all booked up!'

They went out into the street again, with the accordion player, the guitarist and the cornetist after them. First of all they drank, passing the bottles around, then the musicians started 'Thanks for the Flowers', while the Holy Six had another little pee on the pavement. Then they began to go down the empty street, dancing by themselves, doing fancy steps. 'Come on,' Ugo shouted at the musicians, 'we're paying you by the mile!'

They came along wearily, already a bit drunk, too. When they finished 'Thanks for the Flowers', Lello said: 'Hey, musicians, ya gotta play "The Prisoner's Song" for your boy Lello!'

'To hell with that,' Ugo said contemptuously, 'I wanna hear "Viper".'

Salvatore stopped dancing with the Loon and shouted: 'What's this "Viper" crap? You poisonous? I'll let you hear a song that'll make you all come!' He held out a finger towards the four-eyed guitarist: ' "Twenty Years"!' he said.

'The electric chair!' Lello shouted.

'Fuckoff, you drunk,' Ugo shouted, already pissed off, and turning to the players: 'I said I wanted "Viper", and that's what it is!'

'Play the lizard for that dope!' Lello said, indignant. 'Come on, play "The Prisoner's Song". That's a real man's song!'

Ugo showed his teeth like a rabid dog: he bent towards the orchestra until he was almost touching the pavement with his chin, crawling like a snake: 'Play "Viper",' he ordered.

Lello began to lose his calm; narrowing his eyes, twisting his mouth, he raised his index finger and waggled it negatively. 'No, no,' he said, 'they're gonna play "The Prisoner's Song".'

Salvatore meanwhile had renounced all claims to 'Twenty Years', and gaily, screaming like a siren, he was singing to himself and dancing: ' "Lola, Lola!" '

Then the orchestra took advantage and played the Charleston on its own, and all of them, clasping their dirty hands, and turning this way and that, started to dance. Dancing the Charleston at top speed, some by themselves, some in pairs, they came to the top of Via dei Santi Quattro, at the square of San Giovanni. Here Ugo, all of a sudden, said fuckoff to the Charleston and the rest of it and ran over to the obelisk, climbing up on the pedestal.

He held out his arms, raising his eyes to heaven, like San Francesco from that other part of the square, and shouted: 'Behold the glories of Rome!'

Then he began to sing, his adam's apple bobbing up and down, looking at the sky:

> ' to conquer we have the lions of
> Mussolini, armed and brave ... '

But he broke off at once, frowning and grinding his teeth: 'This is the obelisk,' he yelled, 'that we took from the Russians, the shits. We can be as tough as we want. Shitheads! Nobody's gonna shit all over us! ... This is the Eternal City!'

He caught his breath, then yelled desperately: 'Plebeians! The black market is finished! Now you can get bread without coupons! Now you have to dig up your bread with your fingernails! ... Before, my father used to bring it home, but you all know, they killed him ... at the door of my house ... He was there on the ground till the next morning, with three bullet-holes in his head ... Who helped him? Nobody, the bastards ... In Italy there're fifty million people, and we've all got wet asses!'

He had shouted so loud he now shut his eyes and looked like he was about to be sick: instead he yelled louder than before: 'To hell with De Gasperiii!'

He was silent for a little while, then he made a fart with his lips, a long one that seemed never to end, drooling bits of saliva, with a sinister sound, bending over, his hands to his belly. When that ended, he summoned his strength once again, to shout, white as death, to the musicians: 'Play the "March on Rome"!'

At that moment, the Loon, also half dead from the effort of dancing the Charleston with Tommaso, looked around the square of

San Giovanni as if he had only just realized where he was, then his
eyes focused on one point, a building at the beginning of Via San
Giovanni in Laterano, and slowly his whole face brightened at
this lovely surprise.

'Aòh!' he shouted, 'Stop. Stop. This is where my godmother is!'

Then he looked around, as if to make sure, assailed by some
doubt.

'Isn't that where they put the dead people?' he asked.

'Yeah,' Shitter said, who had taken down his pants behind the
column where Ugo was making his speech, 'it's the morgue, where
they put the people who die in the hospital!'

The Loom brightened again, content: 'Then that's where she is,
all right,' he shouted, 'because she died yesterday.'

He was silent for a moment, then turning toward the iron-
barred windows of the morgue at the end of the square, he shouted:
'Hey, Auntie!' Then again: 'Auntie!'

'She died of cancer,' he said.

'Cancer my ass,' Shitter said, 'she died of syph.'

Not content with calling her, the Loon let out a whistle, with two
fingers in his mouth.

'You expect her to answer you?' one of the musicians asked.

'Let's give her a serenade!' Salvatore shouted. Without waiting
further, the Loon started running towards the morgue. The others
ran after him, laughing, dragging the musicians. From the windows
of the morgue, the Loon turned towards the players, who arrived
breathless, white with fatigue and fear.

'Strike up,' he shouted, 'this time it's my turn!'

He looked towards the windows, and began to sing, spitting
whole blobs of saliva in the passion he was putting into it:

> ' My last serenade
> is not for you ...
> The last serenade ...
> What can I do?'

'Play!' Ugo, his face grim, commanded the musicians, who were
reluctant. After a moment's indecision, they started playing the

accompaniment, and the Loon could go on, triumphant, accompanying himself with broad gestures, as if he were on the stage of the Ambra Jovinelli.

> 'I want my song to go ...
> to a little blonde girl up there,
> I'm singing it soft and low
> for her, who's waited to hear ...
> my last serenade ...'

Then they saw at the top of the square, three or four night-watchmen on bicycles coming towards the gardens at Porta San Giovanni.

Shitter saw them first. 'Look!' he shouted, 'there's the parade!' and he began to retreat down towards Via Merulana.

'Here comes the charge!' Tommaso shouted, running after him. They all cleared out, and, since the opportunity had arisen, they dropped the musicians, who couldn't run because of their instruments, so they were left in the shit.

*

Rome was finally sleeping. Only the night-watchmen were still around, under the starry sky, starry after a manner of speaking, because the heavy, dark clouds were gathering densely, stormily, among the cornices and over the squares. Christmas was near, and the weather was really turning nasty. When they reached a safe spot, the friends said good-bye, and those from Trastevere went off on their own, taking Shitter with them since he was about finished, with those shits he had.

Instead, Lello and Tommaso set out on foot along the road towards home.

They didn't have all that far to walk, either to Piazza Vittorio, or as far as San Lorenzo, depending: anyhow it was going to be a while before the trams started running. They went down Via Emanuele Filiberto, and when they reached Piazza Vittorio they went towards the little soaked gardens and stretched on two benches.

one beside the other, Lello had his feet in one direction, and Tommasino in the other, so their heads were close, though they couldn't look each other in the face.

Kiosks, toilets, newspaper-stands: everything was shut up. Nobody went by. The street-lamps among the trees gleamed on their own: only at one corner of the square, at the end, in the midst of some fake rocks, there was a tribe of cats, of every kind, who roamed around, snuffing every now and then like forges. Tommasino and Lello were asshole buddies now: they had sprawled out, their hands clasped behind their heads, legs apart, cocks to the sky.

To pass the time, they started talking about the old days, when they were kids, and life was all rosy, though for that matter they were doing okay even now.

But they soon tired of all this great talk; they started to yawn, arguing a bit, and finally they dozed a little.

Slowly the night passed. When they woke and stood up, on the damp gravel, it was already almost five in the morning, and you could hear the first trams.

Full of life, his mouth ready to laugh, Lello stretched, looked at Tommaso and said: 'How about walking a little way, Tommà?'

'Chrissake,' Tommaso said happily, 'aren't you tired of walking yet?'

'Who's tired?' Lello said, starting off across Piazza Vittorio.

The men and women with their carts were beginning to arrive for the market: one was pulling his between shafts, like a slave, and another ran behind, half-asleep, all neatly combed like he had just come from the barber's. Ghostly, they passed over the wet cobblestones and disappeared along the pavements around the little park in the square's centre.

In one corner they heard some booming sounds. It was the garbage collectors, under the arcades, rolling the big metal drums of garbage and loading them on the truck.

Lello wasn't sleepy now, and he felt light, like when, towards morning, you come out of the dance hall after you've had a bit to drink. He went along under the arcades, his hands in his pockets, chest thrown out, a smartass look on his face.

Tommasino, pleased with his friend's good mood, trotted after him, also in a fine humour, but frowning a little, so as not to give Lello too much satisfaction.

'Fa Chrissake, Lè,' he said, 'you got fire under your feet?'

Lello didn't answer. He could hardly help laughing, and he walked without turning around. He knew his friend was just talking to keep his mouth busy: and if he complained, it was because he was in too good a humour, and basically, he was paying him a compliment, as if he were saying, slyly: 'Jeezus, Lè, you're a real sonofabitch! Don't you ever get tired? What are you anyway? A bersagliere?'

He was singing a song, wagging his head a little, his eyes staring straight ahead, and his hands in his pockets, almost tied there.

They met a night watchman on his way home, then a worker, white from lack of sleep, who was going off to the Lazio railway station, then a little old man with a beard, pushing a pram full of damp rags and other stuff that stank. But each was detached from the other, on his own, frozen, in silence. You could hardly hear the sound of the worn shoes on the damp pavement under the arches.

They left Piazza Vittorio and turned into Via Lamarmora, with the barracks and the Milk Depot, from which came a din of iron racks full of bottles, dragged over the floors of the warehouses and loaded on the trucks.

They stood loosely a moment in front of the Ambra Jovinelli, to look at the posters of the next day's film and the photographs of the vaudeville artists.

'Angel-face!' Lello said, exaggerating, biting his lips, in front of the poster with a half-naked blonde, her face looking over her shoulder, a whore's smile from ear to ear.

Immediately hard, Lello stood there a while, staring, his hands in the pockets of his tight pants.

They heard a tram creaking, from Piazza Vittorio.

'Come on, Lello!' Tommaso shouted then, beginning to run.

Whistling like nuts, they turned the corner of the Ambra Jovinelli and took Via Principe di Piemonte at full speed, along the

tracks of the little tram for Centocelle. They reached the arch of
Santa Bibiana. They were tired and breathless, but there wasn't
even the whiff of a tram. 'Fuck you ... Puzzilli,' Lello said, bending
from the waist, to breathe better.

'How could I know?' Tommaso said, trying not to seem too
exhausted. 'How could I tell whether it was the 12 or the 11?'

Lello sat down on the edge of the pavement. He stretched out his
legs, and rested his back against the rubble of a wall. 'Now we've got
a wait ahead,' he said, with a grimace; but he was soon resigned, his
face brightened, and sprawled on the pavement he started singing
again.

Tommasino made himself comfortable next to him, standing,
leaning against the wall, a bit bent and numbed, his hands in his
pockets and his legs crossed.

He felt pleased with life, replete, and as he waited all he could do
was yawn a little.

Lello stopped singing for a moment, and with his mouth taut,
because he could hardly keep from laughing at the smart crack he
had thought up, he said: 'Who's going to pick up these two bums
here?!'

He gulped gaily, and went on singing. He was a bit uncomfortable, but the position he had taken was smartass, he decided, and he
didn't want to change it.

Opposite them was the Cinema Apollo, which also had its posters
out, soaked, behind a metal grating, and the title of the picture
above the door, in letters two feet high.

All along Via Cairoli, where they had taken their places in the
curve because, even though there was no stop, the tram always had
to slow down, you couldn't see a goddam soul. And it was worse
still on the other side, along Via Principe di Piemonte, with the
Centocelle tram's tracks beneath the white wall of the Stazione Termini, and above, a kind of minaret, all wound around with a spiral
staircase, and rows and rows of lights. There was the Santa Bibiana
underpass, dripping like a wash-basin: a row of lights along the
peeling vault, and the tram tracks that entered it, for San Lorenzo
and Verano.

There was nobody at all. It seemed that instead of day breaking, night was falling: that everybody had gone back to bed, leaving squares, streets, avenues, underpasses to that darkness where, for no good reason, the municipal illumination shone, lighting the cobbles glistening with sticky water bright as day.

You could hear only some trains whistling above the embankments of the Stazione Termini, beyond the big wall. And, since there were no houses up there, you could see the whole sky clearly, still overcast: but you couldn't tell if certain dark stripes were bits of sky or clouds even more burdened with rain.

It was a sky that really had no end: whitish and a bit red. Since it was morning, a cold breeze had risen, freezing everything, and that's why it didn't rain, and everything was clear and clean. But that red that covered the piles of clouds was perhaps the reflection of the city's night-time illumination, which stretched for miles and miles in every direction, or else it was, now, a bit of the day's light: you couldn't tell.

It was barely daylight, if at all, so faint it was worse than night. At the farthest edges — those suspended over the outskirts, past the slums, past the beginnings of the countryside, hanging over the fields or the hills — a pinkish or yellow wisp slowly began to kindle the big clouds. It seemed to breathe up from the city's corners exposed to the north, where some drunk had pissed or vomited two or three hours before; though it was as if a hundred years had gone by, or else it blew from much farther away, from the beaches of Anzio or Fiumicino.

'Goddammit!' Tommaso said, disgusted, overcome with an attack of sleepiness so terrible he could almost cry. But he patted the wad of money in his pocket and was consoled. Lello had stopped singing: and he had also shifted his position. He had crouched over the pavement, pointing his elbows on his knees, resting his face on his fists. Every now and then he yawned idly, patiently.

'Goddamm that 11,' Tommaso said again, clenching his teeth, 'has it got lost or something?'

But at that very moment, as if sent by God, at the distant corner

of Via Cairoli and Piazza Vittorio a tram began to scrape at the
turn, with a *nyiii nyeeeeu* that made your flesh crawl. And the 11
appeared, completely empty.

Lello went on acting indifferent. When the tram came to the
Apollo it slowed down to turn and go under the arch of Santa
Bibiana. Tommasino darted forward, grabbed the railing, and,
leaping on to the running-board, entered the car, smartass, all ready
to stir up a fight with the conductor who, since nobody was there,
was sitting beside his pal, the driver. But suddenly, with a creak that
made your bones sweat, the car put on the brakes so abruptly that
Tommaso was hurled against the conductor's neck. 'Aòh, what's
up?' he yelled. The driver had his hand already on the switch, the
front door opened and he jumped down from the tram. Tommaso
went after him with one leap, and was on the street again, there in
front of the Santa Bibiana arch. Lello was sitting on the ground, on
the wet cobbles, next to the tram tracks, by the second car. He had
his back to Tommasino and to the two men who had got down at
the front: the conductor from the second car was already beside
him, standing there, staring. Lello sat with his back stiff, and his
legs stretched out in front of him. He had one hand against the
damp stones, the other raised to his eyes. Seen from behind, he
looked as if he had found something on the ground and was taking
a good look at it. Tommaso ran up to him. What Lello was looking
at was his hand, but it was in such a state that Tommaso, seeing it,
turned white as a rag and began to tremble. It was a little mashed
heap of bone and blood. Lello, trying to scream, but actually with
a tiny little voice that seemed to come from another world, as if he
weren't the one speaking, was saying: 'Help, my God, help!' His
foot was crushed, too: the shoe, the flesh, the bone made all one
mess, red with blood.

The conductor and the driver were there now and were bent
over Lello: they looked but didn't move, like the other man: he had
put his hands to his face and couldn't take them away, so as not to
see. Then other people came from here and there: in a few minutes
there was a little crowd around the stopped tram. Somebody tried
to pick up Lello under the arms and drag him toward the pavement.

But Lello started to scream louder: then they left him there, sitting on the cobblestones, his hand raised and his leg outstretched.

Two or three garbage collectors, younger men, ran off to telephone from a bar or from the booth at the terminus of the Centocelle tram. Meanwhile, around Lello now, the walls of the damp houses, the walls of the station, the faces of the people, the stones, everything had become lighter, almost white, in the first rays of the sun, which was slowly coming up, as always, over the city.

3

Irene

It was a fine afternoon, not long before Easter: with a tepid sun and a wind, still cool, that chapped the skin.

At the bottom of the swamp, near the sewer, Tommaso stood up, pulled up his pants, and began to climb up the embankment fastening his belt and cursing the stones and the sticks.

His shoes were all plastered with mud, black and stinking: he seemed to be emerging from the mouth of some volcano, with a puddle of water in the bottom, also black: around, among some carpets of watery grass and mould, a few frogs were already hopping as if they were in the midst of open country, and there were even some bugs here and there, the first little winged insects of spring.

Tommasino got to the top with his shoes all full of gravel and, furious, he sat down to shake them out. He cleaned his shoes, singing, put them on again, and started to walk in the direction of Sette Chiese.

He passed quietly the Viale Cristoforo Colombo and started along the level stretch towards Garbatella. This stretch was maybe half a mile long, with a few crumbling walls in the midst, and rows of big new buildings all around, six or seven floors, with some smaller ones only on the longer side, down the Via Maria Adelaide Garibaldi. There some kids were playing with a football, maybe a hundred of them, at the very least.

Tommaso moved into their midst: it was like Easter Monday already, with all of them yelling and enjoying themselves. There were also some who weren't playing football, the little ones, two or three years old, with smocks on and playsuits, and smart faces already, like those of their bigger brothers.

Tommaso, however, didn't even see all those kids. He had taken this direction for one reason only: to have a look at the girls he had glimpsed from a distance.

In fact, there were a lot of them, all over the field, watching the babies, some of them young kids themselves, others almost grown, all in shabby house dresses. They sat in rows or in circles in the midst of the plain, taking care to have nothing to do with the boys, of whatever age, making a racket all around them.

They were sitting on the dry grass or on the beaten earth, swept by the wind, the way women usually sit, or else with their asses on the ground and their knees held tightly together, covered by their skirts, both to one side. But, chatting and arguing, as they occasionally changed position, or as they stood up to slap one another or play some trick, they let the skirts go, and something, underneath, could be glimpsed.

That's why Tommaso was moving slowly along the field, skipping the games, and passing alone by the groups of girls, staring at them. They pretended not to see him at all, but they caught on right away that he had his eye on them. Then they began to joke more enthusiastically or laugh exaggeratedly, without looking him in the face: and they let him look down below, as they moved, since they weren't aware of his presence. And besides he was alone, and they were many. Tommasino walked along, one foot after the other, gulping.

'Goddamm lousy whores,' he muttered, twisting his mouth.

He was really angry, when he got to the end of the field. Here, behind a road that entered among the buildings of Garbatella, there was another open space without any women, and Tommaso then, red as a rooster, was already about to turn and go back, among those animals. But, in the way Fate sometimes works, right at that moment the dogcatchers' car turned in from the Cristoforo Colombo: it passed the heaps of girls and stopped in front of a big building a bit farther on.

All the kids ran after it, yelling, followed by the older ones, also curious as monkeys. From the courtyards all around, other kids had run up already, and so a whole gathering of snotnoses formed outside the door. Among these, however, there were also some girls this time, their hair all done up like starlets, with ponytails or locks falling lankly over their sweaters.

Seeing them, Tommaso moved closer, as the head dogcatcher had quickly gone inside, crossed the long and narrow courtyard among the blocks of houses.

Acting indifferent, Tommaso stood in the midst of the kids' racket, right behind two or three cunts, who, arm in arm, were stretching their necks towards the courtyard.

Slowly, pretending also to look at the courtyard, he closed in on the oldest, his hands in his pockets, his knuckles inside the worn, light cloth of the pants, and he began to do a bit of feeling: she caught on right away, and her eyes melted, looking a bit towards the courtyard and a bit towards the road, snapping her head, tick this way, tock the other, like a hen pecking. Her ponytail flapped from side to side, stiffly, over her little red collar. Pretending to look towards the road, she glanced occasionally back at Tommaso, who stood there, slack and frowning, his knuckles tight, but as if he didn't even exist, or was made of air, like the angels.

The little sun, from the midst of the sky, softly illuminated the houses. There it was sheltered from the wind, and everything, from the pavements to the trees among the buildings, was golden and warm.

Five minutes went by, then ten, a quarter of an hour. The boys had started playing again, pushing and shoving. Conversations had sprung up among the passers-by who had joined the crowd. The girls laughed like idiots, clinging to each other's hands, or rubbing their cheeks together affectionately. The other girls had also caught on that Tommaso was groping their older friend, the redhead with the ponytail, and the more they laughed, the angrier Tommaso looked.

Then, at last, something was happening at the end of the court-yard, beside the stone posts for the laundry-lines and the dried flower-beds. A little group was coming forward, marching: at the head was the dogcatcher with his assistant, behind them two hand-some girls in black aprons, hurrying, all excited. The catcher was carrying a kind of long fishing-pole, like the fishermen use in the

Tiber: but at the end instead of a line there was a strip of leather.

At the other end of this strip, attached by his neck, there was a comical little animal, trotting along, click click click, on little paws like a cricket's.

It was a tiny black dog: a mongrel, all curly, with black tufts at his paws. Like the two girls behind him, he was forced to walk fast, running every now and then to catch up with the man in the lead: and, at times, hanging from that sort of rod, he covered a yard or so in mid-air, like a fish.

When the group, at full speed, reached the entrance, all you could hear was laughter from the bunch of people waiting.

'Look at that!' the kids yelled, all amused, rather than disappointed, at the sight of the little thing arriving.

The dog, seeing all those people waiting for him at the exit, all those eyes trained on him, seemed to have a moment's hesitation. He froze, looked around, with one leg raised. But a tug on the line raised him bodily, and he had to go on his way, running, his little paws moving so fast they could hardly be seen.

However, fast as he ran, he still looked around and even pointed his eyes on the people waiting for him: but you could tell he felt embarrassed, as his big black eyes, shining through his thick coat, glanced here and there. And he was trying to hide his shame and his mortification, assuming an almost merry manner: he seemed to smile at the people looking at him, to show that nothing bad was happening to him; in fact, he was almost happy about it.

So he went past, half choked by the leather strap, through the audience, his chest out, tail wagging.

Only when he was very close, among the people's feet, you could see that his back was all raw, with patches of grey, mangy skin, among the scattered clumps of black curls.

The catcher sent him flying into the little truck, where the other prisoners were scratching the sides with their paws and panting.

The little truck shifted into gear and drove off. A moment later all the people, or almost all, had gone off, laughing: the boys back to the field, the girls along the pavements outside their homes, in the sun.

But the two who had followed the dog remained standing there at the entrance.

Tommasino, more and more aroused, coughing with emotion, went over and leaned against the wall, with one foot against the peeling plaster and one hand in his pocket.

The two girls stood there chattering, happy and calm, as if their mothers weren't waiting for them upstairs, as if they were just enjoying the sun and the fresh air.

Lousy tramps, Tommaso thought again, looking at them with disgust, his face flushed.

One was short, black as an African, with long hair, two tiny, pointed tits under her summer blouse, and a low, hard ass that almost came down to her heels. But Tommaso didn't get his hopes up about that one, not even to the point of looking at her. She was too cute and too wise: for him, he had glimpsed at once, the other one would do, who was also short, but plump, sturdy, almost like a boy, her hair curled by a permanent, standing up, toasted, all around her red, square face.

The two of them had noticed Tommaso right away: but they didn't pay him the slightest attention. They stood there, chatting the way grown women do. The little African was telling her friend about the telephone call she had had, the day before, from a boy-friend of her cousin's fiancée, and then about the phone call she had made that same morning, reporting the call to the cousin's mother. Tommaso was all cocky, and she went on talking and talking: he looked the other one in the face a bit, and then let his eyes wander around a while. The one that was talking also glanced towards the street now and then, as she talked, with a snap of her head, like a chicken.

Since they were dressed for staying at home, in their light blouses, they trembled in the cool air.

The African had a cold, but she seemed all pleased with the tight, slightly dry voice that came from her blocked nose with its red nostrils. The other, Irene, was listening to her, half-numb, pressing her elbows against her sides, her arms over her tits, her hands clasped. She was bent slightly forward, her head hunched between her shoulders, the tips of her feet both turned in, her thighs together and her belly sucked in. Tommaso, silent as a cell, took a cigarette from his pocket, lit it calmly and began to smoke, in slow, measured drags.

The two girls were a bit eager, they laughed, rubbing themselves on the shoulders and tits with their hands because of the cold. As they chatted, an old bag went by, her hair long as broom straws, as lean as Good Friday. The two greeted her, shouting and coming almost outside the gate: 'Ciao, Celeste!' The woman returned their greeting, gravely, from afar. And even more gay and sly, the little African shouted: 'How about giving me a kiss, Celeste?' But the woman went on about her business, frowning, catching on.

This was the right moment. Taking slow, calm drags of smoke, Tommaso detached himself from the wall and took a step toward the two girls.

'Was that dog yours?' he asked, seriously interested.

The two looked at each other. 'It's hers,' the African said. Irene became still more red in the face, and she burst out laughing. 'Why?' she asked.

'What was wrong with him? Hydrophobia?' Tommaso inquired.

'No, he was getting mange,' Irene answered.

Tommaso was silent for a while, looking at her; but then he continued at once, nice and polite: 'How'd he get that, for Chrissake?'

'I dunno,' she said, 'my kid brother was always taking him around, and he probably picked it up from some other dog.'

She talked fast, vibrantly, while the other girl, who had done so much talking before, now looked on in silence, glancing up at her friend.

So Tommaso and Irene started talking, making some remarks about dogs, about the advantages and disadvantages of having one around the house: she had her recent experiences with Fido, and Tommaso had known plenty of dogs where he lived.

'Eh,' Tommaso said, 'lotsa times you get attached to a dog, like he was one of the family! I had this dog, when I was little; but then he got too big, so my Ma gave him to a man with a wine cart. You won't believe it, but I cried all day that day!'

'Yes, indeed!' Irene confirmed, 'and they're smart too, dogs are!
Lots of times', she added, 'they understand more than some people,
who the world could do without. They ought to hand some of
them over to the dogcatcher.'

'That's the truth, all right!' Tommaso said.

All of a sudden, at that point, the African turned serious, impatient, stamping her feet on the ground as if to warm them up in
her open, run-down shoes. She said: 'I'll be saying goodbye,
Irene … ' She had made up her mind once and for all, and it was no
use arguing.

'You leaving?' Irene said, out of politeness. The African made a
kind of little bow, bending her right knee and drawing her other
leg back abruptly: 'Naturally,' she said, 'I can't stay here all day.
With the work I gotta do at home!'

She was almost cross and spiteful. But she promptly changed her
tone, and became intimate and sweet again, in spite of her hurry:
'Ciao, Irene,' she said, 'see you later.'

Proud of her voice, choked because of her cold, and proud of her
haste, she ran and dragged her ass after her, low and big, throwing
her legs out the way women do when they run, like they were
coming loose from the body, and holding her arms straight, elbows
against her sides, like a pair of plucked wings: it took her half an
hour, running like that, to reach the little pavement at the end of the
courtyard, where she vanished inside the door of a block of flats.

Tommaso lifted to his lips the cigarette now reduced to an ember.
He kept his other hand in his pocket, loosely, half in and half out
red and yellowish like a cabbage-stalk. He resumed their conversation about dogs: 'Would you like another dog, Signorina? If you
do, there's this friend of mine at Pietralata who has about half a
dozen puppies; they're nice dogs, too. Thoroughbreds!'

'I should hope not!' she said, half shouting, as if she were a bit
insulted, sticking out her tits. 'Don't let my brother and my father
hear you, or else they really would take another dog. I don't care
about dogs, really, not in the least. They just make work, they
climb on the beds … they dirty the house. And they eat!'

She talked like a little girl who is saying things to spite a play-

mate: her face was all fiery, in her outburst: 'What does a dog
mean, after all?' she went on. 'It means another thing to worry
about, that's what!' She was almost speechless, in her excessive conviction, and she pressed her chin against her throat, shaking her
head: no, no.

Then Tommaso had a stroke of genius: seeing that on the subject
of dogs they were in agreement, he looked at her, laughing, with his
little round, greasy face, and observed thoughtfully: 'If I hadn't
been coming here, to Garbatella, to see a friend of mine, and if I
hadn't stopped to see the kids play ball, and then if the dogcatcher
hadn't turned up, when would we of met, the two of us?'

He was pleased with this philosophical observation: he didn't say,
of course, that he had stopped on the field to look up the girls'
skirts and not to watch the kids playing football.

Nor did he think it wise to say who was the friend he had come
to see, a certain Settimio Augusto, a Jew who lived in one of the
houses beyond the Cristoforo Colombo: every now and then Tommaso lent him a hand with his cart, picking up a few hundred lire
this way: and he particularly didn't mention it to her, because with
the four hundred lire he had in his pocket, he had already worked
out the whole programme.

'Why?' Irene said, at the end of Tommaso's philosophical speech,
acting naive, the nice, homey girl who doesn't know anything about
these matters, and doesn't even give them a thought.

Tommaso let her have her own way, because he too was playing
the role of the good little boy. 'Why?' he said, 'aòh! ... haven't you
ever seen the way Fate works?'

Before the mysteries of Fate, Irene could only remain silent: but
keeping quiet, all full of herself, meant two things: 'So what?'
and, at the same time, 'I know, I know.'

In short, she didn't want to commit herself: Tommaso, for his
part, came a step closer to her, with his face all red over his pimples.
He stared hard, his eyes narrowed like two slits because of the smile
that swelled his cheeks under their grease. Looking at her like that,
up and down, he asked, as if casually and without any personal
stake: 'What's playing at the Cinema Garbatella tonight?'

'*Quo Vadis*,' Irene said quickly, as if happy to be able to give him good news.

'That's a good picture, all right!' he said, a connoisseur, also glad to receive the news.

He was silent for a moment, his smile becoming more intense and more sly: 'Why don't we go together, tomorrow? It's Sunday,' he asked, trying it out, since Irene must already have been expecting the question.

Irene frowned, made a kind of bow, serious, cross, almost severe: 'I can't,' she said, a bit sadly, hinting at certain facts, also fated, in her life.

But, of course, it would have been impossible for her to say right off that she would come: that much was understood.

Tommaso, however, didn't insist immediately: instead, he showed he understood the facts of life, a man who knows how hard it is for a girl to have a bit of freedom in the family, and the way people think, the neighbours.

He pressed the butt between his fingers and flicked it away, on to the pavement.

He dropped the subject of the movies, and asked: 'Do you work, Signorina?'

'No, I stay at home; but I have plenty to do, all the same!' Irene said, sadly.

'A homebody then!' Tommaso said, still playing the nice boy.

'That's right,' Irene said.

'And what does your father do?' Tommaso inquired, discreetly. Irene frowned and said, in a faint voice, very dignified: 'A city employee.'

Tommaso's eyes shone, at this happy surprise: 'So's mine!' he cried. This fact brought them still closer together, gave him more confidence, and they were both pleased and moved.

'My brother works, too,' Tommaso said then, 'a tailor.' 'As for me,' he added, bitterly, 'I've been doing a bit of clerking. But I've been going to technical school, at Tiburtino, and now I'm hoping to get a better job. I'm waiting for the answer to my application now ... '

He was silent for a moment, killing time by lighting himself another cigarette; then, smoking, he looked at her for a little in silence, with the question he had still to ask written all over his face: 'So tomorrow then ... ?' he said, 'nothing doing, at all?'

Irene was immediately a bit less negative: 'I'm afraid not,' she said.

'Why not?' Tommaso asked, innocently.

Irene was pensive. Then she shook her head again: 'No, no,' she said.

'Why not?' Tommaso repeated, 'we could meet here, at the tram stop, and go straight to the movies. What's wrong with that?'

'I don't know,' Irene said, 'it depends ... '

'On what?' Tommaso exclaimed, simple and innocent as a cherub.

'You can wait for me, if you want,' Irene said, 'tomorrow, around four, there at the tram stop ... If my father goes out ... and my girl-friend goes to see her cousin at Alberone, then I can think up an excuse for my mother ... and maybe I could come ... and meet you ... '

Tommaso was all red with emotion: 'I can wait even two hours,' he said, 'it doesn't matter, so long as you come .\ '

'Aòh!' Irene said, pressing her chin against her throat, 'if I can come, I'll come, if not, that's that ... ' But it was clear she would come. Like the African, she too suddenly became all serious and hurried, and a bit mysterious. 'Now it's late. I gotta go,' she said. 'So long.' And, a bit awkwardly, she held out her pudgy, red hand.

Tommaso understood this time too, a man of the world, and he didn't insist.

'So long,' he said, shaking her hand, with a long look. So they separated, and he stood and watched her hurry across the courtyard, but not running, very dignified, her permanent bobbing up and down. When she was at the end, realizing that he was watching, she couldn't help herself, and she ran a few steps, pretending to be in a hurry to go up to her home, wiggling her whole body, embarrassed at being observed from behind, with her elbows a bit tattered and her shoes with holes in them.

When she disappeared around a corner, Tommaso went off, smoking, and digging his hands into his pockets, acting like a smart bastard. He was thinking only of the next day: and he had time to think about it for more than two hours, until it was almost night, because he went all the way to the Tiburtina on foot, to save the tram fare.

*

All Garbatella was gleaming in the sun: the ascending streets with the little rows of trees, the houses with the pitched roofs and the tile cornices, the clusters of big, brown buildings with hundreds of windows and holes, and the big squares with arches and porticos of fake rockery all around. In one of these squares, at the tram terminus, next to a little parish movie-house, Tommaso was smoking nervously, all decked out, waiting for Irene.

She was already about ten minutes late, and Tommaso was grumbling angrily, casting nasty looks around, especially towards the Via delle Sette Chiese, where she ought to appear. 'Goddammit,' he was thinking indignantly, 'is she gonna stand me up?'

Under that fine sun, everybody had taken off not only overcoats, but jackets too, and they walked around, handsome, sloppy in their jerseys, with blue jeans. They walked up and down in groups, or maybe two or three on a Vespa.

Tommaso, who hadn't had even the sight of an overcoat all winter, and who had run around on the coldest days at most with a dirty scarf around his neck, was now covered from neck to heels by a handsome overcoat, really great, with a low martingale. He had borrowed it from Alberto Proietti, that friend of the young Fascist students in Trastevere, who was a full-fledged book-keeper by now. Because Tommaso, though he lived, if you'll pardon the expression, in the lower depths, on the level of starving bums, had friends in high places. Partly for this reason, and partly because of the woman he was waiting for, his face was blackly grim, and he wasn't looking at anybody.

From above, the 11 arrived, creaking, half empty, and stopped there on the slope, outside the fleabag movie house. Seven, eight people got off and, among them, Irene with her girl-friend of the day before.

Tommaso became as red as a pepper and stepped forward, nervously sniffling between one drag and the next. The two girls also came towards him quietly, almost laughing. They shook hands politely, saying hello. Then the African, all dolled up, with a purse that hung down to her shoes, promptly gave him her hand again, to take her leave. 'I gotta be running along,' she said, a bit embarrassed, with an air of complicity. And once her hand had been shaken, since nobody tried to stop her, she went towards the square of the Sette Chiese, her hair lashing the air.

The two of them remained alone. Irene made her habitual sideways gesture to arrange her hair, which was annoying her, over her collar. She was all dressed up, too: wearing a grey skirt and a light jersey of black wool, very tight. Tommaso was getting hot just at the sight of her. Jeezus, what boobs! he thought to himself, still more red and grim.

'Shall we get going, Irene?' he said, starting to walk towards the Cinema Garbatella, about three hundred yards away.

Irene fell in at his side. 'If my Dad sees me!' she said, rather than answer yes. They went up slowly along the tram tracks. Tommaso had some ideas on the subject of fathers. 'First of all,' he said, 'older men don't go strolling around the neighbourhood! They stay at the tavern, drinking their wine and playing a game of cards!'

'Sure,' Irene said, with irony, 'but my father comes to the tavern right in this neighbourhood, because his friends live at Piazza Pantero Pantera.'

What if we really did run into him Tommaso thought. Goddamm him! He let out a little laugh: 'Well, what of it?' he said, aloud, 'What if we did run into him? All the better. Then you can introduce me, and that'll be that!'

'Sure!' Irene said, sceptically. Tommaso's whole little speech was, in brief, the one men usually make when they want to convince a girl. But Irene was wide awake. And after she had spoken, a bit mysteriously, she remained silent, with an expression half incredulous and half bitter, as if she were saying: 'Yes, I'm game, and here I am, but I wasn't born yesterday!'

Tommaso chose to go no further into the argument. Now I'll

work her over, he thought, with those tits of hers! 'She's very cute,'
he said, aloud, 'that girl-friend of yours!'

'Yes, isn't she?' Irene said, agreeably, posing a little.

'What's her name?' Tommaso asked.

'Diasira,' Irene answered, proud to have a friend with such a
lovely name. 'She's engaged,' she added, again with her sly little
laugh, a bit stupid.

'Really?' Tommaso said, good-naturedly.

The incredulity deepened on Irene's face: 'To a boy from Tormarancio,' she said.

Tommaso dropped the subject again, not asking further information about this boy from Tormarancio. But Irene went on: 'But
he's not such a nice boy! He works for a week, then for a month
he's out of a job. He was fired only yesterday. If you ask me, he just
doesn't feel like working!'

Uhhhh, Tommaso thought, what a pain in the ass! then, aloud:
'Not every girl can be lucky. Times like these.'

Irene was silent again, her features hard with scepticism and bitter-
ness. But they had reached the theatre, with the posters full in the
bright sunlight. In the little square in front there was a bar, and
around it, maybe twenty boys. Tommaso's face became even more
glum, and coughing, he piloted Irene towards the entrance, to the
box office, putting his hand ever so lightly, with a protective air,
on her hip. Irene immediately assumed a cross, suffering manner,
the way engaged girls act.

She stayed like that all the time Tommaso waited to buy the
tickets: then they went up to the gallery, not condescending to
glance at the poor bastards sitting in the cheaper seats downstairs.
But there weren't many people, most of them had already seen
Quo Vadis when it first came out, especially the boys, because nearly
all of them had worked in it as extras.

When they went in, it was the interval between the shorts and
the feature, and they sat in the front row, against the railing, grim
and reserved. As soon as the lights were lowered Irene began to look
contented; she gave a glance at Tommaso, pushed her hair back
with the usual flick, settled in her seat: you could see she was pre-

paring to enjoy the film, and her good humour increased when
Tommaso called the vendor, who was about to go away, and
bought fifty lire of peanuts.

'Look,' Irene said, politely, between one peanut and the next,
reading the names of the actors: 'Leo Glinn's in it, too!' Tommaso
didn't even know who this Leo Glinn was. But Irene went on, full
of admiration, bubbling: 'I love the way he acts.'

'He's good, all right,' Tommaso admitted, agreeably.

As long as the peanuts lasted, that is to say almost to the end of
the first half of the picture, Tommaso, his hands and mouth occupied, good-humouredly looked at the film like Irene. But when he
had finished the peanuts, his nervousness began: Irene was there
beside him, innocent as a dove, with those tits that seemed to climb
over the railing, and those thighs that stretched over the seat and
grazed Tommaso's coat. Tommaso made a disgusted face, mentally,
and, also mentally, drew his head down between his shoulders, as if
he had been hit, thinking: She's stacked, all right. My God, she's
stacked!

He began to press his knee harder against her thigh. She understood, gave him a sidelong glance, but let him do it, because that
was the least she could concede, and it didn't clash with the innocent
pleasure of sitting and enjoying the picture. So, after a little while,
taking advantage of a scene of Christian martyrs in the Colosseum,
Tommaso put his arm around Irene's shoulders, as if driven by a
sudden outburst of affection, holding her tight. She accepted this
too, only becoming more serious and glum, continuing to look at
the film, her eyes glistening with emotion.

Tommaso had a mean hard on: as he held Irene tight with his left
arm, with his right he was smoking nervously. Then, all of a sudden,
for the first time in his life he threw away a butt over an inch long
and, very slowly, slipped off his overcoat. 'It's hot,' he grumbled,
carefully folding it and putting it against his belly.

Then he replaced his arm on Irene's shoulder; lost in her admira-
tion of Leo Glinn at work, she leaned a bit towards Tommaso.
Tommaso didn't stay long, however, with his arm on her shoulder.
He removed it and, this time, sought Irene's hand, which he pressed

in his. Her hand was like a man's, but it was sexy all the same: Tommaso squeezed it tight, holding the back of the hand against her thigh, down by the knee, and pressing on it.

'Cute, eh?' Irene said, alluding to Saint Peter. 'He's a marvellous actor.'

'He's okay!' Tommaso said. And, calculating Irene's remark as an encouragement, he moved the back of her hand a bit higher along the thigh.

But Irene, casually, pushed her hand down towards the knee, carrying Tommaso's, clenched, with it.

Fuck you! Tommaso thought.

'Oh, my goodness!' Irene said, putting her free hand to her mouth, in apprehension for the fate of the Christians, just about to go into the arena to be torn to pieces.

'It's not a true story!' Tommaso said, accustomed to consoling himself in this way. 'It's only a movie!'

'Only a movie!' Irene said, resentfully. 'Not a true story? I suppose the gospel is all made up?'

'Well,' Tommaso said, briskly, because he didn't give much of a damn, 'maybe these things really did happen, but when? About a thousand years ago, at least!'

'So?' Irene said, but she was too upset by the sight of the martyrs going up the narrow steps, singing hymns, so she was silent.

Tommaso exploited the moment to shove the two clasped hands up again: but Irene resisted, though she was all caught up in the film. Aha? Tommaso thought, grimly, trying to act smart with me, eh?

He began to get tough: he was really worked up and was sprawled in the little seat, his knees against the railing, so he had Irene's tits almost under his nose. Beneath the light wool jersey they were nice and big and firm, twenty pounds of meat apiece. Tommaso then removed his hand from hers again and put his arm back around her neck, but this time he held her tighter, so that with his fingers he reached the place where the tit met the shoulder. 'Jeezus,' he said, referring to the Christians, 'they really believed in God, all right, eh?'

'Sure they did!' she said, moved at feeling her sentiment shared by

Tommaso. Tommaso pushed his fingers down a bit farther and
began to run them over the flesh of her tit.

At that point the seats behind them were occupied by a father and
a mother with four little kids, three boys and a girl; the girl sat
down right behind Irene.

Goddamm these bums! Tommaso thought privately, grinding his
teeth. He had to stop the movement of his fingertips and withdraw
his hand a bit to the shoulder. Then he had to resign himself to
taking her hand again, on her thigh. And as for the tits he had to be
content with looking at them, two inches from his nostrils.

Then, getting harder and harder, though he was seriously enjoying the film, and with a whole family behind them, he started trying
to shift the two clasped hands from Irene's thigh to his own. Irene
resisted: she resisted twice, three times. Tommaso was really getting
mad. You shithead, he thought, you think you're out with some
shy dope? And meanwhile he went on tugging. Finally, all of a
sudden, Irene gave in, and Tommaso could press her hand on his
thigh. You dumb cunt, he repeated, to himself, didn't you know
you had to come across?

Now that he had Irene's hand there on his thigh, he began slowly
to pull it up: he had taken the other hand from his pocket, and was
holding it on his overcoat, for greater protection, keeping his eye
on it. He was wearing a light brown suit with white pin-stripes,
which he kept for holidays, socks and shoes bought the year before
from Zimmìo, who had stolen them from a faggot. But it was so
dark you couldn't see very clearly. As the two hands were a bit
higher, towards his cock, Irene began to free hers. Now whaddya
doing? Tommaso thought, menacingly, not letting go, red from
the strain, changing your mind?

Stubbornly, Irene went on trying to free her hand. Tommaso had
to squeeze it with all his strength, and he could hardly manage it.
When Irene tired and her hand relaxed, for a little while Tommaso
had to be content with holding it still almost on his knee. They
went back to watching *Quo Vadis* in peace, temporarily.

Meanwhile the balcony had slowly filled up, and now there
were even people standing, packed like sardines, with a stink of

sweat filling the place. One of the kids behind them, the smallest, was crying softly, taking advantage of the fact that his father, yellow from drink, had fallen asleep.

So when an important scene was over, now that you could see an ancient Roman aristocratic lady in her palace with slaves playing the harp, Tommaso started trying again.

Irene turned her head towards him and said: 'I don't want to. Keep still, Tommaso.'

'Why not?' he said.

'Because I don't,' Irene answered, and started freeing her hand again.

Goddammya, Tommaso thought, furiously, I'm gonna give you a kick in the face in a minute! Then, aloud: 'What's wrong? We're not doing anything!'

'Let go of me,' she murmured, 'I'm never going to come to the movies with you again!'

'What's wrong?' Tommaso repeated, more and more red from the effort he had to make to hold her tight, without moving too much. Who gives a big fat shit? he thought, whether you come back or not? You're here now, you bag, and that's enough. And while you're here with Tommaso, don't try any tricks!

He clasped her still harder, until he made the bones crack in that fat hand of hers. Irene grimaced with pain and stopped pulling. She sat still, looking at the screen, slumped down, her eyes shining.

Caught on at last, eh? Tommaso thought nastily. And he slowly began to rub her hand, the way he meant: but she really wanted none of it.

'Tommaso,' she said, in a different tone, 'I didn't think you were like this! If I'd of known, I wouldn't of come to the movies with you!' and she started the pulling and tugging again.

Tommaso turned really mean: 'Whadda we doing wrong? A little thing like this!' he said to her, almost yelling. And he yanked angrily, until her hand had gone where it was supposed to go. Lousy whore, daughter of a whore, Tommaso thought, feeling his honour was at stake by now, why'dya think I paid your way in here? Three hundred lire, and that's not shit! Gimme ya hand! he added, with a new, angry tug. Three hundred, he repeated to himself, furiously, I suppose you think that's nothing? And what for? To sit and look at you, for chrissake, because you're so cute? And I paid for those peanuts, too, he remembered, with a new access of rage. Fifty lire. Fuck you ...

He pressed the clenched hand under his.

'Just for a minute,' he said to her, 'only one minute, I swear by my Ma, who's dead!' But, at that same moment, he saw in Irene's eyes and face, now, a kind of resignation; and then he added, affectionately, a bit gaily: 'A man's gotta have his satisfaction, right?'

Little by little, still watching the film, Irene let Tommaso have her hand, as if it weren't hers, and he said to her, aloud this time: 'Jeezus, you're stacked, Irene. I really like you, you know that?' And he even added: 'Irene, I love you. I'm not kidding. I really do. I swear.'

Irene huddled down in the seat, silent as a shadow, grieving in every part of her body, from her chin to her tits, and from the tits to the thighs, looking at the picture with her eyes glistening with tears.

Quo Vadis was good and long, and when it was over and Tommaso and Irene came out of the Garbatella, it was already so dark it seemed late at night.

The little bar on the square opposite the theatre shone like a rhinestone, with all its tubes of neon, and Garbatella, all around, was a heap of lights scattered in the night. The groups of young guys had increased; some were astride their motorbikes, ready to go into Rome, others were coming back, all making a racket.

Along the street into which Irene and Tommaso now turned, the Via Enrico Cravero, it was almost dark, with only the slits of the closed windows and an occasional headlight. They walked in the centre, along a kind of fishbone of dirt in the midst of the crumbling asphalt, with a few skinny trees. Tommaso walked quietly, his hands in his pockets, and Irene came along behind, holding his arm. They walked in silence, like a couple long engaged, who have nothing to do with the rest of the world, all closed in their thoughts, and who have nothing even to say to each other, since all has been

4

said, except a little word here and there, pss pss pss, yes, no, said with a concerned expression, slightly bitter and full of many unsaid things.

In this way they reached Piazza delle Sette Chiese, where two more bars gleamed against the emptiness of the fields, with the immense outline of the hospital under construction in the distance and the lights of the Cristoforo Colombo; then they turned into a little road, still darker, without even street-lamps, with freshly excavated earth.

Along there, they stopped every now and then to say to each other those heart-rent words, psss, psss, no, yes, and an occasional kiss, but not too many because Tommaso felt lighter, since in the movie what was to happen had happened. Scowling, they came in this way to the top of the dark street, to the gardens of Piazza Sant'Eurosia where, already in agreement, body and soul, they said goodbye: they fixed an appointment in a low voice, said ciao almost breathlessly, and Irene went off along the fence of the gardens, on the gravel path, moving faster, and even running a few steps every now and then.

Tommaso watched her go, took out a butt and lighted it, going slowly down towards the tram stop, very smartass.

*

Full of his first Sunday spent with his girl, Tommaso arrived at Pietralata, and, on his arrival, Zimmìo and Shitter with another two or three of the band stopped him and asked him if he was willing to go with them to knock off some chickens at Anguillara. Tommaso said, 'Sure, why not?' It was already night and they set off in a Fiat the others had collected that afternoon.

The theft of the chickens at Anguillara went off fine, and they did it again the next day at Tivoli, and again at Settecamini, still nearer home. Holy Saturday then, without going to the trouble of driving all that distance, they went to knock some off at Ponte Mammolo, which was only a few steps away, beyond the Aniene.

Joking aside, this is how things went. Shitter, Greasy, Cazzitini,

Buddha, Hawk, Hyena, and Nazzareno, along with the younger ones, Tommasino, Zimmìo and Zucabbo, who in the meanwhile had grown up, too, had all gone to Tiburtino to rent a truck, since there was work to do in another direction, around Ciampino: three or four hundredweight of bronze. It was raining. Soaked to the marrow, the friends reached Tiburtino, and outside the window of a building that overlooked the countryside, they started whistling. Deaf Carlo came out, to the covered entrance, but when they asked him to give them the truck, he refused.

'No, no, no, I'm not giving you the truck. Three times I've lent it, and then the job falls through, and I'm stuck!'

'But we're not like those other bums!' they said.

'Well,' Deaf Carlo said, 'give me the five thousand here and now, and you can take it!'

'But we don't have five thousand,' the friends said.

He says: 'Then I'm sorry, kids, but the truck stays where it is!'

'Look,' they insisted, 'you'll screw up the deal for us. Tomorrow's Sunday. Monday's a holiday. What'll we do, without a lira?'

'You come with us,' Hyena suggested, 'if you don't trust us!'

'No, no!' Carlo said, 'I'm in trouble enough already. If we got caught, I'd be in for years!'

'We'll leave you our overcoats!' Shitter said.

'What good are they to me?' Carlo answered. 'Tomorrow's Easter, and I want to enjoy it nice and peaceful. I don't want to lay awake all night, worrying about the truck!'

And so it was good night, good night, and they had to go off, empty-handed. Shitter, Greasy, Hyena, Buddha, Hawk, Cazzitini, and Nazzareno went to the Bar Duemila, there opposite Monte del Pecoraro, at Tiburtino. The three younger kids stayed on the street, outside the building of Deaf Carlo, unable to make up their minds to move.

'Nothing doing,' Zimmìo said, dejected.

'You gonna go to bed? You crazy?' Zucabbo said, 'Let's get busy, we gotta think up something. The money's gotta come from somewhere!'

'You know,' Tommaso said, who was the greediest of all now that he was going with Irene, 'when you do a job without planning it ahead, it's easy to get caught!'

'Tomorrow's Easter,' Zucabbo said, 'I'd rather spend it inside than go without a lira!'

'We can't even hook laundry,' Zimmìo said, bitterly, 'it's raining, so nobody's left their washing out!'

They were silent for a moment, all depressed, and it was so quiet you could only hear the rain fall.

Then they heard a cock crow: it belonged to Deaf Carlo.

'How about knocking off the Deaf man's chickens?' Zucabbo said, his eyes shining: 'that sonofabitch wouldn't rent us the truck, so why don't we screw him?'

'Aòh, that reminds me,' said Zimmìo, who, with Tommaso, still stank from their chicken thefts, 'you two feel like coming with me? Now that I think about it, at the church of Ponte Mammolo, at the priest's house, there's some chickens. I know where. I went to knock off some eggs, a few years back. They've got a yard full!'

'How many?' Tommasino asked.

'Two, three hundred,' Zimmìo exclaimed.

'Let's go then. It's worth it,' Tommaso said. 'Five hundred apiece, that makes a hundred and fifty thousand!'

'Where'll we put them?' Zucabbo asked, already moving.

'I got a mattress ticking,' Zimmìo said promptly, 'my Ma took the wool out to wash it, and it'll hold all the chickens you want. We can even put the sacristan inside with them!'

So, full of hope, they set out. They went along the Via Tiburtina, huddled in the rain, with their hair soaked; they passed the Fiorentini factory and came to Zimmìo's house, next to a field, behind a rubbish heap. Tommaso and Zucabbo waited outside, while Zimmìo went in to pick up the necessary: a crowbar weighing sixty pounds, a chisel and a torch. As he went in, he glimpsed the flask of wine on the sideboard and began to gulp it down, one swallow, then another, then another still: and so he came out half tight, acting smart.

With the tools rolled up in the mattress cover, they came back to the Tiburtina and quickly walked the mile or two to Ponte Mammolo. The road seemed a river, over the darkness of the countryside as the lights of the slum quarters all around flickered on the horizon.

Crossing the bridge over the Aniene, they continued till they came to a pizzeria, then they turned left for Via Casal dei Pazzi. There were no lights there yet, as there was no electricity in the whole quarter, which was made up of little white-washed houses, half built and half not, with some taller buildings here and there. Halfway down Via Casal dei Pazzi there was the church, all white, and next to it the priest's house. On the other side of the road, only fields and gardens, with the lights of Montesacro in the background.

Around the church and the priest's house ran a little wall. The three followed it to the back, where the henhouse was. The little path that flanked it was a stream of mud, and the two or three hunks of new houses near by looked like ruins. It was still raining. Zimmìo got to work with crowbar and chisel, while Tommaso gave him a little light: Zucabbo had taken his position at the corner of the street in the distance. Zimmìo hammered loudly, not worrying: it didn't take long to make a fifteen-inch hole. He was nearly finished, when a light came on in one of the half-built houses.

'Watch out!' Zucabbo came back to say.

Zimmìo didn't even look at him: 'Who gives a shit?' he said, 'That's Bove's father, the worst robber since Ali Baba. If he sees us, he'll want a cut!'

Zimmìo knew all these things because his girl lived there at Ponte Mammolo, and they'd been going together for more than a year.

'Then get moving!' Tommaso said.

When the hole was finished, Zimmìo turned to Tommaso: 'Now I've made the hole,' he said, 'I'll keep watch, and you go inside. I gotta headache, after all that wine!'

'Whaddya mean he goes in?' Zucabbo said, 'You go. You're the one who knows all about catching chickens. By the way, don't they squawk or something?'

'No,' Tommaso said, 'they don't squawk. Not if it's dark. If you turn on a light, they holler; but in the dark they just go cluck

cluck, quiet. Besides these are Catholic hens. Religious, know what
I mean? They're good!'

So Zimmìo wriggled in on his belly: once he was inside, Tommaso climbed through the hole and followed him. When they were
both in the yard, they turned on the flashlight.

In the henhouse, there was a lot of straw, a couple of empty
baskets, and a tool-rack, but no sign of a hen. In the back there was
a wooden gate with a chain, and the other wall was of hollow
brick.

'Hurry up,' Zimmìo said, 'they're in this next little room. Cancha
hear them?'

'Goddammit,' Tommaso said fiercely, 'you could hear them before, too!'

Anyhow, they broke through the hollow-brick wall, and went
into the other little cell. Here, in a section of another tool-rack,
there was a single hen. They turned on the light again and, in a
basket, they saw an egg. Tommaso fell on it and sucked it dry.
Zimmìo tried to stop him: 'Gimme some,' he said angrily, 'goddammya!'

But Tommaso pointed to the hen, and said: 'Stick a finger up her
ass and see if she's got another egg in her!'

Then he went over to the hen and grabbed it: in the darkness, she
allowed herself to be taken, clucking softly, and Tommaso started
to wring her neck so hard the head almost came off in his hand:
'Ya dope, whydja kill it?' Zimmìo said, 'I woulda taken her for
myself, put her in the yard, and I'd of had an egg for breakfast
every morning!'

Tommaso was so angry he preferred not to answer: there was a
deep silence, and they could hear the drops of rain outside. In that
little cell the gate was open: there was no need to break the wall to
get into the next one. Zimmìo noticed this, overjoyed: 'The hens've
gotta be here!' he said, hitting the gate with his shoulder. So they
went into the third room, and here were four hens. They took
them and killed them. ''Let's break this wall, too,' Zimmìo said
then, disappointed at having found only four, 'where the fuck're the
others?'

'Come on, let's get outta here,' Tommaso said grimly, 'the priests'll start saying Mass in a minute. They get up early!'

They came out of the henhouse, and Zucabbo was gone.

'Come on, come on,' Zimmìo said, 'where the fuck's Zucabbo gone?' They began to put everything into the ticking, the tools and the hens, and then Zucabbo appeared. 'It's nothing!' he said, coming over to them, 'I saw somebody, and I followed him to see where he was going!' 'What about the hens?' he said then, turning white with disappointment, when he saw the ticking.

'Where are they?' he repeated, with desperation in his eyes.

Tommaso answered him, with a seizure of nerves that made his voice shake: 'What hens? There weren't even any moths in that dump!'

Zucabbo couldn't take his eyes off Zimmìo, who was crouching over the tools, putting them back. 'What?' he said, unable to resign himself, becoming more and more depressed, 'you said there were three hundred chickens. So where are they? You bring us to catch years in stir, not hens!'

'The shithead!' Tommaso added, angrily, his voice quavering.

'Shithead yourself!' Zimmìo snapped, dropping the tools. 'What of it? Last time I took you on that oil job, and it worked; so I wasn't such a shithead then. And there weren't any years in jail!'

He knelt over the ticking again, his knees in the mud, quiet for a while, then shrugging, he muttered to himself: 'It didn't work out, goddammit!'

Tommaso looked at him, hard, his eyes filled with rancour, becoming narrower and narrower, almost squeezed shut. Finally he blurted: 'Another time you get one of these fits, pick on somebody else! Goddammit. Tomorrow's Easter. The next day's Easter Monday, I gotta go out with my girl, and we're broke!'

He said these last words almost with tears in his eyes, like a little kid. They were all quiet for a while: it had stopped raining, the clouds had broken up, leaving patches of clear sky here and there with a little moonlight, and a breeze was blowing, glueing their icy clothes to them.

'Aòh,' Zimmìo said, hoarsely, 'you won't be dead broke; you got a chicken to eat. Thank God we're still free!'

At these words Zucabbo lost control of himself, his nerves broke, he trembled, and he hurled the chickens at Zimmìo, shouting: 'Eat the chickens yourself, bum! I got plenty to eat at my house!'

The chickens, having slammed against Zimmìo, fell into the mud with their wings open, at Tommaso's feet. Seized with rage like Zucabbo, he gave them a kick that made them roll down on the field. Then he turned and went off along the road, without even looking back to see what the others were doing. He walked a good way like this, his face green with rage and with the cold, because the wind was blowing strong, racing over the fields and the countryside soaked with icy water. Then he turned a moment, to look: Zucabbo was still arguing with Zimmìo, who was holding him by his clothes. 'Let him go!' he yelled. Zucabbo, with a shove, freed himself from Zimmìo and came running, wet as a pullet, towards Tommaso. Tommaso walked with his hands in his pockets, filled with water, and his soaked hair over his forehead, crushed. 'What'll I do tomorrow, with Irene?' he said aloud, talking to himself, 'Let's hope Christ helps me; a man can't go on living this way!'

At these thoughts he had another fit of anger, stopped, and turned to Zimmìo to yell again: 'Lousy son of a whore! You're gonna make us rich, eh? Goddammya!'

Zimmìo, in the distance, looked up from the ticking that he had been folding, and yelled back, prompt, not taking it too hard, since the words were already in his mouth: 'Stop shitting your pants, you Spy!'

However, the next morning, Tommaso and Zucabbo, asshole buddies again, had second thoughts. Tommaso was in a good humour, because so long as there are dopes a smart kid can always get along: in fact, his guardian angel had arranged for him to meet a guy with a camera, a Northerner doing his military service at the Fort. The soldier had said to him: 'How about taking my picture for me?'

'Sure,' Tommaso said, and the character had hardly turned to pose when Tommaso was gone with the wind.

So he had picked up a thousand lire: now he could go to the date with Irene happy and swaggering; a thousand. The soldier had put a fortune in his hands.

Zucabbo said: 'Why should we give all the hens to Zimmìo? We can eat one apiece. With a chicken inside us, we'll have a better Easter than anybody!'

It was a pretty nice morning, with the sun among the clouds, burning a little. Zimmìo lived outside Pietralata, in some houses on the Tiburtina, beyond the field, in the direction of the new village the INA-Case had been constructing for about a hundred years and where, for the moment, all you could see was gaps for windows, peaked roofs, and skylights.

Tommaso and Zucabbo came to Zimmìo's house and called him. He was asleep. Since he had his girl at Ponte Mammolo, and she and his mother-in-law were real Catholics, he had had to get up early and go with them to Mass, half dead with sleep, over at Ponte Mammolo.

Then he had come back, maybe half an hour ago, and was under the blankets again, having fallen asleep at once. Tommaso and Zucabbo woke him up. 'What about the hens?' they said to him. 'How about giving us ours?'

'I gave two to my Ma,' Zimmìo said, swollen with sleep, grey, with a funny face that didn't look right, 'and I left the other two there, at Via Casal dei Pazzi.'

He looked at them for a moment, his eyes beginning to laugh and laugh. 'By the way ... ' he said, and he burst out laughing aloud, like a nut, 'by the way, you know what the priest said at Mass?'

And he went on laughing so hard he couldn't say another word: the others knew he had been to Mass right where they had pulled off the job three hours before, and they looked at him, already red in the face and laughing, too.

'He said ... ' Zimmìo began to narrate when he had calmed down a little, 'that they stole thirty hens from him last night. That blasphemous thieves had broken into the henhouse, and that these sinners had taken thirty hens, exploiting him, who lives only for charity. Thirty hens, he said, the sonofabitch!'

Tommaso and Zucabbo were bright-eyed with joy at the idea
that the priest had spoken about them at Mass in front of all those
people.

'Aòh, Tomà,' Zucabbo said, 'You hear that? We're worse than
the bandit Giuliano! That's us!'

'Aòh,' Tommaso said, 'how about going to Mass to hear him?'

'Let's go!' Zucabbo said, enthusiastically.

'Come on,' Tommaso said to Zimmìo, 'come back with us!'

So they walked to Ponte Mammolo, and they weren't content
to hear only the sermon of the second Mass, but they stayed also for
the last one, at noon. The priest talked about them each time, these
terrible robbers, these lost souls, these blasphemers, and so on and
so forth ... They really got a bellyful of Masses, considering it had
been ten years since they had been in church, when they made their
First Communion, and they couldn't even remember who was the
creator of heaven and earth.

Then, all content, they walked out under the fine sun that had
cleared out the clouds and was shining gaily over the little white
houses scattered over the clean-washed countryside.

Zimmìo bought coffee and buns for all at a bar in Via Selmi,
crowded with young guys in good suits, full of God's Grace. But
Tommasino was impatient: he had things to do, not like those
hopeless bums Zucabbo and Zimmìo, who could think only of
pulling off some job. He felt a great calm inside him, a happiness
that made his stomach tingle at the thought of what he was going
to do. So, he said goodbye hurriedly, wished them both a Happy
Easter, and took the bus for Garbatella, to the appointment with
Irene, all loving and giving.

4

The Battle of Pietralata

It was Sunday, but all of Tommaso's friends, Shitter, Greasy, Hyena, Buddha, Hawk, Cazzitini, Zimmìo, Zucabbo, were broke and hadn't stirred from Pietralata. Maybe most of them had new suits, but what was the use of going into Rome without a cent? That morning they had taken their places at the bar opposite the bus stop, which had tables outside, and they were sprawled there, talking about football, and kicking up a bit of a fuss. About eleven Greasy and Hawk got fed up hanging around there and had ventured off. The others didn't feel like moving, and they sat at the bar with their bellies in the sun and their hands on their crotches.

Then, to take the place of Greasy and Hawk, some others had come, Prickhead, Pincher, Cianetto, Chestnut and others.

Even though it was April, the weather wasn't very good: it was colder than it had been at Christmas. It was one of those days with the sky all full of clouds and an occasional orange stripe here and there; the whole city seemed illuminated by candles. Pietralata lay in a lake of mud. But with the excuse that it was spring, they had all put on their new clothes, light poplin suits, and yellow sport shirts or cowboy blue ones. There were lines of people coming and going, from Tiburtino, from Ponte Mammolo, or waiting in a bunch for the bus to go into Rome; and others, like Shitter and his friends, who were without a lira, flat, mooching around the place, acting elegant in their new clothes.

Shitter and the rest, then, were sitting outside the bar when they saw three people coming along Via di Pietralata, in plain clothes; but the friends recognized the trio at once. Two were policemen, and one was a carabiniere of the neighbourhood, also in civilian clothes. They stopped to buy some olives, at a stand at the beginning of the section and then, slowly, eating the olives, they headed for the bar.

All the bums sitting at the tables signalled each other, with sad eyes, rubbing their tongues lazily over their teeth, or half yawning. They muttered: 'What's up? What's up? They picking up somebody?' There wasn't a one who didn't have a record, and the police could be coming there for anybody in the bunch: so nobody moved, all looking around with sharpened eyes, acting wise.

The cops came in among the chairs and tables, very calmly. Shitter, watching them, kept his seat and asked himself, a bit with uncertainty and a bit with fear, as his eyes shone blissfully: 'Who're they taking? Me? Him? Or him? They're here to pick up one of us, all right!'

In fact, the men came over to the tables where the gang was, and already the rumour was spreading: the people at the bus stop, the women going by to do their marketing, the swarms of kids, the other customers of the bar, all had sniffed the situation.

As if nothing were happening, meanwhile, the men went to Shitter's table, and with the same casual manner, they stood one on either side of him, and one behind his chair. They were all joking, and the first words they said were: 'Eh! Long time no see.'

Shitter was huddled down in his seat: with his grey jaws, his few, sickly curls over his neck, his eyes asleep. But you could already see that his hands, clasped, were trembling.

The policeman, however, had been addressing Cazzitini, who was near by, not Shitter, and in fact, had given him an affectionate slap on the cheek. Then they turned to Shitter, all of a sudden, and said serenely: 'Come along with us!'

Shitter was alert, because he had been very busy those past few days and he even had some hot stuff at home. So as soon as the men opened their mouths, he yelled: 'No! I'm not coming with you. Why should I?'

Meanwhile he had half risen, ready, in the hope that his friends would help him get away. People were already beginning to gather around, to look on. You could hear voices everywhere: 'Aòh, what's going on?' 'They're picking up Shitter!' 'The dope, he lets them pinch him like that?' One said one thing, another another, until there was a general racket. 'What's he done? What's wrong?' One man spoke to Shitter, who had sat down again, white as a candle: 'Go with them!' he advised him, and another said: 'Don't go, dope. If you do, they'll never let you out again!'

The crowd pressed tighter and tighter, especially the women: those already out, and those who lived in the houses near by, who now came out to see. All poor slum women, dishevelled, with black housedresses on, greasy and dirty, slippers on their feet.

The policemen began to shout: 'Clear out! Make room!' But the women who had crowded around wouldn't move; instead, they also began, in voices still a bit subdued, to yell a few words at the flatfeet: 'Shame on you! Bums!' They looked ready to cry, their faces red and drawn, their hair falling over their foreheads, their knots half undone.

Then, without wasting more time, two of the men grabbed Shitter under the arms and lifted him bodily, trying to drag him away, to tear him from the chair, where he was clinging like an octopus. The chief, a Neapolitan smartass about forty, speaking in a cancerous voice from his nose, yelled: 'Clear out! Bugger off!'

Shitter wouldn't submit, and he began to wriggle like a madman: they had already torn his shirt and his T-shirt, and he still writhed in the chair, his arms clasped by the policemen, twisting his body to be free, as if his ass was on fire. His friends sat still, not moving. In fact, they had huddled around the table; they had a right to stay there and they watched carefully, a foot or two from the policemen's shoulders. More people had come up, attracted by the racket. Between the bus stop and the bar, there were already about a hundred people, because it was Sunday and they were all outside in the streets. The men, especially the younger ones, stayed behind, keeping their distance. But the women came forward, forcing their way, determined to make themselves heard, to take Shitter's part. The policemen meanwhile had managed to get him out of the chair: but he had grabbed the legs of the little table with both hands, and if they wanted to drag him off, they would have to drag the table with him. The woman who ran the bar began to yell with fright: 'You're ruining the place!' so angrily, with such hate in her voice, that the other women also started yelling louder along with her.

Dazed by all that noise, the three policemen decided to get it over with. One bent down to grasp Shitter's wrists and tried to tear his hands from the table's legs. But Shitter, with an animal-like jerk, when he saw that man's wrist near his mouth, sank his teeth into it.

But he caught it clumsily, sleeve and all: he drew his head back, twisting his mouth, spitting, then bit again, this time farther down, towards the hairy hand. He got as much skin as he could, with his nose wrinkling over his bared teeth, biting, drooling spit: until his saliva was mixed with blood.

Crazed with pain, the policeman gave Shitter a slap that broke him clean from the table, which rolled to the ground, crashing and bouncing. The others still didn't move, calmly watching the scene.

Shitter was suspended in mid-air, held up under the arms by the policemen, but he kept on kicking and wriggling: one of the policemen holding him had to use a free hand to clear the way, because the other guys wouldn't budge an inch, and the women kept pressing closer all around. So Shitter half succeeded in freeing himself again and grabbed another table, scraping along the ground on his belly, over the muddy pavement.

He got a better grip than before: if the two policemen tried to detach his hands, he kicked with such fury he upset all the chairs; if they held his body tight, they couldn't detach him from the table. Finally the one with his wrist dripping blood gave him another jerk and pulled him loose. Shitter found himself all of a sudden lying with his belly in the air, his legs held fast, his back dragging in the mud.

Then he began to squirm like a fish: his eyes were rolling, and he was so white in the face he looked like he was about to die on the spot. He yelled, almost crying: 'Mamma! Mamma! Help! Let go of me!'

The women were now beside themselves, out of their heads.

'Bums!' they shouted. 'Don't hurt him!' 'A poor mother's son!'
'Clear out! Make room!' the policemen shouted. But one woman
grabbed a policeman's arm with both hands, pulling at him and
shouting: 'Let go! Let go, you killer!'

A stone whistled over their heads, thrown hard, and smashed
against the wall of the bar: and the women yelled still louder:
'Traitors! You'd betray your own mothers!'

Shitter, twisting on the ground, grabbed the policemen's pants,
and if they managed to drag him a few steps, he bit them, like a
mad dog. Then the policemen really had to try to finish it off: one
raised his fist and hit Shitter, who threw up, and when he opened
his eyes again, he was without strength, merely moaning as if he
were about to die: 'Mamma! Help! Mamma! Save me!'

But with blows and jerks, the policemen now succeeded in dragging him along, forcing their way through the crowd. The women
then began to get nasty, urged on by the men, who were shouting
from behind. 'Kill them! Hit them!' the women who were farther
away shouted. 'Carry him right, you lousy bums!' others shouted,
more pityingly. 'Leave him alone. He has eppapleptic fits!' 'He
doesn't have a father or mother!' 'He's a poor orphan, and he's sick,
too!'

'Kill them,' the more venomous women shouted, because all of
them had sons in jail, or on the wanted list, who hadn't been able to
find work for years and were starving to death.

One woman, crying, took off a clog and began to hit one of the
policemen, Behind her, some others charged, all together. Things
were taking a bad turn, and the policemen had to let go of Shitter,
if they didn't want to be torn to shreds. Shitter lay motionless where
they had dropped him. 'They've killed him!' one woman yelled at
the top of her lungs. 'He's losing all his blood, from his head!'
'Come on, we'll kill them, too! Goddamm them, we'll make them
lick that blood up with their tongues!'

The policemen began to swing the chains of their handcuffs all
around, shouting: 'Stop this, you nuts! We'll lock you all up!'
And one of them, drawing his gun, yelled: 'Stop, or I'll shoot!'

He should have kept his mouth shut: all the women fell on him in a body, kicking and biting. They pressed the men from behind, from the sides. Two or three times the men fell to their knees or flat on their backs, with the women around trampling on them and spitting. Then they started to run, freeing themselves, and moving faster and faster. The women threw stones after them, bricks, pieces of wood. There was another woman on the road, with a baby in her arms, near a metal hod where she had lighted a fire.

'Set fire to them, Crocefissa!' the women yelled at her.

Without having to be told twice, Crocefissa set down the baby and began throwing burning sticks at the policemen. Then, not content, she grabbed the whole pan with both hands, full of glowing, crackling coals, and hurled it right at the feet of the three men, with all the fire spilling on the ground, spreading and exploding, in a burst of ashes, smoke, and sparks.

Meanwhile Shitter, lying there like a dead man, opened one eye, shut it again, reopened it and looked around, indifferently. Hyena was spread-legged over him, looking towards Montesacro; as if speaking to the air he said: 'Clear out. Run to my house.'

Shitter slowly got up; in the midst of the riot, and quick as a fox, he ran off: he dived among the houses, ran along all those streets, jumped over puddles, until he was almost in the open country towards Via delle Messi d'Oro; he climbed over a fence and jumped into a garden, crouched in a field of cabbages, and came within sight of a farmhouse. It was old, crumbling, like an ancient ruin: in its midst it had a dirty courtyard strewn with manure, two or three sheds, a watering-trough: next to the old house, there was a new one built on, a kind of storeroom, just opposite the pump. Shitter dug into a hole under the pump, all cracked and stained with copper sulphate and litter, took out a key, and opened the storeroom's broken door.

Hyena was living alone temporarily because his father was locked up. The room was a big, black kitchen, with a cot, a chest of drawers, and a radio, the whole place full of butts; on the chest of drawers a package of hand-made cigarettes was ready for his father. A real cigarette, a Nazionale, was fixed to the wall with a nail; a friend of Hyena's had stuck it there, when he swore he would give up smoking. In another corner there was a coat hanger without the rod for pants, and a carpenter's bench with pincers hanging from it, and a whole bazaar of stuff on top. On the wall beside the door there was even a little washtub with some clothes soaking, because Hyena did his own laundry.

Once inside, Shitter drew breath, then immediately went to see if he could find anything to eat: but there was fuckall. So he stretched out on the cot with a butt in his mouth, and waited.

After a while Hyena arrived, with a packet containing slices of salami and two or three rolls: they ate like two pigs, chatting about everything that had happened; then, around two, some other friends came and, since, on this earth, what must be must be, and a man who worries about it is a dope, they immediately started playing cards with the gummy pack belonging to Hyena's father.

It was afternoon, the sun was shining, and here and there you could hear radios broadcasting the football game. The farmer and his family, all dressed for Sunday, in black, had come out into the courtyard, under the badly swept, stinking sheds, with the babies in their arms, and there were some friends of theirs, more hayseeds, who farmed somewhere near Ponte Mammolo: there were also some Southerners, some stupid bums who worked for the farmers on starvation pay and who spent their Sunday there, chatting on the mud.

Inside Hyena's kitchen they were playing a good game of zecchinetta, when they heard a voice yelling outside: 'Hey, Shitter!'

Shitter was in his shorts, because, while the others played cards, he was mending his pants that had split, and was there with the needle between his fingers.

'Hey, Shitter, they want you!' Hyena grumbled. Shitter, his pants in hand, went to the door, opening it slowly and thinking: 'Now who's coming to bother me?'

He stuck his head out and saw an unfamiliar face; he was about to shut the door again, thinking: 'Who spilled on me like this?' but the newcomer stuck his foot in the crack and grabbed Shitter by the neck, half-pulling him out. When he was outside, he gave him a rabbit punch and slammed his head against the edge of the door. Shitter sank down, his stomach churning: this was it.

Meanwhile other policemen came, took him while he was dazed and helpless, dragged him over the mud and manure by the armpits, before the eyes of the hicks, who kept their mouths shut as if they hadn't seen anything, then loaded him into the wagon.

*

It was two or three in the morning. Zimmìo was asleep in his little house. He was sleeping soundly when he heard a loud knock at the door. He was so sleepy he couldn't keep his eyes open, as if they had been sewn tight with gut, sealed. 'Goddammit,' he thought, almost crying. Since he had a year's parole, he had to answer the door in person, presenting himself, if it was the police.

He pulled himself up on one elbow, almost ready to vomit. White as a corpse, because, obviously, all his blood had gone to his feet, with his hair plastered over the red pimples on his forehead, wrinkled like an old man's. He staggered to his feet, crossed the room towards a curtain that divided the cell where he lived with his mother and sister. They had waked up, too, on the beds next to Zimmìo's, and they were watching, wide-eyed. They didn't have electricity: some light came in through the windows of the flimsy wall. Outside, they kept on knocking at the door like wild men, almost breaking it down, it was so rickety. 'Get dressed, Maialetti!' they shouted from outside. But Zimmìo stood there, dazed, in a pair of loose shorts, the two hundred lire kind.

'What's up? What've I done now?' he asked, looking around for his clothes and his socks, between the two urinals on the floor.

'We don't have any time to waste now; get dressed and come outside!'

'I'm dressing!' Zimmìo said. He had found his pants, and as his mother and sister watched, frightened, he got dressed, sinking down on the grimy cot again. He dressed lazily; on the wall behind him there was a tapestry picture of two Arabs and a camel resting at an oasis.

The others, outside, began hammering on the door again. His feet on the floor, holding his shoes in his hand, Zimmìo went to open it, and since all over the kitchen, on the other side of the curtain, the laundry was hung out, blind as he was, he banged against the stand with the basin full of filthy water, knocking it to the ground. Cursing, he opened the door and almost fell to the floor himself, sick.

There were four or five policemen, all armed, in full kit, with helmets and straps and automatic rifles, some slung over their shoulders, some at the ready. Zimmìo took a couple of steps backward, half dead with fright, into the kitchen, against the big old stove with the tube of compressed gas over it; he stood there, breathless.

The others came inside, guns in hand, and glanced beyond the curtain at the two women, who in the meanwhile had also started to get up. Then they gave Zimmìo a shove and said: 'Let's go.' Without a word, Zimmìo bent down to tie his shoelaces, that is, the laces of one shoe, because the other was still on the floor, by the overturned basin.

But they weren't waiting, two grabbed him on one side, and two on the other, under the arms, and another covered his mouth. So they dragged him out of the shack, with his mother and sister after him, still half naked, holding his shoe and shouting: 'The other shoe! The other shoe!' almost in tears.

They dragged him under the shed in front of the house, six inches of mire, four planks nailed to a piece of wall and another wall of planks with a roof of sheet iron over it, and all around rags, scrap-iron, a few old chests, some ancient tyres, a quilt full of snot, a dozen bricks in a pile, a broken washtub: the entire wealth of Zimmìo's family. They dragged him through there, and then along the little muddy road in front.

Around the other huts there were at least forty carabinieri, also wearing their helmets, their cartridge belts, with their fire-spitters in their hands: some were knocking at the doors of other houses near the field, some were carrying off other kids, even a few women. Others were turning the dogs loose over the field, in case anybody had jumped out of a back window, and others were flashing light around with their lanterns. The dogs were barking away at full tilt, and the women were screaming inside the houses or under the sheds.

Buddha was also sleeping peacefully: he was sleeping fully dressed, because he was tired, and the night before he had had a drop or two. He was wearing his overall with a cap on his head, drawn down over his eyebrows, with his curls standing up behind. So he slept, in the larger bed, stretched out lengthwise, with his wife and two kids. In the other cot, without a mattress, slept his mother.

He lived in a farmhouse near the housing development, where the countryside began, towards the Aniene and the Messi d'oro. The floor was without tiles: he had sold them. In the big room there were only those two beds, one against the wall, the other against the first, and two chairs to put clothes on: nothing else. All the wiring had been stripped away, and there were two patches of wax on the chairs by the beds, because the family got along with candles.

At Buddha's house they came straight in, because the door was open. They set the lights inside, their guns aimed, and asked: 'Does Virginio Postiglione live here?'

Buddha woke up, rubbed his eyes, pulled his cap up and down two or three times, shifting its position on his head, until it was down over his eyelids again; then he had to hold his chin up to see. 'No,' he said, 'there's nobody named Postiglione here. This is where Giovanni Di Salvo lives ... '

'What's the name of your wife?' they said, turning towards her with their guns.

'Teresa Spizzichini,' Buddha answered, 'the guy you're looking for isn't here?'

'What? What did you say your name was?' a little lieutenant asked.

'Giovanni Di Salvo,' Buddha repeated.

The lieutenant looked at him: 'Come along. You come along too,' he said.

'What?' Buddha asked, all amazed and innocent. But two policemen took him, one on either side, and Buddha had to give in. He turned towards his wife, who was watching, with the two kids, who had waked up and were also looking at their father, and he said: 'Good night, honey!'

Outside Buddha's house, which was joined to the last plots of the quarter, there was a whole lineup of police, with dogs and lanterns, automatic rifles, wagons.

Zucabbo, who had once lived at Little Shanghai with Tommaso, Lello and the others, now lived right in the centre of Pietralata, at Block B, in one of the streets parallel to the main one that cut straight across the quarter. Zucabbo was under surveillance, too. He was asleep. When he heard them knock, he also had to open in person, half-dressed, staggering, sleeping like a log. He opened the door, and the policemen came into the house. They entered, but they couldn't go any farther than the kitchen. Facing them was a little partition with an old curtain for a door. They clustered there, with their guns bumping against an iron drum like the kind they roast chestnuts on with a little stove on top, a tub full of dirty clothes, a table covered with bottles of tomatoes, and a cupboard with doors of red and blue glass checks, all around like a frame: they couldn't go any farther because beyond the partition, in four or five square yards, there were three cots, two daybeds, forming, you might say, a single bed, with a tangle of sheets and warm blankets.

There were about twenty of them sleeping there, Zucabbo's father and mother, his grandmother, four or five sisters, a whole tribe of smaller brothers. A sergeant stuck his head into the room, gave a look at all those half-naked little beggars, who were scattered there like worms, staring at him.

'You two. You and you!' the sergeant said, pointing to two girls about seventeen or eighteen, all dishevelled. 'Get up!'

The two girls looked at him wide-eyed, sitting on the beds. Zucabbo stepped forward, saying: 'What? What for? How dare you? What's up?'

'Come on, you two,' the sergeant said.

As for Zucabbo, two of them grabbed him by the arms and dragged him out across the kitchen, then through the shed full of rags, which was attached to the front of the house: and they held him there, in one of those little streets that crossed the main one at right angles. All the houses around there were being searched and turned inside out by the policemen. There were four here, ten there, more than anybody had ever seen at once, milling around and giving orders. The lights of their little lanterns darted over the peeling walls, on the bits of tarred paper and slabs of corrugated iron that hung from the roofs, on the rubble, on the underpinnings, on the miserable patches of yard. The dogs barked like damned souls, and on all sides you could hear shouts, curses, orders. After they had held him there less than two minutes, Zucabbo saw the other policemen with his two sisters, half-dressed, their feet stuck into their shoes as if they were slippers, their stockings hanging down, their hair rumpled. They were crying. 'What've they done? Let them alone!' Zucabbo shouted. With a yank they dragged him off, not even answering him. The others dragged along the two girls. They went about a hundred yards across the little streets, some of mud and some paved with blocks of tufa, under the laundry lines, among the soaked walls. There was a storm raging all around them. They came into the main street, which ran from the bar by the bus stop to the church door.

On either side of the street there were rows of Jeeps, maybe a hundred on each side, lined up like in a parking lot from one end of the street to the other. Patrols of policemen came and went everywhere, some dragging people, others going after somebody, with guns and dogs. Zucabbo was forced into one truck, his two sisters into another. A lieutenant shouted: 'Load up as many as you can and take them away!'

Zucabbo didn't have time to shout anything to his sisters, to say goodbye to them before the truck they were loaded into drove off, with a police Alfa after it, its bright headlights blazing.

They loaded their catch everywhere, in trucks, in the Jeeps, in the red police wagons, in the cars, even the big ones. They packed them up and took them off. Every vehicle took a different route, maybe so the people in the other neighbourhoods near by wouldn't realize what was going on.

There were four checkpoints, formed by a number of Jeeps lined up at the four entrances to the neighbourhood, towards Monte-sacro and towards the Via Tiburtina. And two other lines of Jeeps, long as the one in the central street, were at either end of the quarter, beyond the market gardens.

In his truck Zucabbo saw Zimmìo, still missing one shoe; his mother and sister were below, holding the shoe, trying to give it to him, but the police pushed them back into the midst of a whole crowd of women and little kids, yelling and crying.

'His shoe! His shoe!' they said.

'Eh, he can do without it tonight. He can go barefoot,' a police-man answered, a Neapolitan.

Zimmìo was grim, so angry he wouldn't even talk. Until finally a sergeant went past, saw the two women with the shoe trying to get closer, and he shouted in a fit of rage: 'Take those two and cart them off right away, too!'

They led them to another truck farther ahead, half-naked as they were, mother and daughter: Zimmìo, spitting with anger, was about to climb over the tailgate of the truck and throw himself, kicking and biting on the policemen, but the others inside held him back: 'Shithead, you wanna ruin yourself? Cancha see what's going on around here?'

To draw him back, they pointed to Cazzitini, sitting stupidly on a bench in the truck. He was naked, with only his shorts on, the brown, hairy ones with the stamp of the Pontifical Charities.

Behind each vehicle that went off, the police wagon took its place, its bright headlights on, to illuminate the interior: in the truck there were fifteen cops for every ten men, but still they kept the truck lighted all through the neighbourhood for fear somebody might manage to jump down and make off.

Vehicles of every sort kept coming and going, and between the headlights of the squad cars, the searchlights of the Jeeps, the lan-terns, it was so bright that it seemed a holiday: only the fireworks were missing.

Cazzitini was trembling from the cold, and was silent. 'Aòh, your sister-in-law's coming,' said Hyena, who had been picked up all dressed, coming back from Rome.

The sister-in-law was half naked, too, but she brought Cazzitini a jacket: 'Here, put this on!' she shouted to him, managing to pass him the jacket at a moment when the police were looking somewhere else; poor bastards, they were half dazed themselves in the midst of all that confusion. But a little later his wife arrived, too. She was yelling and lamenting, clearing a path for herself; she had his clothes clutched tight against her tits, and she was running for all she was worth. 'Stop, stop!' Zimmìo and the others shouted at her. 'Stop, or they'll pick you up, too!'

But she wouldn't listen, and she came to the truck and handed the clothes to Cazzitini, crying and yelling: 'Here, Mario, here!'

'Clear out!' he shouted at her, 'go home, ya dope, the kid's all alone! Who's looking after him?'

The five or six policemen who were around there came over and asked her to give her full name; with her hands clasped over her skinny tits she shouted: 'I came to bring some clothes to my husband, who was all naked!'

'Naked, hell!' they said to her, 'you come along with us, too!'

She began to wriggle and to go into convulsions. 'Let go a me, let go a me,' she shouted, 'I left my baby at home!' 'Let her go,' they yelled from inside the truck, 'she's got a four-months baby at home!'

'We'll take care of the kid,' the policemen said, and they picked her up from the ground, where she had dropped, raving, and loaded her into a Jeep.

The sergeant of that afternoon, the one who had come with two other policemen to take in Shitter, marked the houses of the women who had started all the riot: he was an old drunk, who got down two litres a day, with a rough voice that came from his nostrils. He pointed out the houses, the policemen went inside and arrested mothers, adolescent girls, old tramps.

They arrived, surrounded by guns and dogs, with the lanterns in their faces: some were collected in a bunch, some had already been carried away. Others were still arriving from every side, frightened, like condemned prisoners in the midst of the firing squad.

Hyena's grandmother was trotting along meek and mild among all those armed men, and she looked even smaller than usual, a bedbug, an ant with her hands clasped as if she were going to pray; she looked around, her black eyes staring, embarrassed, apologizing to the men, like a little girl. She walked, her slippers trailing in the mud, with her little green dress, and all that white, wispy hair, falling uncombed around her face as black as a coal, almost smiling with her toothless mouth, as if she were in the May procession.

In the midst of another squad, cursing like a Jew, came Anna, who worked as a labourer in the General Market, with six or seven kids scattered around the city: a real piece of woman, who wore lipstick up to her nose, her makeup falling to pieces in her sweat, and all her rotten teeth in her mouth, always filthy, yellow; but she was a fucker, and her eyes always had black bags, her hair was of all colours, because every so often she changed, and some was black, some brown, some platinum blonde, some red, all burnt till it looked like the hairs on an ear of corn, or like plumber's straw.

Who could control her? She was pouring out everything she had in her: 'Cocksuckers!' she shouted at the policemen who were taking her off, her hands struggling, 'Fuck you and yours! Bunch a lousy traitors! ... Go back to picking beans, lousy hick bums! Go see what your lousy whore wives are doing. Go on.'

Behind her some other policemen were taking off Nazzareno's mother. She, too, had hardly had time to get dressed: she walked along, crying, her hair dishevelled but lank, down on her neck, with hairpins hanging from it on every side. She had a plump face, but very pale with bags under her eyes. Her dress had been torn in front, a piece was missing, because when she did the washing, she got wet, and with her wet dress, she rubbed up and down at the tub, at the pump and everywhere: so you could see her belly; she was wearing an army undershirt as slip. She had thrown a wrinkled red wool jacket over her shoulders; it came halfway down her back. Got up like this, she came forward, among the carabinieri, crying, out of breath.

Behind her, here and there in the midst of the policemen, there were lots of other women, young and old, taken from all the houses of the neighbourhood: some protested, some wept, covered with rags, like animals driven from their dens.

By now night was almost over. The sky had already brightened a little over towards San Basilio, above the clouds, which were violet, blue, with tattered edges; but it looked as if the day, instead of being born, was about to die. Then, a little at a time, the air was tinged with light, and the light stuck to everything, still without any sun. It was dry, weak whiteness, sticking to the mud, the haggard faces, the headlights still burning.

A few at a time, too, the police began to clear out: the Alfas, the squad cars came and went less often, the big trucks had scattered, others were still in the area half empty, and the Jeeps, too, in groups of three or four, first the ones in the outside lines beyond the gardens, then those in the line along the main street, shot off like curses.

The policemen made their last pickups, half dead from lack of sleep: a boy in Via Feronia, who had got up to go to work was taken with his lunchbox in his hand and carried off: he cried and yelled: 'I gotta go to work!'

'No, you're coming with us,' the policemen said, by now almost exhausted themselves.

'I got the keys to the storeroom in Piazza Vittorio,' the kid repeated, crying, under the light of the sun, now cheerfully warm. 'If I don't go, the others won't be able to work, either!'

'Doesn't matter!' they said to him, and loaded him into a wagon.

The sun was good and high and shone down on a Pietralata which seemed that of the war period. The walls of the houses were silent, because walls are silent. But on the mud there were the marks of the tyres and the feet of all those poor bastards who had trudged back and forth during the whole night.

*

During the raid, Tommasino had been absent. He knew nothing of what had happened. As on the past two or three Sundays, he had been with Irene, and then he had hung around, over at Garbatella, after dropping the girl, with that friend of his, the fishmonger named Settimio. He had slept at his house and then, together, since they were both completely broke, flat as their feet, they had gone around Rome all day, after foreigners.

When he came back to his neighbourhood, alone, the sun by then had firmly decided to clear out behind a grey mattress of tattered clouds, after shining reluctantly all day on the mud.

The first lights hadn't yet come on in the slum, but it would soon be time. And there was, now, a deep calm, a silence.

Everybody was attending to his own business, inside the houses or in those few feet of yard in front of them. The women, if they talked, from the windows or at the pump, spoke in low voices, as if somebody had died. At the bar there wasn't a soul, and the blinds were half pulled down.

Tommasino and the others who had got off the 211 with him, about four, four-thirty, knew nothing, looked around, their chins jutting, aghast, staring one another in the face.

Then the majority of them hurried home, fearing the worst: some stopped along the street to ask what had happened, what was wrong. Among them, Tommasino. But he understood at once what it was all about. We're finished! he thought, with his legs trembling. If they were after Shitter, then they had me on their list, too!

A kind of mist descended before his eyes, his head began to swim, he felt a lump of lead inside his body.

He ran towards the house and didn't even know himself where he was going: he couldn't see what was around him, the grey façades of the buildings, the puddles, the crumbling slabs of the pavements, the people talking, seared by the cold, their skin white and drawn, dirty little shawls drawn around their necks.

He couldn't stop thinking those same words, looking around: We're finished!, nothing else, like an imbecile. Running, with that obsession, he came to Little Shanghai. He hadn't been home at that hour for God knows how long: he couldn't remember. Maybe since he was a little kid, when he used to come home from school.

He usually stopped up at Pietralata with his friends: Shitter, Zimmìo, Zucabbo, Lello and the rest. If they weren't around, he lingered with others whom he knew by sight. He sat at the bar even if he didn't have a lira, not ordering anything, the manager overlooked it. Or else, especially if the weather was good, he stayed in the street. He went home either early, for a bite to eat, going away again at once to be up at the bar by this hour, or else very late, well into the night, because his mother left out a bowl of cold soup for him and a slab of bread on the table.

He felt funny, coming home at this time of day, when, in the last light, you could still make out clearly the almond trees and the dried-up peaches in the gardens, the canebrakes: and farther on, the aqueduct bridge over the Aniene, that flowed off icy and dark.

With his hands in his pockets, taking the side-paths where the thin crust of mud broke beneath his footsteps, transforming the way into a muck so slippery you could hardly walk, Tommaso walked the whole distance, all the way to Little Shanghai, like a blind man.

Little Shanghai, at the bottom of the muddy slope with its few ragged bushes, couldn't even be made out, it was so grey and messy in the swamp.

It crouched there, as if in hiding, at a curve in the road, which followed a bend in the river: a depression, already completely in shadow, while, on the other bank, the expanse of fields towards Ponte Mammolo with a little house here and there was immersed in a strange yellowish light, as if struck by a row of distant searchlights.

I'll go there, Tommaso thought, distraught, if I see things look bad, I'll fling myself down the slope towards the river, hide in the canes, and nobody can see me. I'll have a bath. Then, on the other side, who can find me? They won't catch me. They can go fuck themselves ...

However, in the central clearing of Little Shanghai, composed of about thirty hovels at most, some of wood and some of brick, there were only a few kids playing and some old women talking with their feet in the mud.

At Tommasino's house, too, all was quiet: they were eating supper.

When they saw him come in, they were so surprised they could hardly believe it, but they still didn't say a word and went on eating as quiet as before.

His father was at the table, with Tito and Toto on either side of him, also quiet, intent on scraping their bowls with their spoons. The older brother ate on a piece of bench by the door, partly in the light, with the bowl in his lap. His mother ate standing up, by the little charcoal stove.

As soon as Tommasino was inside, she said: 'Whaddya doing here this time of day?'

Tommaso shrugged slightly, more frozen inside, in the pit of his stomach, than outside, and said: 'Aòh, Ma ... ' His mother said nothing else and fixed him a bowl of beans and stinking sausages. Tommasino sat at an empty corner of the table and began to eat. But he couldn't get it down and, instead, he wanted to vomit. He swallowed a few mouthfuls of the soup, nauseated, then bit into the dry bread. His mother said to him: 'Wait,' and put a couple of spoonfuls of cold greens on the bread. Tommaso took it back and went on eating it, with this condiment, slowly, trying to overcome his nausea.

His older brother finished and went off. The other two, the little ones, when supper was over, began roaming around the room, like a couple of moles. 'Put the kids to bed, for crissake,' the father said.

'Wait till I've cleared up,' Sora Maria said. The father, still grumbling, went and threw himself down on the bed.

Tommasino stood leaning against the door-jamb, careful not to press too hard, or else he would knock it down: he stood there calmly, his hands on his head, observing what the neighbours were doing. In one shack they were yelling happily: maybe it was a baptism, or some relative had arrived from their home town. Here and there, in the open space outside, there were people moving: young guys especially, going towards Montesacro. Passing the neighbours, they said hello: 'Good night, Sora Lina! Good night, Teresa!' Or else they acted cocky: 'How about taking some fresh air?' 'Eh, you're lucky, all right!' the woman answered: and they went off along the slimy road, hands in their pockets, huddled in their work clothes, with little short, light jackets, summer clothes probably, and worn-out shoes on their feet.

Tommasino wanted to display himself, there, calm as he was, at the door of the house. He was trying to make it clear that he wasn't going around at night, at least not this time, and he was going to bed with no foolishness: that he was a good boy in other words.

From the shack next door a woman came out to take some clothes hanging from a string in front of the door. 'Hello, Sora Adele,' Tommaso said at once.

'Hello, Tomà,' she said, agreeably: both felt they were sage people, old-fashioned, minding their own business and not looking for trouble.

'Eh, Sora Adè, always got your hands in hot water, eh?' Tommaso said.

'Tell my husband that,' she said, pressing her chin against her neck.

'I hear Sor Armando's buying a T.V. Is that so?' Tommaso asked.

'Yeah, an invisible one!' she said.

'Eh,' Tommaso sighed, sly, 'you're lucky, all the same ... '

Meanwhile Sora Adele had collected the two or three pieces that were hanging out, now frozen, and as she went back into the house she said hastily: 'Night, Tomà!'

'Good night, Sora Adè,' Tommaso said, and slowly, still with that sage, resigned manner, he took a butt from his pocket and lit it.

Meanwhile Tito and Toto, obviously tired of trotting around the room, peered out. Toto, his head lowered, immediately banged into a rotten, crumbling bench, which was in the shed beside the house: he settled there, crouching in the black, frozen mud; he grabbed a piece of tin can and began to scrape the sharp part against the bench.

Tito paid no attention to him: he wandered around a little in the yard's five square feet of mud, slamming his head here and there, all content, with laughing eyes, letting out an occasional cry of satisfaction. Then he too huddled down, bare-assed, his stomach hanging out, because he had just sat on the pot and nobody had straightened up his clothes afterwards. He was staring at something in the muck: then all of a sudden he stood up straight and, with his little foot, he started stamping, stamping on the thing he had been looking at: he hit it with his heel a lot of times so hard that once or twice he almost fell over. When he had finished, he let out another yell, which seemed to mean: 'Fuck you' and began to run around and around the open space in front of the house, making a sound like: 'Rrrrrrr, grrrr, yaaaaa': he still couldn't say Mamma, but he knew how to imitate the sound of a motorcycle.

All of a sudden Sora Maria came out of the house, bumping past Tommaso, and going straight to Tito, who was racing around. She took him under her arm and, with his little drawers over his knees and his other rags under his armpits, she picked him up and carried him inside. After two minutes she came out again and did the same with Toto, who was still scraping the bench with the piece of tin; this time it was less easy: as his mother grabbed him, Toto opened his mouth to its full width, and began to cry his guts out. 'Take it easy with those kids, eh?' Tommaso said, sternly.

'Mind your own goddam business,' his mother said, concerned with dragging Toto, who was nothing but one big mouth, inside the house. Tito was already dozing off in a little bunk prepared under the table. Toto, instead, slept in a packing-case, half full of household things, summer clothes, blankets and, over these, a kind of pillow, all filthy and torn. Toto, however, didn't keep it up for long, and after two minutes, he was already pacified too, poor thing, and his mother put him in his box, as quiet as a puppy.

Outside it was night, though it wasn't much after seven. You could hear only the voices of those people who were having a big time two or three hovels farther down. All the rest of the village was lost in silence. Tommaso still couldn't make up his mind to go to bed, although he had turned into a piece of ice: he was pretty much relieved, however, and it seemed a miracle to him that everything should have gone smoothly so far: he couldn't even believe it himself. He looked around, acting the nice boy who has a last smoke before going to beddyby: but there wasn't even a whiff of cops about. The heap of shacks was all dark, you couldn't tell it from the side of the hill where it was huddled: a fissure glimmered here and there, and the puddles in the midst of the black mud. The only light was the electric lamp over the scabby road to Montesacro.

Beyond the Aniene, which was encased at the bottom of the embankments, the meadows were lost in the darkness: of the light that had struck them, even after the sunset, like a glow of searchlights, there was still a kind of yellow dust sizzling: perhaps because over them there was nothing but sky, and the plain stretched as far as the eye could see, to the hills of Tivoli.

The sky above was cloudy and whitish: only here and there a clear patch could be seen, much darker. In one of these patches, just above the roof of corrugated iron and tarred paper of Sora Adele's shack, at the tips of some shredded clouds, there were a few little stars, shining all alone. And around that wretched pile of huts there was a silence, a peace, a solitude that were frightening. After a little while, without even realizing it, while he stood there alone and downcast, Tommaso felt something like a tear rising in his throat. But he promptly swallowed it again.

5

A Real Serenade

In the rose-perfumed air, Tommasino started running and caught up with Zimmìo and Carletto, who were going towards the bus stop.

'Carletto!' he said, as he joined them, 'I gotta tell you something. Got a minute?'

Carletto stopped and looked at him, waiting, affably: and Zimmìo stood a bit off to one side, chewing some gum, his eye immediately sharpened.

'You catching the bus?' Tommaso inquired.

'No,' Carletto answered, still polite, with a hint of curiosity.

'Listen, Carletto,' Tommaso began then, brisk and confidential, 'I'm after this girl ... over at Garbatella ... She's a real piece ... pretty and all ... '

'Aw, fuckoff ... ' Zimmìo chanted, stopping his chewing for a moment.

'Cut it out, Zimmì,' Tommaso said fiercely, but with laughter about to burst from his mouth, 'stop shitting around ... So,' he went on, to Carletto, 'as I was saying ... Listen, I want to knock her out with something extra, and you gotta help me. Tomorrow I wanna give her a serenade: we'll turn up outside her house, and have a real serenade—your speciality!'

'Haw, haw, haw,' Zimmìo sniggered, splitting his gut, his belly bent forward, and his legs spread.

'Lay off, Zimmì,' Tommaso commanded, his mouth wrinkled to keep from broadening in laughter. But there was a nasty glint in his eyes, all the same.

'Well?' he said then, to Carletto.

'Okay by me,' Carletto said, 'but we'll have to see ... '

129

'Whaddya mean, have to see?' Tommaso asked.

'Aòh, I'm flat. Not a lira! My guitar's in hock. How'll I get it back now?'

'We can ask Bambino to lend us his!' Tommaso exclaimed, optimistically.

'Yeah,' Carletto said, 'when'll he give it to you? He's tighter than a pair of pliers, don't you know him?'

'How much would it take to get yours back? Go ahead, tell me,' Tommaso asked then.

'Four hundred, at the most!'

He said: 'Well? Can't we scrape up four hundred?'

'It's up to you. I don't mind coming and singing the serenade for you, at Garbatella. Shit.'

Evening was falling, and Zimmìo was in a hurry.

'Carletto, come on!' he said, already walking off. But Carletto wanted to close the deal with Tommaso.

'So how'll we work it?' he asked.

'Aòh, I'll see you tomorrow morning and give you the cash. You think I can't collect it, Chrissake?'

'Sure,' Carletto said, 'I'll be expecting you.' And he went off after Zimmìo.

The lights came on and shone in the mud, along with the light of the sunset which was mirrored especially in a big puddle, there near the bus stop where Sora Anita had her stand. After Lello's accident, she wasn't herself any more: she sat there, all dressed in black, her mouth pulled down, brooding, full of wrath against everybody and everything, in silence.

Tommaso dug the change from his pocket and counted it: 'Seventy lire, goddammit,' he muttered, his teeth clenched, 'it's enough to get there, and I'll pick up the ten lire to get back, all right.'

He took the 211 to Portonaccio, and from there, with the 9, he reached the Stazione Termini.

First of all he lit a butt, and walking calmly, slowly, a man going about his own business, he ventured forth, crossing Piazza dei Cinquecento.

Life was smiling at him, for once, On the subject of Lello at the
General Hospital, nobody had got interested, and Shitter, in stir, had
kept his mouth shut: he had been forced to admit about the others,
the guys from Vicolo della Luce, since they had brought him face
to face with them: but he hadn't given a name, also he was play-
acting, bringing on epileptic fits in jail, and two or three times he
cut his wrists with razor blades. And not even Salvatore, or the
Loon, or Ugo had spilled, when they were caught, so maybe the
cops had even forgotten about Puzzilli, Tommaso.

They had picked them off not long ago, one after the other, like
ripe cherries. Salvatore was in the square, buying some prickly pears
from a cart. They came over to him and said: 'What're you up to
these days? Working? Or still on the street?' 'I'm working!' 'Could
you spare us five minutes, at the station?' 'Whaddya mean five
minutes? Five minutes really, or five minutes of your time?' 'No,
no, no, the sergeant just has to ask you a little something, a for-
mality. Don't worry: we know your father!'

They went off. As they stepped inside the entrance, Salvatore
caught on that instead of taking him up the stairs to the offices, they
were leading him along the corridor where the tank was. When he
saw this, he realized at once: 'They're locking me up!' He jerked
around and ran. At the door there was another cop, who took fright
and stepped aside. Salvatore ran as far as he could, the others after
him, yelling, and another guy, who was going by in a car, a civilian,
who also turned and followed him. But they couldn't stop him, and
the car raced alongside him; when it approached, Salvatore climbed
on the pavement, and the other guy lost ground. They got to a
school run by some nuns, the Sisters of the Little Deflower, no
doubt, God save them, and Salvatore, so pumped out he couldn't
breathe, started to jump over the wall, but he couldn't make it, and
the man said to him: 'Take it easy, kid, take it easy. What've you
done?' Finally, with a supreme effort, he managed to get over it just
as the cops were arriving, and he landed in a garden; he stayed there,
hesitant, looking all around: there were some masons mixing cement
and throwing down gravel with a spade, and they said to him, too:
'Aòh, whaddya doing?'

Then Salvatore saw a tiny little door; he flung himself inside and
found a flight of stairs; after that there wasn't anything else, a door
on one side, locked, and a door on the other, open, which he went
through into a long, long corridor where, from the other end, he
heard singing. He ran, reached the end, there was a window and
some doors to the classrooms: the window was barred, and he
couldn't get past it, so Salvatore then turned and was about to run
back down the corridor: but he heard the police coming up the
stairs. He opened the first door he saw, and inside the little girls
were singing some hymn, Ave ave ave, and as Salvatore entered,
they all shut up. Now he was trapped, and there was nothing he
could do about it.

The Loon, on the other hand, was in a car looking for some
action the next night, with certain friends of his from Borgata del
Trullo. As they went by Porta Maggiore there was the squad car
stationed behind an ancient arch. They saw them pass, and right
after that the boys heard a siren wailing behind them: 'Jeezus, we've
got them on our tail!' they cried: they stepped on the gas and took
the tunnel at top speed, rounding the curve at a hundred per, to
shake off the car, aiming at the narrow streets around San Lorenzo.
But the tram turned up in front of them, and they had to go on the
main street by the freight station: they swerved and hadn't gone
two hundred yards when, all of a sudden, they crumpled up against
a tree. They were all dragged out in pieces. The Loon was dead.

Ugo was having a shampoo at his barber's, and was all covered
with suds, bending over the basin: then the policemen came into
the shop, there by the Fontanone, and one of them asked: 'Is this
one almost finished?'

'Just wait a moment,' the barber said, 'I'll be with you in a few
minutes!'

'Hurry up. We need him!'

Ugo caught on, looked at them sideways, in the mirror, out of
the corner of his eye, and said: 'Who wants me so badly?' He
finished having the shampoo, and all fresh and brilliantined, he followed the cops to the station to make his statement, and he even
bought them a coffee. Then, when they were at the entrance to

Regina Coeli Prison, and were about to shut him in, on his way up
the steps, to show he wasn't scared, he started singing at the top of
his voice:

' Scapricciatiello mio, Scapriciatiello ... '

and, still singing, he was locked up.

All the trees in the Piazza dei Cinquecento stirred in a light breeze
which lifted the scraps of paper over the cobbles of the square and
on the platforms of the buses. There was that good odour you can
smell on the first spring evenings, when everybody starts going
around without an overcoat, maybe even in shirtsleeves, because the
air is warm, almost hot, and there's already that feeling of holiday
you get on summer nights.

Tommaso headed straight for the little park in Piazza Esedra, and
first of all, he went down to the toilets. Very serious, almost frowning, because there wasn't anything wrong with going down to drain
your tank. The underground toilets were so full you could hardly
move, and you had to wait in line for a while in the urinal department. There were a lot of soldiers because the Macao barracks were
not far away, and the trams from the barracks in the suburbs arrived
there, and this was the hour of liberty for the men.

There were other transients, peasants, workers, or clerks with their
briefcases under their arms, on their way to take the train at the station.

All of these men came in and did it quickly, chatting and calling
to one another. Some, however, as Tommaso noticed right off,
took more time staying huddled against the marble of the latrine
between the two little screens, also of marble. Among these characters, there was one who had been there for some time, an old man
of about fifty, tall, his hair mostly white, with an overcoat, a dog
face, a pair of eyes that seemed to burn whatever they looked at.

He was flushed, with red ears, like he was a little drunk or had
bad heart trouble: and all over his face there was a wet smile that
squeezed his eyes shut. A place became free next to him in the row,
and Tommaso moved into it, opening his pants with a serious,
absent manner. The old man, from his place there on the right,
gave him a look, and Tommaso, as if by chance, returned it, then

immediately looked away, at the wall in front of him where there was an ad for MOM, the crab-killer.

The other guy went on looking at him, staring hard, like a horny old devil: Tommaso gave him another glance, then buttoned up, and without looking back, started right up the steps.

When he was outside again, even more serious than before, he went over and stood on the pavement under a plane tree, where a swarm of people went by towards the station or towards the suburban buses. He leaned against the trunk, his hands in his pockets, as if he were keeping look-out for somebody.

After a little while the old man appeared from the steps, and he walked along the pavement. He noticed Tommaso and came past him: and Tommaso stayed still, a statue. The old man went on a little way, then turned around. Tommaso didn't look at him: he was looking towards the other pavement, across the street, with even more people, outside the glistening shop-windows, at the fruit stands. But from the way he was standing and the way he was looking, you could see he was available and was only waiting for some move from the other guy. At that moment, however, past the old man, and past Tommaso, came two bersaglieri in uniform: nice and square, a couple of rocks, and with a bundle in their pants that seemed to make it hard for them to walk. When they saw the toilets, they disappeared down the steps. The old man, passing Tommaso again as if he had never seen him, followed the two soldiers.

Tommaso stood there like a dope, hesitant, with a face on him, ready to cry like a kid.

After a while the two bersaglieri came out again, passed the rows of tables of a bar, and went towards the station. The old man also came up the steps, after them.

Giving the tree trunk a little push with his shoulders, Tommaso moved away and muttered, grinding his teeth: 'Goddam fucking faggot!' Starting to whistle again, he went down through the little park. Then, thinking of the Garbatella, he was a bit consoled and even began to sing in the people's faces, with his hands in his pockets:

  ' ... and my song goes off among the boughs ... '

But there was nobody around. Just people coming home from work: it was still early. Yes, he saw a pair of queens near the newsstand, arguing between themselves, but then, suddenly in a hurry, they went off on their own.

'I guess I'll try Ponte Garibaldi!' Tommaso thought, 'you can't find fuckall around here! And I'll kill some time walking there.'

Full of high spirits, he started to take this little walk: he went down Via Nazionale, the whole length of it, crossed Piazza Venezia, and down the Via Botteghe Oscure, and after maybe half an hour, so exhausted he could have taken a nap, in his weakness, he reached Ponte Garibaldi.

'For Chrissake!' he said, when he had taken a little look around, disgust dripping from his nostrils down his chin, 'Have they all lost their way tonight?'

In fact, at the corner of Via Arenula and the Lungotevere, at the Bar Mancinelli, there wasn't even one of the usual habitués: namely, those four or five bums between fourteen and twenty, who were there every night, waiting for the faggots: a little redhead with freckles, half nuts, who grabbed the clothes of those who cruised around there and wouldn't let go till he'd been given at least ten lire or a cigarette; and Bigfoot, a tall guy, with clothes that walked by themselves he was so skinny, and hair on his dirty face and a broad mouth with a tooth missing right in the middle, always laughing; and then another two or three, with clothes that stank because they never took them off, not even when they slept, since they slept outdoors, under a bridge or inside some cave.

Besides these, sometimes there were the good-looking kids from Trastevere or Campo dei Fiori, who arrived on motorbikes, ready for the assault, and woe to those who crossed their path.

The whores, however, were usually a bit farther on, in the shadows at the tram stop, between a gas pump and a flower stall, on the Lungotevere at the level of Piazza Giudia.

But not even they were to be seen. Aha! Tommaso thought. Inside the Bar Mancinelli, half empty, you could see the counters full of pastries, and the woman at the cash desk, a fat redhead, who was reading the *Messaggero*, spellbound.

Tommaso went over and, at the end of the counter, he saw a couple of policemen hanging around.

Outta here! he thought.

He crossed the street, full of traffic, of people going back to their holes at supper time, and turned down the Lungotevere, along the embankment towards Ponte Sisto.

And there, in fact, peering from behind a tree trunk, he saw Clementina.

She barely stuck out her big head with its wispy, solid permanent, glaring hard and crossly at the Bar Mancinelli.

She was all dressed in black, because somebody or other had died not long ago, a black blouse, black ankle-socks, with a pair of run-over galoshes.

She was observing certain goings-on she knew all about, hidden behind that tree like a crummy little girl: in one hand, red as fire from the winter's chilblains, she held a black purse, clutching it tight, because you never know what sonovabitch might get ideas and try to grab it from her, with what little cash she had scraped up.

Staring fixedly down there, to follow the actions of the police-men, she had to move a bit, but, raising one foot which, obviously was hurting her, she made a grimace and almost had to lean against the tree trunk, biting her lips. All this, apparently, reminded her of her recent loss, and she looked so glum she was about to cry.

Here I'm not gonna pick up a lira! Goddammit, Tommaso was thinking. How much've I got! Twenty and twenty makes forty. I've got thirty lire left, fa Chrissake! Might as well buy a couple of butts; I'm dying for a smoke!

He went into a tobacconist's at Ponte Sisto and bought himself two Nazionali.

Four hundred for that sonovabitch Carletto's guitar, fuck him! In hock. I wish he was in hock, getting his ass fucked off, the bastard. Four hundred for a guitar! Two litres, maybe three, of gas, that makes another five hundred. How'll I get it? Tonight I'm gonna make somebody cry. I don't give a shit ...

With his feet hurting enough to bring tears to his eyes, he went to Campo dei Fiori, then to Piazza Navona, from there to the Corso, and when he reached Piazza di Spagna, it was already late, night, and the flower vendors were shutting up their stands.

He sat down to catch his breath a minute, and to look around to see if the cops were out. None in sight. He stood up and began to climb the Spanish Steps.

Sitting on the first steps there were two or three foreigners. Above, on the landing halfway up, under the balustrade, some tattered kids were playing with a ball, yelling.

Grim, Tommaso went up, step by step, and when he reached the top, he glanced at the game, with the two goalies tense under the light of the street lamps and the others in a heap after the ball, sweating, laughing or pulling up their pants when they missed a play. The ball reached Tommaso, who, with a classy kick, prevented it from rolling down the steps; having done this, in no hurry, red in the face, he headed towards a little group he had noticed sitting on the low wall.

At that moment, from the top of Trinità dei Monti, their cassocks fluttering, two priests came down.

'Mmmmmmh, the priestesses!' a drawling voice said. It was one of the group Tommaso had noticed on the wall.

Tommaso moved over, and there, off to one side, there was a poor sonovabitch like himself, with a little black coat over his overall, reading *Il Corriere dello Sport* in the light of a street-lamp.

Other sonsabitches, a fatty with a forelock a foot long and a skinny character with his hands in his pockets, were also standing along the wall.

Sitting down there was the one who had said, 'Mmmmmmh the priestesses!' and who had now assumed a haughty manner, with his chin on his shoulder, as if they were going to take his picture, and two others, also very snooty and grand, who dominated the scene, detached from it; and still two others who, instead, were leaning against the wall, talking with the trade.

One of these last two, a blond with his hair combed like Gina Lollobrigida's, was maybe a woman, and Tommaso looked at him uncertainly: for that matter, the blond began to look at him too, though he continued his conversation with the others, hitting

Tommaso's face with glances that were direct yet casual, as if he weren't seeing Tommaso but something beyond his shoulder.

It wasn't, however, that this blond was talking with the others: his friend, who was very swish, took care of the conversation. The blond was silent and gave his approval, and every time he had to approve, making a sign that meant yes, he not only lowered his head, but also his shoulders and his whole body, as if he were sinking into a hole, like ladies-in-waiting in a movie when they have to curtsy before the king.

Then, to resume his normal position, he shook himself a little, with a slightly defiant air, very haughty, but with laughter ready to burst from his eyes and mouth. His glances at Tommaso became more and more frequent, and Tommaso, moving without haste, all puffed up, came closer, lighting a butt.

The other boy looked at him a bit longer, and less absently: his eyebrows had been shaved then done with a pencil, the lashes were inches long, like those of actresses, and his cheeks, smooth as a peach, were all made up, with powder and a bit of rouge. He was a real beauty. His Lollo coiffure fell over the upturned collar of his camel hair topcoat.

The other one, who was talking so much he seemed a radio, with the two pieces of trade listening to him in silence, seriously, also began to glue glances, like stamps, on Tommaso, here and there, all over his body.

He was all indignant about the story he was telling, but when he looked at Tommaso his indignation suddenly faded for a moment; he seemed to have four eyes, two for talking about this quarrel in which he had been in the right, and two for glancing all around.

Suddenly, he broke off and turned to Tommaso, saying: 'Now tell me who this butch number is? We've never seen him around here before. My goodness, he's lovely, all right!'

Tommaso leered, raising the cigarette to his mouth, then puffed the smoke into the face of the queen who had spoken.

'Might as well introduce ourselves, while we're about it, don't you think? I mean: we're all civilized, mature people here!' he said this, pulling his chin down below his shoulder and wriggling his whole body: then he held out his hand to Tommaso, saying: 'I'm Miss People's Choice. Pleased to meet you!' And so Tommaso entered their circle: the other little queen, the one who had been quiet all the time, still kept quiet: but he gave Tommaso a shattering look.

'Where you from?' the People's Choice asked, agreeably.

'Pietralata,' Tommaso said, grimly.

'Mmmmmmmmmh!' P.C. exclaimed, looking at him with new interest, and with a pleasant shudder of terror, writhing all over.

'What's wrong? Doncha like it there?' Tommaso asked.

'I like it just fine, handsome!' the People's Choice said, in a shrill voice.

'What's up?' one of the two seated off by themselves on the wall asked, 'ya cunt itching tonight?'

They all talked like girls, half in Neapolitan dialect, with voices like soubrettes, as if they had a bean pod in their throats.

'I feel like an Empress tonight,' Miss Choice said, putting a hand on her hip, and addressing her sisters. Then, coming back to Tommaso, 'Are you the brutal type?' she inquired, caressing and provocative.

'I'll whip you!' Tommaso said, snickering.

Miss Choice felt an electric shock run through her and said: 'Mmmmmmh' again. Then, with no more fuss, she came straight to the point: 'Let me feel!' she said. With her left hand over her stomach, she continued to hold the flaps of her overcoat, thrown loosely around her shoulders to create a décolleté; and with her right, quick as a stab, she groped Tommaso, not looking at him, acting modest.

When this was done, she went back to her conversation with the other trade, Fatty and Skinny, not concerning herself with Tommaso any more.

The other little queen was still silent. She was lost in a tranquil ecstasy, suspended over the world like a spirit: she also had her hands in her lap, holding the flaps of her overcoat as if it were an evening cape, thrown back against the wall.

She seemed to want to preserve that state of bliss, which might break off if she spoke. She participated in the world with gestures, with her eyes, with her manner: that was enough; in this way her participation was more complete. It was also an opinion on the world: 'Blessed art thou amongst males!'

Tommaso, while Miss Choice was talking, went over and also leaned against the wall.

'Aòh, kid,' he said, 'can I ask you something?'

'Yess,' the other one said, snapping her head, framed in the coat-collar.

'Let's go over there a way,' Tommaso said, unctuous and confident.

'Why? It's nice here,' the queen said.

'I wanna talk to you alone,' Tommaso said, offended. 'Why not?'

The other shrugged. But Tommaso took her by the arm and dragged her a bit farther on, towards the second flight of the steps. The queen moved and, when she did, you could see she was lame, a cripple, with one leg half-a-yard shorter than the other, and as she walked, she seemed to make a complete revolution with every step.

When they were a bit off to themselves, in a slightly dark spot, they confabulated for a while, very tense. But then after a while, Tommaso came slowly back towards the group, smoking, surly: and the cripple came after him. After manœuvring for five minutes on the pavement, spiralling, she resumed her place among the others.

She ran a hand through her hair, and laughed tenderly at her sisters, a bit depressed, but acting bored. One of these put a hand on her shoulder, drew her over affectionately, and they stayed there, cheek to cheek.

'What did he want?' Miss Choice said, rearing herself up.

'Ask him!' the queen said.

'L'arjawnt,' Tommaso said (his single French word), 'whaddya think I want?'

Miss Choice didn't even answer him. She turned her ass on him, drawing her coat around her, rising on the tips of her feet and making two or three pirouettes, spinning like a woodpecker with the stammers, one leg drawn up like a stork's: then she stopped all of a sudden, with a half-split, before Tommaso's nose.

Fatty raised one leg, said: 'Watch out', and let a fart.

They all burst out laughing and said to him: 'You crude bastard, that's no way to behave in front of ladies!' and Tommaso took advantage of all this gaiety to clear out of there, too.

He quietly went down a flight of steps, then another flight, thinking: 'Goddam fruits. They oughta be lined up against a wall! What the fuck are they around for, on this earth?' 'And now, how'm I gonna make the eight hundred?' he added, 'Where's it gonna come from?' He was desperate, things were beginning to look really black.

Meanwhile, it had turned cool: and with the coolness, a new, strange vein of warmth. Down the steps, the breeze bore certain perfumes, God knows what they were, damp grass, burned wood, alleyways with the mud dissolving.

And Tommasino walked on. His shoes were like vices: he had calluses on his toes and his left heel was one big sore. Obviously the leather worn and soaked by the rain and dried by the sun had become harder than iron and, behind, it rubbed against the skin of the foot, which moved up and down inside that little onion-coloured package, with the laces that hadn't been untied in months and had become all one with the leather.

Dragging those poor feet along, Tommaso covered the length of Via Due Macelli, crossed Piazza Barberini, then up Via Bissolati, and back to the station, to the little park at Piazza Esedra. He still had ten lire in his pocket, so he went into a bar to buy his last Nazionale: and he almost felt sick as he passed the case of pastries, because it must have been the night before when he last ate.

It was almost eleven by now: but in the park and even down there around the fountain, its jets of water illuminated till they looked like ice, there were still people. It was the first warm night of the year: and then with the station near by and the bus terminal, there was always some movement around. A number of people continued to and from the toilets, though you didn't have to wait in line now.

Tommaso went down, very seriously did what he had to do, even if he didn't feel the need; but he couldn't find anybody, so he came back up again.

On the bench near by, next to a flowerbed, off to one side, a row of people were sitting, and another two or three were standing up.

Tommaso, angry, went over to have a look. The seated ones were all trade: the standing ones were three faggots, about ready to leave. In fact, as Tommaso came up, they said: 'Ciao ciao,' and went off, all in a hurry, like three girls whose mother is waiting for them at home with a switch.

One of the seated ones was a queen, too. But he didn't look it. He had a smartass face, with dirty curls over the turned-up collar of a grey duster, its colour now unknown because of its age. This one was holding forth; the others with one eye were paying attention to him respectfully, and with the other looking around, not giving a fuck.

The queen, in fact, was talking seriously: sitting at the edge of the bench, on a piece of his ass, so he could thrust his chest and his whole body out farther, he had put one hand over his heart.

His eyes glowed with pride: but he was acting modest all the same: 'I'm nobody,' he said, 'because I'm nobody. Still I've always done my dooty!'

He looked around, pressing his chin against his neck, already beginning to be moved by his own sense of duty: 'I've worked since I was eight years old, I tell you,' he went on, 'since my father died, and my mother had eight kids to bring up ... I've been a barber, a mechanic, furniture-polisher, carpenter, elevator man ... labourer ... every kind a job. When there was work to do, I didn't run away!'

He turned angry, winked, and ratatatatat, hitting himself on the chest again and again with one bent finger, he continued: 'But yours truly has always had one idea, and he's never gonna change it. I'm not one of them that says bread and work, and only want the bread! I'm a hundred per cent Italian! But show me the Italians in Italy nowadays. Italians with real principles, the ideels Italy teaches us!'

Nobody answered: but at that moment, from the end of the little park, a blond character appeared, satisfaction personified. His eyes were smiling, and he was smoking a cigarette like he was a chimney. He seemed to be eating it, smoke and all, he was so happy.

He heard the faggot's last words and said: 'Aw, knock it off; you don't have enough wind to fart with!'

Tommaso, serious and reserved, went over with his unlighted cigarette and said: 'How about a light, kid?'

So happy he couldn't contain himself, the blond held out his cigarette, not looking at him, looking instead at the faggot, who paid no attention, erect as the statue of Anita Garibaldi on the Janiculum, as he went on saying: 'The communists, as far as I, Luciano Plebani, am concerned, make me sick ... '

Tommaso wasn't listening: smoking like he was chewing poison, he looked around. He was pissed off with everything. They were all lousy bastards. What did he care about Left or Right, the one or the other? He was a free man, an anarchist, and that was that.

'Aòh,' said the blond guy, the last to arrive, as if he couldn't keep back the good news a minute more: 'the Seal's out tonight!'

'How much did you make?' one of the listeners asked at once, emerging from his indifference, with a yawn.

'Seven hundred!' the blond said, and all content, since life had been good to him for that night, he went off, smoking like a king, and holding the cigarette between his fingers, which trembled slightly.

The one who had asked how much got up, stretched, completed his yawn, and went off slowly across the park towards Piazza Esedra.

Tommaso sat down in his place, at the end of the bench.

'Say,' one of the kids asked the faggot, 'What's happened to Sabrina?'

'What?' the fag said, jumping as if they'd stuck a pole up his ass, 'doncha know? Doncha ever read the papers?'

'Who reads the papers?' the kid had to admit, a bit ashamed.

'Jeezus,' the other said, sparkling, 'it was a real scandal.' And saying this, he waved his little hands before his face, palms out, raising his eyes to heaven.

'A scandal!' he repeated. 'Imagine! They caught him with a man, and he was in drag, in a short skirt and a plaid bolero, in the park at Trionfale! There was even a photo in the paper! You oughta of seen it!'

At that moment the famous Seal arrived. He was a ball of fat, with a sunburned face, bald: he looked like My Son Nero. He had a sports shirt over his pants, and you could see all the hair between his tits.

He came up to the bench in a big hurry, his eyes and mouth yellowish: he greeted hastily the two or three he knew, shaking their hands hard. They looked at him very friendly, ready to go off with him. In fact, he said: 'Let's get going,' and headed towards the place where he had left his car.

Tommaso did everything to attract attention, smoking calmly, and looking out of the corner of his eye.

But the Seal was in a rush: like an officer who had come to collect a couple of soldiers for some detail. The three stood up and went after him. At that moment the fourth arrived, the one who had gone off to look for the Seal's car in Piazza Esedra, who had risked being left out. The Seal glimpsed him in time: 'Franco,' he said, 'get moving.' This Franco, all delighted, joined the party, and with the Seal in the lead, they ambled towards the fountain.

The other faggot, left alone, also stood up, politely gave his hand to Tommaso, introducing himself, then went off singing, turning up the collar of that duster whose colour was unknown.

Tommaso remained on the bench, by himself.

It was late now, and the later it got, the sweeter and milder the air became, among the little trees and the lamps of the square, now almost without any people around.

Tommaso stood up; six or seven times he went up and down the steps of the urinals. It was midnight, and he couldn't find anybody, or else the men there didn't see him, and walked away.

Then he headed for the station, which was a good place day or night. He walked back and forth for more than half an hour, outside under the awning, and inside.

There was a big crowd where the trains came in, and piles of people asleep on the marble benches: all poor hick bastards with their bundles around them, stinking of sheep and mouldy cheese. There were also some people strolling up and down like Tommaso, but they were mostly thieves or pimps: in fact, at either exit of the passage, at Via Marsala and at Via Giolitti, the place was full of whores. Tommaso looked at them one by one, as he walked, and especially one who was aiming at an old man who could hardly stand on his feet, by the little wall around the steps down to the lower level.

She was little, with a pair of tits bigger than she was, and an ass that drooped over the high heels of her shoes; all dressed in red.

She walked around and around the little wall, and the old boy, his nose dripping, was after her. Then she went towards the arcades across the street and disappeared in the shadows. The old man looked around, frightened, then also began to cross the street, so thin a gust of wind could carry him off.

It was half past twelve, maybe one. And a police patrol came along. Tommaso cleared out just in time. And when he looked into the station again half an hour later, it was all over, for that night.

There was a great silence, and the whistling of the trains and the clumps of travellers who came and went seemed to have silencers on them, too.

Tommasino was cross-eyed with weakness and hunger. And now he would have to walk all the way back to Pietralata.

He came out of the station again slowly, walking on the rubbery pavement, got a light for the last stub of cigarette from a porter half asleep on his cart, and turned down Via Marsala.

There were still a few stragglers about. But in those little streets beyond, towards San Lorenzo, that Tommaso had taken to save time, there was nobody.

You could hear only his footsteps, weary, his feet all sore.

But suddenly from a corner of one street, a woman's form appeared: Tommaso recognized her at once, because of her loose red overcoat. It was the little whore who had picked up the old man and who now, having done him, was hurrying home, clutching her black patent-leather purse.

Tommaso thought: Look at that! and hurrying, softly, he almost caught up with her. She half turned and gave him a funny look, walking on, faster. Tommaso watched her, also increasing his pace.

That lousy tramp, he thought, looks like a mixture of tin cans and roast chestnuts! Got a low ass, too, and that's always a bad sign ... Where the fuck's she going?

He followed her, already a little short of breath, not taking his eyes off her for a moment: she had caught on, and was almost running, turning into another street, towards San Lorenzo, deserted, without a soul in sight.

Tommaso was angry: his mouth was twisted in a grimace that bared his teeth. 'She makes me wanna spit!' he said, spitting. 'Where's she going, this bum? I hope she gets run over by a tram, to grease the wheels; the world's better off without people like her, goddamm her! She even goes with old men. Filthy pig! She's a disgrace to her trade, she makes you vomit just to look at her ...'

He had caught up with her and had only to reach out to grab her. She looked at him out of the corner of her eye, frightened, clutching her bag tight.

Aha! Tommaso thought, afraid of me, eh? You see I'm gonna make you cry ... you'll pay for your sins, all right. Slow down, dope! Where you running to? Slow down, you can't get away from me! You gotta do what I want...

His face was distraught: he looked around: there wasn't a fly in the whole street.

'Aaah,' he yelled, when he fell on her, grabbing her bag and giving her a shove with all his might. But she had been expecting him and she wouldn't let go. She clutched the bag with both hands and started to scream. Tommaso punched her in the mouth, then punched her a second time. She fell to her knees, still not letting go of the bag, which she was holding by the handle. Tommaso, pulling on it, gave her a kick in the stomach, but that only made her yell louder. 'Goddamm you,' he shouted, 'I'm gonna kill you!' But she wouldn't let go, and she went on screaming. Then Tommaso bent down and bit her, first on one hand, then on the other, biting

off a piece of flesh. With that, screaming in pain, she let go. Tommaso darted off at top speed to the end of the street, then down the
Viale dell'Università, then, still running, to Verano. He didn't even
look around to see if anybody was after him. At Verano, behind a
bush, he took off his shoes, and holding them too, he started running
again, along the wall of the cemetery. In sight of Portonaccio,
under another bush, he put his shoes back again and stuck the bag
inside his jacket.

In this way he reached the terminus of the trams and the buses to
Pietralata: half dead, he went another fifty yards, down under the
Tiburtina overpass, along a garbage dump.

There, in the darkness at the bottom, sitting on a bit of stinking
ground, he opened the bag and began to go over the contents, and
as he did, little by little, a great happiness bathed his face, making
all his pimples glow like matches over his swollen jaws. Chrissake,
this one was well off, he said to himself, six thousand in her bag, and
she was too cheap to take a cab. Look at all the cash. Tommaso,
you've struck oil! Besides the money, there was powder, rouge, a
lighter, and a change purse with some coins. There were also identity papers, with her picture, smiling, all dolled up in a little white
collar and earrings. But Tommaso threw this stuff in the mud along
with the bag and pissed on it.

*

It was evening at Pietralata: some had had their supper, and some
hadn't, but all were happy and noisy, going back and forth on the
streets of the quarter. And the air was mild, if the slightest breeze
sprang up, it had a flavour of quinces and salad bathed by the
dampness.

Zimmìo was straddling his Vespa, chewing gum, open-mouthed,
his clump of lank hair on his forehead going up and down, following the movement of his jaws.

He had his hands clasped on his belly, a patient, calm expression.

Behind him sat Tommaso, and third, his ass half-out of the
saddle, was Carletto, with the guitar around his neck.

Beside them, on another Vespa, there were three others.

'Hey, shitheads,' one of these three said, with a disgusted face like he wanted to throw up, 'shitheads,' he repeated, wearily waving one hand in interrogation, the fingers clenched in the air in front of his eyes. He had pale blue pupils which, in his disgust, seemed about to turn white, then melt. His face was a triangle, all smooth, and his hair was blond, cut short. 'You gonna pay the gas?' he went on, in a fit of nerves, 'we don't have the cash!'

'Aòh, Dresser, keep your cock on ... ' Tommaso said.

'Let's get going!' Dresser blurted angrily. 'Let's go,' and he wriggled free of the other two he was squeezed between, trying to grab the handlebars to start the Vespa and go off, the three of them, about their own business.

'Wait a minute and take it easy!' said one of the two, Smoky, looking at Dresser with a mouth ready to break into laughter. 'What's eating you?'

'Hey, you guys,' he said, to the others, 'we'll come along on our own, okay? Why not?'

Zimmìo lost his patience all at once, kicked the starter a couple of times, and went off, zig-zagging in front of the bar at the bus stop, almost throwing off the two sitting behind him.

The other Vespa came after him, though Dresser went on yelling: 'Let's tell them to fuckoff ... eh, Smoky!'

Smoky, green as a cake of Palmolive, paid no attention to him. He followed Zimmio, biting his lips because of the care he had to take, picking his way among the people and the cars. Dresser soon got over his annoyance, his eyes became blue again, the wrinkle on his puppy-like forehead smoothed out, and gripping Smoky's overall, he began to laugh and insult the people on either side.

Behind him, the third, the American, maintained the fuckemall air he had had since the beginning.

He was a little kid, not much over fifteen, with a tuft of hair that palpitated over his forehead like it was alive. Black, wavy, with a straight parting to one side.

The warm air struck him and his eyes laughed.

Zimmìo zoomed like a madman down the Via di Pietralata,

passed the Lux Cinema, and took the Via Tiburtina. Here there was
an endless line of cars, trucks, and creaking buses.

Tommaso slumped behind him, thinking wisely of his respon-
sibilities as leader of the expedition: I pick my horses good, he said to
himself, some show that fucker Tommaso is gonna put on!

Behind them, the others were acting smartass. The American,
placidly, had started ripping leaves from the oleanders that hung in
tatters over the road, and he flung them at the girls they encoun-
tered. Dresser, every time they struck home, let out a shrill whistle,
and Smoky, as he drove, shouted: 'Do it again!'

They passed Portonaccio, San Lorenzo, San Giovanni, went
through Porta Metronia, along the Passeggiata Archeologica,
buzzed around the whores a few times, then sped off like rockets
towards Porta San Paolo, passing the General Market and entering
Garbatella.

Where Garbatella begins, in a field naked and empty among two
or three rows of identical little buildings, and four or five others
under construction, there was a house like the ones back at Pietralata; it looked like a beach hut, all patched up. At the corner of it,
all chimneys and peaks and full of windows, there was a pizzeria and
a little bar with a kind of arbour in front.

All around there were patched huts, all flowers and decorations,
some as small as a family tomb, brown, next to the big box-like
blocks of new housing, white as refrigerators.

In the bar, around the arbour, all the young guys who lived in
those buildings were gathered.

As Tommaso and his partners turned into Garbatella, the first
thing they saw was the neon light of the bar, alone in the midst of all
the night's darkness.

'You could at least buy us a coffee!' Zimmìo said, spitting out his
chewing-gum.

'Let's go then,' Tommaso said, 'come on!'

Zimmìo slammed on the brakes, almost making Smoky crash
into him.

They left the Vespa outside the arbour and went in, Carletto with
the guitar over his shoulder.

'Aòh, Heart-breaker, who taught you to sing? The police-chief?'
one of the Garbatella characters said, in a low voice, seeing them
go by.

'I get by, I do my best,' Carletto answered, calmly, in the accepted
manner among smart guys.

'So long as you got a good voice!' the other one muttered. 'Sing
us something, like you sang out at Headquarters!'

Meanwhile the other three, Smoky, Dresser, and the American,
had also put on the brakes, got off, and followed their friends.

When they passed the entrance with its four or five dry trunks of
wistaria around, Zimmìo stopped for a moment, yawned, and with
his mouth wide, adjusted his cock, pulling like it was elastic. Then
he went into the bar.

It was a little place, with a circular counter, and behind it, two
dopes, one old and one just a kid.

Crowded between the counter, the wall, and the cash desk another four were playing cards at a little table.

Tommaso, Zimmìo, and Carletto took their places, all men of
the world, stretching a little, immediately followed by the other
three, who stood off by themselves, fresh and good-humoured.

One of the four card-players looked up a moment and, when he
had glanced around, lowered his eyes again on the king of clubs in
his hand with that saintly manner a priest has when he raises his
eyes for a moment from the missal; then he said to one of his three
friends, in a low voice: 'Aaaah, you know Irene?'

'No, who's she?' the man said, agreeably curious, and assuming
at once a polite, conversational tone.

'The one that lives near us, up at Via Anna Maria Taigi ... '

'Well?' the other asked, with a neighbourly interest, already
dying to laugh.

'Sunday I saw her with one of the better-known characters
around here. They say she's an easy lay ... '

With this, he drew his head down, resigned, between his shoulders and slapped his card on the table.

Tommaso, who was jammed in near by, couldn't help hearing,
he turned red as a turkey; controlling himself, he addressed the man

at the cash-desk, with a bitter expression. 'Three brandies,' he said; in a bored voice.

'Three cognacs,' the cashier said to the two dopes at the bar; coldly he took the money Tommaso held out and put it in the cash register.

The other three, after some consultation, ordered two orangeades with three glasses.

Meanwhile a couple of guys from the bunch outside under the arbour came into the bar to buy cigarettes, and the place was so crowded you couldn't move.

'We got Roberto Murolo here!' one of the newcomers said, looking the other way.

Carletto laughed, a bit nasty, moving to the counter with the guitar in his hand.

'Hey, barman! You gonna give us that cognac?' Tommaso said, partly to redirect the conversation, to the old man, who was resting after his exertion in serving the orangeades. He looked at Tommaso for a moment, wet his lips, and with a stealthy look, started to serve him, too.

Meanwhile the newcomers, having bought their cigarettes, repeated their tactics. The one who had said: 'We got Roberto Murolo,' now said: 'Aòh, how about playing something for us? I got fifty lire in change here.'

The other burst with laughter. 'That's right,' he said, 'you look ready to kick off from starvation!'

And the card-player who had talked about Irene now couldn't hold himself back and, slamming a card on the table, he added: 'Cut it out: he's the royal minstrel!'

Carletto's only answer was to take the little glass of cognac and drink it, his eyes smiling very bitterly.

Two others came in, from Tormarancio. They saw the situation right off. They went to the counter to buy five Nazionali, and casting an absent look around, one of them added his bit: 'Ah, here're the bastards that keep people awake nights!'

Tommaso looked at the last two who had come in, clicked his tongue against his palate, as if to taste if it was bitter, nodded his head, yes, and then slowly turned towards the counter and took his glass in his fingers.

The one who had talked about Irene was a postman: he was dressed in black, in his uniform, and he had set his vizored cap lightly over his sparse blond curls. He glanced up a minute from the flush he was holding, saw Tommaso drinking, and said: 'Done your gargling? She's a heavy sleeper!'

Tommaso gave him a deep look. He was silent for a little while, clicking his tongue, like somebody who has just waked up and is rolling over to go back to sleep. 'Listen,' he said, in a deep and passionate voice, 'I think you guys are going too far ... ' The postman looked at him, decided apparently Tommaso wasn't all that tough, so he let out a syphilitic laugh.

The three extras, Dresser, Smoky, and the snotnose, were enjoying the scene, playing dumb; the other three from Pietralata didn't even look at them, like they'd never seen them before in their lives.

The postman finished his forced laugh and, with shining eyes, went back to his cards. 'Somebody around here,' he said, 'has breath that stinks.'

Zimmìo, having drunk his cognac, went over to the cash desk. 'Gimme ten Nazionali,' he said to the owner, a young man about thirty, half-bald. He threw a pack on the bit of marble that was free and collected the money. Meanwhile Tommaso and Carletto, with the tear-jerker on his shoulder, were going towards the door. This time addressing Zimmìo, the postman said, playing his cards: 'Where's the money come from? Mamma's pocketbook?'

Zimmìo was going out, but instead of going straight towards the door, he lost his control, turned blind mad, and threw himself on the sonovabitch postman, grabbing his collar with both hands; mouth against mouth, spitting, he said: 'Aòh, I'd fed up, see?' The other guy grabbed Zimmìo's wrists, couldn't free himself then grabbed his neck, pushing him back and trying to pull himself up: the others jumped to their feet, knocking over all the chairs, and began to pull Zimmìo by his sweater, giving him four or five punches in the ribs. Tommaso and Carletto came to the defence of their friend, pulling at the clothes of the postman's pals. But the

owner and the barman were fastest of all; they came from their
places, and one grabbing the postman by the shoulders, the other
grabbing Zimmìo, they tore them apart.

Once he was off the other guy, Zimmìo started wriggling like a
mad horse, eager to fall on the postman again; and the postman, who
wanted to do the same to him, tried kicking out at full strength.
The barman, holding him tight, said to him in a low, breathless
voice: 'Whatcha doing anyway? Hitting somebody weaker than
you ... It's not a fair fight ... It's not like you were hitting a man; it's
hitting a kid ... '

And at the same time, the owner, also embracing Zimmìo to
restrain him, muttered to him, bitterly: 'Listen, kid, it's not worth
getting your hands dirty! You don't know that guy ... He's so sick
he can hardly stand up ... it's a crime to hit a guy in his shape!'

At these words, the adversaries calmed down a little. And so did
the others around them. The owner suddenly became sociable
and full of chat: apparently he had profound convictions on the
subject of fighting: 'kids,' he said, as a start, 'you wanna get in
trouble over nothing?'

'Who started it?' Zimmìo said, interrupting him, still full of gas.

'Listen, shithead, I didn't lay a finger on you,' the postman said.
The owner made a very vague gesture, as if brushing a fly off his
nose: 'Eeeeh,' he said. Convinced by that 'eeeeh', the two became
calmer and kept quiet, adjusting their clothes, frowning.

'What'd he do?' the owner said, 'he didn't curse you bad or anything.'

'No,' Zimmìo said, still black as a sky after a storm, shrugging.

'Well then?' the owner went on, 'Can't you see he was just
joking? You and your pals come in here with the guitar for a
serenade, all full of piss—you can't blame them? They have to have
their say on the subject. Wouldn't you of done the same?'

'No,' Zimmìo repeated, disgusted, shrugging again with a jerk
and looking at the owner, ready to sustain his no against them all.
But the owner gave him a foxy glance, almost affectionate: he
made a benevolent and disbelieving grimace, as if to say: 'Come on,
kid, you'd of done the same, admit it, what the shit ... ' Then

Zimmìo gave in, angrily dusting off his black-and-red striped sweater. 'These fellas,' the owner concluded, 'are all good boys!' The good boys all made a face worthy of a chain-gang, and one of them, half outside the bar, let a fart.

'We're good boys, too,' Tommaso said.

'Well then,' the owner said, 'what's all the fuss about?' He came to a sudden decision, moved over to Zimmìo, with a face that said: 'What? Are we a bunch a hicks here? Listen, we've all come up the hard way! Listen to what I say, don't act silly!', he took him by the arm, with an eye lost in the distance, and brought him over to the postman, whom he slapped on the back at the same time, with more intimacy, pushing him toward Zimmìo.

'Come on,' he said quickly, 'we're all Italians! Shake hands, and forget it!' He was almost angry himself now, because if this reconciliation didn't succeed, it would make him look bad.

Tommasino gave Zimmìo a shove. 'Go on,' he said, 'don't be a pain in the ass … shake hands!' The two, bitterly, stuck their hands out, shook, first moving their fingers in the air, as if they had glue on them.

'Seven coffees!' Tommaso ordered from the barman, who in the meanwhile had gone back behind the bar. As he was making the coffees, the contenders introduced themselves, exchanged a few remarks, told where they lived, what they did, and all that sort of thing.

In the end they asked Carletto to sing a song or two, since it was still early. Carletto took the tear-jerker off his back, put his foot on the rung of a chair, tuned the guitar a bit, assumed an expression like Giacomo Rondinella, and began to sing 'Maruzzella', with plenty of feeling.

*

Half an hour or so later, they came out, saying goodbye and shaking hands all around. They got back on the Vespa and went off towards the centre of Garbatella.

Immediately after that, the other three, who had stayed in the bar a bit longer, acting indifferent all the time, overtook them.

'Aòh,' Dresser yelled, his little tiger-cub face all happy, 'you know what they said, when you went out?'

'Fuckoff!' Tommaso yelled at him.

'They said you were three little shitheads, and next time they'll beat you to a pulp!'

'Fuckoff!' Tommaso yelled again.

'And you know what they said about you?' Dresser answered. 'They said your face looks like a dish of lentils!'

'Fuckoff!' Tommaso shouted at him for the third time.

It was still early. They zoomed around the neighbourhood for a while, from Viale Cristoforo Colombo to the Passeggiata Archeologica, having some fun with the whores.

Then they came up along the Colombo towards the Via delle Sette Chiese, passing through that open square, big as a village, which in the darkness looked like a deserted lake with rows of lights all around it.

At Via Anna Maria Taigi not a soul was in sight. The gate opened on to two or three courtyards, one after the other, all empty and silent, below the yellow walls, high as cliffs, full of closed windows.

The friends entered the first courtyard, then the second, then the third: in the middle there were two or three dried-up little trees and instead of a flowerbed a patch of beaten earth, hard as rock. Along the cracked pavements, the half-basements, there were some low walls. They propped the Vespas against them and took their places, some sitting on the wall, some on the edge of the pavement, some standing.

Irene lived on the third floor, next to the stairway's row of lighted windows.

Carletto took his guitar, pressed it against his waist, with one knee raised. He tuned it. Pling plong plang, the plucked strings hummed gaily, like a kind of shudder in all that silence. Then Carletto played a couple of chords, which spread all around, even more gay and exciting. Tommaso waited, red in the face, frowning, intent on having everything come off right, his hand trembling as it held his cigarette. After these chords, Carletto bent over to hold the instrument tight between his chest and his thigh, then turned and asked: 'Whaddya want me to do now?'

'The serenade!' Tommaso said, venomously, his little mouth twisted.

'Sing "The Prisoner's Song"!' Zimmio said, 'that's a real man's song!'

'Shut up,' Tommaso said, furious, spitting saliva. ' "Prisoner's Song"! my ass. Sing a serenade, go on!'

Carletto lowered his head a bit over the guitar, as if he had to think a minute, then with his whole face changed, his eyebrows dropping, till he looked like the Baby Jesus, he lifted his head and began to sing:

> ' ... My sleeping beauty, you're dreaming
> My kiss is touching your brow.
> My song must sweeten your slumber,
> My song so sweet and so low.
>
> Every flower's aroma
> Around you flows ...
> And my song goes off
> Among the boughs ... '

He had a sweet, loud voice, that rose up in the courtyard, along the dirty, yellow walls, beyond the stairways' lighted rows of windows, over the roofs, from courtyard to courtyard, in all that silence.

People began to gather right away: boys who maybe had been playing cards somewhere under the stairs, little kids; and then older people, and some girls coming back from the movies or from the pizzeria. Under Irene's windows, which remained shut as if they were all dead inside there, a little crowd formed, and while Carletto sang they remained fairly quiet, respectful, trying to figure out who had arranged the serenade and for whom.

Tommaso, because of the way his heart was pounding, had a nasty face that made it immediately clear he was in charge. There were maybe five or six girls in that block, and some said it was for

Irene, some said for her girl friend with the ponytail, the African, and some said other names. Then people drifted away and others came. Only the boys had taken their places there, standing or sprawling on the walls, to listen to the songs, meaning to stay till the end.

They were pretty well behaved, except every now and then one of them wouldn't be able to restrain himself and would have to let out a bit of a song too, eyebrows drooping, chin upraised, moving his head as if he were saying no, no, while his hands passionately caressed the air: then he would give up, with a smile that wrinkled his forehead, patiently, as if to say: 'Look at me!'

By now there were the permanent ones, and the transients, who stopped for a little while and then went off because they had to go to bed, which was more important. Especially the women, with their sleepy girls after them.

After the serenade proper, Carletto began:

> 'Gateway amid the roses ... '

melting everybody's guts with emotion. After that, he played a few chords, was silent for a moment, then sang:

> 'O wave of the sea,
> so beautiful, so enchanting to me ...
> What strange spell sets you apart,
> Such loveliness ... without a heart ...'

And then:

> ' Nightingale,
> What tears are in your song!'

All around there was a gathering, like in films where the thieves meet at night. Serenades weren't too frequent, but everybody stood around quietly all the same, as if it was something that happened every night: only they felt a tingling in the stomach, and a great contentment, like at Christmas or at Easter.

They sprawled around, with ironic expressions, their eyebrows drawn up, up to their black forelocks, and their hands on their cocks, acting bored. But you could feel them getting gooseflesh; they all melted, hearing those songs. Right at the climax of 'Nightingale', they saw the cracks in Irene's window light up.

After a moment the light went out again, but the shutters were opened just a little. The girl was there, listening. Carletto then put his whole heart in it, till he was about to go to pieces.

'When I hear that song,' a blond, smartass kid near by muttered, 'I feel bad!'

They were all in agreement on that score. And Carletto sang, all in ecstasy, till he seemed ready to take off like a helicopter and fly through the air.

'Angel of Paaaradiiise, my scarlet flower!' another kid said, putting himself in Tommaso's shoes, addressing the girl. 'For you I'd kneel and pray, every night and every day ... to make you a queen!'

> 'Nightingale,
> what tears are in your song! ... '

repeated Carletto, transported by the holy beauty of the song: and all the people around were flying with him, like helicopters, in the sky, over the buildings.

When that song ended, Carletto had to start another at once, because this was the crucial moment, and if he let it slip, it was all over. He sang the first one that came into his mind, and since everything was going well, and he was happy, like everybody else around there, friends, strangers, and all, he sang in phonetic English:

> 'Ai kaym frum Alabama
> weet a bancho awn mai nee ... '

When that was over, too, having spread a feeling of satisfaction and well-being, he promptly broke into a third, which he had had time to select in his mind, and he had made a wise choice:

> 'My lady, Love,
> the moon glows at your window pane,
> beyond the curtain's veil you lie ...
> Singing, I come, to say: I love you!
> Appear, to listen to my song.

> My lady, Love,
> the hour for sleep has not yet come,
> and if your heart allows,
> I'll stand and sing
> the song of night ...
> Why have you not appeared,
> to still my sighing heart?
> My lady, Love ... '

But, halfway through it, the shutters up above closed very slowly, and didn't open again: the lights were all out.

'Look who's here! Look!' they heard shouts suddenly in the distance. From the street, from Via Anna Maria Taigi, in fact, a band of older boys was coming into the entrance. The moon was so bright you could read a newspaper: and Tommaso and the others, who were already preparing to get the Vespas and go, saw at once it was the postman and his friends from the Bar, up at the beginning of Garbatella.

They must have had plenty to drink, since they came in shouting with the cancerous voices drunks have. One had remained behind, maybe to piss before going up to his house, and was also singing full blast, yelling. Some of the others were snickering, holding their bellies with their hands in their pockets. Then they came up to Tommaso's bunch, the postman looked around and, red in the face, under the blond curls peeping from his vizor, he said: 'Listen ... send us off to bed happy ... We really got a passion for music,' he added, with a greedy smile, round-mouthed, his eyes happy, 'it's in our blood. How about letting us hear a good song, eh?'

'Sorry,' Carletto said, 'but we're all tired, not just me. And besides we gotta go.'

'What? You not gonna sing?' the postman said, with a grieved air, sadly surprised, 'you won't do this little favour for us?'

'Listen, fella,' Zimmìo intervened, 'we don't live here at the corner, you know. We got an hour's ride ahead a us, see?'

'Eeeeh!' the postman chanted, 'the sun hasn't come up yet, and you wanna go away? Don't you like our company?' he added.

At that very moment, after having worked over it for a while, Zimmìo managed to get the Vespa started.

'Come on, let's go,' he said, his sly face full of pimples, white with anger and sleep, under his hair that had been cut with a razor.

'Whaddya mean go?' the postman said, with embittered patience, 'Don't be a baby! I don't think you're a baby!'

'Sing the song for him, go ahead,' Tommaso said briskly, rather than act shitty with these new friends.

Carletto, hesitant, displeased, got off the seat; with his hands doing one thing and his face saying another, he struck a couple of chords.

'Come on, we'll buy you a litre!' the postman said.

'Sure, tomorrow!' a friend snickered, ironically.

Dresser, Smoky, and the American, hugged together on their Vespa, were enjoying themselves like three bastards, seeing the others give in.

Carletto played another chord, then sang the first song that came to him, gradually warming to it:

'Strings of my guitar ... '

When he had finished, the postman showed his contentment, and so did the rest of the bunch. 'This boy'll go a long way! He's got promise, all right!' one said, about as tall as his cock, hard and assy. 'He's got a voice, eh?'

Zimmìo started kicking the starter again, but the Vespa wouldn't start.

'Whatcha doing?' the postman asked resentfully, 'What? You wanna go off like that? You wanna leave us? No, no! It's still early!'

'Early my ass!' Zimmìo said.

'Whaddya mean?' the postman said, then smiled sadly, with a bittersweet look. 'That's not right!'

'Listen,' he said then, all friendly, to Carletto, 'let's have another song. Sing "Ownly Yew" for us,' he said this title even more emphatically, his mouth round, almost biting his lip in pleasure.

'We gotta go, you!' Carletto said weakly: he and the others had to put up with it, because the other group was much bigger, almost double.

The postman went on acting like a victim: 'It's only midnight,' he exclaimed, 'he's looking for excuses!' He was grieved, full of commiseration, and so he urged the guys from Pietralata to be more broadminded, to rise to his height.

'One more then,' Tommaso said, 'and after that, we're going.'

'Okay, okay,' he said.

Carletto sang 'Only You'.

'Eh, this boy's got a big future!' another friend of the postman's said, a certain Dyer, who had green eyes, and when he got a hard on, one stayed green and the other turned red, like Siberian cats. 'Sing "Timber Jack" for us. Let's hear how you sing that!'

Zìmmìo farted, and he had to laugh a bit.

'What? Did you mention love?' a little guy said, all eyes and hair, in the shadow of the postman.

'Come on, let's go,' Zìmmìo said angrily, kicking the starter some more with his heel until the motor caught: he jumped on the seat.

'Wait! Act nice!' the postman said. 'Didn't you hear what my friend said? He expressed a wish to hear "Timber Jack"; you don't wanna go off like this?'

'Listen, Air Mail,' Zìmmìo said, calm again, 'whatever your name is, you haven't taken us for dopes, have you? Let us go, and drop the argument!'

'Ain't you nasty!' the blond said, his mouth widening, shocked, like a priest or some respectable character, his eyes filled with amazement. 'Just look at the people we've met up with ... You'd never think it to look at them. They seem so nice!'

'Get on,' Tommaso said to Carletto, as he got on behind Zìmmìo. Carletto started to get on behind him.

With this, Dyer, very calmly, almost delicately, took the guitar from Carletto's hands. Caught off guard, Carletto let go, so as not to break it. Dyer turned it in his hands, this way and that, looking at it.

'This is a fine guitar,' he said, calm and detached, filled with a purely artistic interest. 'Whodya steal it from?'

6

'Your cocksucking mother!' Tommaso yelled, jumping down from the seat.

Dyer looked at him, aghast: his smile dropped, flaked from his face, which remained a piece of white flesh, the mouth bent down, the nose straight under the peroxided head, and the eyes filled with a profound, awestruck attention.

He shook his head a bit, as if to drive off a mosquito buzzing around him, annoyed but still calm, then barely twisting his nose, he asked: 'What did you say?'

Tommaso ground his teeth fiercely. 'Your cocksucking mother!' he shouted again, spattering saliva.

Dyer snapped, grabbed him with both hands by his tie and pulled his face to his own, torn with rage. 'Listen, turd,' he yelled, 'don't say that to me! Don't say it!'

'Cut him up!' a friend yelled.

Tommaso was trying to free himself, but caught like that, he couldn't do it: he grabbed Dyer by the wrists and tried to pull his hands from his clothes, but the other guy was getting madder and madder, and kept clinging to him with all his strength.

Then Tommaso went blind and kneed him with all his might in the stomach. Ready to vomit with pain, Dyer bent over, writhing, and rolled on the pavement with his hands on his belly.

They all began to feel their blood rise; Tommaso, when he had finished kneeing, jumped back against the wall of the house, and he was just in time because the postman, to defend his friend, was on him.

He had darted forward, turning his back to the others, giving a kick with all his strength, to catch Tommaso where Tommaso had caught Dyer: but the kick went wild, because Tommaso dodged it, huddling still closer to the wall of the steps.

The postman then threw himself on him to work him over, and he was already giving him punches that should have broken him into four pieces, turn him to ashes and rags. Tommaso seemed to disappear inside him, since he was half the other guy's height.

But, all of a sudden, as the others had formed a circle to slaughter Tommaso in the event that he got the better of the blond, the postman stopped, clasping his hands to his ribs: 'Oh God, Mamma!' he shouted, half breathless, and stood still, paralysed.

Tommaso was there against the wall, his knife in his hand. Dresser and the other two friends, seeing the bad turn things were taking, cut off at once and disappeared down Via Taigi at the end of the courtyard.

Tommaso started to run off on the other side, but there were no exits.

'Grab him!' Dyer yelled to the others, who didn't know what to do: the postman was standing there, still; he had put his hands under his jacket, on his shirt, and had taken them out all stained with blood.

Then he began to yell for help and leaned against the little wall to support himself with his back: he slipped slowly down the broken bricks, and sat there, with some of the others looking at him, trying to help, and some trying to catch Tommaso.

Meanwhile Zimmìo and Carletto had gone off too, at top speed, vanishing at the end of the yard.

Tommaso, alone, chased by two or three of the gang still at a distance, made a wide curve, was confused for a moment, watching what was happening: then, seeing his chance to escape, he ran off desperately, gasping for breath, towards Via Taigi, all in darkness.

PART TWO

1

Stink of Freedom

Tommasino's father, Torquato Puzzilli, was a municipal employee and, as always when somebody says municipal employee, that meant he was a street-cleaner. Of course, he had been better off before, back in his village: he came from a working family, true enough, but he could hold his head high, and when noon came the table was always set, and there were always two full bowls on it.

Torquato had been the owner of a little house, probably made of slabs of tufa, in the midst of the countryside half a mile from Isola Liri, which he had been left by his mother: around it there were a few square feet of land that he worked, and he had built a shed for the hogs, the sheep, and the hens. And along with this Torquato had also been named beadle of the Isola Liri combined schools, so he was able to marry Sora Maria after they had been teasing each other quite a few years: in 'thirty-four the first son was born, and in 'thirty-six Tommaso; then they had a girl, who was born dead. When the war came, Torquato was called up, and on September eighth, of 'forty-three, he came home, a deserter like everybody else. But he had to move off right away, and this time with everything he owned, in the caravan of refugees escaping towards Rome.

When they reached Rome, all exhausted, hungry, barefoot, worse than gypsies, they were herded along with some other homeless into a school building at Maranella, the Scuola Michelazzi which then, after Fascism fell, was re-named Scuola Pisacane.

Back at his village Sor Torquato had lost everything: the planes had razed his house, shells destroyed the stables, and the tanks had wiped away the last traces of it all.

When the Americans reached Rome, he, his family, and all the other peasants there in the school were told to get out because the troops needed it: to persuade them to move, they were given some packages and few lousy lire. But they weren't fooled, and they really didn't know what to do, where to turn: then, on one of those summer days where the air boils and every stone is a glowing coal, the police came, charged in on them, and flung them into the street with the few rags they had left.

Everybody then worked out something, as best he could. Every man for himself and God for all. Some found living-quarters in a cellar for two thousand lire a month, some built shacks under the old arches or in some bombed-out building, using the same rubble.

So the Puzzilli family went to live in the shack between Pietralata and Montesacro, on the bank of the Aniene: a fellow-villager left it to them, a man who had made money on the black market and had drunk it all away. From then on they stayed there: at first Torquato made ends meet somehow, then they got him a city job, and he became a street-cleaner.

At that point he began to fill out all sorts of application forms, at City Hall, at the Registrar's Office, at the Vatican, appealing to every saint in heaven, to have a house once the war was over: months had gone by, years, but their house was still that shanty, in the little settlement where in the summertime the heat nearly set the place on fire, and in winter the rain and the mud threatened to shift the houses into the river. Now he had resigned himself to putting down roots there, with wife and children, for the rest of his life.

But then one day they started flinging together new buildings around there, along the Tiburtina a bit above the Fort: it was an enterprise of the government-sponsored INA-Case, and the blocks of housing began to sprout on the fields, on the little hills. They had strange shapes, pointed roofs, little balconies, skylights, round and oval windows: the people began to call those buildings Alice in Wonderland, Magic Village, or the New Jerusalem, and everybody laughed, but all the people who lived in those slums began to think: 'Aaaah, at last they're gonna give me a palace!' And there wasn't one of the refugees, the shanty-dwellers, who hadn't tried

presenting an application to get out of the miserable heaps of junk
they lived in.

In fact, when the development was almost finished, when it stood
all empty and neat and clean amid the rubbish and the mud, one
night all the inhabitants of the area got together and worked out the
plan: they went and occupied the place, like staking claims in a
Western, and the one who got there first occupied what then became his.

Most of them were women, and they entered the buildings of the
project, where there still weren't any streets, pushed aside the watch-
men, and biting and kicking among themselves, pulling out hatchets
when necessary, they occupied the apartments and squatted.

For five, six days they stayed shut up in there. The police came
and surrounded the buildings: there were Jeeps and patrol wagons
all around, blocking the access to Jerusalem.

Sora Maria, too, with the other women, had gone to occupy a
house: her older son looked after Tito and Toto in the shack, and
took her some bread and odds and ends to eat when he could, because the police sometimes let you past and sometimes stopped you
and asked for your identification papers.

Then, one fine day, or rather one evening when it was raining
cats and dogs, orders came to clear them out: the chief of police in
person turned up, and in a few hours everything was back to
normal: about fifty women were carried off in the wagons, and the
village was empty and deserted again, with the last squatters moving
out, carrying their crummy mattresses rolled up on their heads.

More months went by, then the first authorized families came to
live there: nearly all city employees, people who weren't so needy.
A few apartments were still empty, but there were thousands of
applications. And then one of those many saints to whom Sora
Maria had been praying for ten years or more, finally presented
himself.

Who would ever have imagined such a thing? One of the INA-
Case apartments was assigned to Torquato Puzzilli! Jeezus! Old
lady Bad Luck had got tired of running after him with her cane!
Singing with happiness, Sor Torquato bought wine for all his

neighbours in the shacks, broke a few old plates as a precaution against the evil eye, distributed other stuff among his friends, and in the end even made a deal, selling his shack: fifty thousand, goddammit, more money than he'd ever seen at once! He pulled out all his belongings and loaded them on a pushcart: that done, he stood at the door of the shack, with an aluminium pot brimming with water, which he flung to the ground, as if to flood the place, because he didn't ever want to go back there again, not even feet first.

So Tommaso's family was settled in the INA-Case project; in two rooms and kitchen, which seemed nice and spacious for the whole family, because in the meantime, while Tommaso was still locked up, Tito and Toto had kicked the bucket, and they no longer played around inside the house all day.

First Tito had felt sick: one morning when his mother came to pull him out of the box, where he slept, she saw him crying, all covered with snot and vomit. She took him in her arms right away, trying to console him, but he went on crying, his little head against his mother's shoulder, since he couldn't hold it up.

Then Sora Maria had put him back in the box and had given him some hot wine to drink to warm up his blood.

The little boy, half drunk, had dozed for a while, but when he woke up, he was worse than before, and he threw up the glass of wine, too.

He felt worse and worse all that day and the following night. The next morning, when he could hardly see and was only a little bundle of rags, his mother took him to the clinic at Pietralata.

It was winter, and it took her a while to get there, in the mud, under the rain. She stood in line at the clinic, which was in one of the buildings near the bus stop, and when it was her turn, the doctor told her the boy was in a bad way and it was best to take him to the hospital. In the hospital, two days later, Tito died, after suffering all night, yelling and writhing in pain.

When his brother was gone, Toto seemed dazed: he was left all alone in the little yard in front of the shack, among the walls of sheet iron and the drying laundry, and he couldn't seem to get his bearings.

He had always been with Tito, and he went on believing Tito was still there beside him. From time to time, he called and called him, then went to cling to his mother's skirts, as if to ask her what was wrong. After a while, he would forget, go back and play about in the mud, alone, then he would start looking around again sadly, calling for Tito.

In the house there was still an old broken valise, found on a rubbish heap, where he and Tito used to sit, pretending they were in a truck: he would sit here now, too, alone, going 'rrr' and 'nyaaaa' for a while, then he would be quiet, and maybe fall asleep, covered with rags like a ball. Or else he would wander around blindly in the shack or the yard, calling his mother for hours on end: 'Ma! ... Ma! ... Mamma!'

A little ragged ball had also remained: and one day, when a bit of sun had come out, he had started playing with the ball, which he had come across accidentally under a rusty sheet of iron in the shed. He threw it in the air with both hands, then went to pick it up where it fell: he tried to kick it, his face became red and fierce with the effort, zzack, and he missed, zzack, missed again, almost breaking his neck: finally he struck it with the tip of his toe and the ball darted off into the distance.

So he left the yard, ran out among the other shacks, passed the little bridge over the ditch that separated the shack village from the road, and started playing where he was.

As he was trotting after the ball, the bus arrived from behind the curve towards Montesacro; the driver didn't have time to put the brakes on, and he side-swiped him with the bumper, flinging him into the ditch.

Toto banged his head against a stone buried in the mud and lay there, still, all padded in his undershirts one over the other, his shorts caked with dirt, the socks hanging down over his patched boots: he didn't move, he seemed asleep, only a little drop of blood came from behind his ears and stained that patch of crushed grass under the stone.

Tommasino was away all this time: he was in stir, had been there so long he was beginning to get mouldy, but only a few months were left before the big day.

Eh, Sora Maria was right, when she used to say to him always: Death lies in wait when you stay out late. He never used to listen to her, but that knifing at Garbatella had cost him plenty, and he had had lots of time to cry over it.

From Via Anna Maria Taigi, to tell the story in a few words, he had headed towards Cristoforo Colombo, surprised that he was still loose in the world; and, thinking that the police would come to comb that area, he had hidden in the little drainage ditch under the big boulevard, connecting two filthy streams: against the wall of the little tunnel, over the black, stinking water, there was a little earth, even blacker and more stinking. Tommaso crouched there, moving away from two or three dry turds, and he slept, numbed with cold.

When day broke, very slowly he walked all the way back to Pietralata, and reached the vicinity of the shanty village. He walked with his eyes good and open, ready to cut out at the first sign: 'I hope nobody's around, maybe they didn't recognize me,' he said to himself. 'But first I wanna have a good look, if there's anything funny going on, I'll keep away from home ... '

He approached and saw that all was calm, only some kids making a bit of racket, playing among the stakes of the little yard.

Reassured, he started to go into the house; he opened the door, and saw the uniforms right away.

Without thinking twice, he ran down the bank of the river towards the canebrake: but the police had seen him and were on his heels. He ran, turned, saw them behind him, and at the same time the other guy who had stayed out of sight in the Jeep started the motor and sped forward: he blocked Tommaso, with a nasty smile, while the other two were already on him, yelling: 'Stop, Puzzilli! We ain't gonna do anything to you!'

They caught him, took him to the station and, in short order, sent him off to the cooler.

After a couple of months, a guard one evening brought him a notification of his trial, and the most experienced prisoner, a guy who knew the laws better than a judge, seeing the paper, said: 'Jeezus, this is a first degree trial, that's Section Three! Wednesday, an odd number, so you draw Old Funny ... He'll murder you, my boy ... Better report sick, make them postpone it!'

In fact, this Old Funny really did murder him: the District Attorney threw the book at him, and they just about gave him the three days in the Sardinian calendar: today, tomorrow, and always.

So, limply, Tommaso came back to his cell in the third wing, with two years on his neck. 'Aòh, how much did they give you? How much?' everybody yelled at him. 'Two years.' 'That's nothing; time you've had a good shit, you'll be out!'

It was evening, the first in his two trips around the calendar, a nice, mild evening in summer, with a bright, serene light that seemed never to die. Around, you could hear the usual noise of the prison: the guys talking in the cells and calling to one another calmly, and those in transit, crying, because it was dusk, the prisoner's bad hour.

Then, louder and merrier, the voices from one wing to another could be heard. 'Hey, you spies in Wing Five!' one shouted, 'ya wife lays the whole city!' 'Doncha know me? I'm ya brother-in-law!' they yelled back. And the first answered: 'Your wife brought me a package today!'

Then, little by little, they all began to cling to the bars and to yell all at once, in the evening air that was like a caress. 'Hey, smelly, I'm in here because I knocked up ya sister!' 'Wing Five! Today they sent ya a couple stool-pigeons. They turned in a lotta our pals! Work 'em over!' 'Hey, Red, take care of them!' 'Hey, Weakass! Ya got some shampoo? Didya wife bring ya some? Send me some hairpins!'

From the Janiculum, in the distance, all full of lights, over the evening breeze came the voices of people who went up there to call to friends and relatives, specially the whores, who came to yell messages to their pimps.

They could hear a kid shouting, leaning over the wall: 'Hey, Papaaaa! Sunday Ma and me're commin to see ya! Don't feel bad!' And one whore, with a voice that drowned out all the rest, sharp as a drill: 'Hey, Tiger! I left two thousand for you today, at the gate!'

And then the voices of the women in the Mantellate prison next door: the men in the Seventh Wing, nearest them, started it. 'Hey, Maria!' one yelled, 'I wanna die!' 'Hang yasself!' the women yelled back.

And so the night went on, and around midnight, there was always one guy, who started yelling at the top of his lungs: 'Brothers! What does the voice of the spirit say to you?' And from all the wings, the jailbirds answered in chorus: 'Fuck you!'

*

When Tommaso was let out, it was a fine May sunset. This was the first time Tommaso had seen the INA-Case development finished: when he was picked up, it was only a pile of bricks and scaffoldings, that people looked at with irony, knowing what was going to come of it. Now it was there, all nice and completed, with a little wall around it, on the fields that had remained what they were before, full of filth. The brand new streets curved in among the pink, red, yellow houses, also curved, with lots of balconies and skylights and rows of railings. Arriving with the bus, looking at it, you really thought that quarter was Jerusalem, with its mass of cement flanks, one above the other, serried in the fields, against the old quarries, and struck directly by the sun's light.

Tommaso got off at the Fiorentini factory, came back a bit, and took the first street that went into the quarter. He looked at the sign: it was called Via Luigi Cesana. 'Via Luigi Cesana,' Tommaso said, gulping a bit in his contentment. 'Well, let's take this Via Luigi Cesana here!' His heart was pounding, his head almost swimming. He knew his house was in Via dei Crispolti, number 19: but he hadn't the slightest idea where the fuck that was. He looked around, frowning, pulling the corners of his mouth down, and widening his eyes. 'Ha ... ' he said. He didn't know whom to ask; he was a bit embarrassed with people, because of the jail business. It's true that, in the end, he hadn't been in for anything like two years, and now he was coming out with the stink of freedom still on him. But he was worried all the same that the people in the new neighbourhood where he lived now might find out about it. So he confronted a little snotnose kid, running home with a bottle of milk. 'Hey, kid,' he said curtly, 'Where's Via dei Crispolti?' The kid explained: 'Over there, to the right!' Tommaso calmly followed this direction, but first he lighted a butt: and so, smoking, he reached this Via dei Crispolti.

It was one of the last streets of the INA-Case: it curved towards the fields, all rippling and baked under the sun. There were six or seven little dark-red buildings, set at a slant, with rows of round windows, five or six little steps up to the doors, and lots of zig-zag railings joining them all: then, behind these buildings the road ended abruptly in another road, without houses, cut from the tufa. Then fields, all around. Farther on there was an old farmhouse with some oak trees, and on the other side, towards Pietralata there was a wooden church, tiny, with a metal fence all around it, isolated in a kind of yard.

The air was hot, sweet: on all sides there was sun, only sun, yellow and tranquil.

A few women were singing, at the windows, because the sun was beginning to set now; and the kids were playing in the street: here in Via dei Crispolti the little kids played with shovels, down in the half-paved street between the walls of tufa a gang of the bigger kids were having a game with a patched football. Under a pump at the beginning of Via dei Crispolti, a kid was singing like a finch in the mild air, a new song that had come out during these past months, a song Tommaso didn't know:

'Oi Lazzarella ... '

Tommaso had stopped to look at his building, one of the two or three painted a dark pink: it stood near the end of the street, against the fields, all nice and clean and new.

Then, with a lump in his throat, moved almost to tears, Tommaso went inside, frowning slightly to conceal what he was feeling. Ever since he could remember, he had lived in a hovel of rotten wood, roofed with corrugated iron and tarred paper, in the midst of garbage, mud, turds: and now at last, he lived in a building, no less, de luxe, with the walls all nicely plastered, and the steps with railings neatly finished, to perfection.

He climbed up just to see, he knew it was pointless, because he didn't have the key and there would be nobody at home: they were all working at this hour. He came to apartment twenty-nine. Here another lovely surprise was awaiting him: on the door there was a card with Puzzilli written on it: PUZZILLI, in big letters, elaborately printed. 'Jeezus!' Tommaso muttered, laughing, red in the face, his eyes still glistening with emotion.

On the landing there was a little oval window, just about the height of his nose. Tommaso went over for a look. From there you could see half of Rome: a pile of houses in the light, the ground already a bit dark, endless; the city seemed to float on the clouds, bobbing up and down, from Montesacro to Piazza Bologna, to San Lorenzo, to Casal Bertone, to Prenestino, Centocelle, Villa Gordiani, Quadraro ... Some sirens wailed down below, a little bell started ringing, making a racket that was enough to deafen you.

Happy, Tommaso detached his nose from the window, and with his hands in his pockets, ran jumping down the steps. He would have to wait till almost seven to get in, because nobody would be coming home before then, for sure.

He trotted happily down Via dei Crispolti, after taking a drink at the pump, singing, too, under his breath. He turned again into Via Luigi Cesana, crossed the Tiburtina at the Fort, and headed for Pietralata.

On his way, he thought about his affairs: or rather, he thought about a single affair, something that made his heart beat like a hammer and so filled him with joy he couldn't stay in his skin. He sang louder and louder, while in his imagination he visualized Tommaso going in and out of the new building, bored-looking and calm, all dressed up, as if he had always lived in houses like that.

With an indifferent air, he looked at those who were still there, in the refugees' shacks, or maybe down at Little Shanghai, hard-luck cases, walking around without a lira, trying to scratch up some cash. It was the hour when work stops: the buses began to arrive packed, with people clinging to the doors, and in the Fort the bugles were signalling the hour for the soldiers to come out on evening passes.

The neighbourhood was beginning to come to life for the evening, though the sun still shone hot and placid; so Tommaso found them all in front of the bar, standing there as if they were awaiting the visit of their newly-sprung friend.

They were scattered about, some at the little tables, some against the trunks of the crummy trees.

Zimmìo, his yellow jersey hanging out of his pants, along with another two or three, broke like him, was throwing some stones to a dog that had shown up, making him chase them. The animal was exhausted, his coat standing up, his tongue dragging in the dust; he didn't realize they were teasing him, exploiting his innocence, and he knocked himself out, running up and down like crazy, bringing back the stones between his teeth.

Zimmìo, the sonovabitch, tried to throw the stone farther each time and put all his strength into it, so he was pretty much worn out himself. When he managed to throw the stone beyond the corner of a crumbling house, three or four little walls, towards the fields white with dust along the Aniene, he was overjoyed and his mouth fell open in a grin of contentment.

Shitter was sitting on a piece of wall, reading a comic book he had stolen off some kid.

'Look who's here,' said Zucabbo, standing there, legs apart, in the middle of the street waiting for God knows what.

Five or six faces, Buddha's, Hyena's, Prickhead's, Cazzitini's, Nazzareno's, turned towards Tommaso, all sleepy-looking, pale, with an expression of weariness and boredom. 'How's things?' Zucabbo asked, shaking hands with Tommaso, the old jailbird. 'Fine,' Tommaso said. 'Who'd you spill on?' Buddha said, talking with his belly.

The others laughed a bit. But Tommaso, looking them in the face, laughed harder than they did. Go ahead and laugh, bums, he was thinking, his eyes narrowed, I'm screwing the whole bunch of you! He was thinking, calmly, of his house: of the nice new house he had, while all the others were still living in huts, one worse off than the other.

At that moment the bus arrived, and most of the bunch vanished, running towards the stop like a flight of crows, Zucabbo included.

Very calm, Tommaso went and shook hands with Zimmìo and Shitter, who greeted him yawning. Zimmìo forgot about the dog, and it promptly flopped down in the dust half-dead, still looking at its killer with shining eyes. To pass the time, Zimmìo started peeing against the wall where, a bit farther on, Shitter was busy reading his comic book; every now and then, still grinning, he swerved and sent a jet against the dog.

The sun was low now over the crusted fields. All through the slum you could hear a murmur of voices and, now and then, somebody singing. Tommaso sat down on the wall, pressed one leg against his chest with his chin on his knee, and also started singing again softly, full of happiness.

After a while Lello turned up there, too. Since he was crippled, Tommaso, seeing him, dropped the leg he had been holding in his arms, stood up, and went towards him.

'Hey, Lè, Lè,' he said, very friendly, slapping him on the shoulder, 'How's things, Lè?'

'Ciao, Tomà,' Lello said, shaking his hand.

Tommaso had assumed the attitude of the old buddy, who acts jolly to show the other guy that, after all, his misfortune is nothing, nobody notices it.

'So, whaddya have to say, Lello?' he said.

'Whadda I say? Shit ... ' Lello said, still dragging his shattered leg towards the bar.

'Jeezus, it's lousy being inside!' Tommaso said then, to keep the conversation going.

'I believe you!' Lello said, still grim-looking, greasy and pale the way cripples are.

'Eeeeh,' Tommaso sighed, 'shit.'

They came to the open door of the bar, which was crowded with people.

Tommaso, not knowing what else to say, and with his heart still full of the new house and with nothing else, sighed again, then lit up another butt. 'What a life!' he said.

Lello stopped and looked at him for a moment, sideways.

'Say Puzzilli,' he said, 'I gotta go someplace. So long.'

He turned around, going off about his business along a muddy little slope beyond the bar, between two big buildings abandoned there between the dust and weeds of the first fields.

He went off, dragging his leg, among the folds of dried mud and dirty bits of paper, and disappeared around the corner.

Tommaso stretched, yawned, breaking off the yawn to click his tongue against his palate, like somebody who has just waked up after a good sleep; and killing time, his hands thrust as deep into his pockets as they would go, he went back very slowly towards the INA-Case.

He felt a great calm in his heart, and he was savouring at the same time his freedom and the thought of the house.

Slowly he reached Via Tiburtina, full of bersaglieri who came out on passes at sunset; he turned into Via Luigi Cesana, and now taking a good look around at the neighbourhood where he was to live, he went towards his house and Via dei Crispolti.

He looked again at the building, all lovely and painted a bright pink, outlined with its balconies and windows against the still-bright sky. All around now, besides the snotnoses, there were some older boys who had come back from work. Five or six were playing cards, sitting on the ground outside their house. At the bar in the distance, at the corner of the low building in the centre of the INA-Case, where there was the market, the first bunches of guys from the buildings had gathered, sprawled in the chairs.

Tommaso wanted to observe the surroundings well: he walked up Via Luigi Cesana a bit farther, to the last houses, which looked over an expanse of fields and caves, with the old villa surrounded by oaks in the background.

From there, too, you could approach Tommaso's building: you had to step into the field, a mass of bumps, hillocks, filth, then climb down to the right, along the little embankment dug out in the field of tufa, where they had taken the stone to construct further houses.

Tommaso's building had an entrance on that side, too: through a vertical row of plate glass panes, you could see the stairs. Tommaso swelled, seeing this luxury: 'Jeezus, look at all that glass!' he thought.

From up where Tommaso was, however, a kind of black trail of beaten earth began, crossing the field and leading from the end of Via Luigi Cesana to the little wooden church in the centre of the field.

Along that black path, which wasn't necessary now, since the field was dry, Tommaso decided to go towards the church. This was a kind of long, narrow storehouse of pale blond wood, the planks marked with long indentations, The roof was pointed, and at the top there was a cross. All around it there was new wire fencing, which enclosed the church and a bit of yard. Behind the church, you could see another building – similar, but lower – attached to it, probably the rectory. Crossing the field, Tommaso approached along the fence, because he could hear some voices there in the back. Behind the little church, opposite his building, the field – a kind of plateau – had been dug up and there was a hole with some foundations, some planks, and in the midst a crane. Everything was still because by now the workmen had stopped work and gone home. At the highest edge, solitary as a lookout, from which you could see most of Rome, there was the building site's latrine, of white, dusty planks.

The voices he had heard were coming from behind the wooden rectory, next to the pit. Some kids were playing under a shed at the end of the little yard of the priest's house. The last light of the sun, red and a bit cooler, illuminated that area obliquely. Four smaller kids were playing table-football, and another two were playing ping-pong: others were watching, sitting on some packing-cases.

Tommaso knew that two categories of people lived at the INA-Case: on the one hand the government employees, railwaymen, tram conductors, who had been assigned houses through their departments, and among them there were even bookkeepers, surveyors and high-class people like that. On the other hand, there were those who had lived in caves and dumps, to whom the City assigned new houses every now and then, all bums or petty crooks.

The kids playing in the church yard must have been students, daddy's boys: and they were all Tommaso's new neighbours, more or less.

They were playing, concentrating on the table-ball and ping-pong. They too were dressed smartly, in American jeans plastered with shiny studs, with broad belts and jerseys: but they were all spick and span, soiled a little only on the ass or on their knees, not from work, but because they sat down wherever they felt like it, playing, or because they had touched themselves with dusty hands.

One kid, so pale he was green, with a pair of black eyes that made him seem a little Arab princeling, looked sarcastically at a friend of his playing ping-pong: 'Aòh, Iacobacci,' he said, 'You got a home? Then go home!' He laughed a bit to himself, chewing some gum: 'You're lousy!' he added.

Iacobacci was too busy playing to answer. But when the ball fell and bounced towards the end of the shed, he bent over to pick it up and said: 'Screw you, Di Fazio!'

'Fuckoff!' the other boy said. And he went on calmly chewing his gum. After a while he stood up and went over to his friend, saying: 'My turn!'

'I haven't been playing five minutes yet!' the other boy said, pulling up his eyebrows and pressing his elbows against his chest, with his racquet in his hand.

'Five minutes, my ass!' Di Fazio said crossly, though he sat down again abruptly, with his hands in his pockets.

'We'll finish this game, then you can play, okay?' Iacobacci said, conciliatory, resuming his game enthusiastically, because his opponent was already getting pissed off.

Tommaso stood beyond the metal fence, watching.

He stayed there, a bit awkwardly, his little mouth half open, thinking his own thoughts while he looked at those kids. Then he stirred a bit: Whaddam I doing here? Acting like a bum? he thought, but not giving much of a shit, because his heart was light.

To give himself some excuse for being there behind the fence, he

went slowly towards the latrine, entered as if he had to do something, and stayed in there a while, faking. He lighted a butt instead,
looking out of the cage of dusty planks at the pit below, and farther
on at the sea of fields and countryside, and in the background,
against an intense, yellow sky, at the quarters of Rome. The sun by
now had almost set, but that beautiful, evenly-diffused light remained, clear as milk, coolish.

Tommaso came out again, and this time assuming a smartass
manner he began looking at the kids in the rectory yard, trying to
make himself noticed. But the kids still paid no attention to him
at all.

Now it was the ones around the football table who were talking,
arguing like puppies. A blond kid in blue shorts yelled at a friend
playing on his side: 'Are you asleep? Wake up!'; and the other kid,
thick-lipped, tall, also blond, his hair down over his forehead, said,
with calm disgust, knowing he had made a bad play: 'Cut the
fucking around!'

Meanwhile one of their two opponents, quiet and happy because
they were winning, caught by a frenzy, had hurled the little ball
into the centre of the table again, shouting: 'Come on, Romagnoli!'

Tommaso observed, rigid, his heart pounding. He realized that
staying there beyond the fence like a beggar was no good. But he
wanted to strike up a conversation with those kids, get to know
them. He took a few steps towards the church, still looking at them
sideways, though they hadn't noticed him except for a glance the
kid named Di Fazio had given him, chewing his gum. Tommaso
considered himself a real expert, or rather, a champion, both at
table-football and at ping-pong: he looked on with a detached air,
half-yawning, thinking of all the games he had played: these guys
were nothing! So now he could allow himself to stay there and
watch, almost as a protector, an authority, with his hands in his
pockets. But still he couldn't manage to say anything. He talked
within himself, alone: and the more he talked the more he felt
those kids ought to have understood, as if they had already made
friends with him, since he lived in one of those new, de luxe houses,
just like them.

I'd take another two years inside, he was thinking, to know why the other guys take them for shits! Anyhow, shits or not, here they are! They don't have a thing to worry about, they play and have fun, make the girls at school! And they have their Daddy who gives them money! If you ask me, he went on thinking, these kids are nice to each other ... Whadda they know about life? All the same, I'd like to mix with them. Goddammit, I wish I'd been brought up like them, to be a good boy, the way they are!

However, he was thinking all this, not saying it. Those kids kept racing around, playing, as if he didn't even exist and had never come there. Tommaso snickered a little, at a silly return by Iacobacci, who had sent the ball slamming against the ceiling: but he snickered calmly, almost affectionately, forgiving him, the way you have to forgive a young kid, and thinking of what ping-pong really was, for somebody who knew how to play it.

Meanwhile he was beginning to get an idea. He thought it over for a minute, frowning, then he gave it up and said to himself: No, no ... frowning still more.

He went on watching, absently: then he thought some more and said: Why not? and added: When I get a thing into my head, that's how it's gotta be! I wanna try. Why not? He had another, brief doubt: What can I think up, though? It's not so easy! Aòh, he concluded, I'll try it, if worst comes to worst, I can tell him to fuck himself ... He glanced towards the church, then, calmly, as if he had come to the decision earlier, and had stopped there to watch the kids playing only by chance, to kill a few moments' time, he headed for the main entrance.

The yard in front of the church's little façade was scattered with piles of gravel and plaster, cases and tools, like the back. Tommaso crossed it, and glancing around, went to the door. He threw away the butt, coughed slightly, and went inside.

The church was empty: there was only one woman, with a shopping bag on her knees, praying, resigned, as if she were a bit ashamed of the requests she was making of the Madonna or of some saint. Beyond this woman there was nobody else. Tommaso made a face, saying to himself: 'Hmph', then he remembered to make the Sign

of the Cross: pray, no, not that, because he could remember the
Hail Mary only as far as 'the Lord is with Thee': but he pretended,
just to show that he had come in for a reason. Inside, the church
wasn't bad: all clean, with its rows of pews, pictures along the white
walls; it looked like the kind you see in cowboy movies, with
whaddyacallem, with Protestants. Tommasino came out again and
looked around in the yard hesitantly, then he started down along the
other side of the church, towards the pit of the building site and the
parish house. He went inside: there was a corridor, a little empty
room to the right with some pool tables and equipment and with a
sign on the door that read 'Realm of Christ'.

The corridor ran the length of the little building, freshly white-
washed with doors in the walls, looking like the doors of a gym's
locker-room. There was nobody around. Tommaso went forward,
undecided, still grumbling to himself. In the end, two or three red,
plump characters came out of the door at the end, and Tommaso
said to them: 'Where's the priest?'

'There,' one said, going off without looking at him. Tommaso
walked forward and said: 'May I come in?'

The priest glanced up at the door, looked at him gravely, and
said: 'Come in.' Tommaso, beneath his gaze, entered a little room
which looked out over the fields with the wooden privy at the end.
It had a table, a shelf with maybe thirty books, two chairs, and a
little cot, plus, obviously, a crucifix almost as big as the priest
himself.

Outside, the kids could be heard yelling, playing in the yard, and
all the voices of the INA-Case.

The priest gave Tommaso a sidelong look, white as the rubble
around the rectory. Tommaso was a bit embarrassed but, with a
priest, it's not hard to seem pretty smart. 'Hello, father,' he said …
and swaying, kinda smartass, he held out his hand: 'I'm Tommaso
Puzzilli,' he said. The priest took the hand with his fingertips and
clasped it slowly. Tommaso was acting like a good boy, a bit jolly
and easy, a man after all and, as a man, with his bad habits: gambling,
smoking, women …

'Sit down,' said the priest, who still didn't know what Tommaso wanted, but was used to these things. Tommaso at first wanted to refuse, because he wasn't tired, but then he gave a look at the chair, with an elastic gesture, and he sat down, again elastically, shrugging. 'Thanks,' he said.

As he sat down, he felt a bit embarrassed, because sitting like that at the edge of the chair, he was fully exposed to the priest's gaze: the brown suit with white pinstripes, bought second-hand two years ago at Campo dei Fiori, the down-at-heel, cracked shoes, so faded you couldn't tell if they had been brown or red, of suede or antelope, the crummy socks, stuck a bit too far into the heels of the shoes so you couldn't see the holes, the old shirt with a tie dating from three hundred B.C., from the days of the god of hunger. In this state, Tommaso didn't know where to put his hands and, to be doing something, he dug out his cigarettes, blushing to the marrow.

He was still the good boy who, being a man, can't resist his weaknesses. 'Mind if I smoke, father?' he said. 'It's a dirty habit ... ' and, meanwhile, he held out the pack towards the priest uncertainly, to offer him one, not knowing if he was being polite or if he was insulting him, since priests aren't supposed to have dirty habits.

The priest indicated with a gesture that he didn't smoke, and at the same time, he looked around, uneasy and serious: he must have been sick, because his skin beneath the sparse beard was white and grey, his eyes hollow, his lips pale as a cat's. He was small, and so thin he seemed lost inside his cassock.

Tommaso started smoking, very relaxed. Usually he was affable and polite like this with people towards whom he had evil intentions. But now, since his intentions weren't the least evil, but in fact, were good, he was hesitant.

'You wanted something?' the priest said, as if it cost him some effort to speak, taken up as he was with other thoughts: perhaps the church he was building, down below, at the end of the project.

'Yes,' Tommaso said promptly, 'I wanted to talk to you about something important ... '

'Go right ahead,' the priest said. 'If I can be of help to you ... '

'Eh, if you can't help me, being a priest ... ' Tommaso said.
'That's why I came to you ... '

'What is it then?' the priest asked.

'Well ... ' Tommaso said, wrinkling his forehead and shaking his
head, 'I don't know how to begin, father ... '

'Speak up, what are you afraid of?' the priest said, simply.

'Well, father,' Tommaso made up his mind. 'I've made up my
mind to marry a girl ... I came to you for a bit of advice ... Listen,
father, if you'd do me the favour of explaining to me, helping me,
I don't know, tell me what I should do ... '

'How old are you?' the priest asked him.

'Twenty in November,' Tommaso said.

'Have you thought seriously about what you're doing?' the priest
said then, 'do you realize the step you are about to take?'

'Sure,' Tommaso said, acting smart, out of habit.

'This is the right path to take,' the priest observed, very calm,
'bringing you close to the Lord: you're young, and you could form
a fine family ... How old is the young lady you're engaged to?'

Tommaso couldn't remember the girl's age very well, he hesitated
a moment, then said: 'She's twenty, like me ... '

'What about the parents?' the priest asked, 'Do they know? Are
there any family objections?'

'No, no,' Tommaso assured him.

The priest hesitated a moment, then gave it a try: 'Do you want
to make your Confession now?'

Tommaso recoiled: he hadn't been expecting this: 'Well, no ... '
he said, 'better tomorrow morning. I'll come tomorrow morning ...
By the way, father, what papers do I need to get married, what
documents do I have to get together?'

'You'll need ... ' the priest said courteously, 'your birth certificate,
baptismal certificate, confirmation ... '

'How'll I manage that?' Tommaso interrupted him, beginning to
be confused, 'Where'll I find all these certificates?'

The priest explained, as if it were all very easy and natural: 'You
go to the parish where you were baptized, confirmed, and they'll
give them to you at once ... In all, you may have to pay about a

thousand lire ... And then you have to have a certificate of your civil condition, that is, certifying that you aren't already married ... '

Tommaso smiled, tranquilly, thinking: Sure, I suppose you'll give me the cash to go back to Isola Liri!

'That certificate,' the priest went on, 'is given you by the city registry office, like the birth certificate ... '

Tommaso indicated he had understood it all perfectly, acting very interested and respectful: 'Does it take time,' he inquired again, 'to get all these papers?'

'Nooo,' the priest said, 'you can do it quickly. In a few days you can have them all ... '

There it was, there was nothing else to be learned from the priest on the subject of marriage: unless he wanted to confess himself then and there, while the iron was hot. But Tommaso was a bit sorry to finish that conversation so fast. He assumed a sweet, good-boy face and asked: 'Father ... you think I'm doing the right thing?'

The priest looked him in the eye for a moment, then lowered his gaze: 'You haven't got into any trouble, have you, with your fiancée?' he asked, 'Has anything happened?'

'Nooo!' Tommaso cried, shocked. 'Nothing like that! You're kidding, father? She's a nice girl! I'm marrying her because we love each other ... '

'So much the better,' the priest said, his head lowered, 'everything is done with the grace of God ... ' And he lowered his eyes still farther, remaining silent. Then, after a few moments, Tommaso coughed a bit, stood up, and started to leave, holding out his hand to the priest.

'Well, so long then, father,' he said, 'I'll see you tomorrow morning ... '

'Goodbye, my son,' the priest said.

Tommaso left and went down the corridor towards the door, all content, thinking to himself, almost aloud: Nice guy, that priest!

He came out of the rectory, jolly, full of himself, red in the face as if he had been drinking. Sniffing and coughing, he put his hands in his pockets and went towards the field.

There, between the dirt track, the church, and the houses, in a crummy, gravelly piece of field, there was the bunch of little kids. Now it was almost evening, the light arrived there as if from another world: the mothers were beginning to call the kids, and the first lights were being turned on. Tommaso stopped to light a cigarette: it was the last, and he didn't have another lira in his pocket. While he was there, the kid named Di Fazio came from behind the church, by himself. Tommaso looked at him, and the kid came over, taking a butt from the pocket of his shorts.

'Gimme a light?' he asked Tommaso.

Tommaso calmly held out his lighted cigarette, and the other kid, very seriously, without looking him in the face, said 'Thanks' and started to go on.

'Say,' Tommaso said, clearing his throat and coughing again. The kid turned. Tommaso was very affable and nice-boy.

'You gotta sign up?' he asked, 'to go to the church yard back there?'

'We're on the list,' the kid said, briskly, running his thumb under his forelock, to adjust it.

'Ah!' Tommaso said. 'You live around here?' he added.

'Over there,' the kid said, 'In Via Luigi Cesana.'

'I live there,' Tommaso said, as if he were a bit bored, though the other kid hadn't asked him anything. As he pointed to his house, Tommaso's heart started pounding again: he half-yawned, and started down the path with the other kid, who didn't know what to do and who wanted to go off about his business.

'Maybe I'll sign up, too,' Tommaso said, pointing to the church. The other kid, having nothing to say to him, spat, with a deft spurt, whimsically. Tommaso was all happy at this intention that he had announced. If I sign up, he was thinking, I'll show you how to play table-ball, ping-pong, and the rest! I'll smash you all! In the end, I'll be the big shot around there; what're you and those others anyhow? A bunch of little turds!

They had come down from the field into Via Luigi Cesana, and from the railing of a little terrace which was joined by little steps to other terraces in front of the houses a kid climbed down yelled: 'Hey, Marcelloooo!'

Di Fazio looked up, recognized him, and ran off towards him, barely turning to wave to Tommaso. The other kid meanwhile had come down from the terrace, all dolled up for the evening, in neatly pressed grey slacks and a red pullover with a white shirt. He put his arm on Di Fazio's shoulder, beginning to talk intently, and arm in arm, they headed for the centre of the INA-Case.

It must have been seven by then, and Tommaso turned towards home. He climbed up: the front door was open. His mother was there, waiting for him.

Tommaso hugged her, and as she hugged him, she started to cry. When she had calmed down a bit, still crying, she took Tommaso to see the house: there were two nice rooms, the kitchen, the bathroom, the balcony ... In one room the father and mother slept; in the other, Tommaso and his big brother.

What a night Tommaso spent! The most beautiful, you might say, of his whole life: because, even if he slept, he wasn't really sleeping, but was always a little bit awake, so he could always remember he was there in his house, a nice house, big and well-made, like rich people have.

2

Spring at the INA-Case

The next morning, by seven o'clock, Tommaso was already up and in the bathroom, washing. A strong sun, of full spring, was beating down on the INA-Case. And since everybody had waked up early, there was such a racket of voices, songs, shouts that it seemed midday.

Tommasino did everything calmly, dressed, put on a shirt and tie: he had decided now that jerseys, T-shirts, all that smartass, kid stuff was no longer right for a respectable young man with his papers in order. His shirt was old, gnawed along the collar, and the tie was a memory, you couldn't tell what colour it was, blue or purple: but looking at himself in the mirror on the bathroom wall, Tommaso was nonetheless pretty well satisfied.

Then, as he was about to go out, without a lira in his pocket, ready to walk all the distance he had to go, which was no jaunt, his mother called him gaily: 'Commere a minute, Tommaso!' She took him to the bureau with the photograph of Tito and Toto on it, in their good clothes, smiling, half-blinded by the sun; and she pulled out a thousand lire she had saved up in those months, for him.

So when he went out, Tommaso was a prince.

He came to the Tiburtina, and without glancing at anybody, but very courteous and reserved, he started waiting for the bus with the others, as if he had never even dreamed of the necessity of going all the way to Garbatella on foot: he had the money for his fare, going and coming, and a nice wad of hundred-lire notes in his pocket.

When he reached Garbatella, he went straight to the market, which was in the midst of some old buildings, all with big windows like chapels, under the roasting sun: he passed the various departments, and reached the fish section, which stank till it hurt.

One of the stands was near a pump, and the fish-seller at that moment wasn't yelling like the others, right and left, sweating and sly: 'I'm selling liquid gold, that's what!' 'How about some live bass here?' and so on. Instead, he was bent over the chest of ice, pounding with a little pestle.

'Hey, Settì!' Tommaso shouted, looking at him, very friendly.

Settimio raised his close-shaven head, his pale-blue eyes. He was tiny and quick as a mouse, but you could see right away he was big-hearted, even though he looked sharp-eyed and dressed like a crook.

'Tomà!' he said, standing up, his eyes a blue flash, 'Whaddya doing around these parts?'

He stammered a little at times, because his father and his mother, Jews, had been killed by the Germans in a concentration camp: and the shock had affected him for life.

'Tell me, Settì,' Tommaso said, when he had shaken his hand, 'you know a girl named Irene, who lives in Via Anna Maria Taigi?'

'Irene?' Settimio Augusto said, thinking it over, his face grave.

'Yeah, Irene. Last name Bondolfi. A kid ... kinda short ... with black hair ... She's not a real beauty, or anything, I mean she's okay ... A home girl ... '

'Well,' Settimio said, still thinking about it, rummaging in every corner of his brain, to see if he could dig up this Irene.

'She's got a girl friend, short, with a ponytail,' Tommaso insisted, 'who lives in the Via Taigi development, Stairway C ... I think they call her the African ... '

Settimio brightened. 'Aaaaah, the African,' he said, 'Diasira! Sure, I know her! I must of danced with her a thousand times!'

Tommaso was happy. He waited while Settimio served a lady who had come to the stand to buy a pound of whitebait, then said: 'Will you be seeing her tonight, or tomorrow?'

'Maybe right away, when I close up! I gotta go right by her house!' Settimio said. 'Why?' he added, looking at him happily, 'You need something?'

Tommaso coughed slightly. 'Well, yes, I'd like to take up with Irene again,' he said, after thinking it over for a moment, 'and you know how it is, all the time I was away ... you see what I mean ... I never wrote to her, not even a line ... I mean, for over a year I've been out of it. So how can I just show up out of the blue? I'd have to arrange a meeting, if somebody could put in a good word.'

'Natural,' Settimio said, looking at him carefully.

'Now, if you talk to this Diasira, and Diasira talks to her, I'll find the ground broken, sort of, you see?'

'I'll talk to her, sure,' Settimio said, kneeling again to pound the ice in the box.

Tommaso pulled out a pack of cigarettes and offered one to his friend; they began to smoke.

'Aòh,' Tommaso said, 'tell her I'm back, that I'm still serious about her, that I love her, and all that sort of stuff, you know what I mean ... '

'Don't worry!' Settimio said light-heartedly.

'And tell her I'll be outside her house tonight, when she goes out to buy the wine ... ' Tommaso went on.

'Don't worry!' Settimio said, 'When I talk to her, it'll all work out; it's as good as done!'

'I'm leaving it up to you!' Tommaso said with a slightly cross manner, but melting with contentment: it was all arranged, and life was smiling at him.

'Whaddya doing now? Working?' Settimio asked, after a while.

'Working!' Tommaso cried. 'Whaddya think I am? I only got out yesterday. I wish I was working! I hope I can find something to do ... '

Settimio was quiet for a while, pensively crushing the ice. When he had finished, he started spreading it over the fish he was putting away for the next day. Then he said: 'Aòh, if you really wanna work, go over to San Paolo. There's work for everybody there!'

Tommaso looked at him, full of hope.

'We guys in the local markets,' Settimio said, 'we got friends there at the General Market. If you feel like it, Tommaso, I can talk to somebody who can lend you a hand!'

'You're kidding? You'd be saving my life!' Tommaso said.
'Really!'

'Well, tomorrow, I'll talk to the wholesalers, I'll take a walk around the stands. Somebody always needs a porter.'

'Is it hard work?' Tommaso asked, very sweetly, just to be asking.

'Well, kid, nobody's giving away money these days! Eh!' He sold a woman some fish for a mixed fry then went on: 'They try you out, for two, three days ... then, if you're okay, you're in for good ... '

Tommaso already knew more or less what the work was like at the market, but he listened anyway to Settimio, who, while he kept busy at his stand, explained what it was: you had to show up there around four in the morning, and, first of all, go straight to the refrigerator and take out the cases of fish left over from the day before. Then you went to arrange the chests in the fish shed in the wholesalers' section. Around five, six, the trucks of fresh fish came in, and they lined up outside the shed: you had to unload the new chests and arrange them along with the others. Then the selling began: the retailers came and bought; and so you had to help them, shifting the cases, weighing the ones they bought, and loading them on carts. Last of all, around ten, eleven, you had to carry the left-over fish back to the refrigerator and throw what was rotten into the sewer.

'Well, let's hope the fish like me!' Tommaso said at the end, full of joy.

'Of course, if you come into our line of work,' Settimio added, 'you'll never die of hunger. Because everybody eats fish, rich and poor people alike!'

'Eh, Tomà!' he added then, slapping him on the shoulder. 'The future belongs to the young!'

Well, things didn't work out quite as easily as Tommaso was imagining them by now: on this earth, there's rough and smooth. But in the end everything was clear sailing.

Irene was now working in a medicine factory on the Via Casilina, and she got off a bit late in the evening. Two or three days went by while Diasira carried Tommaso's message to Irene and then Irene's message back to Tommaso.

As Diasira then told it, laughing, the minute she heard the name of Tommaso, Irene looked mad, serious, and stopped talking for a while, concentrating and thinking about her own business, and then she started talking again, a few words at a time, very reserved, sniffing like she was about to cry.

Though she tried not to show it, and she lingered on certain things half-said and half-unsaid, on those sad events she was pondering and that upset her a lot, she was really very excited and happy that Tommaso had got in touch with her again. Two or three evenings later, in fact, with Diasira, she waited for him, as she got off work, at the gate of the factory: she was all dressed up, in her little white overcoat and wearing earrings. When she saw Tommaso coming towards her, she turned melancholy and haughty, but sweet at the same time: they shook hands politely, greeting each other like old friends.

The following Sunday, without telling her parents, they went into Rome together. It was a really fine day, with a warm sun, so warm you could already see bunches of people going to Ostia. Especially around the station, where Tommaso and Irene arrived with the number 11 from Garbatella, there was a pile of people, all enjoying themselves. Tommaso had saved most of the thousand his mother had given him: he had spent only a little on trams and butts, because at the Market, where he had already started working, they still hadn't paid him a lira.

They got off the tram at Piazza Vittorio and walked up towards Piazza Esedra.

Tommaso was very serious and grim, partly because he was happy to be there, in his shirt and tie, strolling with his girl, and partly because, since that morning, he hadn't been feeling so hot: maybe because in his excitement he didn't shut his eyes the night before. He felt funny: he broke out in a cold sweat, and his legs and his whole body trembled a little, God knows why.

Respecting his seriousness, composed and elegant, Irene walked at his side, just a bit behind, with her hand through his left arm, half stuck into his pants pocket. With his right hand Tommaso was smoking, red as a rooster, proudly taking his girl out for a walk.

However, he really didn't feel good: and when they came to the Piazza Vittorio toilets, all decorated like two little Indian temples, he frowned even more deeply: 'Wait!' he said to Irene, and very reserved, she stood sadly and waited for him.

'Have I got the trots, like Shitter, now?' Tommaso thought, angry with himself, when he was in the filthy little can at the corner of Piazza Vittorio. 'Am I gonna have a fit and die?' In any case, when he came out in the midst of all those cats among the flowerbeds, he was already feeling a little better, and he walked on as if nothing had happened, with his girl on his arm.

Shall I tell her, or not? he was thinking, clenching his jaws: on the one hand he was happy and proud at the piece of news he wanted to give her; on the other, he was growing cold and, almost, without wanting to, he had half a mind to drop her. Irene instead, was thinking about having a nice Sunday out with a boy, and that was all.

'Look at that little girl! Isn't she cute?' she said, seeing a dolled up kid walking along, holding on to her father with one hand and her mother with the other, both big characters with gold all over them. Or else: 'I just love these rugs!' when they went past some rug shop. All like that. Tommaso, in his heart, was happy to have a girl with ideas of that sort, like nice people, with money: and he agreed that the little girls with ribbons and the older girls were cute, and he liked the same kind of rugs she did.

And so they reached Piazza Esedra, where there was plenty of life. Just at the beginning of the arcades there was a dance hall on the fourth floor, and outside the entrance some guys were beginning to collect, wearing black suits like jailbirds, with some more classical types in their midst, in blue serge and antelope shoes.

Some servant girls, some slobs came along too, with a boy or with their girl friends.

Farther on there was the Moderno, a first-run movie-house where the best seats cost six hundred lire: a little farther still under the arcade, there was the Odeon, a little cinema full of soldiers and kids, where *The Woman of the River* was playing. Tommaso and Irene stopped outside to look at the posters, to see if they liked it: Irene's

eyes brightened immediately, in happy surprise, seeing the actress
in rolled-up slacks, a handkerchief tied around her head and a straw
hat over it, cutting cane with a sickle. Beyond her you could see a
lovely lagoon, still waters under a dazzling sun.

'This is a nice picture, you know,' she said warmly, since she knew
all about the movies, 'it has Sophia Loren and Rick Battaglia!'
Tommaso also looked at the posters, and he caught Irene's enthusiasm. 'Let's go!' he said, determined and pleased, coughing with
excitement.

They quickly bought their tickets and went inside: Irene ahead
and Tommaso afterwards, directing her with his hands on her hips,
like a good boy, guiding and protecting his girl.

They found two seats, because it was still a little early, and they
sat down, happily watching the film. A little later, when the lights
came on at the end of the first half, they looked around: they were
really a handsome couple. And there were another seven or eight
around them, downstairs. The soldiers and the kids, on the other
hand, were making the usual racket, sprawled in their seats:
Tommaso looked at them with anger, almost with hatred. Compared to them, he felt superior, a person who had given up all that
foolishness: if he had been the usher, he would have made them
behave: by now he would have kicked them all out into the street.

But while he was thinking this, he felt another attack of pain in
his belly: slowly he turned white as a corpse, and he really felt he was
dying, that his guts were coming into his mouth; his eyes had
clouded over, and he nearly banged his forehead against the seat in
front of him. He couldn't move very much, even if he had wanted
to, because during the night some boils had developed on his neck
and his back, and they hurt him.

As soon as he was feeling a little better, his head still fuzzy, and a
bit of saliva drooling from his lips, he grasped Irene's hand, pressing
it so hard he half-crushed it, clinging to her.

'Irene, I gotta tell you something ... ' he said gravely, when he
could speak, half-whispering.

Irene, moved but not showing it, as if she had always been
expecting this thing, turned slightly towards him and looked at him.

'I don't know how to begin ... ' Tommaso said.

'What about?' she said.

'Well, you know ... ' Tommaso began, 'now I've seen you again, and these days I've had this idea in my head, that it's time for me to settle down ... I mean, I wanna change my life ... You know, in the old days, I was kind of wild ... But you understand, I had to behave like that and ... well, I couldn't come right out and tell you I was running around like a bum, could I? I couldn't tell you I hardly ever worked ... But almost everybody's like that where I used to live ... '

He was silent for a bit, pensive, but excited, red in the face. Then he went on: 'I knew I liked you a lot, Irene, and if I had told you the truth, I don't know how you'd of taken it ... '

'Well?' Irene asked, all attentive and sweet.

'Now,' Tommaso said, 'everything's changed ... Now I know what it means to have everybody respect you, and like you ... Look, what I'm getting at is this: you know what I mean: I love you, and that's why I want to change from what I am, why I don't wanna be Tommaso any more!'

'I know, Tommaso,' Irene said, understanding, 'you've got good principles, and you didn't do anything really bad; see, it was all to the good that you kidded me a little ... I know all boys, even the real good ones, act like you the first times ... '

'Irene,' Tommaso said, happy at those words, 'would you be willing to be serious, with me?'

Irene was too overcome with emotion to answer right off, then and there. 'Serious?' she said. 'Whaddya mean?'

'If we got engaged, at your house!' Tommaso cried. 'I'll come and talk to your father and mother ... We'll do things the way they ought to be done ... '

'Well, Tommaso,' Irene said, 'if you really feel you love me ... ' But she couldn't go on because she started to cry.

Tommaso was quiet for a while too, with a lump in his throat: he put his hand on her shoulder and pressed her to him.

'You know something, Irene?' he said, happily, looking at her, 'the other day I went to talk with the priest, and I told him what my intentions are!'

'To get the papers?' Irene asked, sweetly, softly, hardly touching her teeth with her tongue.

'Yes!' Tommaso said, 'it isn't hard, you know!' he added, content. 'Birth certificate, baptism, confirmation, civil condition ... And it doesn't cost a lot either. A thousand or two. Nothing!'

But at that moment the lights were turned off again, and the film resumed: Tommaso and Irene huddled one against the other, holding hands, and settled down to enjoy it, like respectable people.

*

When they came out, the weather was even finer, the air more mild. The sun was still high, and all Piazza Esedra and Via Nazionale were full of light and noise.

Since Tommaso was feeling better and his strength had returned, before going to the Number 11 stop, they walked a bit along Via Nazionale for some fresh air. They strolled and looked around at the shop windows, the people, all that luxury and that life.

They passed a little bar all full of Americans, with the windows crammed with stuff Americans eat and drink, sitting on those high stools by the counter. They went past a men's clothing shop, where there was a dinner-jacket in one window, with patent-leather slippers, a white scarf, black gloves, walking stick; and in the other window, a light suit, for afternoon, with brown moccasins beside it and a red and black tie that was something special. Then a shoe store, a big department store where they had everything, until slowly they came to the Exposition Hall, its flight of white steps shining in the sunlight.

But then, as he walked along, Tommaso saw suddenly a familiar face, flung back against the low wall of some steps that went down below the level of the street. He took a better look and, sure enough, it was Lello.

What's he doing there? he thought, frowning immediately; in any case, he didn't say hello, but turned even grimmer and walked straight on, holding Irene by the waist, without her noticing anything.

'Nice, isn't it?' he said, alluding to the façade of the Exposition Hall, white as a bathroom.

His back against the little wall, Lello had stretched his misshapen leg out on the pavement, his trousers drawn up so you could see the stump where the foot was missing; and he had also rolled up his sleeve, to display his handless arm.

With this arm he was clutching a little kid, maybe a year or two old: the other hand, his good one, was held out towards the people passing by, for alms.

Lello didn't see Tommaso either, because he didn't see anybody.

The little kid he was holding was nice and quiet, dressed like a girl, with a tiny face so pale it was almost green, and black thoughtful eyes like an old man's. Every now and then he glanced to the left or the right, his curiosity caught by something, but he didn't show his curiosity, and was content to look around in silence.

Lello seemed not even to notice the kid beside him: he had rented him, and he held him like an object, not a little boy. And the kid knew it, too, and behaved himself.

How Lello had changed, from the days when he used to go venturing into Rome with his friends! He was worn, thin; even his hair, which he used to take such good care of, no longer looked the same. He hadn't shaved for six or seven days at least, but his beard was blond and fine and you couldn't see it very clearly: he was filthy, and his skin was covered with a kind of greasiness, something it exuded that wouldn't go away not even with lye, since it had soaked into him now for a long time, like with all cripples, all deformed people, the same as him. The smart pants he used to wear, when tight pants were the fashion, the striped jerseys, the scarves knotted around his neck like a sheriff's: none of that now: he was wearing an old pair of grey, filthy pants and a checked jacket with swollen pockets, maybe containing something to eat wrapped in old newspaper.

He didn't beg by moaning or by looking at the people angrily, nastily, the way some do: he did it as if it were a profession, a habit, thinking of other things, with that crook's face, God-forsaken.

'How about a coffee?' Tommaso said to Irene, expansively, generous of pocket and of spirit.

'No, let's walk. I like to look around!' Irene said, sweetly.

'Pretty de luxe around here, eh?' Tommaso said, giving a last, insistent look back at Lello, then moving on. 'They have a different way of behaving around here,' he continued, 'they're different from us! The way they dress, the way they blow their noses, the way they sit down in a chair ... you can tell they're not like us ... Different, that's all there is to it.'

'Well,' Irene said, 'they were born ladies and gents. You see how the kids act? Saying Daddy and Mammina ... They keep them nice, give them everything ... Make them study till they're grown up ... '

'They're all Demochristians,' Tommaso said, 'That's why ... '

'Whaddya think?' Irene asked. 'Would we ever be able to act like them? I don't think so ... '

'They're too high above us,' Tommaso observed, 'How could you compete with them? In the old days, when I used to see them, I'd call them no-good bums, dopes, but now I'm beginning to see the difference between living back in the shack and living in the midst of people like these! These people live honestly, and wherever they go, people take their hats off to them.'

Irene was silent for a while, meditating. 'Howdaya know?' she said then. 'Maybe one day, if we work at it, maybe we'll be lucky and be able to look nice and all!'

Tommaso was silent too, intent, pondering a little. 'You wanna know what I'm thinking, Irene?' he cried. 'I'm gonna talk to the priest, and sign up with his Party, too!'

At Irene's house they were all communists, and she had always thought that way, since she was little, the way her father had taught her. She reflected a moment, very optimistic and sage, then said: 'That's not a bad idea, Tommaso! And besides, when you belong to their Party, one of these days they may help you ... give you a job ... And anyway, the Church is always a comfort!'

*

Tommaso and Irene met also the following Sunday, to spend the afternoon together, like a properly engaged couple.

But this time Tommaso wanted Irene to come out his way, to the INA-Case: at first Irene made a fuss, saying she was embarrassed, that it was too far, and one thing and another, but in the end she agreed, also secretly happy to go there, maybe to see Tommaso's mother and father, though he hadn't said a word about that.

This Sunday wasn't so nice; the sky was all full of grey clouds so you couldn't see a ray of sunshine if your life depended on it. It threatened rain, but didn't rain, and the cold breeze that blew occasionally through all that greyness was chilling and made you sniffle.

Tommaso didn't feel right that day either: he was numbed by the cold air, which after all can't have been so very cold, since the other kids went around calmly in jerseys and light clothes, which they had started wearing by now and were determined to keep on even if it snowed: and they weren't shivering at all. But Tommaso was shivering, and he coughed a bit. So he was grim, while he waited outside the INA-Case on the Tiburtina for the bus that was to bring Irene.

He was huddled there with his hands in his pockets and his collar turned up, cursing to himself at every bus that stopped without Irene getting off. Finally there she was, all got up in her new red dress. She stepped down from the bus and hurried to Tommaso, running a little, slightly out of breath, to apologize for being late. But Tommaso didn't pay much attention: these things happen, as everyone knows, when you're engaged; he took her by the arm and led her up Via di Pietralata, turning before Monte del Pecoraro, towards the Cinema Lux.

He walked ahead, serious, concentrating, his hands in his pockets, pale with the cold, and she a bit behind, her hand thrust under his arm.

At the Lux there was a comic film with Totò, and Tommaso and Irene thought they would get a few laughs. They stayed there for over two hours, because they wanted to see the first part twice. When they came out finally, the air was even colder and darker but

there were lots of people around, whole families going to the
pizzerias, soldiers who didn't know what to do, snotnoses of
Pietralata going to the Tiburtino movie, and Tiburtino kids going
to the movie at Pietralata.

Now Tommaso and Irene were walking arm in arm, close. He
had caught her below the waist, where she was nice and plump, and
he held her tight, as if he were afraid she would fall down. They
were silent and grave, the way couples are, going slowly off where
they were to go.

When they walked the length of Via di Pietralata and turned into
the Tiburtina, Tommaso's arm was aching badly, after holding the
girl tight like that, supporting her like she was sick. But he wouldn't
have let go, not even if the police had come. The passers-by glanced
at them, and if they didn't, Tommaso, faking and pretending to
think of other things, looked at them frowning, nasty, until they
took a look at the couple. And Tommaso then started looking
straight ahead, completely taken up with holding his girl. Some
boys, smartass kids, once they went past, made wisecracks: 'Looks
like a bad case of ivy!' Or else: 'Made of glue?' or even that old one:
'Don't trust him!' But Tommaso and Irene paid no attention to
them, and more and more sad and reserved, they went on their way.

Usually the couples around there went down along the Tiburtina,
beyond Tiburtina Terzo, towards the Aniene: after two or three
hundred yards, a good bit before Ponte Mammolo, there was a
little bridge over the road: beside it, a steep path down the embankment towards the countryside, around Via delle Messi d'oro. There
the country was beautiful, all green, full of wheat, fruit trees,
market-gardens with cabbages, fennel, turnips, in the midst of
piles of manure and clumps of olive trees. However, the path led to
a kind of canebrake, thick with tall reeds, slightly smelly, between
two ploughed fields. It was so long it almost stretched to Pietralata,
and narrow. The couples went there to make love. And, in fact,
along with the shit, the dirt and the mud, you could see, here and
there, the pallets they made with newspapers.

Tommaso and Irene, their clothes soaked with the damp, went
slowly down along the path, following the canebrake. Tommaso

was feeling colder all the time and was coughing, turning angry:
but now he was determined they were going to make love, and so it
had to be: he hadn't the slightest idea of giving it up. They came to a
place where they were alone, and they sat down on a soaked pile of
tall grass in the midst of the canes, as still as beams, with ragged
leaves.

When they were seated, Tommaso clasped Irene by the hips
again.

'You comfortable? You okay?' he asked her.

'Oh, yes,' Irene reassured him.

'Come closer. Come here,' Tommaso said, grasping her with his
arm that was aching so he could hardly use it.

She allowed herself to be hugged, putting her cheek on his
shoulder, and Tommaso began to kiss her: one kiss, two, on the
mouth. But he was uncomfortable, and he broke off a moment to
shift his position: 'Shut your eyes,' he said to her, 'Doncha know
that when you keep your eyes open it means you're thinking of
another man?'

Irene shrugged gently: Tommaso started kissing her again,
putting all the enthusiasm he could muster into it, all his feeling.
He began to push her around, tonguing her a bit. But he had to sit
all crooked on the little mound, and his back was hurting.

'Aòh, relax,' he said, straightening up, 'Whaddya doing?'

'It's all wet, Tommaso,' Irene said, 'I'll ruin my dress. Let's stand
up ... It's all the same, isnt' it?'

'Whaddya mean, stand up?' Tommaso snapped. 'We're okay like
this ... wait a minute!'

He rose to his feet, got out a handkerchief and, handkerchief in
hand, looked around: a little farther on, beyond two stumps of cane,
there were some pieces of cardboard, carried there obviously by
somebody; he took them and arranged them on the ground, and he
also put his handkerchief over them because they were damp.

He began kissing her again: but they still weren't right, with
nothing to lean on, their legs stretched on the damp grass.

'Aòh! You been eating nails?' Tommaso said, becoming nervous.
He wasn't getting hard at all, and he blamed it on her. Without any

ceremony, he wanted to push her down, made her stretch out on the
grass: 'Get down, lie down!' he said to her, already breathless, in a
fit of anger. But Irene resisted with determination; she said: 'No,
no, Tommaso!' So, for a moment, Tommaso let it go: but, meanwhile, he began to move his hand up under her slip. 'Pull up your
dress ... ' he said, to her, 'go on, pull it up ... ' And, at the same time,
he was pulling it slowly over her knees, up to her thighs.

'I could eat you!' he was muttering, grabbing in his hand all that
white, white flesh, that was going to his head.

'Loosen that belt, goddammit!' he said then, with his hand on it,
'I can't do anything with it ... '

He couldn't manage to loosen the belt, his hand trembling with
excitement: and, with the belt tight, he couldn't pull up her skirt
the way he wanted it.

Her legs were already all exposed, her stockings held up by
suspenders. Looking at her toes, Irene kept her legs stretched out,
together, partly to show how straight they were.

Tommaso had one hand on her thigh, where the stockings ended,
and he began to thrust the other under her neck, in her hair. She
was quiet for a while, then she began raving. 'No, no not like this.
No, not there, stop, keep still ... '

With a hoarse voice, half-whispering, like her, Tommaso said:
'Found your weak point, eh?' And he went on stroking her neck,
beneath her hair, smiling.

Still raving and defending herself, she said: 'Give me your
comb ... '

'Afterwards, afterwards ... ' Tommaso promised her, 'don't be
afraid, I'll give it to you after ... '

Meanwhile he had begun to look down, between her legs, with a
lump in his throat: 'Aòh,' he muttered to her, 'pull down your
pants ... ' And seeing that she promptly looked cross, he anticipated
her objection: 'You don't have to take them off ... just a little ... '

'It's cold,' Irene said crossly, 'and then whaddya wanna do?'

'Nothing!' Tommaso said, still hoarse. 'Whaddya think? Don't
be afraid. I won't even touch you ... I just wanna see ... '

Without waiting for Irene to answer, slowly, delicately, like a

trainer with an animal, he took her by the pants, held her above the
elastic: then he lifted her a little, heavy as she was, and pulled them
down.

'Jeezus, honey, what thighs!' he said to her, 'so nice and hard.'

He began to pull down her suspender-belt, too.

'Whaddya wanna do? Strip me?' Irene said.

'Take it easy, take it easy,' Tommaso said, 'this is enough ... '

He began hugging her again, keeping her hands in the middle,
biting her neck, and murmuring, almost crying: 'Baby, baby ... '

But he still wasn't worked up good, though usually by now he
would have done it twice. 'Goddammit!' he thought to himself, his
mouth already drooling with anger. Irene had half eaten him up,
with bites, kisses, working her tongue. 'What the fuck's happening to
me? Why can't I get hard?' he kept thinking, trying to joke about it.

He grabbed Irene by the tits and squeezed them so fiercely she
almost cried. He made her take them out, and he began to kiss them
and lick them.

Sure, it's a long time since I've been with a woman, he was
thinking. But what's come over me? Maybe it's the cold ...

He had another fit of anger, put one hand against Irene's shoulder
and forced her down, making her stretch out in the wet grass.
'Lie down! All the way!' he said furiously.

'You'll get me all messed up ... The ground's soaking ... ' Irene
complained, trying to pull herself up.

'So what? Even if you get a little wet, it's not the end of the
world! You can dry out afterwards!'

He held her down, sucking at her neck, kissing her, now all on
top of her.

'Aòh, do something. Move!'

Irene began to work, kissing him on the neck, touching his hair,
holding him tight. They lay like that for a while, hugging, piled up,
almost digging a hole by their writhing.

Jeezuschrist! Tommaso thought, what's wrong? What've I done?

All of a sudden he let go of her and pulled himself up, sitting on
the mound as he had before, on the damp cardboard. He put his
hand into his pocket, pulled out the pack of cigarettes, took one

with trembling fingers, lit it, after spitting two or three shreds of tobacco that had stuck to his lips, and began to smoke.

Irene, all sweet and resigned, pulled herself up from the soaked grass, brushing off her back, looking at him sideways: but he didn't even glance at her, smoking, his forehead wrinkled, his eyes venomous, white with the cold. In the end Irene decided to say something to him: 'What's wrong?' she asked sadly, with a hint of accusation in her voice.

Tommaso looked at her. 'Nothing's wrong,' he said. He was silent for a while, puffing out the smoke, then added: 'You're the one who's changed!'

Irene was dumbfounded, immediately angry, and she answered back: 'Me? Changed? I'm the same as always ... This is the way I am, doncha remember?'

'No, when I met you, you were different!' Tommaso insisted, acidly.

Irene adjusted her clothes, which were a mess. Then she stopped, to say: 'I tell you: I'm the same!' she cried, with tears in her voice.

'No, no, no,' Tommaso said, shaking his head, his mouth twisted, 'it's not like you say! You can't fool me. There's gotta be something. I'm not wrong ... '

'But why?' Irene said, 'What could there be? I don't think I've changed ... My life is what it is, the usual thing ... The only difference is that before I didn't work, and now I have a job! But my job hasn't changed me ... '

Tommaso was silent for a little while, bent over, his elbows resting on his knees; his forehead was all wrinkled, and his gaze was cloudy, pensive.

'How'd you get the job, in this place where you work?' he asked all of a sudden, looking at her.

Irene explained, rather happily, despite the sadness of the situation: 'There's this family that lives near us, and their nephew drives a truck, carrying the medicines, and he put in a good word for me with the manager ... '

'And in all of this,' Tommaso interrupted, 'you didn't have to do anybody any favours?'

Irene didn't even want to understand what Tommaso was hinting at. She blurted: 'What kind of favours could I do for somebody who's well off already?'

'A woman can do favours for anybody,' Tommaso said.

Irene looked at him: she took her purse from the wet grass, wiped it a little, and started to get up: her chin was trembling, she was ready to cry, but she was determined to break off the argument and go away.

'Let's go home ... ' she said.

'No, you stay here!' Tommaso said, grabbing her by the wrist and forcing her to sit down again, almost making her fall. 'You gotta tell me,' he went on, grinding his teeth, 'everything you've done from that night I came to your house for the serenade up till this afternoon!'

Irene resigned herself to giving all these explanations, sad, insulted, but calm, because she knew her conscience was clear. 'All I have to do is tell you about any one day,' she said, 'because they're all alike ... and besides I don't even have to tell you, you know the road I take ... '

Tommaso turned mean: 'My name's Tommaso, and I have my doubts,' he said, raising one hand with the palm open and striking it with the thumb of the other hand, hard: 'Listen! For eighteen months I was out of things: I don't know anything about you for all that time. And I'm not asleep on my feet! You gotta put your cards on the table with me!'

'I don't understand you,' Irene said, distressed, 'You're talking to me like this ... Why? What's come over you? Has somebody said something about me? Tell me ... '

'No,' Tommaso said, 'you tell me: how old's this nephew, this driver?'

'Why, he's married!' Irene exclaimed. 'He's got a wife and grown-up children. And besides he's a friend of my family's. He used to know me when I was a baby ... '

'And the manager?' Tommaso interrupted her.

'I've never seen him. I don't even know what he looks like!' Irene said.

'Then tell me something else!' Tommaso went on, 'at that drug factory, are you all women? Aren't there any men working there?'

'The men're in another section,' Irene explained, 'they're the porters ... '

Tommaso wheeled around and looked her in the face, furiously: 'You see?' he yelled. 'Now you want me to believe that for more than a year you've been The Little Flower of Jesus? You haven't even talked to anybody?'

'What's that gotta do with anything?' Irene said, shaking. 'Yes, I've talked ... I'm a woman, after all ... And, anyway, I wasn't so friendly with you before ... How was I to know you'd be coming back to me?'

Tommaso knelt with his face to hers, his mouth twisted and his teeth sticking out like a corpse's: 'You see?' he yelled again, 'There is something!'

'Well,' Irene said, almost trembling, 'one fella did try to strike up acquaintance with me, but there was nothing doing ... '

'You let him talk, though,' Tommaso blurted, drooling, 'You stopped and had a nice chat with him ... '

'Yes,' Irene admitted, 'but it was just an accident ... '

Tommaso didn't let her finish: he was all ready, and he gave her a slap on one cheek that almost spun her head around.

Irene at first didn't understand: she looked at him, hesitant, frightened. Then she took her face in her hands and began to cry softly.

'Cry. Go ahead, I'm glad!' Tommaso was thinking, infuriated, looking at her, standing over her.

It had become dark, almost: among the reeds now there was shadow. In the silence, as Irene wept, you could hear distant voices, cries, and people singing: maybe they were groups of young people going home along the Tiburtina, and other young people farther off who, hearing them, teased and mocked them, laughing loudly. As evening fell, the air was less cold, because the breeze had stopped blowing: it was almost warm, in the dampness that dripped over the weeds.

After a while Irene stopped crying, stood up, her purse in her hand, and walked off. In silence, Tommaso went after her, lighting another cigarette, still grim. They went up the path, which could barely be seen, a faint mark among the tattered walls of cane and the piles of weeds. They struggled up, because the mire was slippery, along the embankment above the Tiburtina, and they headed slowly for the bus stop.

They walked quietly along the road where the cars were whizzing by, the first lights shining, and groups of friends coming and going, pushing one another, arguing, laughing.

After about a hundred paces, as Tommaso walked along frowning, his hands in his pockets, Irene stopped, with the excuse of putting a finger in her shoe, which was tight and hurt her: to hold herself up, with a little grimace, she grasped Tommaso by the elbow. Then walking on, she continued to hold him by the arm with her red, pudgy hand.

Still silent, Tommaso let her do it, his face flushed with anger and emotion. He went on like this, not talking, a little farther, then finally he said in a hoarse voice: 'You got money for the bus?'

'Yes, I have it,' Irene said quickly, with an expression of relief in her eyes, almost ready to start crying again.

They were silent a little longer, walked a dozen yards or so, then Tommaso grumbled: 'Irene, you know how I am ... I don't know if you realize, but when I gotta say something, I gotta say it, I don't wanna explode inside, because of you!'

He was silent a moment, moved by his own words, then he started again: 'I'm not the kind of guy you can cheat on! Get that straight! When I love a person, then I'm serious, it's not just for a day or two ... I made all this noise, this fuss, because I love you ... If I didn't give a good goddamm about you, I'd be satisfied with what I get ... It would be just some fun, and I wouldn't give a damn about the rest!'

Irene listened in religious silence, understanding everything Tommaso meant: 'You know,' she said finally, moved, half-whispering, 'I love you, too.'

For all the time they stood at the bus stop, under the shelter at the beginning of Tiburtino, they were silent, frowning as usual, a bit

apart from the other people waiting there like them. Then the bus
arrived, half empty because they were only two stops from the end
of the line, and Irene got in: They said 'ciao' 'ciao', barely, as
everything between them was established, and there was no need
for many words. Tommaso stood there until the bus was far away,
then looked around, and still red in the face from excitement, his
eyes burning, he put his hands in his pockets and very slowly went
towards Monte del Pecoraro, just opposite.

Already, as he had gone by before, he had glimpsed the situation:
there were some kids playing a game, and his friends were sitting
around the edge. ·

Tommaso went and sat down too, on the wet, dirty grass behind
the goalposts, among his pals. He was very calm and easy, since he
had just left his woman: but he still didn't feel good, he was burning
up in a cold sweat.

The Hyena, standing with his hands in his pockets holding his
cock, was imitating a radio broadcast of the game; he broke off,
opened his mouth to its full width, stood motionless for a moment,
then with a movement of his Adam's apple, let out a belch, like
gargling.

Another boy from Tiburtino, a friend of his, specialist in belches,
called The Patient, gave a little demonstration, to be one up on him,
belching three or four times in a row: the others all looked at him,
regaining their faith in life at the end of an afternoon spent without
a lira, dragging their asses on the dirty grass or in the little chairs of
the bar.

But the kids who were playing ball had become fed up all of a
sudden, and they were clearing out, off towards the houses, quarrelling. It was really dark now, and the light dying behind the hill was
a purple colour. Now I'm gonna go to bed, Tommaso thought,
Whaddam I standing around here for? But singing at the top of his
tuberculous voice, an old drunk, blind on wine, was coming along
from the direction of Ponte Mammolo.

'Ah, Cunappa!' the friends all shouted, delighted at seeing him,
just as they were about to go off too: 'Cunappa, come over here and
give us some of your crabs!'

They all knew him because he was the night-watchman at a warehouse at San Basilio, where they had been going to steal since they were little kids. Cunappa, however, didn't see or hear them. He went on, veering abruptly now and then, his knees bending weakly, and at any moment he was ready to bang his forehead against the cobbles. His filthy grey pants flopped as loosely as skirts, and his jacket with its torn pockets hung to his knees. He had a cap pulled down to his nostrils, old, ancient, and so greasy that lard came out if you squeezed it.

His presence boosted everybody's morale, even Tommaso's. 'Hey, Cunappa,' they yelled, 'Hey, you old stool-pigeon, come over here! ... Your turn's come! Tonight you die!'

They had lined up, legs apart, along the ragged edge of the hill, as if to be passed in review. Suddenly, without warning, the old man, Cunappa the stool-pigeon, sat down on the worn edge of the pavement, which was all mud. With a deathly flush, he stayed there, swaying, rummaging in the huge pockets of the jacket, which you could smell two miles away.

'Hey, Stool,' The Patient shouted at him, 'You've been enjoying life, eh? You've had people licking your feet!' Then, with a disgusted manner: 'Whatta they waiting for, to lock up these lousy old drunks, these bums that go around disturbing people?'

The old man looked at The Patient cross-eyed: God knows how, but he had heard him and was staring at him: you could tell he wasn't able to make him out clearly in the shadow of the hill among the other devils in that sliver of purplish light where the street-lamps had already come on.

'I gotta eat, I gotta eat!' he said, or something like that; he sounded like he had a piece of tyre in his mouth.

'Whattya eating? Bread and crabs?' the Hyena asked.

This time the old man managed to pronounce, loud and clear, a single word: 'Fish!' he yelled, spitting, as if his tongue were red-hot.

In fact, he managed to take a paper packet from his coat, and only to see it was enough to turn your stomach: it was wrapped in old newspapers, collected from the mud.

'You mean there's fish in there?' they asked him, inquiring politely.

Speaking with his nostrils, his chin, his ears, his ass, the old man laughed contentedly and said he had bought it in the square the day before and had been saving it for his supper.

Half bald, pointed chin, face greasy as a piece of egg-shell, The Patient went over to him: 'Let's have a look at your jacket,' he said, 'I wanna see if it fits me!'

Since the old man was helpless and they could dress and undress him like a baby, The Patient slipped off the jacket and put it on. He walked about for a moment, spiralling, clowning, while the others all split their guts; then he was off like a shot along the little path of Monte del Pecoraro, dark, brown, with the corpse-like light which barely reached it from the street-lamps along the Tiburtina. And the others after him, yelling. Blindly, the old man picked up the packet that he had dropped and began to run after The Patient and the others, yelling: 'Gimme back my coat! My coat!'

The others let him overtake them at the top of the hill, among the hummocks all scattered with fresh turds that stank beautifully. Though he felt very weak, Tommaso ran with the others, laughing like them.

Then the old man arrived, gasping, about to cough up shreds of lung. But he didn't notice it. He rasped angrily, like he was talking through somebody else's mouth: 'My coat, my coat.' He didn't know who he was talking to. Maybe he couldn't even see, like when you address some saint, praying for a favour. And he kept on insisting, as if they had thrust a stick in his gullet: 'My coat, my coat!'

The Patient continued twirling around in the jacket that came down to his heels. Then he stopped abruptly, concentrated, and let a fart. The old man stood still, yelling out his guts.

'Here!' The Patient said, going to him: he took off the jacket, disgusted at its stink, and as the old man, silent because the saint had heard his prayer, held out his hands to grab it, The Patient laughed and yelled: 'Fuckoff!' and hurled the jacket far away. Leaving a wake of stink, it landed against the electric pole. Without looking at

anybody, as if he were going after a living person, Cunappa chased
his jacket and flung himself headlong under the pole to pick it up
again.

Half-yawning, his mouth twisted, an expression of pleasure on
his face, Tommaso said to himself: 'I'm gonna go home, I'm gonna
go to bed. Now I'll get under the sheets,' he went on, wisely, 'and
sleep so hard I'll come.'

He was about to leave but, at that moment, laughing like an ape,
Nazzareno threw himself on the old man. Cunappa was bent over
his jacket: Nazzareno took him by the belt and began to tear off
his pants. 'I wanna see how these pants fit me!' he said. 'Where'd
you get them? From Pucci?' The old man tried to resist, as if some
malignant spirit from Purgatory were making his despair: but
Nazzareno rolled him over on his back and slipped the pants off his
filthy legs. The Patient grabbed the jacket again and threw it into
the air. The old man now didn't know whether to chase jacket or
pants: meanwhile, he collected first of all the package of fish and
began to run here and there, yelling this time: 'My clothes! My
clothes!'

'Let's burn them up!' the Hyena yelled. 'Where's your lighter?'
he shouted to one of his friends, who quickly produced his lighter.
'All of them! Let's burn them all,' Nazzareno shouted, inspired.

They made a pile of jacket and pants: and while two or three of
them held the old man by the arms, the others finished undressing
him, laughing like whores. Nauseated by the stink, they added his
shirt to the pile, his filthy undershirt, his shorts, cap, shoes. They
left him only his socks: they then pushed him to one side, naked as
his Mamma made him, with all that white hair, and they lighted
the fire. The old man watched wide-eyed, and illuminated by the
tongues of flame from his burning clothes, instead of shouting
anything, he let out a kind of groan. 'The package of fish!' Nazzareno yelled, interrupting their laughter: he picked it up and threw
it too on the fire. Then one of them started running off down the
hill, holding his nose with his fingers: 'The stiiiink!' he yelled. All
of them went after him, running among the bushes down towards
the Tiburtina, howling and busting their guts with laughter. They

scattered as they ran down among the black mounds of the hill, on the mud, the piles of rotten sticks, like a pack of old jackals. Tommaso also ran off laughing: but he was feeling worse and worse: the boils on his neck were gnawing at him, he was all red in the face, burning, and he felt cold even while he ran, as if he had the fever.

3

What Was Tommaso Looking For?

From that day on Tommaso felt a bit funny all the time, especially in the evening: around four or five in the afternoon, he felt overheated, dry, and at the same time he would shudder with the cold. It wasn't that he was downright sick; he just felt strange, that was all. So he went on as if nothing had happened: as soon as day broke he went to work at the Market just the same, shifting fish, and he stayed there until late morning. Then he went home for a nap and woke up feeling nauseated, chilled. Yelling with his mother, he dressed again and went off on his own, up and down Pietralata, with his friends.

Just about that time the pink postcard arrived: it was time for him to do his military service.

He presented himself at the draft board one morning, in Via della Greca, for his physical, with Zucabbo, Prickhead, Hyena, and the others of his age: they stripped naked, and one by one they passed into the little room to be examined. The others were all more or less declared fit, at once. But Tommaso was sent to the Celio, because they had discovered something they didn't like, and that was where they sent the ones who had to have a more thorough examination.

A few days after that, he reported at the Celio: here they gave him a real going-over, X-rays and everything: in the end they said a word he had never heard before, namely that there was something in his lungs that made him get those boils and he had to be treated right away. Tommaso didn't understand: he acted a bit worried, kind of smart: 'Aha!' Then he made them explain it more clearly, and finally they said he was tubercular and that he had to go into the Forlanini Hospital right away.

Right away. After a manner of speaking. He had to fill out a series of applications, to the Health Insurance people, and here and there, then wait a week, a month, two months.

He didn't say anything to Irene, to anybody. It all seemed foolishness to him: and everything made him angry, got on his nerves, that was all. He would go to the Forlanini, yes, because he had to go there: but he was going bravely, because he was sure that there was nothing really wrong with him: it was something that might last from Christmas to New Year, but he wasn't tubercular, never had been.

He got to the Forlanini one evening around five on the Number 13, which went from Acqua Bullicante all the way there, to Monteverde Nuovo: they got off, he and his mother, and walked along the broad new streets to the entrance of the Forlanini: a barred gate, with a kind of guard-house next to it, like a barracks. Inside they could see gardens, trees, and at the back, a big building, full of columns, as big as a theatre.

Tommaso started to go inside, impatiently, stiffly, with his mother after him, almost ready to cry, heading for the colonnade at the end of the flower-beds. But an attendant stopped him crossly and told him to wait. Huffing, Tommaso lit a cigarette. The attendant went and called a young man, the doctor on duty, who calmly checked that Tommaso's papers were all in order, that he had the certificate from the National Health Insurance saying he had to be hospitalized, and all that. Tommaso knew he was okay, and he waited angrily, but putting on a patient expression.

From the entrance, they sent him to the Business Office: an attendant showed him there. They crossed the whole garden, where at that moment you could smell the stink of gas from the Permolio, with its flame reddening the sky, already glowing in the sunset, a bit farther down, behind the Trastevere station. They went inside the colonnade and walked about ten minutes through reception rooms, entrances, steps, halls, corridor, then they came out into another garden, semi-circular in shape, and at the back on the opposite side, towards the Via Portuense, there was the Business Office.

With his mother after him, not saying a word, Tommaso went

inside and found himself in a little room that looked like a Post Office, where you go to send telegrams and special deliveries: a man examined his papers, asked him vital statistics and in the end gave him a number and said to go to Reception.

This, he explained, was just outside at the beginning of the horse-shoe garden: it was in the first pavilion of the men's section, a tall building with one flank all covered with balconies. Tommaso went there, frowning, impatient, furious, with his mother still following silently, bundled into that dress which had been her best for the past ten years.

Inside, there were corridors again, steps, big windows: he wandered back and forth, not encountering anybody, becoming more and more irritable. Finally he saw a nun and asked her nastily: 'Say Mother, where'm I supposed to report?' She pointed to a little door in a corridor along the garden, then she went off in the other direction.

Beyond that little door there was an office, with a woman in charge, nice and pudgy, broader than tall, with hick's eyes: this was the end of all Tommaso's wanderings. He was supposed to stay in that pavilion for a few days, under observation. The woman in charge, checking all his papers again, was ready to take him to his place in the little ward where he had been put.

She was quiet for a minute, because the time had come for Tommaso to say goodbye to his mother, who had to leave. At first, Sora Maria was so shy she didn't understand: the nurse had to tell her. Then she gave her son a desperate look, hesitating: 'So long, Tommaso,' she said in a low voice, 'be good!' She hugged him tight, close to crying: she turned right around and, drying her eyes with a handkerchief, went into the garden, taking the wrong direction two or three times, walking fast, all embarrassed.

As soon as they were alone, the head nurse said to Tommaso: 'This way,' and led him towards a corridor that opened on another little internal garden, full of benches under the withered trees. Before they had gone two steps they were at a door, half metal and half glass.

She pushed it open and made Tommaso go in. There was a room with six beds, one next to the other, and a window at the end overlooking the garden along Via Portuense. Some patients were lying on the beds, grey-faced, thin as finches, unshaven.

Tommaso's bed was the first as you came in, by the door; the one next to it was empty. 'Here you are, now get settled,' the head nurse said to him. But Tommaso couldn't grasp it all. He couldn't get it into his head that this was his place, his bed. 'You've got a table,' the nurse said, 'and a locker.' In fact, along the wall opposite the beds, there were six little metal lockers, painted white.

'Supper's in an hour,' the nurse said, and she went out in great haste, to deal with other matters.

Tommaso stood there like a fool, his bundle in his hand. One of the patients said from his bed: 'Put your stuff down.'

Mind your own business, Tommaso said to himself, grimly, get fucked ... But slowly, he began to take his few belongings from the bundle and put them inside the locker, which was narrow and tiny but remained half empty, nevertheless. When he had finished, Tommaso had nothing else to do. He could only wait, there in that corner of the hospital, half out and half in, with those other patients, rotten with T.B., all around him.

Now evening was beginning to fall, and as the light gradually died, the beds seemed whiter. You couldn't hear a sound, not a voice, nothing.

In this way Tommaso passed an hour, lying on his bed, his hands beneath his neck, angrily thinking of his troubles. Look where I've gotta go and end up, he was thinking, in the midst of all these wrecks! How the fuck am I gonna manage? I'm gonna have to kill somebody to get outta here!

Then, following the others who were allowed up, he went to supper: the refectory was at the end of the corridor where the head nurse's office was. It was a big room, ninety feet by a hundred and twenty, full of big metal tables in long rows. More than five, six hundred patients gathered there to eat.

After supper, Tommaso, who didn't know anybody, went back to his little corner in the ward, and although he was wide awake, angry, rabid, without even giving a look at the others in the room with him, he got under the covers.

He was sick, but he didn't know if it was really sickness or fury he felt. Two or three times he was ready to collect his stuff and clear out, go home. Who's making me stay here, for Chrissake? he thought. I'm not like these other characters!

Then he controlled himself, but his anger and his contempt for the others and for that place increased. He lay stretched out, motionless, looking at that high, white ceiling, which didn't even seem a ceiling; it was like being outside, in the corridor or in the garden: this was no place for sleeping, not here.

Finally, after quite a while, he did fall asleep. He dropped off, but it wasn't like sleeping: he dreamed and, at the same time, he was almost awake, with full awareness.

Little by little, he began to feel he was outside the hospital in the open, in the sunshine, healthy as he had always been.

He was at home, not at Via dei Crispolti at the INA-Case, but in the old home in the shanty village on the Aniene.

'Aòh, I don't live here any more!' Tommaso protested, almost crying, 'I don't live here any more!'

It was a lovely day, with a clear sky from which a sweet but too-strong light fell on the earth. Try as he would, Tommaso couldn't see the fields beyond the river, flowing between embankments and little hills: everything seemed to end just after the shacks of the village. But the shacks, instead, went on much farther than usual, as if it were all a great city of hovels, muddy yards, packing cases, rotten planks, poles and lines with rags hung out in the sun to dry.

The light that came down from the sky, however, made everything larger, cleaner, almost majestic. The little brick walls, the roofs of sheet metal and tarred paper, the partitions of filthy wood, flimsy with age, all seemed made of some magnificent material and shone clear and beautiful in the light.

Tommaso's shack looked like a palace: the bench of black mud mixed with piss was as comfortable as an easy chair.

Tommaso was seated there in the sun, half dozing, feeling better than he had ever felt in his life: he wanted to cry, there was something in his throat tickling him, but it didn't bother him at that moment.

Inside, there was Tommaso's mother, cleaning up the house: you could tell she was happy, talking to somebody or other.

Tito and Toto came to play at Tommaso's feet.

They were wearing their usual rags: Tito was buried up to his chin in a little overcoat with more holes than a sieve. The other kid had on flannel pyjama bottoms from an E.C.A. package, and over them a dirty sweater, also American, with two football players on the back of it. All those rags, for some reason, seemed made of silk, and the rips, the frays, the stains were like embroidery.

Tito stuck his head in the mud, getting all dirty, raised his little legs in the air and, kerplonk, fell over with his belly up, lying there in the muck for a moment, laughing, his mouth wide with happiness.

Toto, instead, was playing dog: he ran around on all fours, over the yard, under the mouldy little shed, between the slimy poles, against the walls of the shack: and he barked until he sounded like a real puppy.

Every now and then the two little brothers ran into each other, by accident, bumping their heads together; then they would look at each other and hug each other. They stayed there, clinging, as if they were obeying somebody who said: 'Come on, kiss your little brother!' and they went on kissing each other even when the older person who gave the order had forgotten all about them. So, hugging, and kissing each other from time to time, they looked around, laughing like two little monkeys.

Suddenly, from one of the little paths among the shacks Tommaso's father appeared: he was all dolled up in his black suit, black hat, a nice tie and gloves, one already on his hand, which held the other glove.

He was smoking, and he walked as if he had new shoes on and they were hurting his feet a little.

'Tommaso, you had your breakfast?' he asked Tommaso, as he came up.

Tommaso looked at him in amazement, because it was the first time in his life his father had asked him that question.

'Sure,' he said, swelling and pretending to stretch, to hide his pleasure.

Meanwhile all the neighbours had come into the yard; and they were huddled there in silence, laughing softly among themselves and looking towards Tommaso's house.

'Whadda they want?' Tommaso thought, looking at them. He got up and went inside. His mother was sitting by the table on a little chair, its straw seat half-gone. She was all cleaned up too, in her white dress. But seeing her, Tommaso was suddenly seized with fear, God knows why; he looked at her, almost trembling and asked her: 'Hey, Ma, are you dead?'

Sora Maria burst out laughing: she got up from the chair and went to the sideboard. She opened it and began to take out stuff to eat, what looked like an endless supply.

'Eat, Tommaso,' she said, all sweet and loving. And she put noodles on the table, eggs, chicken, salad, peaches.

'Thanks, Ma,' Tommaso said and began to eat, while his parents stood and watched him, smiling.

The house seemed bigger, and Tommaso could hardly recognize it: the little partition that divided it was very high and yet it didn't end: it seemed unable to reach the rooftree, and up above there was a hollow space you couldn't tell what for.

'What's in there?' Tommaso asked his mother, as he began to eat the noodles.

'Whaddya mean?' his mother said, 'that's where you sleep!'

At that moment, pushing and shoving gaily, the neighbours began to crowd into the house: they were all happy, and their eyes were laughing: 'Long live the bride and groom!' somebody began to shout. And after a moment it was like a big party. 'Long live the happy couple!' everybody was shouting. 'Go get Carletto, with his guitar,' somebody cried. But Carletto was already there with his guitar, playing and singing, his hair flapping and his eyes bright.

The bride and groom were Tommaso's mother and father. They smiled, a bit moved at all these festivities, and Sor Torquato clasped Sora Maria by the waist, in her fine white silk dress, tiny and pretty, as if they had to strike a pose for their photograph.

Meanwhile Tommaso went on eating, keeping a bit off to one side so as not to disturb the celebration with his presence. He ate carefully: before him he had a dish of noodles as high as a hill, and he couldn't wind them around his fork: when he did succeed, it was a problem getting them down.

But they were good, better than any Tommaso had ever tasted: there was an inch of grated cheese on them, and you could see they had really been made with eggs: nice and yellow, smooth, tender but not overdone, they melted in your mouth as you chewed them. They were smeared with a nice mixture of butter and tomato sauce: and there were an extra three or four pats of butter still unmelted, dotting the mound. And there were pieces of chicken liver, with bits of mushroom and sheep-milk cheese, that made your mouth water just to look at them.

But much as he liked them, Tommaso had trouble swallowing: his throat was gripped by something like a vice, and he could hardly breathe. He kept looking towards the partition, with a furious desire to get up and go to see what was in there.

While all the people around were laughing, shouting, dancing, making such a racket you couldn't hear yourself think, his mother came and bent over Tommaso and whispered in his ear: 'Don't look at the partition, Tommaso.'

'Okay, Ma,' Tommaso agreed politely.

'I can't eat any more noodles,' he said then, a bit embarrassed.

'Leave them on your plate,' Sora Maria said, 'eat the chicken now.'

Everybody was happy: and Tommaso was becoming a bit dazed, though he didn't want to show it. He picked up a chicken leg and began to eat: and at the same time he was thinking how he could manage to go in the other room, beyond the partition. The chicken was wonderful, too, like the noodles, but Tommaso couldn't get it down.

'Goddammit … ' he thought all of a sudden. 'Why not? This is my house, isn't it? That's where I sleep, isn't it?'

The room in there, like the first room, like the whole house, was much bigger now: the partition rose up and was lost in the void, and the brick floor was nice and polished, without gaps. In the back there was the bed where Tommaso slept, against the wall of wood and tarred paper. Tommaso went to it, having clearly realized from the beginning that there was somebody lying in the bed. He started shaking all over, until he could hardly walk or even stand on his feet.

He approached the little bed all the same, took the sheet trembling, and pulled it down. Lello was lying there motionless, his mouth open, and all dirty from his hair to his feet, stained with black blood. Lello sat up at once on the mattress. He stayed there, sitting, staring hard at Tommaso, his mouth gaping: he looked at him as if for the first time, full of surprise and fear. He seemed to want to say something, but his voice couldn't get out of his throat. He sat bending forward slightly: and held his right hand in mid-air, all mangled, a little heap of bones and tatters of flesh, dripping blood, staining the cuff of his shirt, his pants. He held his legs out, still: and one foot was all crushed, too, and you could see only the shoe leather mixed with a bloody pulp.

Lello looked first at his hand and his foot, then at Tommaso; but when he finally managed to say something, he stared only at Tommaso, looking into his eyes and shouting: 'Run, Tommaso, they're coming to catch you!'

'Why?' Tommaso asked, trembling.

'Go on, Tommaso, run!' Lello kept shouting, frightened and urgent.

The little bed, the wall of rotten planks, the corner of the shack, everything had vanished, and Lello was sitting on the cobbles of Via Principe di Piemonte by the tram stopped outside the arch of Santa Bibiana. With his crushed hand in mid-air still, he kept urging Tommaso in terror to escape: but now his voice was drowned by a very loud scream which rang against the walls, the streets, the squares all around: it was the siren of the police Jeep, dashing up and down in the neighbourhood, growing softer and louder, but coming steadily closer. Tommaso's mother was there too, and she hugged him, holding him tight to her, and kissed him, leaving a bit of saliva on his cheek. Now the police siren was only a few feet away, there beyond the corner of the street; it was about to arrive.

'Let go of me, Ma, let go!' Tommaso yelled, 'Oh my God, help!'

So he woke and sat straight up in bed. He looked around, not recognizing anything: the walls, the windows, the rows of beds.

A black-haired boy near him was watching, one hand supporting his cheek.

'Jeezus,' the boy said almost gaily, as if saying something welcome. 'You been yelling for half an hour!'

'Where am I?' Tommaso asked, almost without realizing it and yet understanding it was a pointless question.

The other guy's face was filled with a kind of happy amazement: 'At the Forlanini!' he answered. 'Where dya think you are?' And he looked at him, his eyes laughing with surprise.

Tommaso was silent for a while, recovering himself: he straightened out the sheets that were all twisted and damp with sweat.

'Aòh, did something happen?' the black-haired boy asked a bit jokingly, resuming the conversation.

Tommaso, though dazed, understood the guy was all right: 'Yes,' he said, 'I just about had it.'

'Where're you from?' Tommaso asked then, turning his pillow over.

'Villa Adriana. What about you?'

'Pietralata.'

He was silent for a moment, concentrating, his whole body still trembling. 'You been in here long?' he asked his neighbour.

'Six months and a few days,' the other guy said, surly.

'Six months?' Tommaso almost shouted, his eyes wide. 'They can't screw me like that ... I'll jump over the fence and clear out!' He waved his right hand, knife-like, against the palm of his left three or four times, indicating flight. 'They can keep anybody they like in here,' he continued with disgust, 'but not Puzzilli Tommaso!'

'You'd be the only one!' the other guy said calmly and a bit sarcastically. 'Here, the people fight to stay in. They throw them out the door and they come back in through the window!'

'Maybe outside they never had a good meal!' Tommaso said.

'When you get out, whadda'll you do?' the boy asked, expansive. 'You think they'll make you a present of your food? Don't you know we're sick? Nobody'll hire us! At least in here, rain or shine, you don't have any worries. You know what they give you when you're outta here? Three hundred lire. Try living on that ... '

Tommaso shrugged, grinning: 'I don't give a shit,' he said 'I don't want any charity. When I get out, I'll start stealing!'

The other guy didn't pay any attention to him, however: he had something else on his mind.

'But they're gonna have to listen to us now. With all the yelling we're doing, they'll have to give us our rights! Here they've all got their hands in the pot, but they can't screw us. We've had enough. And when we get out, they gotta give us what we're entitled to. And right away, the minute we're cured, they gotta give us a chance to work!'

Tommaso listened in silence and, looking the boy over, he was thinking to himself: Is this guy crazy? What's he talking about?

'We've had hard luck,' the dark-haired kid was saying, now well-launched in his talk, 'because the guy who ran everything around here just died. Day before yesterday, while they were operating ... He had a friend stand by the table with him so they wouldn't bring in a priest to confess him when he didn't know what was going on ... '

Jeezus, you're a talker, all right ... Tommaso thought.

'He was our age, maybe twenty ... He was a real man, all right ... When he was quiet, he was quiet ... But when he made a move, he smashed up everything ... I'll show you his picture ... '

From his bedside table he took a little identification photograph with a death announcement printed under it, and handed it to Tommaso. To be accommodating, Tommaso looked at it, turning the photo in his fingers. 'Bernardini, his name was ... ' the other boy explained, more excited than ever.

Tommaso glanced at the photograph of the dead boy: a long, determined face, with glasses, he looked a little like the Pope. The other guy went on: 'You shoulda seen him the way he made them send back two truckloads of stuff because it wasn't first quality like we're supposed to have. Aòh, they couldn't do anything with him. They just had to turn around and clear out!'

'Eh, I bet,' Tommaso thought. Then he said, aloud: 'What's your name, kid?'

'Lorenzo,' the boy said.

8

'Eeeeh,' Tommaso said, yawning, 'you're lucky, all right ... '

After he had told his name, this Lorenzo fell silent as abruptly as he had started chatting and giving all those explanations. Perhaps he had fallen asleep again, suddenly, the way little kids do.

Tommaso, instead, wasn't sleepy; he remained awake, hoping the guy would start talking again. After a little while, he even called him: 'Hey, kid, hey, Blackie!' But the other guy didn't answer, he had really fallen asleep. You could see the dark patch of his hair and his face against the pillow, unmoving.

Tommaso still felt bad. He would have given a year of his life, if he had one left, for a cigarette.

He lay there a long while, maybe over an hour, motionless in the bed, burning in sweat.

Then something changed: he felt that outside it wasn't all dark any more, that a faint light was whitening the air. Or else it was an impression: maybe it was only the Permolio burning more brightly, with its jet of flame flickering in the middle of the sky. You couldn't hear a voice, a sound.

But then, slowly, some bells began to ring. The tolling came weakly, muffled, as if from a distance, beyond the pavilions and the gardens, maybe on the Portuense, from the church next to Vigna Pia or from some new church that had been built around there, at Casaletto, or Corviale, or at Santa Passera ... It was a sound Tommaso had never heard: or maybe he had heard it when he was a little kid, and now he didn't remember. It seemed to come up from the bottom of the earth or from some point above the early-morning clouds, where the sky is just taking on colour and already seems the light of a good and happy day. It was the sound of Matins. It still wasn't clear whether it was a sign of celebration for the returning day or whether it was announcing a misfortune, a death. Maybe it was both things mixed together, cancelling each other out as they mingled, and that sound was only a sound, repeated, faint but constant. Tommaso couldn't make out what it meant, because he had no words for it, no way of understanding; he had never paid any attention to these things, nobody ever talked to him about them: it was as if they didn't exist. But now it was there, and loud, that sound, dong dong dong dong, passing through all those sleeping neighbourhoods, that old air which was beginning to brighten, barely, from within, as if from itself, becoming grey and cleansed, rediscovering all the things around: walls, trees, buildings, streets. And it had to be ringing for someone: for the priest, who made it ring, for the sacristan, for some old woman, for the workers on some night-time job, coming off work at that hour, for those who had to catch a train for somewhere.

But ... how to say it? ... it seemed that those bells, that mysterious dong dong dong dong that re-announced the life of every day, were saying instead no, that everything was in vain, that all were alive but already dead, buried, lost souls. And at the same time the smell of mud, of rain, of coffee, as if borne by the tolling of those bells, began to be perceptible all around, giving a sense of calm and of freshness.

As if dazed by that sound, which seemed never to end now that it had begun, and by other bells from other churches, from Trastevere, Testaccio, San Paolo, which had also begun with the same sound, the same melancholy, Tommaso felt himself slowly gripped by a profound, irresistible sleepiness: he lay there like stone, falling asleep while he grumbled within himself at the sounds of those bells, cursing them. He dozed off and slept for a good while, in that sleep that had fallen on him, full of peace.

When he woke up he thought he had heard another bell. And, in fact, when he was completely awake, he realized that there really was another bell ringing. But this one was closer: it seemed almost over his head, maybe in a pavilion nearby, in the hospital's chapel.

It was morning: from the window came a light that hurt his eyes, all white: and on the tile floor, the beds were even whiter, with the shapes of the sleeping men in them. Some of them, already awake, were sitting up or standing by their tables, in the light as pale as milk.

The bell was a single one: it rang loud and fast, three rings in one way, ding ding ding, and three in another: dang dang dang. It would be quiet for a while, then resume the three alternating sounds. And so on and on, always the same. It was tolling for the dead: this was a sound Tommaso recognized all right, one he knew.

The tolling seemed even louder, since everything was fairly silent, though you could hear life starting up. And it seemed to strike you, coming from all sides, from the window, from the corridor, with its shrill and strident sound.

It wouldn't stop: sure, it was telling that somebody had died, had turned up his toes, poor bastard, and rest his soul: but it was so insistent that it made your head swim. Every time it paused, you thought it had stopped for good, the bell seemed swallowed up in the silence of the morning, resigned, docile. But then, again, the first ding, the first row of dings; then the dangs.

The sky was now light, but grey: perhaps because it wasn't full day yet or because it was covered with clouds. The only life in all that new brightness was that bell, which rang and rang, fell silent as if to catch its breath a moment, then started again, ringing, ringing.

*

It was time to get up: Tommaso had no idea what he was supposed to do. He lay there in the bed, still looking around, angrily. The four T.B. cases in there with him got up slowly, except one, who was on the critical list. The kid in the next bed had already gone off: God knows where. That was his business. Those others, in silence, did what they had to do: with white shirts down to their heels, they went to the wash basin one by one, washed their faces, like so many Zombies, then dried themselves and put on, over their shirt or their white drawers, a jacket or a sweater, or only a scarf.

They didn't say anything, not to Tommaso, merely exchanging a few words among themselves, resigned. Tommaso looked at them, ready to throw up. These poor slobs! he was thinking. They have the nerve to be satisfied with themselves? Whadda they think they are? Bankers on a holiday?

Then, all of a sudden, he made up his mind and got out of bed, too. He threw off the covers and, in his shirt, barefoot, he went to the basin and gave himself a wash, drying himself with a new towel, which was surely his. Then he combed his hair, and took his time over it, as usual. He saw, too, that he needed a shave, like those other

bums. Am I supposed to look ugly like them? Ha, they'll see, he said
bitterly. He went to the locker and found the razor his brother had
lent him to bring to the hospital. In no time he shaved off his beard,
a few wisps among the pimples.

Then he dressed; he wouldn't stay in his shirt. They only put on
their good suit to be buried in, eh? he thought, his mouth twisted in
contempt.

He went back to the locker and took out the best suit he had, best
after a manner of speaking, since he had had it for two years and
had bought it second-hand, at Porta Portese: he fixed himself up
as smartly as he could, with his tie and a clean shirt. Finally he was
ready. Now whadda I do, for Chrissake? he thought.

He left the ward, stuck his nose into the corridor beyond the
metal door which had no key or keyhole, and looked around,
frowning. Some people were hurrying back and forth, dragging
their ragged clothes after them. 'Well?' Tommaso said, with a
venomous grimace. He took a few steps towards some sounds he
heard, some voices. He walked a little way down the corridor,
peering around: then in the distance he saw a short girl, dressed in
white, walking along, holding against her belly a tray bigger than
she was, full of cups and saucers. Now we eat! Tommaso thought,
thank God.

With his face still longer, he went in the door where the girl had
come out, careful not to compromise himself too much in case he
was making a mistake; he saw, in fact, that the corridor widened
at this point into a kind of little room, all full of tables. The patients
were seated at them in silence, having their breakfast.

Two tables were full of young men, more or less Tommaso's age.
Tommaso looked around a bit, red with emotion, because he didn't
know what to do, whether he should stay there or whether his
place was somewhere else. Then he thought: Whatta fuck! I'm
gonna sit here, okay?

There was a place at the end of one of the young guys' tables;
and he sat down there, waiting. Nobody paid any attention to him.
Pretending to be absorbed in his own affairs, Tommaso listened to
their talk. They were all talking about this Bernardini who had died

two days ago, and who was about to be buried. Whadda they all
talking about him for? Who was he anyhow? Garibaldi? he thought:
and meanwhile he kept his ears pricked.

One guy was saying that with Bernardini gone, it was all over,
they could forget everything, all the plans they had had. Another
was saying that if he had lived, he would have become a member
of parliament or a cabinet minister, at least. Eh! Tommaso thought,
Why stop there?

The squat waitress brought him some coffee and milk, with bread,
butter, and a little dish of honey: at that sight Tommaso forgot
about Bernardini and everybody else and started eating like he had
two mouths. The others finished eating in silence, hastily. Then, as
if by some secret agreement, they all got up and went off together:
some of the older men followed them, too. Where the fuck're they
going? Tommaso thought, goddam them. Is Rome on fire or
something? Meanwhile he ate faster, to follow them. He swallowed
the last scrap of bread and honey, wiped his mouth with his sleeve,
and was off, along those corridors, those stairs, not knowing where
he was, until he reached the front door and went out.

Outside, there was the garden with Via Portuense at the back, the
cheap housing blocks with laundry hanging on the balconies.

There were evergreen bushes, pines, cypresses, oaks: along the
streets and the paths, between the Business Office and Reception,
between the great wing of the Men's Ward and the Orthopedic
Ward, you could hardly see anybody at that hour. Only occasionally a gardener passed, an old man the size of a peppercorn, his
face yellow with ancient illness under a blue skullcap; he would
slowly sweep the paths and walks with a huge broom about six
feet long.

What sun, what light there was! They seemed to increase minute
by minute before your very eyes: the green became greener, the
blue, bluer. Not a cloud in the sky, not even if you looked for it with
a telescope. The air was taut as the skin of a drum: you could hear
the faintest voices of the neighbourhood, far as they were, and all the
sounds, the hum of the day that was beginning. Everything seemed
too limpid and beautiful under that sun so radiant it was immodest.

And a smell of warm earth, dry, clean grass, a breeze from the sea. It was really one of the most beautiful days of the year, the kind when you go to Ostia, when everybody feels a kind of itch in his heart, a fury to go and have fun.

Tommaso wandered around the garden at random for a while, trying to find the path the others had taken: the garden wasn't so big, but if you weren't familiar with it, it was fairly hard to get your bearings. Luckily he saw another group of patients, almost all of them young; he watched them for a moment or two letting them pass him, then, as if casually, he started following them, an expression of boredom on his face.

Walking after them, he went along a side path for a bit, downhill, obliquely, neither in the direction of the main entrance in Via Ramazzini, nor towards Via Portuense. Here the garden was a little wilder, the smaller trees mingling with huge old pines, and here and there some half-buried pots with prickly pears. And on the other side of the wall, beyond a slope there was a little road which certainly went from Via Portuense to Monteverde: the garden path ran parallel to it, and at the end, in an open space outside a big door, there was a crowd of people.

Tommaso approached slowly, trying to maintain his reserve: he had immediately realized they were there because the body of that Bernardini everybody was talking about was going to be taken away. The patients, the dead boy's friends, were huddled together: some were in the little yard by the gate near a tiny construction like a cake, maybe the gate-keeper's house; others had gathered near another construction near by, oval-shaped, with smooth walls and big coloured windows: some went inside. That must have been the place where the body was laid out. In fact, a little later, the gate was opened: in the street outside there was the hearse with the priest, and they went inside that oval building for the coffin. They put it in the hearse, followed by the patients, all of them crying: and the funeral moved off. There were lots of cars with wreaths on their roofs: and the flowers gleamed, bright, glowing, like corals, under the sun which was warmer all the time, dominating all that peace.

Tommaso remained alone, with some of the worst cases, who

weren't able to follow the funeral; then they went off about their business, back towards the hospital.

Tommaso also turned and started up the path that he had walked down. Now he was all alone, and he had nothing more to do. He was in despair because he didn't have a cigarette, panting for a smoke. 'Goddammit,' he muttered through clenched teeth, almost crying, 'I'm gonna go crazy. I can't just lie down and take this!'

The place was deserted all around him, empty under the sun's blaze. At the beginning of the path there was a pile of cabbage stalks, two yards high, still green and fresh, beginning to rot in the heat.

A little farther on, in another open space he hadn't noticed before, there was a hut with a kind of little bridge in front of it: it looked like a workshop or a kiln. Over it there was a funny chimney, cone-shaped, broad at the top: from it came a thin, peaceful thread of smoke. Two characters, garbage-collectors, so thin that their smocks could walk by themselves, with their heads full of bumps, and with little crooked legs, were pushing a cart with a sack in it. When they got to the kiln, they took the sack and, all exhausted, gasping, but working and without haste, they rolled it in where the oven was: then they also disappeared inside without a word, with their birdlike little shoulders all bent over.

Tommaso turned his back, went up through the garden reaching the flank of his pavilion. And now whaddam I gonna do? he thought, Where'll I drag my ass?

With a lump in his throat, ready to cry, though he couldn't have said why, he climbed up the two flights of stairs to that big entrance hall that looked like a Ministry and entered the corridor where, after a few steps, there was the little door to his ward. He had no other prospect, no hope, except to stay there, to fling himself down on the bed again. Meanwhile it was becoming so hot you broke out in a sweat even if you weren't doing anything. He went in and lay down. In the ward there was also Lorenzo, the kid who had talked with him during the night. 'What're you doing?' this guy asked, 'it isn't rest hour yet?'

'Whadda I care?' Tommaso said, shrugging one shoulder: he

didn't know what this rest hour was and he didn't give a shit. He didn't even ask.

'Aòh,' he said, instead, after a while, in a hoarse voice, 'what ward was that Bernardini in?' He pronounced Bernardini's name with scepticism and some anger, because he couldn't stomach the way they all talked about him so much.

'Upstairs!' Lorenzo said, raising his head from the comic book he had begun to read.

Tommaso lay on the bed a little longer, then got up again: he reopened the door and went back into the corridor.

He spat on the floor briefly, out of embarrassment and indecision, then he looked around, a bit scared, thinking he might have done something wrong: there was nobody around, and he shrugged, saying aloud, disgusted: 'Who gives a shit?'

He took his bearings for a moment then went to the end towards the steps: he climbed up one flight to the floor above, where he found another, identical corridor.

Again he looked around, stretching his chin: there were some patients going back and forth, entering the wards, but Tommaso was ashamed to ask, because it was a silly thing he was doing, just something to kill the time.

From the windows up there you could see streets and houses along the Portuense, almost to the Tiber, which flowed in a green ditch, between clusters of building sites, sheds, green fields steaming in the strong morning sunlight.

In the corridor, a little farther on, there was a glass door, with grey, opaque panes: it couldn't have been a ward, or a dining-hall either. In fact, printed on the glass in clear, white letters there were initials: U.L.T. and some others, inside little circles. Tommaso put his hand on the knob and opened it; he peered inside: nobody there. It was a big office with three desks and some posters on the walls behind the desks. His hand still on the knob, Tommaso looked around a bit: an old patient was leaning on the sill of a large window.

'Say,' Tommaso said, 'where's everybody?'

'All gone to the funeral,' the man said, turning his long yellow face towards him.

Tommaso shrugged and went inside, thinking: Who's gonna keep me out? I'm coming in anyhow!

Inside there was only the sun, festive, absorbing everything, flashing over everything. There were some flowers, too: on one of the desks, the last one, by the window, the smallest. Carnations: some red carnations in a little vase and behind them the photo of that guy, that Bernardini. Tommaso recognized him right off, and, his curiosity aroused, he began to look at what was on it. Nothing: some typewritten papers inside a folder, faded by the sun. The drawers were all full of books: old ones, worn and dirty. Tommaso tried to read them, skipping here and there. He couldn't make head or tail of them: they were books about politics, social facts, with hard words he couldn't understand. He opened a bottom drawer and there, all dusty, rolled up, wrinkled, he found a new flag, red, with the hammer and sickle.

Tommaso pulled out one end, looked at it. At that moment, a bell began ringing again full blast, the hospital bell, loud and continuous.

Tommaso went to the window. Down below, in that sea of light, he recognized the piece of slightly wilder garden, the little kiln where they burned the infested rubbish of the hospital, the buildings at the back gate, the street along the Forlanini where, a little while before, he had seen the boy's body taken away.

What if I died, too? he thought, What if I'm gonna end up here, that same way?

Sweating in all that heat, Tommaso felt a shiver run through him, like a chill, as if, around him, night had suddenly come back again.

*

Some weeks went by, a month, two months, and Tommaso became hardened to life at the Forlanini. However, towards July, some events occurred that upset things all over again, and for a long while, and Tommaso had to pay the consequences.

As it happened, the patients, Tommaso included, had been smelling a rat for some time. At the headquarters of the Union of

Tubercular Workers they were making a cause of it, because
Bernardini wasn't the only boy around there who was on the ball,
and the others, more or less like him, got busy; they increased the
struggle, as they put it. Tommaso didn't much care, but he had good
ears and a sharp nose. One day, as he was walking in the little gardens
around the Disbursement Office, he had seen a group of those guys,
Boneschi, Triggiani, Taddei, Guglielmi and some others, with a
camera, taking a picture of something inside a Mercedes: the car
belonged to the Assistant Director of the sanatorium, a certain Fani,
a Jew who during Fascism had joined Mussolini's party, had been
purged, and had then got back in again, in a stronger position than
before.

Tommaso kept his mouth shut. Finally, one morning, what had to
happen, happened: they had been expecting it at the Forlanini for
months. The male nurses, the orderlies, as they were called there,
had made some demands, in the natural order of things: there had
been a lot of talk, but nothing concrete. Until one fine morning they
called a strike, and out of the eight hundred workers, only about a
hundred showed up, maybe less.

To take their place, from the Via Portuense entrance, two or three
companies of soldiers turned up: Medical Corps, grenadiers. They
got out of the trucks and were led into the kitchens. But they
couldn't manage things: they took the stuff and had it moved from
the storeroom to the various sections. The grenadiers worked well,
but the patients began to yell, to rave: they knew you have to be
careful about hygiene, that it took only a little oversight, maybe
in washing a dish or a pan, to spread the disease: and specially those
who were convalescent or who only had pleurisy weren't at all
satisfied that guys with no training, who didn't know a thing, should
come and work in the place of the strikers. And for that matter,
more than a few of the orderlies had died, infected: and so for the
soldiers, too, it was no joke. The patients all began to protest, to
yell out accusations. Nobody, not even those who were worst off,
stayed in his bed: they all got up and started walking back and forth
in the corridors, gathering at the windows to watch what was
going on.

Others, the less serious cases, went around the gardens in squads, among the sections, to see what the soldiers were up to. Meanwhile at Union headquarters, where there was also the 'Felice Salem' cell of the C.P., whose secretary, after Bernardini, was a guy named Guglielmi, they were all arguing about what to do. They decided to set up a delegation and make a big noise in the office of the Director.

They went along all those corridors, through those entrances, up those stairs until they arrived at the main offices: they were received at once and softened with plenty of fine words. But, when they went out, this time they used the front door, towards the main gate, because they could hear one hell of a racket. There, in the open yard among the flowerbeds, various groups of patients had collected, looking towards the street and shouting: in fact, beyond the gate, there was a big police Jeep.

Nobody liked this. And, in fact, some were already going to the fence, shouting at the cops: 'Whaddya doing here? Whaddya here for? Clear out!' The men shouting were yellow-faced, living skeletons, their hospital shirts flapping under their old clothes.

The cops had got out of the Jeep, and were keeping the men calm, at the open gate, with the barrier raised.

The guys in the delegation arrived, and, seeing them, the others got even more excited: 'Get out, you dirty bastards!' they yelled at the cops. 'You're not afraid to push sick guys around, eh?'

There were maybe a hundred, hundred and fifty patients gathered there. Somebody got the idea of throwing the police out of the garden and slamming the gate in their face: 'Let's gettem outta here! Throw the murderers out! Why don't they go chase thieves?'

The policemen, seeing the nasty turn things were taking, decided to grab one guy and take him with them. They took Guglielmi, who had come forward, to talk with the chief from the Monteverde station, to try to persuade him to make his men leave: and it was the chief, instead, who yelled: 'Grab him! Arrest him!' But the others got involved too, and they drove the cop away with his uniform torn.

They didn't think twice about rebelling against the forces of law and order, they didn't give a damn, they were sick anyhow, and some of them didn't even have a hope of ever getting out of the Forlanini.

At that moment, however, another police truck arrived, at full speed; obviously it had been lurking in some side street or around the curve of Viale Ramazzini. More cops got out, with night-sticks. All hell broke loose. Some of the patients attacked the police, hitting them as best they could, poor slobs, barely able to stand up on their feet.

Others cleared out, scared, along the paths and the roads under the trees, with the cops after them, waving their sticks and making them run at top speed this way and that.

At this point the sanatorium's alarm siren began to sound: it sounded so many times, it was enough to make you deaf. Now almost all the patients who could walk had collected outside the windows of the office, in the yard before the main entrance: there were all of fifteen hundred, two thousand. The ones who had run off, seeing the crowd advancing and gathering in the yard, now mingled with it and started coming forward again. They were bound and determined to get the police out of the hospital grounds and close the gates, and they had almost made it. But meanwhile, apparently all ready and waiting, a lot of other Jeeps, and even some big trucks, loaded with cops, turned up, along with two hose-trucks.

Five or six hundred cops lined up in front of the gate, sticks in hand, and nozzles aimed.

The patients had managed to shut the gates and had taken up their position inside. But the police didn't give a shit; they brought up two or three trucks, rammed the gates, which immediately gave way, the locks broken; and the cops swarmed in, not giving a damn about anybody.

The patients retreated, taking refuge where they could, some towards the Invalids Department, some inside the main building, running in every direction, along the corridors, up the stairways. But there were lots of them, and those who were more exposed, towards the entrance or in the garden, couldn't evade the police

charge. Over a hundred, the smartest, ran off all right, but then
turned up again, shouting more and more menacingly: 'Hey, you
bums! You killers! We're gonna spit blood in your face!' These
guys were hit by the hydrants, and they ran off into the wards,
soaked with foaming water, their clothes glued to their bones.
They were crying and yelling.

Now there were only a very few left racing around the gardens,
with the police and their sticks still on their tail: most of the patients
had slipped into the wards at random, the women with the men.
They barred all the doors. The police tried to open them and
occupy the buildings. Then the patients grabbed anything they
could get their hands on, anything they could lift and throw and
that didn't belong to them: chairs, tables, cases, night-jars, urinals.
The police ran off wildly, withdrawing among the trees of the
garden. But some things hit them even there, hurled by the patients
from the windows and the balconies where they took their sun-
baths. They were about to empty and demolish the whole hospital:
and they managed to hit some of the police on the head or the neck,
yelling: 'Take that, you sonovabitch! Take it home with you! Go
tell Mamma all about it!'

Partly to keep everything inside the hospital from ending up in
the garden, the cops did an about-face and went back towards the
offices, towards the main entrance: and as they retreated, the
patients once again came out from the wards and followed them,
still throwing stuff.

Little by little, all fifteen hundred, or two thousand, however
many they were, returned to the big yard outside the Director's
offices and lined up along the entrance gates in Viale Ramazzini: they
were content, and in their contentment, you could see even more
clearly how much emotion, how much weeping, how much venom
they had in their eyes.

They went on attacking the police from the distance, or else they
yelled against the management of the hospital or against the
government.

Each had to have his say, and they all waved their arms, yelled,
screamed till they couldn't scream any more: their nerves were

keeping them going, with those ragged clothes on their backs, those white, floppy pyjamas that made them look like a crowd of Pulcinellas.

Meanwhile a group of orderlies, for whose sake all this stink was being raised, went into the main office to talk with that famous Fani and a bunch of others, to say they would suspend the strike if the Riot Squad would clear out and go back to minding its own business. The bosses said no, they couldn't do anything, because by now the responsibility for the Forlanini had been turned over to the mayor, to the chief of police. But then other factors were considered and, what with one thing and another, they finally came to an agreement: the police moved out, left the grounds, and the patients, more content than ever, went back, some of them, to their wards for a little rest, while others lingered in little groups around the main gate.

Half an hour went by, an hour: it was noon; and then, all of a sudden, the police vehicles showed up again, speeding straight into the hospital grounds, not leaving time for the word to get around; they parked their trucks at strategic points and occupied the interior of the various buildings.

Some patients tried to put up a fight, especially the women, who were the maddest, but the cops, who everybody said were being commanded by Fusco, the city chief, were determined to settle things once and for all.

From mouth to mouth, the word was quickly passed that there was nothing to be done, that these cops were ready to kill you even: they said that one woman in the surgical ward had been dragged along the floor by her hair, they had torn off her clothes and she was left in her slip, all in shreds. That another woman had taken such a fright she had gone dumb and couldn't talk any more; and another, a pneumothorax case, had been carried off and beaten with night-sticks.

The fact was that all the wards were occupied by the police: there were ten to thirty flatfeet in each ward. They stayed there all that afternoon and through the night, while the trucks patrolled the grounds, with their headlights glaring.

They had set up camp there, with tear-gas bombs, machine guns and sidearms.

Towards morning, with lists all drawn up, they started investigating, to arrest those held responsible: these were all marked down already, the heads of the U.L.T., the Union representatives, the officers of communist cells, needless to say, and all the rest: they were picked up and led out with their hands over their heads. Then they were taken away.

The room which had been used as an office for the organizations and the parties was broken into by the cops; they entered, tore up papers, and confiscated everything.

At the gates of the Forlanini, both in Viale Ramazzini and in Via Portuense, hundreds of people had already collected, patients' relatives; but they weren't allowed inside. Then a little later, when the sun was already high, a truck came to the side entrance, and they began to pack into it the patients who were being sent away: some arrested, others discharged, or transferred to other hospitals. There must have been two hundred of them. The police grabbed them and carried them off, without looking at them, even though in some cases, they were vomiting blood while they were being carried off.

For their meal, the patients ate with the cops: a plate of cold pasta, worse than slop, and some canned stuff.

Meanwhile the cops were still hunting for the guys they wanted to make pay, who had hidden.

Any sort of place was good to hide in: the hospital had become chaos, confusion everywhere: those who had to hide to avoid arrest changed places with friends in other wards, trying to conceal their features with bandages, with dark glasses: or they stretched out in the deck chairs on the balconies, huddling under the blankets.

Tommaso was sitting on his bed eating his cold pasta, grumpy and silent as an old whore. One mouthful after the other, swallowing hard, bitterly, with a jerk of his Adam's apple that seemed to say: 'You all make me throw up!' On the blanket beside him he had a little can of meat, in reserve, with some pickles.

The other old patients also gulped down their food, hunched

over, each turning his back to the other, like workers, old labourers, when they eat on the building-site, resting against a dusty plank fence. You could hear the chomp chomp of their mouths chewing slowly, patiently.

Lorenzo was eating on his feet, standing by the wall, glancing intently every now and then beyond the panes of the little door. Guglielmi had come with another guy, a certain Pezzo, to hide there in the ward; the two of them had run in there, while some cops were looking around for them: they knew Lorenzo and so had ducked in.

The cops on guard in that wing were also eating, a bit farther on, at the end of the corridor. They had set their metal dishes on the sill of a big window and, leaning on one elbow, they were chewing and swallowing too, hungry, being young, with dark peasant faces; and they were silent. You could tell they were also a bit upset at everything that was going on.

'Action! Action!' Lorenzo suddenly shouted in a low voice. Immediately, Guglielmi and Pezzo dived headlong, one under Tommaso's bed, one under Lorenzo's.

Tommaso sat still, motionless as stone, staring, blind and dumb: he ate. He put food in his mouth, chewed, swallowed. All this without changing his expression, disgusted and resigned, a face that looked like D'Artagnan.

In fact, a little later the patrol came along and paid a visit to Tommaso's ward: they saw only some people eating, behind Tommaso's back, in order on their beds; every face, stuffed, was turned towards them. There was also a hospital supervisor, a character with a sharp face, and you could see he had sniffed the funny atmosphere in the room: but he stuck to his own business. Instead, the police looked around, asked the names of those present, and went off: they had done their duty: if there was somebody under the beds, fuck him, leave him there.

The waitress with the big tits came and collected the dirty plates, sloppy and gabbling away.

An hour went by, two hours. The police up and down the corridor, and the news kept coming, more and more desperate: everything was over at the Forlanini. The strike had furnished the authorities an excuse to wipe out everything, send away the undesirables, restore order and resignation.

Some comrades, older men, who weren't compromised, moved around, bearing the news. One of them came and said the police were about to come back, with the lists all ready: and this time they were really going to search. 'Come on,' he said, 'I'll take you to a good place!'

'Where?' Guglielmi asked.

'Come with me,' the old guy said, smartass.

'We have to take somebody else, too,' he added, 'to see where this place is, so afterwards he can bring you some food and keep in contact with you! They're beginning to catch on to me. They keep giving me dirty looks!'

Lorenzo was too well known; he had been running around with the leaders for some time, working hard. The others were old, already half-corpses, ready for the oven.

'You come, kid!' the old man said to Tommaso.

Tommaso felt his heart leap, as if they had stabbed him; he twisted his mouth in a grimace so serious and disgusted that he seemed ready to spit venom, and blushing, he turned as dark as a coal. He jerked his head towards the door, then said in a muffled voice: 'Let's go!'

They went out into the corridor like they had to go to the can or take a bit of air, sauntering. The two cops at the end of the corridor looked up and said nothing, good as gold, as if they had no eyes or ears.

Tommaso tried to fix into his mind the route they were taking: they went downstairs, out into the garden, walked the length of the horse-shoe-shaped courtyard between the Men's Wing and the Women's Wing, which they entered through a little side door. They had made it. They disappeared inside as if it were nothing, as rigid as if they had swallowed nails. There was a narrow corridor which led to the Supervisors' Office a little farther on: but just inside there was another little door to a store-room.

Guglielmi was a tall guy, with a broad back, a bit stiff, and with a pensive, kid's face: you could see he was really sick, his skin was grey, bloodless, and his lips were the same colour, small and thick. His companion was blond, with pale eyes and a long face; he spoke with a Veronese accent. They slipped inside, as if they had been doing things like this all their life, and the old man locked them in and took away the key.

When he and Tommaso were back at the ward, the old man said goodbye and added: 'Now you've gotta take care of those two: I got other things to do, and by now I'm on the shit list myself, I'm sure. Here, take the key. Remember to take them food: don't let them starve! So long, kid, and don't forget: do things right!' He went off.

Tommaso stayed there with the key in his hand: half yawning, he stuck it in his pocket, thinking to himself, but not angrily, almost laughing: Jeezus ... I've made a big deal, all right!

It was four, maybe five in the afternoon. Evening came, one of those lovely full summer evenings when the darkness never descends, and, if the moon comes up, it stays up there near and warm, too, useless, because its light isn't necessary, but it's beautiful, all the same.

At the Forlanini the arrests went on, the beatings, the clubbings, the tears. To be kicked out of there, for a sick man, for a convalescent, meant a lot: not to mention those who ended up in jail, like thieves.

Tommaso had made an arrangement with big-tits, speaking only in signs and hints because he was sure they were all stool-pigeons around there and even the walls pricked up their ears.

At supper time, the waitress brought two extra portions into Tommaso's ward: she was putting up a big pretence, and as she did, she let them all know it. She was swollen with pride at what she was doing; almost winked at the cops, too. Tommaso, with Lorenzo helping him, made two very tight packages and put them under his jacket, then ventured forth.

He retraced the route of that afternoon, across the garden, he reached the store-room, and unlocked it stealthily. The two friends were still in there, like a pair of old jailbirds. They immediately asked a lot of information of Tommaso, how things were going, if they were still making arrests, and so on. Tommaso, to tell the truth, didn't know all that shit. He answered them the way you answer little kids, agreeing with them to keep them quiet. He left the food and went off, looking around carefully, on the alert, because the Supervisors' room was near by.

He went back to the ward to sleep. The next morning, the same story. The waitress came in with extra food. But, a little before noon, the patrol showed up again, six or seven cops with an officer in civilian clothes, and this time, entering the ward, he asked the patients to produce their identity papers and also looked them all in the face, 'Do you know a certain Aldo Guglielmi here?' The sick men stuck out their chins, twisting their mouths with pursed lips, with a grim expression in their eyes, almost spitting, all of them, because of the bad taste in their mouths. 'Who's he? Never heard of him? Who knows who he is?' they said. The officer went off, after giving them a nasty look, with a blue eye that boded no good, accustomed as it was to considering everybody a thief, an insect pest. He went off, with his little pigeon shoulders and his shaved neck, his peasant's face. 'Fuckoff!' Tommaso said behind his back, one corner of his mouth pulled down in disgust, almost twisted off.

Then, after half an hour, when things had calmed down a little, he took the two packages and went out again.

The two friends were really in bad shape, white as spirits. The little room had only one long, tiny window, up above, and there were only two benches and a little table, with some showers behind: it was a dressing-room out of use at that time. There was nothing else in there, and those two bastards had had to sleep on the floor. They couldn't stand much more. But they weren't depressed at all: they asked news of the others, of the situation, of the newspapers: as if they didn't have their own troubles to think about. They began to eat in haste, not even looking to see what was in the packages. While they ate, they didn't speak, so Tommaso could say to Guglielmi: 'Aòh, they're after you, you know!'

Guglielmi then wanted to hear everything, from start to finish. When he had eaten, he stood up calmly and said with that fleshy, purplish little mouth: 'The office of the Internal Commission ought to be near here ... Wait for me a minute. I'll go there and be right back.'

He went out, came back after a while, even whiter, carrying a typewriter. He put it on the little table and bent over it, writing for quite a while, writing and then rewriting. When he had finished, he turned to Tommaso and said: 'It's a proclamation: I'm asking the patients to maintain their calm, and I appeal to the police to try to avoid violence with the patients ... You've gotta post these papers somehow in the glass cases of the Internal Commission, in the Men's Wing and the Women's ... Can I count on you?'

'Sure,' Tommaso said. Kid, he then said to himself, you still don't know who Puzzilli is!

'Give the stuff here!' he said, taking the papers Guglielmi held out to him. 'See you later!'

The two locked themselves in again, and Tommaso went off, acting indifferent, along the corridor and across the garden. He put his hands in his pocket, and, as if he had stepped out of his house to go to the movies or to meet his friends at the bar, he started whistling, happily and absently:

'Maruzzella, Maruzzeee ... '

Whistling, at times muttering the words of the song, he went back into the Men's Wing, his eyes darting here and there, alert while his mouth sang, to see if there were any cops or stoolies around. The cops as usual were stationed at the end of the corridor, where Tommaso's room was: he passed in front of them, his mouth stretched in a slight yawn, his eyes stewing in boredom and well-being beneath his wrinkled forehead.

He also passed the door of his room, with Lorenzo and the other carcasses looking at him and wondering: he went to the other stairway, and climbed to the floor above. Here there were two more cops at the end of the corridor: but the Union's room, with the glass case in front of it, was around a corner. There were more wards, and so more confusion.

Aaaaa, Tommaso thought, Is something up?

Beyond the corner there were fewer people: only a bunch of

young guys near a big window, getting some air. Tommaso knew them, knew they were communists. I'll give them a heart attack now! he thought happily, so red he was catching fire.

One was the Banana, another was Fatty, another, Magpie; they were from Quarticciolo. One of them, when he was a kid had belonged to the Hunchback's gang: he had been there when the Hunchback died, pierced by bullet-holes like a sieve.

The disease had wasted them, their bones stuck out below their eyes, almost tearing the skin, and they had all become big-jawed, with holes in their cheeks: so skinned, gnawed, that with that grey flesh, their long hair over the collars of the worn, tattered clothes they were wearing, they looked even more deathly.

But just as Tommaso was about to pass them, the cops appeared from the end of the corridor: the same hick official with the pale blue eyes, thin as a weasel, and the other cops after him, all armed, obeying him but, at the same time, willing to let things ride.

'Who farted?' Magpie said, looking out of the window. Banana, wrinkling his nose with disgust too, slapped him on the shoulder: 'Eh, some dirty bastard!' he shouted, aiming the corner of his eye at the cops. They were all amiable and content, laughing with swollen jaws, looking at one another or out of the window. 'Eeeeeeh,' Magpie said again, slapping his hands loudly, palm against palm, his elbows raised, then rubbing his hands together good-naturedly, 'eeeh, nice little game!'

'Remember,' Fatty shouted all of a sudden: 'it's six months!'

And he started laughing peaceably, his tongue between his lips in such a way that, as he laughed, he slobbered saliva. They were now all in the grip of this hilarity: an expression of contentment and of general optimism had come into their eyes and had settled there with a light full of innocence and virtue. They went on laughing, looking at one another; and as they laughed, they pressed their chins to their necks or else shook their heads, no no, as if to say: 'We're great, we are!' When the laughter tended to die down, there was always one who repeated: 'Hoeing is hard work, all right!', and they were off again, with fine, innocent, cordial laughter, as their eyes stared into the air, just the slightest bit sharp.

The cops passed by them: would they stop or not, they're stopping, no, they're not, my God, there they are, this is it, no, no, they're going off, thank God, now what're they doing? Changing their minds? Fuckoff, goddammya! And they went on laughing, calmly. Tommaso had mingled with them, one shoulder against the wall, his hands plunged into his pockets, also laughing calmly.

When the cops had passed and were far enough away, Tommaso went pss pss with his mouth, stopping his laughter, patiently. Then he moved from the group, and under the vaguely curious gaze of the others, he went slowly to the glass case by the sealed glass door.

He took a rapid look around, opened the case: the thumbtacks were already there in the old papers. He pinned up the new sheets, shut the case, and went off.

The others meanwhile came over cautiously. Tommaso walked past them and muttered calmly, like the Scarlet Pimpernel: 'Say, kids, spread the word: everybody should come and read it!'

And he went back to his ward.

Next day the search at the Forlanini went on, and it was even worse because things had naturally calmed down, so it was easier for the police to work. The orderlies, without having won anything, had come back on the job and were under police surveillance. Now it became harder for Tommaso to carry provisions to the comrades.

The sun blazed, nice and high, and it was time for Tommaso to take his walk: God knows how hungry those two living skeletons were, locked in there. Carrying the usual lunch packages, Tommaso went towards the room in the Women's Wing. He did everything right, but when he was at the little door, bending to knock, he turned to look around and saw, ten yards farther on, a Supervisor, a certain Saletta, standing there looking at him.

Tommaso went in and said: 'One of the Supervisors saw me; he's the worst sonovabitch there is around here!' He stuck his head out, but Saletta had gone.

'He's gone to call the cops!' Tommaso said. It was no use for them to think of staying in there now: they darted out, on the run.

They ran up one flight of stairs, then another, narrower flight, then along a corridor till they came to a ward. There were three

beds, with women in them, having rest period. Guglielmi knew
them, and was known. They hid there. For two hours Guglielmi
discussed politics with one of the women, from Milan or from
Genoa, who had fought with the partisans.

It was time for the doctor's rounds: the only thing to do was hide
under the beds again: there were three cops, and for about ten
minutes the boys lay huddled under there, until the doctor had gone
away. Meanwhile another woman came to warn them that the
police had already started around the pavilion, obviously informed
at once by that Saletta, and now they were coming nearer. The
friends couldn't stay there, either: this time the police were looking
under the beds, too. 'But I know a good place,' the woman said.
They ran off. They ran along another corridor, up some stairs,
a short flight with shallow steps: they ran to the end and there, under
more stairs, the woman showed them a little, broken door, half-
open: it was a closet, so low that your head banged against the
ceiling, and completely dark. The woman went off, and they stayed
there, in that kind of cell, still talking politics.

Evening was falling: it was so dark in there you couldn't see an
inch in front of your nose. They didn't have anything to smoke,
and hunger was beginning to make itself felt.

We can't spend the night here! Tommaso was thinking. We
can't stay here!

The Veronese, Pezzo, was a glum type, and Guglielmi did all the
talking, calmly, with that head that looked like a round cork on a
square jar, those thick lips that moved fast, beneath his steady,
little kid's gaze.

And then they heard a soft knock at the door: they opened it
slowly, and in the last light, falling in the stair well, they saw a dark
squat, young guy. He wasn't a patient; he wore a black smock over
his suit. In fact, he was the hospital switchboard operator: and
Guglielmi knew him, too. 'The women told me,' he said, 'let's go!'

Go where? Tommaso said to himself, falling in with the group,
stiff, his blood up, but keeping cool.

The young guy led them along a corridor: at the end of it there
was a low door; to reach it they had to go down three or four steps.

They opened it, then went down an endless flight of stairs in darkness. But the switchboard man had a flashlight, and he walked ahead, lighting the way.

So they came to an underground passage, then to another: under all the Forlanini there were these tunnels, so that you could get from one end to the other, underground. They walked a good fifteen minutes, and finally they climbed up another stairway. At the top, the door opened into a kind of cavern, but all nice and clean, like a little room. It opened on to the garden below the balcony side of the Men's Wing. They stuck their necks out into the open air, under a beautiful moon shining in the midst of the sky over the city. They could hear voices, laughter, the noise of the buses along Via Portuense, all the buzz of summer evenings.

About fifty yards off, at an entrance to the Wing, there were two cops: they were far enough away, there were plenty of bushes and little trees in between, but the boys could see them all the same. 'I'll go,' the switchboard man said, 'and put them off!' He shook hands with the two comrades, wished them luck, and went off, lighting a cigarette. They saw him go slowly up to the cops, talking with them and standing so that he cut off their view.

Tommaso and the other two, all hunched over, promptly slipped among the bushes, the tree trunks: to reach the end of the garden was easy: a couple of jumps among the flowerbeds, over the dry grass. They reached the fence that enclosed the grounds, tall, with a bit of barbed wire on the top. Beyond it, there was the street, the Via Portuense, with lots of people coming and going outside the houses; there were some old buildings, red and peeling, and some brand new ones, gleaming white. In front of a mechanic's shop, a bunch of kids were discussing, arguing, astride motorcycles, the engines running. The buses went past jammed with people; from the open windows, where the lights were turned on, came voices, songs, fading in the warm air, under the light of the moon.

Tommaso was about to climb over the fence like the others: but Guglielmi stopped him and said: 'Whaddya doing? Whaddya running away for? They don't know you; you better stay here and get treated, the right way ... ' For the first time he smiled a little:

'You don't wanna act crazy like me, do you? I've even got the
Party against me for wanting to do too much, instead of lying with
my belly in the sun and thinking about my health!'

To tell the truth, Tommaso really felt like climbing up and going
off in freedom, but he realized the other guy was right, and he shut
up, helping the others to climb the wire.

But, before he went off, Guglielmi turned again to Tommaso,
looked him hard in the eye, with that poor, rubbery face of his.

'Thanks, Puzzilli,' he said, 'you're one of the best!' and he shook
his hand.

He climbed up on the fence; the Veronese was already on the
other side, waiting impatiently. Tommaso watched them run across
the street: they reached the other side, near the mechanic's, and
headed for the bus stop: all around them there was the bustle of
traffic and people at the supper hour. From some old tenements a
troop of little kids came down towards the stop, heading for God
knows where.

Their faces dirty under their forelocks, they walked arm in arm,
all talking eagerly, paying no attention to anyone. Some talked on
and on, others just laughed. And those little smartass faces, above the
filthy, coloured collars, were the very image of happiness: they
didn't look at anything, and they went straight where they had to
go, like a herd of goats, sly and carefree.

Aaaah, Tommaso sighed, I was rich, and I didn't even know it!

4

Old Sun

The August sun set afire the dust, the sheets of corrugated iron, the refuse and the grass, the cane-fences and the rubble. Pietralata lay there, against the mounds of the Aniene and the grey sky: the old buildings to the right, and beyond, all the arc of the development's blocks and the rows of little houses, like a kind of native village, with an odour of heated garbage so strong it was overwhelming. Every now and then there was a puff of cooler wind, a breeze from the sea, and then the stink of the houses full of rags, rubble, and kids' pee mingled with the smell of the mud and the canebrakes along the river.

To tell the truth, at that time, the slum had changed a little. In the centre, they had torn down the seven or eight rows of refugees' little huts, had broken up their paths, and had constructed three or four big, new buildings, dark and huge as mountains, all full of little windows, with lots of narrow yards, entrances and stairs, taking away the sunlight from the other shacks still left in the neighbourhood, and from the fields, yellow as hunger.

The Cinema Lux, farther on, had changed its name, and was now called the Cinema Boston. The little factory below Monte del Pecoraro had closed down, and its old sheds had become the garages of the Zeppieri bus line.

Tommaso walked happily along the deserted, sun-baked street, his hands in his pockets, fairly pleased with all these changes: he looked around, like a landowner who returns to his property after an absence, and since he knows the area inch by inch, he notices everything, sees everything, the things that have changed, and the things that have stayed the same. All dressed up, even to a tie, he came forward without haste, but briskly: with his calm, content, almost bored manner, though underneath it, his heart was pounding so hard it almost dazed him.

And as he gradually approached the bus stop, the pounding he heard between his ribs became louder and louder. He even began to feel his legs trembling a little, and although he went on sweating like an open tap, his cheeks had turned a little white and his eyes were glazed.

He yawned again, stretched, smartass, then, without any hesitation, turned into the central street of Pietralata, towards Party headquarters, among the refugees' shacks.

There, on the little brick yard, the sun was blinding, and there was nobody around. Silence everywhere. Tommaso sniffed, took another two or three drags on the butt so short he could barely hold it in his fingers, then threw it away and went inside. The sun also entered the two rooms of the shack and made the dust glow like the red flag and the picture of Uncle Joe in one corner. There was nobody to be seen there, either. 'Aòh, can I come in?' Tommaso said in a hoarse voice, taking a few steps into the first room.

After a moment, he could see a man sleeping in a bit of the shadow behind the rickety counter. It was Cazzimperio, the man who ran the section's bar-room. He was asleep in a tattered straw chair, between the counter and the barrel, both dry, without a wine-stain, in the heat.

His skull-like grey head was thrown against the back of the chair and you could see only his moustache, his nostrils with dried snot and hairs, and two teeth sticking out of his black mouth. He was snoring softly. 'Chrissake!' Tommaso muttered and went into the other room, the big one where they held dances: nobody was there either, but the door of the office was open. Tommaso went to it and stuck his head inside, repeating: 'Can I come in?' Inside the office there was only one guy, bent over the desk sticking stamps on envelopes and, at each blow, light as it was, the whole desk shook.

'Aòh, Persichì,' Tommaso said, recognizing a kid he knew only by sight. The kid glanced up, examined him for a moment, then looked down again at once, going back to his job.

'Aòh,' Tommaso said, 'tell me something: whaddam I supposed to do?'

And the other guy kept his mouth shut, sticking on stamps; he stuck on another two while Tommaso waited, not knowing what to say, a bit confused, torn with emotion. Then the guy looked up and said, pulling his pale jaws down around his half-toothless mouth: 'There's nobody here now.'

Tommaso also pulled a long face and said: 'When am I supposed to turn up then?'

But the kid was again bent over his stamps: and again he stuck on two or three, then raised his head as if he had to say something important, official: 'Later. There's a meeting.'

'When later?' Tommaso insisted.

'Around five, six,' this Persichini said, looking at him in silence, his mouth open slightly, very serious.

'Okay!' Tommaso said after a moment, starting to leave. 'I'll come back later,' he added: but the kid wasn't even listening to him, licking the stamps, frowning, severe.

Outside, it was an inferno. Everything was grey, limp: the rows of faded houses along the deserted streets, among the gardens without a leaf, without a shred of green. As you walked, the heat stuck to your skin like a rag soaked in hot water.

The streets wound into the slum, all yellowish against the piles of rubbish and garbage, with the little wooden church in the background.

From one of those streets a kind of native emerged, with ragged rubber shoes, jeans, his chest bare, a jersey in his hand. As he came closer, walking under the sun, Tommaso saw it was Zucabbo: he had become fat and full-faced, and his hair, instead of being brown the way it had always been, was blond and glistened in the sun.

'Aòh, where you coming from?' he asked Tommaso.

'Aòh, whaddave you done?' Tommaso said instead of answering, staring at his hair.

'I bleached it!' Zucabbo said, grinning. 'At Porta Portese,' he added, 'there was this blond kid, Roberto, from Mandrione, who had blond hair, real blond like gold, with a curl that fell down to his eyes. I liked it, so I bleached mine, too. But not just me! There must be twenty-five of us around here, all bleached!'

'Okay!' Tommaso said, 'Now where're you going?'

'Swimming,' Zucabbo said.

Tommaso hesitated a moment, thinking. 'I think I'll come along, too!' he concluded.

They went past the last fields, crossed the Montesacro road, and turned into the open country.

There everything was parched, the grass yellow, and the only green was a few canes along the river. The little trees, peaches, cherries, all black and twisted, as if it were winter: dry, without a leaf. The grass all around had been burned out, you could see the black patches of ash among the ragged bushes.

There wasn't a soul in all the blackened stretch of fields, along the Messi d'oro, except for a kid or two, tattered like Zucabbo.

Walking along, Tommaso and his friend talked of this and that: mostly about mutual acquaintances that Tommaso, having been out of circulation for over a year, hadn't heard about. By now hardly anybody he knew was living at Little Shanghai: in the shacks there were new people, mostly peasants, hayseeds who had come up from the lousiest villages in Puglia and Calabria.

Lello still went begging downtown, and all the others more or less were in and out of jail.

Talking, they reached the aqueduct bridge, went down along the canebrake, and came to the little beach.

The stinking sand among the turds was all full of naked, blackened kids, jumping in and out of the water. Zucabbo took off his jeans, then the rubber shoes, with a smell that took your breath away.

'What about Shitter?' Tommaso asked, remembering him.

Zucabbo looked him in the eyes with an expression of happy wonder. 'What? Don't you know?' he asked.

'No,' Tommaso said.

'You haven't heard anything about Shitter?' Zucabbo repeated, already naked. 'Listen to this! Just listen!'

And, taking off his socks, his ass on the filthy sand, he began to tell about Shitter.

Shitter's mother, old Granny, worked Via dei Cerchi. She'd been there for four, five years now: that was her zone, and every evening when it got dark she was there, on the job, and she stayed till the last tram took her back to the little sheds at Piazza San Giovanni di Dio, at Monteverde Nuovo, where she lived with a crook, her pimp. There were another five or six like her, old companions: the Spic, the Capitana, Marisa. They placed themselves above, towards the Passeggiata Archeologica, on the crumbling wall around the street, or on the big oval lawn by the embankment below Piazzale Romolo e Remo, or on the mud among the bushes.

Sometimes customers came by the dozens: there were little fields, including a half-paved one: in the morning the kids played ball, and at night they were teeming. You could see the white shirts, the jerseys moving here and there in the darkness, the little red dots of burning cigarettes: then if there was a moon, it was like daytime. The kids, the young guys, soldiers, even some old drunks stood in the centre of the open spaces, walking around or waiting. The whores drew back into the shadow of the embankment, and they did it there against bits of ruins or in holes dug in the ground. Often all hell broke loose: bands of young guys came down, hungry, stupid, looking for trouble, and they weren't satisfied till they had started a fight, over any little thing, like kids: and since the whores wouldn't have them, there were fights that went on and on. Then maybe, at the height of it all, the Capitana would arrive running, all breathless, yelling: 'Cops!' or to be smart, 'Vice!' and then they would all run off, this way and that, in the moonlit darkness among the bushes towards the slopes.

One winter evening, when Tommaso was still in the Forlanini, some kids came down from Via Portuense, four or five of them, no more. They left their motorcycles up beyond the wall and came to the centre of the Cerchi, hands in their pockets, singing like chickadees.

It had snowed a little the day before, and on the ground, among crusts of frozen mud, shit and sticks, there were still some patches of grey snow.

Excited by this Christmassy air, as well as by the whores who

could already be seen in the background among other groups of
kids, these guys began to sing still louder, running all around like
horses. There was one with his head cropped almost to the skull,
his hair sticking out over his collar, and a face like a nut's who scared
you just to look at him; another was dark, from the North somewhere, and since he was shy, he acted smarter than all of them; and
the rest were a couple of redheads with bumps on their faces, their
skin white with the cold, maybe brothers.

The nut, in an overcoat that came almost down to his heels, its
collar buttoned tight around his neck, was known as Buretta. This
Buretta, all of a sudden, made a face even more snotty than the one
God had given him. He said: 'Keep your mouth shut, eh?' then
took some snow, packed it into a hard ball and put it in his overcoat
pocket. With the others trailing after him, not understanding what
he meant to do, he presented himself nicely to one of the whores,
who was wandering around by herself, a purse in her hand, in the
midst of the open field.

He acted very proper with her, talked about the weather, the
cold, asked her how much she wanted, and all that sort of thing:
then with a sly, little-kid face, he asked her please would she show
it to him. He insisted and begged so much, that the whore, to get
rid of him, took her dress and pulled it above her bellybutton.

Buretta, who had his hands in his pockets, took the snow, which
had melted a little, and shoved it, wham, into her thing, black as
the gate of hell.

The whore started screaming like crazy, from the cold and from
anger, while the others flung themselves on the ground, splitting
with laughter. Then, since they liked the idea, they went around the
Cerchi, repeating the joke with the others, including Granny.
When they had used up all the snow, they went off.

They came back five or six days later, left their Vespas in the
same place, and walked down into the field.

There was no trace of snow any more. It was nice and warm,
already like spring. Buretta didn't even have on his overcoat; he
was wearing only a jersey and a scarf, for vanity.

They came down singing and laughing. All of a sudden, like the other time, Buretta had an idea: his face turned sly, like when he was making a decision Jesus Christ himself couldn't have made him change, and he said: 'Aòh, look for a piece of paper, but good and strong, eh? The kind you wrap packages with!'

Grumbling some curses, the others started looking for this piece of paper. They found it right away, because a piece of paper is one thing that's never lacking in Rome. It was that yellow kind, all right for packages. Buretta smoothed it out nicely, because it was a bit wrinkled, slapped it a couple of times to knock off the dust, and spread it carefully on the ground. When he had done this, he loosened his belt, pulled down his pants, crouched over the paper, and calmly began to shit. The others, holding their noses and yelling stinker and bastard at him, ran here and there, waiting. When he had finished, Buretta made a neat package, and this time, he didn't put it in his pocket, but held it behind his back, walking lazily in the direction of the whores.

The first he met was Granny. Naturally, with all she had been through those last five or six days, she couldn't recognize him. Buretta began to grope her with one hand, pretending he had serious intentions of doing it with her, then with a sudden movement, he pulled up her skirt, slammed the package on her short hair, so hard, that it smeared her all over from her tits to the wool socks hanging down at her ankles. She began to yell at the top of her lungs, almost throwing up because of the stink. The four guys, with Buretta in the lead, ran off, busting with laughter: and you could hear their haw haw haw haaa to the end of the street, until they vanished towards the Registry Building, their guffaws mingling with the explosions of their motorbikes.

A week later they were back. It was becoming a habit with them. Buretta crapped again on a piece of paper, and with the package held behind him, and the others after him, already laughing, he looked around for the right victim. But this time the young gents were expected, there at the Cerchi. All the pimps, in those four or five evenings, had come and taken up their positions too, in the field instead of waiting in the square above, pretending to mingle with the customers who came and went. There was also Giovanni

Patacchiola, the crook, who was really the moral leader, since it was Granny who had got the worst of it. So when the four smartass kids from Parrocchietta arrived there in the midst of the field and approached one of the whores, she immediately went wild, waving her purse on high and yelling curses. The four were a bit confused by that welcome, caught off guard. Buretta stood there with the package of shit in his hand, looking at her, his eyes shining in his nut's face. At that moment, from the shadows below the embankment, the pimps came forward in a row, followed by Granny and the other women, all screeching like hens.

Patacchiola went straight up to Buretta, who dropped the package: it fell open spattering its contents between the feet of the two adversaries. There was no need for explanations: but Buretta wasn't the type to let things slide, so they promptly began to hammer each other. First just the two of them, then all the others: a massacre. The little northern kid had a broken jaw, spitting teeth and blood; the other two, the redhead brothers, tried to slip off and came out of it better, with swollen eyes and their ribs kicked in. Buretta wasn't tender: at one of Patacchiola's punches he fell full length in the mud. But he pretended he was throwing up: and as soon as Patacchiola turned to go and slaughter the others, Buretta sprang to his feet again, holding a little knife he had opened in the meanwhile; he stabbed Patacchiola four or five times in the back, and now it was the crook who fell down, yelling his guts out.

While Patacchiola was in the hospital and then in stir, Granny thought of killing two birds with one stone: namely, getting free of him, and at the same time getting free of her son, Shitter.

The night of the knifing at the Via dei Cerchi, when the crook fell and the others ran off, some here, some there, Granny, instead of taking the Number 13 for Monteverde, took the 23, then the trolley-bus, and reached Ponte Milvio.

There, under the New Bridge, between the Tiber and Villa Glori, two shanty villages were located, one larger and one smaller, looking like Alice's Wonderland, with these little huts, some round and some pointed, one made out of an old wagon, one from a car,

one blue, one-green, all scattered amid the rubble and the piles of
garbage. In one of these shacks lived an old girl-friend of Granny's,
who had been in the same orphanage with her when they were kids.
For a long time this friend had been saying: 'Come and stay with
me? Why not? You think you're better off the way you are?': so
Granny seized the opportunity and went to live with this friend.
When she was settled there, she began working that area secretly:
Via Flaminia, Ponte Milvio, Acqua Acetosa ...

A week went by, a month, and the day came when the crook
showed up again. He had slowly, calmly made the necessary
investigations, he had questioned one by one the guys around, and
had made an agreement with a pimp who had done well and who
covered all Rome in his own car. So the moment came, one evening,
when he turned up at the shack of Granny's friend: the old woman,
was out beating the streets at that hour. But he sat down under the
shed between a couple of flower pots, smoking in the dark. At
the first light of dawn, Granny, her feet killing her, came limping
to the hut: she was so worn out she didn't even see him at the door:
or maybe she was blinded by the sun, just rising, fresh and sparkling
beyond the shacks and the trees. He stood up, pulled out his knife,
and with a sudden, animal yell, he stuck it ten or twelve times
into her belly.

And so Shitter lost all hope. He had never been a thief, not really,
not a professional: they always took him along at Pietralata, but as
a lookout, as an old expert; on little jobs that brought in next to
nothing, and there were too many dogs quarrelling over the bone
every time!

Besides Shitter was sick: he had always been sick, more or less,
but now he really spent the whole day on the can. And, along with
his bellyache, he had another disease, whose name he never learned
right, that made him all swell up, as if he had a leaking gas pipe
under his skin. His neck would swell up, or maybe his lip, or then
one eyelid: he had lost almost all his hair over his forehead, and the
little curls he had left were all on his neck. After his mother had
gone into hiding and had stopped his wages, the days when he
didn't eat outnumbered those when he did. At noon he managed

to get a bowl of soup from the monks. In the evening, he tried
here and there. When he had some cash, at times even twenty or
thirty thousand, he spent it all in one night on some whore.

One day Shitter vanished, nobody saw him around next day,
the third day he was still missing. On the fourth day some friends
of his had a little job to do, an easy place, a cloth shop in Prati, and
they started hunting for him. They went into the shack in Via
delle Messi d'oro where he lived, and they found themselves with
their noses against his feet. He had hanged himself from the ceiling,
and how that rotten beam had held up for three days with the
weight of that body, nobody could figure out.

Yawning, Zucabbo tied his clothes with his belt and threw them
in the pile, going straight off with a loud whistle towards the diving
plank. Tommaso didn't go in swimming: while Zucabbo swam, he
sat there, crouched on the sand with his back against the steep bank
full of dried roots, a bit in the shadow.

All around there were dried reeds. The stems of the flowers were
dry too, more than a yard high, piled together like a planted field,
on the other side towards the water: black, rusty, they shredded if
you touched them, like ash or like burnt paper.

In the midst of these canes, very thick, there were some other
plants, like a second crop inside the first: they were those white
flowers that come apart when you blow on them, big as fists, on
rotting stems. They had only the skeleton left, because all the white
stuff had fallen on the ground, on the sandy grass and on the turds.
But, apparently, on some bank in the area a pile of straw had caught
fire, a meadow's edge, a tree, and had become a cloud of black dust:
the air, the wind had scattered that dust around and had dirtied
everything: if you put your hand down somewhere, it was black
when you raised it again.

That dust covered everything: the clump of dried flowers, the
white stuff that had fallen on them, the weeds, the kind of grasses
you see everywhere in the summer, that crawl like snakes, dry and
stinking, over the piles of rubbish, with tins, empty medicine jars,
broken plates, turds, everything submerged in that rank brush,

under the baking sun, also black: by now, if you called for September, it was close enough to answer.

Waiting till it was time to go back to party headquarters, Tommaso tried to sleep a little, but he couldn't with that sun cooking his brains. And the hours seemed never to pass. His heart beat louder every time he thought about presenting himself at the Pietralata section to the comrades: it seemed impossible that they wouldn't welcome him with open arms, a brother.

He hadn't even taken off his shoes, which had filled with sand and filth. All around him the others were bathing in the oily black water, with the little strings of slime that swam along on the current.

They yelled like nuts, arguing, the smaller ones at the bend in the distance; closer, under two or three twisted canes there were the bigger guys, like Zucabbo. Then they started playing cards, crouching under the slope among the piles of clothes tied with their belts.

Tommaso started playing, too, with Zucabbo, Brooklyn, and Dope, two half-silly kids who could hardly stand on their feet and who spat when they talked, barely getting the words out, with drooling mouths and shining eyes. They played a few hands of *zecchinetta* until the sun began to go down.

Then a faggot turned up on the other bank and began to watch: the little kids knew him, and, Zucabbo with them, they dived into the water and went to the other side, to steal some cash from him.

It was still early when Tommaso got back to the party offices. But he waited there. Persichini wasn't there any more, but the place was open, and in fact, you could hear voices in the bar-room, beyond the broken door. Tommaso went in, sat down on a little chair, alone with the red flag, and began to leaf through some newspapers piled up in the dust on the floor.

But he didn't feel like reading, because those voices nearby distracted him: he couldn't make them out clearly because a man in the next little house raised pigs, and the animals kept grunting, mingling with the sound of voices.

Then Tommaso stood up and went to sit by the door, to listen.

He began to pick up a bit. One voice, rough like the voice of an old man who has had something to drink, was saying: 'No, things ain't what they used to be! Eh, in my time, in the days of Ponte, there was life around! When I was twenty, you couldn't hold me down, not with chains!' He said: 'Aaah!' as if he had sucked a drop of wine from the glass, and went on: 'All you had to be was twenty then, to know the world; now you guys won't know what it's all about when you're sixty! Look at the knife-marks I've got on me. Look!'

But a younger-sounding voice cut him short and said: 'Listen to the voice from the grave! Let's get down to business!'

The man who had been speaking before was quiet for a while: judging from the voice, Tommaso thought he must be a certain Di Nicola, an old man, maybe fifty, whom Tommaso had known ever since he was a little kid. 'Aòh, boys,' this Di Nicola said finally in a very low voice, 'get this straight: whatever I do, I'm doing for all of you ... because you're outta work and five thousand in your pockets comes in handy! But I wouldn't want a stink to be raised, and my name to come out later! Eh, that's for sure! Not that!'

A grave-like voice answered, Cazzimperio's, who had two teeth in his mouth like an old man maybe a hundred years old: 'How can they catch on? Are you kidding? And besides, even if they found out, one of us would take the blame. You think we'd pay up, all four of us? Eeeh!'

'So who would take the blame?'

The guy talking like a broken gramophone, with a voice so deep it was deafening, was Delli Fiorelli.

Cazzimperio answered at once, angrily: 'The guy who's got the least to lose. That's obvious, isn't it? We can't send him in ... ' He was no doubt pointing to Di Nicola. ' ... or me. One of you two! If worst comes to worst, whaddya lose? You won't be able to come back here again ... whaddya care about that? These guys have to keep their mouths shut, because they can't make a scandal inside the party!'

'Aòh, whaddya say?' said Delli Fiorelli, 'It's good while it lasts! Come on,' he added, impatiently, 'how much came out, for us, last night?'

'A hundred tickets: twenty thousand,' the voice of the fourth guy said, a voice Tommaso didn't recognize. 'That's the amount, and you know it! We can't take more than that!'

He must be the one who takes the tickets at the dance, Tommaso thought.

They were quiet in the next room: they were dividing up the stolen money, and each of them was silent, looking at his share, the packet of tattered hundred-lire notes.

Whadda they doing? Tommaso thought. The tickets? What tickets? They're cheating on the tickets to the dance! Yeah, that's it, all right, the tickets of the raffle ... Delli Fiorelli turns them back in, instead of throwing them away ... The bastards, they're picking up five thousand apiece!

In the other room all was silence now: it was taking some time to count out the money. You could hear the pigs grunting beyond the wall in the other house and the kids yelling, playing outside in that boiling air.

Di Nicola started talking again: 'Boys,' he said, 'here we've got five thousand apiece per week, that makes twenty thousand at the end of every month. With twenty thousand, you can get by ... I can pay my rent! And besides we can pick up something else too, if we can muscle in on the wine ... '

'How many litres of wine do you sell in here a day?' the ticket-taker asked Cazzimperio sharply.

'A hundred. Two barrels,' Cazzimperio said in a dissatisfied, low voice, 'more or less ... ' 'I don't see any way to make off it!' he added, grumbling painfully, full of tender dejection.

'Whaddya mean?' Delli Fiorelli snapped at him. 'You just took your five thousand, didn't you? Because he and I risk getting in the shit, but you don't want to run any risk yourself! I don't like your attitude, not at all! You gotta work too, if you want the money. Eh!'

Di Nicola intervened, to convince Cazzimperio calmly: 'Why not? If we can tuck away another five thousand a month, what's wrong with that? We could pay forty lire a litre to the hicks, the way the party does ... That's my job! All you have to do is sell it

in here! When you've added a thousand litres of our wine, to the
three thousand a month, you know how much that is?'

'Listen to the bastards,' Tommaso thought, 'they'd sell Christ
off the cross around here!'

Then Persichini came back in, all bustling, his face grim, his
pale eyes serious, a good tooth shining in his half-open mouth as
he glanced around.

He saw Tommaso, and setting promptly to work, without
looking him in the face again, he said: 'Help me fix the benches for
the meeting!'

Overlooking that brusque tone because he knew it was the right
one for these situations, Tommaso got busy too. He began to carry
into the hall the benches that were piled on top of one another in the
office and in the barroom. They arranged the benches in rows facing
the desk, and a little later, people started to arrive.

They stood outside in the yard, in a patch of shadow, and waited,
sweating.

After a while, a larger group of people came, along with the
leaders, all from Pietralata. The meeting was being held to discuss
the circulation of the newspaper and to prepare the Celebration
of *Unità* in the area: so there were both young and old. There was
also the press and propaganda man from the Federation: he came
straight inside, and all the others came after him slowly, wiping the
sweat: they huddled in the hall, still standing up; and little by little
there was a stink of dusty, sweaty clothes that took your breath away.

'Is that the guy I should report to?' Tommaso asked Persichini,
pointing to a man who could have been the secretary, since all the
others followed him. He was a certain Passalacqua, and Tommaso
had known him for years.

'Can't you see him?' Persichini said.

'Can I present myself?' Tommaso asked, a bit shy.

'You want me to shove you?' the other guy said, dumb as ever,
with other things on his mind. Tommaso started to go over to this
Passalacqua; but at that moment Di Nicola took the man aside,
licking his ass no doubt and telling him God knows what lies: so
Tommaso was screwed.

Then they soon started the discussion, and everybody began to take his place on the benches. Tommaso had to be patient and wait till it was over, standing to one side.

He stood with one shoulder glued to the wall, looking all around as the meeting began and the man from the Federation laid the groundwork for the speeches of the others.

Ah, Tommaso knew Di Nicola, all right, and he knew the fourth guy too, named Di Santo, sitting on the bench next to Cazzimperio. Delli Fiorelli had sat down with the young guys, waiting, thin faced, a pack of greedy bastards, for their turn to come to talk about the celebration and the dance.

I know you, all right! Tommaso was thinking, as he slyly watched Di Nicola, innocent as Samuel, sitting on his bench, his checked shirt over his black guts. You're smart, eh? Tommaso had got to know him, in fact, three or four years earlier, and as it happened, in a matter involving some hicks. This Di Nicola, with a rented truck, still unpaid for, went to Cisterna, where he had bought some watermelon crops, on the vine, and on credit, too. Tommaso and two or three other bums picked up playing football at Monte del Pecoraro cost him next to nothing. They got to Cisterna, and they had to do everything, gather the melons in the field, take them to the truck, load them. Then they raced back to Rome. On the way, through the villages, they threw hunks of melon at the girls, laughing when the rinds plopped on the asphalt. When they reached Rome, they went to the market at Piazza Quadrata, or Piazza Vittorio, wherever it was. They unloaded the melons, passing them from hand to hand, made a pile, and kept watch over it all night, with some whores for company. The next morning early, when the sun rose, they began to sell, shouting their lungs out: 'Aòh! Fire! Call the fire department! Melons! Watermelons!' Di Nicola watched and collected the cash.

Tommaso had met Di Santo in another way. He was even younger, almost in diapers still. He had banged his head and was crying, covered with blood, at a corner of the street. Di Santo passed by there, picked him up and took him to the first aid post, shouting at the others who were standing around to watch, without

moving: 'You wanna see him bleed to death? Come here, kid!'
'Let's take him to the hospital!' said one guy, all happy at the new
notion. 'Hospital, hell! We'll take him to the first aid!' Di Santo
said, twisting his mouth. He took out a handkerchief, put it on
Tommaso's head, pushing him along with one hand on his shoulder
and leaning over every now and then to say to him: 'Does it hurt?
Eh? Does it hurt?'

Yes, yes, Tommaso was thinking, looking at the pals, his hands
in his pockets. They were all old acquaintances in there, with those
faces that invited bullets, in the stink of dirty clothes and smoke.

But more than the other he looked at the secretary of the section,
sitting beside the young man, who went on and on talking.

I know you, too, all right! he thought with an old foxy smile,
sweet and benevolent below his narrowed eyes. He remembered
the scene as if it were now: the fight they had got into! The ruckus
they had made! Like a revolt at the Santa Calla home for the old,
like a bunch of old drunks. It was an evening like this one, hot, in
August, bright as day. The moon was on fire, purple, and it coloured
everything purple: the dust, the garbage, the shacks. People were
going around half naked in the open. Along the slums, along the
old fields, the world looked like a gypsy camp. Windows and doors,
everything was flung open, with all the rags on display. People
were laughing, crying; in one shack they were boozing up, in
another somebody was about to kick off and on all sides bunches
of young guys were wandering around, singing, undershirts
flapping over their pants.

The old people were outside the taverns under the arbours,
inside the cane fences; and among them was Passalacqua.

He and another guy, an old peasant, had started arguing about
their animals: each of them drove a horse, and each was saying that
his animal could pull a cart faster up the slope of a lot where they
were working. One remark led to another, and little by little, they
got hotter, full of wine as they were, half blind, and they began to
fight.

They started inside the tavern, with all the other old men, drunk
themselves, trying to separate them. They seemed to want to stop,

but instead they went outside, and with the whole bunch after
them, all white-haired or bald, they began again outside the door,
under the little light bulb, dazzled by the moon.

Drunk as they were, they hit each other in jerks, in sudden furies,
wham, a punch on the stomach, bang, a kick in the groin.

Hitting each other and yelling, they shifted here and there, the
crowd after them, trying to break them apart, telling them to cut it
out.

They moved over to some slopes in the countryside above the
Aniene, then back again towards the tavern.

More people had gathered, young guys, kids, and they were
watching, running here and there as the fight shifted, like a handful
of dried leaves blown by the wind, or a flight of sparrows. Tommaso
was there, too, half naked also and black as Sambo.

Now it seemed that the two of them were fed up, and they stood
a bit apart, each among his closest friends, faces red as blood,
teeth bared beneath their grey growths of beard. All of a sudden
Passalacqua gave a leap, ran like a wild man towards the tavern:
there was a fence around it of half-rotten planks. He grabbed one,
tugged at it, and pulled it loose: he began to swing it wildly, and
they all ran off, some this way, some that. The other horse-driver,
too, with his tail between his legs, seemed to be clearing out,
stealthily. Instead he ran inside the tavern and promptly emerged
with a chair in his hands, striking out with it, crazy as the other.
As those blows rained, first one ran off, then the other, with all the
onlookers after them: there was a procession running grrrr in one
direction then grrrr in the other, partly trying to stop them, and
partly hoping to witness the moment when somebody's head was
broken.

Suddenly, as he was running up and down, Tommaso saw a
little pile of clothes on the ground: Passalacqua's jacket and cap. He
bent down, looked around, grabbed them, and raced off.

Somebody who knew him, however, had seen him from a doorway. And when the fighters had made peace, the person told
Passalacqua, who was looking for his things: 'Torquato's kid took
them!' Passalacqua and the other man came to Tommasino's, to the

shack. Tommasino was inside, his mother out in the little yard. 'Is
your kid home?' Passalacqua asked, with one eye like an eggplant.
'He's got my jacket and hat!'

Hearing the voices, Tommasino caught on at once and came out
with the things in his hand. 'I saw them there on the ground,' he
said, all innocent, a good little boy, 'and I knew they were yours.
Then I saw all that fighting, and I got scared, so I brought them
here!'

'You did right, you did right!' Passalacqua said and even gave
him five hundred lire, then wanted him to come and drink with
them at all costs: 'Scared?' he said, 'We were just joking! Come
on, have a drop, too. Wine drives your worries away!'

Now he was there, acting busy, next to the young man from the
Federation, who was keeping quiet and listening to the others talk.
The moment had come to discuss the celebration, the dance: and
it was the young guy's turn. One said one thing, one another, all
the usual crap. But the young man listened to them with respect
all the same, interested. He sat with his elbows resting on the little
desk, paying attention, his eyes very pale, so blue they were almost
white. He must have been pretty well built, you could see he had a
good pair of shoulders on him, but he was shy: when he talked, he
hesitated, and even when he said something funny, now that they
were discussing the dance, he had a kind of sad light in his eyes,
worried, like a kid.

Hey, you shithead, drink it all in! Tommaso was thinking to
himself, watching him. You think these bastards are gonna pay any
attention to you? Anyway, why should you give a shit? All they have
to do is applaud you at the end, for the use you can make of them!

A pal of Delli Fiorelli had begun to make a little speech on the
subject of the dance: hearing him, Tommaso felt happy. Listen to
the bastard, he thought, What a waste of breath? What hick town
does he come from? What was he? A shepherd? Swell! Now he's
gonna tell us about the national situation!

He's talking about the dance! he thought, almost laughing out
loud. He must of led the fun at the village, with the tarantellas and
the wooden pipes! Go spit in the air and stand under it!

The speech was answered shyly, a bit sadly, but with determination, and in book-language, by the man from the Federation. Go ahead and talk! Tommaso thought, here they'll finish you off like Cicero! He thinks they're not smart around here! He collected himself a bit, concentrating and putting on a nasty face. Now when you've finished wasting your breath, I'd almost tell you how matters stand. I could spill a few things that'd bring tears to your eyes!

He took a sidelong glance at Delli Fiorelli. Hey, crook! he thought, if I feel like it, in five minutes, unless you're deaf, you'll hear the explosion I'm gonna set off. Now watch out!

I've got you all in my hand, the whole bunch! he thought again, clenching his fist hard inside his pocket, and casting a sticky look around, a hint of menace in his gaiety.

He was sweating enough to melt: the sun was still bright, a flame, on the horizon of the wretched clump of Pietralata. The comrades went on arguing for a good while before they gave up, discussing this and that in the stinking room.

Finally the meeting ended: it was high time, but they still stayed and yelled a bit, especially the ones standing around Passalacqua. Tommaso went there, stuck to him, waiting for the right moment. As the man was already going towards the exit, Tommaso ran after him, took him by the elbow, thinking: Running off, eh? You're worse than Fanfani, are you? and said to him in a loud voice, blocking his way: 'Excuse me, aaa ... Got a minute?'

Passalacqua looked at him, helpful, with his face like an old shoe, an old sonovabitch it was soothing just to look at.

'Well?' he said.

Tommaso took him off to one side, in a quieter corner of the little yard.

'Listen,' he began, 'I been meaning to come and say this to you for a long time ... But I never had the chance, I just got out of the hospital, and you know how it is, when you get outta place like that, you gotta take it easy ... Well, this is how it is ... I've always had my ideas!' He broke off and looked hard at him, his palms open before him, and his eye scandalized, sacred. 'You mustn't think anything else ... ' he went on. 'I'm a poor kid, working class, too ... And I don't know if you've heard anything, but you can find out easily enough, how I worked down at the Forlanini ... I was all over the place, pinning up the proclamation, helping Guglielmi ... You know Guglielmi, the secretary of the section in the hospital? ... I did everything I could! So this oughtta be enough to show you how I think ... '

He drew breath for a moment, having finished the first part of his speech: the other man looked at him, agreeing, his chin against his neck, waiting to see what Tommaso was getting at.

'But there's one thing,' Tommaso resumed at once, 'I've never signed up with the party, just because it didn't seem so important ... I thought: so long as you think that way ... and that's how it was!'

He clapped his hands two or three times, palms open, as if he had closed a deal and sealed it.

'But now,' he went on, 'I see that's not right. I want a party card in my pocket, like all the rest of you. If there was to be any real fighting again, everybody's got to be in on it, and if things are bad for you, they're bad for me, too; so I want to be in along with the rest!'

He had begun this last part with his eyes bitter, and he ended it, deepening his voice, since he was expressing his right, logical, legal, and that was how it had to be.

Struck by these arguments, the man stood there silent, his big face grey, as if he were chewing something hard, looking at Tommaso with a clinical eye.

'So tell me,' Tommaso concluded, 'what I gotta do, who do I report to, to sign up?'

Passalacqua was quiet for a little while, looking at him, then he said: 'Well, it's the simplest thing in the world. Don't you know two members of the party, who can vouch for you? Come with these two people, get them to present you, and in five minutes you're all fixed up: just have to stick a stamp on the card!'

He looked at him again, friendly, and slapped him on the shoulder, saying: 'I'm glad about this!'

And so it was: a few days later, Tommaso turned up at the section, with the two people who had to be his witnesses, Delli Fiorelli himself and Hawk; he was signed up, paid what he had to pay, and finally he was able to have his slice of the pie: he put the card in his pocket, ready to struggle for the red flag, too.

5

The Eternal Hunger

It didn't take long to figure out: of the four thousand lire the boss gave Tommaso at the last moment of the last hour of Saturday evening just before he stopped work, two thousand went for the suit he was paying for in instalments; of the other two thousand you had to subtract tram fares for the whole week: the 209 was ten lire in the morning, and twenty in the evening, making one hundred and eighty lire a week; the same for the Number 8, because Tommaso got off at the end of the first lap and went the rest of the way on foot: one hundred and eighty plus one hundred and eighty makes three hundred and sixty. Ten Nazionali a day was the least he could smoke, and that made another six hundred lire. Five hundred he kept in his pocket for himself: the other five hundred he gave them at home, because his parents had agreed that for this month they'd be content with that. Before he bought the suit, he managed to save five hundred to spend on the Sunday. But now? With Irene he couldn't just stroll up and down the pavements of the Garbatella all day, or in the fields, from two in the afternoon till eight at night. It was Saturday, and he had to get some cash for the next day at all costs, a five-hundred note at the very least. In his pocket, saved on the cigarettes, he still had thirty lire; plus the forty he had set aside for the tram, that made seventy. The four thousand he had just collected couldn't be touched: he had stuck it in the inside pocket of his jacket, as if that money didn't even exist.

Tommaso got off work late, like every Saturday: he set off, on foot, from Via della Giuliana, where he had found a job with a fruit-seller, because he naturally couldn't go to the Central Market any more. Heading for his goal, he took Via Giulio Cesare, already growing dark: it was September. Then he started walking faster. At the end of Via Giulio Cesare he turned towards Piazza Cavour, passed Castel Sant'Angelo, and reached Borgo Panìco: he crossed Corso Vittorio and was in Campo dei Fiori.

Via dei Chiavari was near there, with its uneven cobbles and its rows of façades, like a maze.

Halfway along the street there were some greenish neon lights over a white doorway: the Cinema Vittorio, a fleabag where they had double features. In front of the posters there were some kids, their hands in their pockets, looking around, waiting for a chance to sneak inside.

Tommaso came along in a hurry, serious-looking, not even glancing at those others waiting outside empty-handed. He quickly bought a ticket, giving the girl at the box office everything he had in his pocket, then went in.

To begin with, he had to try to avoid the usher. So he slowly lifted the big, black-velvet curtain and slid in along the wall, leaning one shoulder against it and pretending he had been there all along, his eyes glued to the screen. *The Road to Bali* was playing, and you could see some Hawaiian girls with wreaths of flowers around their necks, twirling around Bob Hope: and Bob, looking at them, made a silly grimace to show he was enjoying it, rolling his eyes like he was going to throw up.

Since the usher wasn't around, Tommaso moved wearily from the wall, giving it a sharp push with his shoulder; he half-stretched, so he could look the place over. The hall was tiny, with a low wooden partition that separated the cheap seats up front from the more expensive ones, three or four rows at the back.

In the front rows, as usual, there were the kids from Campo dei Fiori or the little jewboys from Via Arenula or the Portico d'Ottavia, with some sloppy old women eating lupins or peanuts. Behind, after the aisle, was seated most of the audience: more women, but without kids, some bums, and a swarm of young guys. In the spaces against the walls, there were also some people standing up: young guys, kids, and a few older characters. Tommaso crossed the hall to the other side and fitted himself into the space between the seats and the wall, where those people were standing. He got in the middle, again leaning, with the other shoulder against the wall, rubbed and polished by all those who had leaned there before him.

Half stretching once more, frowning because he considered himself a serious boy now, and not a kid like these ragged characters in jerseys, sprawled all around, he cast another, exploratory glance.

He took in the situation, moved away from the wall and went up the aisle towards the railing that separated the two categories of seats. In the last rows there was an empty place: grim, Tommaso went and sat there: next to him was a character who, even seen at a distance and in the dark, looked pretty suspicious. Tommaso sat in the empty seat, his knees pushed against the back of the seat in front of him, and he relaxed. At that moment, like a whiplash, the lights came on.

Tommaso immediately sat up more properly, acting indifferent and looking around almost angrily, barely turning his neck inside the collar of his shirt, which looked like it had been rubbed with a clove of garlic dipped in coal: it was Saturday, and therefore he had been wearing that shirt a week with that chewed-up little purple tie.

Under the bright light, the room looked like a stone when it's been lifted up and you find it was covering a pile of worms: one coiled around the other, moving and crawling all around, twisting their heads and their tails, half-crazed, struck by the light like that.

The last two rows of the cheap seats were all full of kids, with some grey-haired old men here and there, still as stones in the midst of a muddy stream. The kids were between twelve and twenty, and they were sprawled out, some with their knees against the back of the seat in front of them, some even with their feet over it, if it was empty, and some with their legs over the legs of the friend beside them.

They pushed and shoved one another, or else, reaching behind the back of the friend beside them, they slapped the head of the kid farther on, promptly acting indifferent and chewing peanuts, their eyes laughing. Their pants were all wrinkled, covered with an inch or two of dirt and grease, worn and shiny in front, so you could even see a little white strip of undershorts. The men in their midst were serious, almost offended, making themselves as small as possible between the arms of the seats.

Along the walls there was a lot of going and coming: a boy stood up with a sudden jerk, and chewing and grinning, as if he planned to do God knows what, he slank off towards the can. Two or three little kids went there together, laughing and talking in loud voices: an older man headed there very slowly, bent over, blowing his nose. The velvet curtains at the doors were constantly being raised and lowered.

The little queen next to Tommaso was smoking, his elbow on the arm of the seat, his hand high and limp, the cigarette between two fingers. Tommaso looked at him, and the faggot also turned his eyes on Tommaso.

The lights went down again. Immediately Tommaso widened his legs, moving his left leg closer to his neighbour's: he sat there, waiting. He remained still, like a cat watching a dog, on the rickety seat. On his face the brown bumps were mixed up with the red that covered the whole surface like a plate. The little round face with the pointed nose and the mouth fleshy but almost without lips emerged from the shirt-collar like an ear of corn from a package: behind, the hair was already a bit long, and hung over his collar: on top, the hair stood up around his pate, like a little kid's. The thin queen didn't say anything. He went on looking around, glancing everywhere with a kind of nervous tic. Tommaso widened his legs still farther, sliding his behind along the seat.

Meanwhile the worm-mass had resumed its calm and silent life in the dark. Every now and then you could hear some laughter, voices fighting over a cigarette, or the cracks of those who had already seen the picture twice and were fed up.

The fag wasn't moving yet. Tommaso watched him, angrily. Whaddya waiting for, shithead? he thought to himself. He changed his position, slamming his back against the seat, almost breaking it, and giving another blow with his knee, almost breaking the back of the seat in front of him.

The character went on looking around, and every now and then, as he looked, he also glanced at Tommaso beside him.

Fuck you! Tommaso was thinking, more and more enraged. Here! And he huffed impatiently, still wriggling. The queen, at all that movement, had begun to look down. And so they went on for about ten minutes. Tommaso had stretched his legs wide and had slid his ass so far down on the seat that a little farther and he would have fallen to the floor, which was covered with spit, peanut shells and maybe some piss, too, for good measure. Meanwhile, Tommaso had caught on where his neighbour was aiming, when he kept pretending to glance all around. He was really looking at a young man who had taken off his jacket, two or three rows ahead of them: you could see only the back of his head, shaved like a soldier's, and his shoulders in a nice cowboy shirt, blue and grey. That was why Tommaso got madder than ever. Go screw yasself … ! he said under his breath, what's that guy got better than me? You think I'm no good, you lousy punk?

Adjusting himself angrily in his seat, every now and then he nudged his neighbour who kept looking at the boy ahead of them but was also lowering his eyes more often on Tommaso. He nudged him hard, like you hit a closed door, so rickety you think it will open at the first push and instead it holds, so you get madder and madder, slamming your shoulder against it. So whadda we gonna do? Tommaso was thinking, almost aloud. The character beside him must have said to himself, finally: Well, let's get rid of him! And, all of a sudden, he stretched out his hand.

When, in no time, he had finished, Tommasino, content, buttoned up again, without haste.

Then he raised his head and looked towards the character at his side.

The other kid paid no attention: now he was seized by a great interest in the movie. Tommaso watched him for a few minutes, his forehead wrinkled, his eyes dazed, and his mouth drawn in a grimace that, all peaceably, meant to say: 'You really like this picture, eh?'

Then, abruptly, he gave him a nudge.

The queen stirred, looked at him as if he had forgotten all about him, and sat still for a moment. Then, just as Tommasino was raising his hand to rub thumb and index finger together, as if he had a little ball of snot between them, the queen said: 'Oh, yes, sorry, eh?' He spoke hastily and politely.

Tommaso then became good-natured: 'Sort of forgot, didn't you?'

'Yeah,' the queen said, with a little shake of his head, wriggling all over, as he rummaged in one of his pants pockets. He pulled out a hundred lire.

Without taking it, Tommaso looked at it, stretching his neck to see it more closely. He wanted to make sure it was a hundred and not, by chance, a five. It was a single, all right, no doubt about that. Slowly he sat back in his seat. Then he said calmly: 'How about giving me another hundred?'

The queen was still holding the first hundred in midair: 'Go on, take it!' he said, disgusted, almost whining.

Tommasino didn't even consider this attempt: 'You think I'm begging?' he said, still calm.

'Jeezus!' the queen said in a drawling voice, with the face little girls make when somebody is nasty to them, 'isn't that enough for you?' 'Whaddya made of? Gold?' he added, like he was ready to throw up.

Tommasino went tchk tchk with his tongue against his palate, sharply. His eyebrows rose still farther among the wrinkles of his forehead.

'Out with the cash!' he said.

The queen looked at him. Tommasino had already turned grim. He couldn't talk loud or else the others around them would understand. But no doubt Tommasino would have said those words in the same low voice and all in one breath like that, even if the two of them had been at the edge of a chasm. The queen dug in his toes. He dug them in literally, against the peeling legs of the chair ahead, and settled in his own, moving his whole body again, this time with an insulted manner and with great determination.

'The cash!' Tommaso repeated.

'Didn't I give it to you? Here take it!' the queen said, nervously holding out the hundred lire again.

Now Tommasino didn't say anything. He just sat more erect in his seat, supporting himself on the creaking chair-arms with his elbows.

The faggot took advantage of that silence to add his reasons. 'You coulda told me before!' he said, 'You got a tongue! I'm not giving you more than this hundred, I tell you! I just can't! You can ask anybody about me, about Idoletto, ask, and tell me if you can find one, just one, who won't say, Idoletto's a real friend! But I like to get things clear beforehand. Yes or no, and that's that. Aòh, whaddya want? I'm so fascinating, I can have all the boys I want!'

He settled himself in his seat, satisfied with this last tirade and still all vibrant with indignation, cocky. Tommasino moved closer again, shoulder to shoulder, and without expression, almost without voice, he repeated for the third time: 'Dig out the cash!'

He was in no mood for joking any more, or for waiting either: he was ready for anything. The queen began to look at him, a bit scared, white-faced, his heart pounding. He sat there quiet, not moving. Tommasino reached out his hand. 'Give me that hundred,' he said. Quickly, the faggot gave it to him, relaxing in his seat then, assuming the manner of a person who has done his duty, and has nothing more to do. At that moment the usher came over that way, showing a fat guy with a woman to their seats, flashing his weak flashlight. He seated them just behind Tommasino and the fag. Tommasino was silent again: and after a while, the queen glancing here and there, started to get up.

Tommasino grabbed him by the arm and forced him to sit down again.

'Where you going?' he asked, calmly.

'Whadda you care? Am I supposed to stay here all night?' the queen asked uncertainly.

'Nooo!' Tommaso said.

'Whadda you want then?'

'Money,' Tommaso said, baring his little yellow teeth, with a bit of saliva round them.

'Jeezus!' the fag said, 'didn't I give you a hundred?'

Tommaso smiled. 'Whaddam I gonna do with a hundred?' he said. The fag sighed. 'Chrissake,' he said, almost crying: he angrily put his hand in his pocket and dug out another hundred, all rumpled, crushed almost into a ball. He held it out to Tommasino. As before, Tommasino took it calmly, and calmly smoothed it out; he observed it carefully to see that it was really a hundred note and, pacified, he folded it and put it in his pocket to keep the first hundred company.

After a little while, the queen started to get up silently and go off again, saying only: 'Ciao, kid, be seeing you.'

But Tommasino, calm as ever, pulled him down casually, like he was brushing off a fly, one hand on the fag's shoulder: 'Eh, what's your hurry?' he said, 'stay a little longer, no?'

'I'm sorry, but I've seen the picture, and I gotta go now ... ' the queen said, in a shaky voice.

'Aòh, knock it off!' the fat guy said, sitting with the woman just behind them. The two of them froze at once, like those animals that pretend to be dead. They watched a bit of the picture, erect and well-behaved. Then, slowly, Tommasino gave a glance behind them, over his shoulder. The fat guy was a dope, all sweating, with a clump of hair on his head, white as a pillow, and if any slaps were handed out, he would get them. Now, determined to finish the whole business, Tommasino twisted towards the fag, his eyes venomous, his mouth taut.

'Come on,' he said, 'you think you're gonna get off that easy?'

'Whaddya want?' the fag asked again, stalling for time, frightened also on account of that dope behind them with the woman: they might start acting up. 'I've given you two hundred now: I think that's enough. Whoever heard of more than that, here at the Vittorio?'

'Listen,' Tommasino said, 'don't make me lose my temper, eh?'

The fag saw Tommasino really was about to lose his temper: he moved closer, to be able to speak to him better, and he played his last card. 'Say, kid,' he said, 'be reasonable ... You think I wouldn't give you the money, if I had it? I don't have another lira, I really

don't ... You gotta believe me ... You think I'm rich or something?
... I'm worse off than you ... I've been out of a job for more than a
year, living off my mother, and ... Come on, be human ... I swear
next time, if I have a hundred, or even two, I'll give it to you ... for
nothing ... We'll go eat a pizza together ... '

'All this talk is doing you no good,' Tommaso growled. 'Gimme
the cash, or it'll be your ass.'

The fag was now trembling with fear. His face had turned grey.
He put one hand in his pocket and dug out another hundred,
almost crying, but before giving it to Tommaso, he said: 'Here,
look.' Tommaso lowered his eyes. The queen turned his pockets
inside out, showing the dirty lining. 'That's the last I've got,' he
said, 'now I don't even have my tram fare, I'll have to walk home.'
Tommasino took the third hundred and stuck it in his pocket with
the others.

Another two or three minutes went by. Then the fag tried to
make friends a bit, why not? 'You think it's nice?' he said pathetic-
ally, 'What you've done? Take a poor guy's money, when he
doesn't even have enough to eat?'

'Eeeh,' Tommaso said, 'What a tear-jerker! You're all alike,
always whining. You always say you don't have a lira, and instead,
you keep your money hidden somewhere ... '

At these last words, an expression of still greater fear passed over
the faggot's face. He had been reassured till then, after he had been
worked over. But he play-acted a bit, pretending he hadn't heard;
he stretched slightly, then rested one hand against his cheek with
his fingertips raised, and looking sideways like movie actresses do
when they're acting coy, he tried to pass it all off as a joke. 'Ah, you
sonovabitch!' he said, 'you really screwed me. But it serves me
right! I'm a crazy queen! As if I didn't know enough to discuss
things beforehand!'

'What things!' Tommaso growled back, 'Discuss! You gotta
come out with the cash!'

'Well now, my dear,' the queen said, still trying to joke a little,
'you won't find a lira, if you turn me upside down and shake me.
You can't get blood from a stone!'

Tommaso looked at him, silent. He smiled a little, acting cordial.
'Out with the cash you've got hidden,' he said, as if it were a bet
they were making, just for the hell of it.

'What cash?' the faggot said, trembling. Tommaso continued to
grin, illuminated from within by a thought that made him choke
with slyness, his dry little eyes bright with gaiety. Then, after
laughing a last time a bit louder, always with this same good
humour, he put his hand in a pocket inside his jacket. He toyed
there a bit, unbuttoning it with the other hand. When it was
unbuttoned, he flapped it two or three times against his chest,
pulling the lapels up with the tips of his fingers, as if he were hot
and wanted to fan himself. The fag looked at him without saying
anything.

'Come on, out with the cash,' Tommaso repeated, still slapping
the hem of his jacket, a bit harder, so as to show the inside part,
over his chest covered with the grey shirt. But the fag went on
being silent, frightened, looking straight ahead. Tommaso then
plunged his hand into the jacket pocket, rummaged a bit in the
torn lining, and brought out a closed clasp-knife in his clenched
fist: he held it, still in his fist, between his thighs just below his belly,
raising his right leg to make a shadow.

The queen looked at him out of the corner of his eye: Tommaso
snapped out the blade, then sheathed it again: he did this two or
three times, as if amusing himself.

'Bring out the money, come on!' he repeated, not laughing any
more, twisting his mouth. The queen was stammering: 'Whaddya
doing? You gone crazy? What is all this?'

Tommaso snapped the blade again, giving the fag a nudge that
almost knocked him out of his seat. But the queen was already
bending over, all trembling, and was beginning to untie one shoe:
but he couldn't manage to do it, because the knot was tight or
because his hands wouldn't obey him. Finally he pulled the shoe
off his foot without untying it and emptied it in such a way that
Tommaso could see it clearly: he had two hundred lire there.

'Jeezus, what a stink!' a boy said, sitting just in front of them.
Tommasino hid the knife between his thighs. In fact, the boy turned

towards the fag: 'Hey, don't you ever wash your feet? Goddammit, you wanna kill us all?' 'Hey, Purfina!' another lounger yelled, beside the first, pressing his nostrils between two fingers.

Tommaso took the two hundred and put it in his pocket too. 'The other shoe,' he said then. The queen obeyed him, muttering: 'There's nothing there.' In fact there was nothing in the other shoe. Tommasino put the knife back in his pocket, coughed a little, looked around, then got up and went straight towards the exit.

It was night by now. A September night that had fallen suddenly, because the season was beginning to advance and it got dark earlier: but it was still summer enough for a kind of light to remain in the dark sky, in the sides of the houses, in certain little grey clouds parked over the Janiculum.

Rivers of cars, of carriages, of motorbikes were tied up along Corso Vittorio, spreading out in Largo Argentina, disappearing towards Via Arenula and towards Piazza Venezia. The kids were whistling, excited by this confusion and above all by the thought that in a little while they would be getting off work. In front of the kiosks, in front of the flower-stalls, outside the bars, there were such thick crowds of pedestrians that those who were in a hurry had to run along in the street: those strolling idly were young guys, almost always in groups, still in their summer clothes, with blue jeans and striped or flowered jerseys, and some of them, who lived in the neighbourhood, even in just an undershirt, all white and clean. Every girl who passed was theirs: they flung themselves on one another, all bending towards her together, and they began to say: 'Jeezus, are you stacked! Honest! Golden cunt! A cooze in a thousand! Angel from Paradise! What an ass you got on you, Marì! You take it even into church with you?'

And yet there was something in the air: something mysterious you couldn't understand very well. There was too much confusion, too much racket. Via Nazionale was a snakepit, and at every traffic light the bus was held up for half an hour: so it took a long time to reach the fountain in Piazza Esedra and the station. Farther on, towards Via Morgagni, Piazza Bologna, the confusion lessened a little, though the streets were filled with long streams of cars: and along the wall of Via Morgagni, plastered with plaques with votive candles under them, there was a procession, with lots of women kneeling and yelling to the Madonna, asking her favours.

There were people again, lots of them, at the end of the line, at Verano: a crowd of pedestrians, getting out of the trams that came from the centre of the city, who then stood for fifteen minutes or more, massed in a dark space without a shelter between a kiosk and a fruit-seller's, waiting for the buses to the outlying districts.

All around rose the big walls of the cemetery with lines of little lights trembling, reddish: beyond, like a great valley, there were the Tiburtina station yards, with rows of new buildings to the horizon: massed skyscrapers, now vanishing, swallowed up by the darkness and the smoke.

There in the distance, as far as the eye could reach, you could see at last what it was that made the fine September evening so strange and uneasy: it was a thunderstorm, bottled up in a corner of the sky down there at the last rows of lighted windows, shining faintly, beyond Piazza Bologna on the Via Salaria. Big clouds, farther away, curled, and darker than the moonless sky, were heaped one on top of the other, crammed there, spreading around a clap or two of thunder and an occasional little, weary flash of lightning.

*

Tommaso woke up at seven: partly because it was a habit with him now that he worked, and partly because he was anxious to put on his new suit.

He pushed the covers aside and sat up on the little bed. 'Hey, Ma,' he yelled, with catarrh in his throat, 'Get the water ready. I'm gonna take a bath!' But nobody answered him from the next room. 'Goddammit!' he said in a lower voice, coughing. He went to open the half-broken shutters, then he looked out, dazed. 'Jeezus,' he yelled, at the sky, which was all white, low, icy.

'Jeezuschrist,' he repeated, his face twisted in anger. From the window of his house, which was right under the roof, you could see a wide stretch of the view. Below, the new development ended with Via dei Crispolti, against the even-shaved embankment, cut in the tufa by the steam shovel like slices of cake, and against the church, almost finished by now.

Everything was dark as if it was seven at night instead of seven in the morning. A darkness that was whitish here and there, almost sparkling. The sky was still wringing out a little rain at intervals: and roofs, fields, streets, everything was soaked. Only from the opposite side, which Tommasino couldn't see but could imagine, came a little light, also milky-white. 'Ma!' Tommaso shouted again, 'hey, Ma!' Nothing. He went into the other room, in his shorts and undershirt as he was. The little kitchen was empty, but he could hear women's voices outside. The door of the apartment was open on the landing, and the racket came from beyond there. Tommaso's under-shorts were almost yellow with filth: and his feet were dirty too, all full of stains and black streaks. He stayed in the kitchen and called again: 'Ma!'

His mother peered around the front door and said: 'Whaddya want?'

'Fix the water so I can take a bath!' Tommaso repeated angrily.

'I better go in,' his mother said to the neighbour, 'see you later, Sora Rosa!' ' 'Bye, Sora Maria,' the other woman said, a weary fat ball, who always stank so of fish you could hardly stand it.

'See you later, my ass!' Tommaso said in a half-whisper. His mother came into the kitchen, took the pan and put it under the tap. Tommasino was chilled. 'Goddammit, it's cold. What's happened? Winter come back?' he said, going quickly into the other room to slip on the pants and shirt of the day before. 'Goddamm rain!' he said again, loud, grim, because he didn't want to break in his new suit on a day like this.

'Didn't you hear, last night?' his mother said to him from the kitchen.

'Hear what?' he asked, curtly.

'The storm!' his mother said.

'I was asleep,' Tommaso said, with a shrug.

'My God, didn't you hear the thunder and lightning? Once it struck right near here, at Ponte Mammolo. I thought it was the end

of the world.' She was all proud of the news. 'You mean ... ' she
went on, 'you didn't hear Sora Rosa come into our house, because
she was afraid? She stayed over an hour, with me and your father.
We even fixed coffee!'

'Good idea,' said Tommaso, sticking out his chin. He was busy
putting on the socks that he had been wearing for a couple of weeks.

'I've never seen a thunderstorm like it, not in my whole life,'
his mother went on in the next room.

'Is the water ready?' Tommaso interrupted her.

'You crazy? I just put it on the fire!'

'You wanna make it boiling for me?'

'No, cold! With this change in the weather, you're gonna catch
pneumonia at the very least; and if you catch it this time, it's your
tough luck,' Sora Maria said, with aggressive irony.

'You wanna make me wait an hour here then?'

'What's your hurry?'

'That's my business!' Tommaso said, fiercely. He went into the
kitchen and took a look at the pan filled with icy water. 'Now we
gotta long wait!' he said in a voice that sounded even meaner
because it was hoarse. He went back into the little bedroom,
opened a drawer in the rickety old chest, and took out the new suit.
It was black with little white pinstripes. 'Christ, this is really
something!' Tommaso said, purple with contentment.

At that moment his brother woke up, in the little cot next to
Tommaso's: he also went to sniff the weather without a word,
then immediately slipped on the pants of his good suit. He went
barefoot into the kitchen. 'What time is it, Ma?' he said, in a voice
also thick with catarrh.

'Almost eight,' his mother said; she had begun to shell beans on
the wormeaten kitchen table. It was beginning to grow light; the
inert roof of clouds was shining, breaking up here and there. After
a little while Tommaso's father also got up and went straight to
the can, where he remained every morning for at least half an hour.

'Goddammit!' Tommaso said, running towards the can. 'Let me
have the footbath, Pa!' he said. Coughing, his father let him come
in, and from the grey wall with its scabby plaster, Tommaso

detached the footbath, which hung from a solitary nail there. The
father, coughing and hawking like a sonovabitch, locked himself
in. Tommaso took the footbath to the kitchen. 'How's the water,
fa Chrissake!' he said, sticking a finger into it. His brother was
heating up the milk. Tommasino, fairly pleased, feeling that the
water was a bit warm, took the basin from under the little cabinet.

'It's still cold!' Sora Maria said, sitting by the stove, shelling the
beans in her lap. There was hardly room for them all in the kitchen,
and if they turned, they bumped each other or stepped on somebody's foot.

'Aòh, Ma,' Tommaso said, 'hurry!' Busily, he shifted the table,
took a chair and placed it by the sink, and on the sink he set the
basin.

At that moment a ray of sunlight came through the window,
illuminated the kitchen with a lovely, clear light for a little while,
dying immediately. Tommaso's good humour mounted at that
first announcement of the fine weather's return. He went back to
the bedroom, slowly undressed again, throwing off his dirty clothes.
'Now we'll have our little bath,' he was thinking, 'and then the
fun begins!' From his working jacket, hanging on the back of a
broken chair, he took his wallet with his party card, the two or
three cigarettes he had left, the red and yellow ballpoint, and the
last five hundred lire notes, neatly pressed. He set everything on the
night-table, and, in his shorts, went back into the kitchen. Here his
mother had finished with the beans, the hulls lay all over the floor,
and his brother was having coffee and milk, almost solid because of
all the bread he had broken into it.

Tommaso drew the footbath under the chair prepared by the
sink, then he poured the hot water partly into the footbath and
partly into the basin. He sat in the little chair, with his crummy
feet in the bath, where he washed himself from the belly down,
with his shorts on. From the belly up, instead, he washed himself in
the basin. When he had finished and had dried himself, a fine,
limpid light, nice and fresh, filtered into the kitchen from the
window, like a little golden rain.

The sky had cleared almost completely. It had been transformed into a sea of light. Around this sea, like strips of sand, there were some clouds, all wrinkled and shrivelled, filled with white light.

The people who lived under Tommaso's family, the Spadaccinis, turned on the radio, which set off at full speed with 'La Cumparsita.' From other open windows all around came voices of girls doing household chores or dressing, each on her own, while from the street below, around the little pump, came the screams of the kids.

Also whistling 'La Cumparsita' in his contentment, Tommaso went back to the bedroom to put on the suit. It took him almost an hour. But it was still early anyhow: and the radio, passing from 'La Cumparsita' to 'Sera 'e Maggio', and from 'Sera 'e Maggio' to 'Maruzzella', kept him company, gaily. The longest and most complicated operation was combing his hair: still singing with the radio, he went into the kitchen, again in shorts, clean ones, and wet his hair like a duckling: then he put a towel around his head, so the hair would stay down. After two or three minutes he removed the towel, and combing his hair with the snaggle-toothed comb he kept in his pocket, he looked at his reflection in the glass of the kitchen window. But, behind, on the knob of his head, the hair was standing up worse than before while in front, soaking wet, it fell over his forehead. 'Goddammit,' he muttered, then beginning to whistle immediately:

'When you say yes, always bear in mind:
to a loving heart, you mustn't be unkind ... '

He wet the hair again, again swathed it in the filthy towel, the same one he had used to dry his feet. In the intervals he sprawled on the wet chair, whistling or singing. In the end his hair seemed to lie more or less right: wet as it was, it outlined the shape of his head, round like a bird–dog's, with his narrow neck and his ears stuck to the reddish bumps behind the temples.

But Tommaso was pleased, and he yelled loud enough for his voice to be heard beyond the wall: 'Hey, Pa, get a move on!' Waiting for his father to get a move on, he started singing again. After a little while he heard the water flushing in the bowl, and his father came out. Tommaso ran to occupy his place, and widening his legs, because the little mirror was too low, he began to work around the parting with the comb, doing it over about twenty times, and bending the hair back in a special way he knew. This took him quite a while, then at last he got dressed.

Outside the sun was blinding. But Via dei Crispolti was almost empty. Two or three little kids who could maybe say Mamma were playing on the central pavement. From the few rickety houses of the Magic Village there to the right, a loud buzz of women chatting could be heard. But, farther on, there was nobody.

Usually, every morning, and especially on Sunday, at least thirty kids were playing ball or cards: and more boys of Tommaso's age, arguing or making wisecracks, were always in the yards or on the steps.

'Well,' Tommaso said, disappointed, since he had really been counting on making his entrance, among his neighbours, all dressed up in his new suit.

Already, he had assumed a calm, relaxed manner, like somebody who has private things to attend to but who nevertheless has time to stop and exchange a few words casually, out of a general benevolence towards all.

To tell the truth, he was impeccable: the sun glistened on the black suit, gilding the rather heavy cloth, as he walked at a calm, controlled pace or as he moved his hand serenely, lifting the cigarette to his mouth. At the end of his pants, his little handsomely-pointed shoes emerged, which he had bought a couple of months ago, but which were still smart.

He slowly went down Via Luigi Cesana, the central street of the INA-Case, where there were only some women; a couple of guys passed by on motorcycles with the exhaust open. The little bell of the church was ringing desperately.

Well, Tommaso repeated to himself with a grimace, seeing the desolation around.

He went into the tobacconist's to buy some Nazionali, though he still had three or four in his pocket. There, too, he found only a couple of old men, their pants sagging. More and more curious, Tommasino took the cigarettes, paid, and came out again.

Outside the barber's, which was next to the tobacconist's, because at the INA-Case all the shops were huddled together in a kind of one-storey bazaar in the centre of the development, it was the same thing: not one of the guys he knew who were usually around, only old people or some characters he knew only by sight.

As he continued along Via Luigi Cesana, which sloped slightly down to the Via Tiburtina, he kept trying to figure it out. To the right, at the steepest point, there were some houses, one against the other, like steps, so that the first floor of the second was level with the second floor of the first, and so on. Along the little painted façades there were a lot of outside stairways that united them, with some landings like little terraces at the entrances, all bars and railings.

On one of these cage-like terraces there was Sparkler, a guy Tommaso knew. Thank God, now let's hear what he has to tell me! Tommaso said to himself. This Sparkler was sitting on his balcony in his undershirt, while the women were yelling inside; he was contemplating the two little streets flanked by huge buildings, baked in the sun, against the naked fields.

'Hey, Man from Mars!' Tommaso said to him, passing beneath one of the railings. Sparkler didn't say anything. Tommaso stopped at his feet, acting indifferent, casual in his shining clothes.

'Aòh,' he said, 'you know where the others are? Francolicchio, Ruggeretto, Ugo Carboni?'

Sparkler looked at him, toasted by the sun like a roll just taken out of the oven: he lowered his black eyes, stared pensively for a moment, his jug-ears behind his forehead, his black hair short and lank, so black it was almost blue. Then, lazily, he began to make a tchk tchk with his tongue against his palate, so lazily it seemed his tongue might stick there. Finally he stood up, yawning like a tiger till he almost broke his jaw, and went off without answering anything, towards the little corridor between the railings at the end of the terrace.

'Hey, sleepyhead!' Tommaso said to him bitterly, going on his way. 'Fuck you,' he muttered, 'Is everybody dead around here?' he said then, almost aloud, angrily.

Flushed and swaggering in his suit, he covered the last stretch of Via Cesana and turned into the Tiburtina.

Along with him a whole bunch of young guys was coming down from the INA-Case, guys he didn't know. They were those little turds, students with mangy heads and jerk-faces, who tried to act smartass. Tommasino didn't even look at them, walking beside them calm and hard. But inside he was dying to ask them what was going on.

Other kids, big and little, appeared from the Pietralata road, farther down, under Monte del Pecoraro, which lay naked in the sun like a garbage heap.

They were all going in groups towards Tiburtino, but without any haste. A little gang of them was walking right in front of Tommaso on the raised pavement at the foot of Monte del Pecoraro. Let's find out if these little shits know anything! Tommaso thought. He glanced at them to see if he knew them: but they were all strange faces. Faces of little shitheads, still wet with milk, but already foxy as grown men. They were dressed up smart, in coloured shirts, jeans full of little pockets and brads on the ass and the cock, partly unbuttoned, beltless, with narrow waists like chorus girls. They were walking arm in arm. 'Prosperello's got the ball!' one shouted, indignant, his face as blond as olive oil.

'Prosperello who?' shouted another, with a forelock over his face as long as a palm-branch.

'Prosperello, the asshole fellow!' answered the first, as his face split in two in a satisfied smile.

'Wait for me, wait for me!' another one was yelling meanwhile, behind them. He ran up.

'Come on,' one of the gang said to him sharply. He was the little brother of two boys Tommaso knew, Francolicchio and Ruggeretto.

'Aòh,' Tommaso said to him, 'where're Francolicchio and Ruggeretto?'

'Whadda I know?' the kid said, spitting, in the conviction with which he said these words; not even looking at Tommaso, he mingled with the others.

'Fuck you,' Tommaso said between clenched teeth, since he

didn't feel like asking for more precise information, out of embarrassment, and also he didn't want to condescend to ask those little jerks.

In short, they were all going down towards Tiburtino, alone or in bunches, in the sunshine.

But now Tommaso was in sight of the Bar Duemila, which was there just at the beginning of Tiburtino opposite Monte del Pecoraro. He hastily finished his butt, shoved both hands in his pockets, and started walking faster.

In front of the bar the street was all full of red motorbikes, with a bunch of guys making a racket under the arbour, joking or arguing.

They were seated at little metal tables or stood in groups, half inside and half outside the bar, at their ease: but there were few of them compared to the usual crowd.

'You buying the coffee?' one guy said, seeing him. He was huddled in a dented chair, his legs out and his hands on his belly. Tommaso smiled wisely, as his face wrinkled, filling with red spots. Without answering, he moved into their midst.

'Aòh, I'm talking to you!' the other insisted, with a grimace to indicate that he wasn't joking about it.

'Ruggeretto,' Tommaso said in a soft, deep voice, 'don't bother me ... '

'You stray dog!' Ruggeretto went on, his face already smoothed, forgetting the disgusted expression of a moment before, 'don't you even have fifty lire, to buy coffee for a friend? What? You show up like this?'

But he wasn't even listening himself any more to what he was saying.

'Uaaaaah,' he said, stretching his upraised arms like a dog. He wriggled a moment or two in the chair, belly up. When he abruptly finished stretching and yawning, he stood up like a jack-knife, pulled the black sweater down a bit over the red shirt, lazily smoothing his pants over his cock, and went off about his business.

His brother, Francolicchio, was fiercely playing cards with three other dirty characters under the arbour. Tommaso went over to

him calmly, looking at the cards, all amiable. He slapped Francolicchio on the shoulder and said: 'Hi there, paisan!'

Francolicchio gave him a rapid glance like a belt-lash: his face
was wrinkled because he had a butt stuck to his lip. 'Whaddya
want?' he asked sharply, and went back to the game, black as a
snake. Tommaso, behind him, full of good humour, peaceable,
burst out singing:

'When you say yes, always bear in mind ... '

The style was ironic, allusive, and another of the players, who
didn't know him, gave him a dirty look, and Tommaso shut up.

Lazily Tommaso moved to the little group of guys with their
asses on the edge of the next table, watching the game. The farthest
away were Ugo Carboni and some others from New Jerusalem.
They were talking, or so it seemed, about something very interest-
ing, under the soaked leaves of the arbour that filtered the sunlight,
in bubbles. Tommaso went over, indifferent. Ugo Carboni, another
of his new friends in the INA-Case, saw him and dropped the
conversation. 'Jeezus, you're dressed up!' he said, blushing a little
at the roots of his pale hair. At last, somebody with the right
idea!

'Eh,' Tommaso said, ironically, 'I'm pretty powerful, all right!'
Ugo looked at him for another moment, complacently, with a
grimace as if to say: 'You're right, all right!', then, with the others,
he moved closer to the fence, to continue their discussion.

Tommaso was left all alone in the midst of the arbour.

He put his hands in his pocket, yawned slightly, and went over to
crumple up in a chair that had remained free in the midst there,
with another empty chair beside it. He stretched out, put his legs on
the other chair, and with his head thrown back, a bit uncomfortable,
really, because the back of the chair was low, he started singing, in
a mocking tone:

'To a loving heart, you mustn't be unkind ... '

As he sang, with more and more passion, forgetting he was just
doing it to act smart, his little brown eyes darted here and there,

especially towards the group playing cards and the others watching, chewing the gum they had been grinding for an hour. Among these there was Alberto, the book-keeper who had been a friend of Tommaso's since the days when he was with the Fascists. After having glanced at him, Tommaso adjusted himself better in the chair, as if he meant to sleep there, crossing his hands on his belly as he went on singing even more beautifully.

But he broke off suddenly, and with his eyelids lowered like a priest hearing confession, all red with pleasure, he said: 'Hey, Albe!'

Hearing his name called, this Alberto—who resembled Alberto Sordi—looked around, innocently. He was the usual idler, all dressed up because it was Sunday, in a nice grey flannel suit, suede shoes, and a yellow sports shirt, a bit open so you could see the crummy hair on his chest muscles.

As he saw Tommaso, he raised his arm and said: 'Aòh, Tomà!'

Tommaso, meanwhile, was yawning again, his forehead slightly wrinkled, a bit out of laziness and a bit out of well-being. He only raised one arm, as if he lacked the breath to say hello.

His friend stood up and came over to him. 'Jeezus, what a suit!' he said. He was silent for a moment, observing expertly how Tommaso was dressed. Tommaso kept quiet, with a mocking manner, allowing himself to be examined.

Then, first the right then the left, he wearily removed his legs from the chair in front of him, and jerking his chin towards it, he grumbled: 'Take a seat!'

'Aòh, Tomà,' the other said, 'why don't we take a ride on the Vespa instead? Whadda we fucking around here for?'

'Let's go!' Tommaso said lazily.

'Let's go see the river!' Alberto said, all ready for the ride.

Tommaso pretended to know what this seeing the river business was all about, and he stood up. But before he did, pleased at that invitation, he sat for just another moment as if he had to gather his strength: then, abruptly, he sprang to his feet, all handsome in his brand new suit. 'Let's go,' he repeated. He stretched one more time, and slowly went outside with Alberto, leaving the other dopes behind making their usual racket.

Tommaso and Alberto were the best dressed there at the Bar Duemila. They could act smartass, with a certain ease, though without carrying it too far. Calm and superior, they went out and climbed on the Vespa, Alberto in front, Tommaso behind. Alberto kicked the sonovabitch starter seven or eight times with his heel, and Tommaso meanwhile settled down, looking around with an indifferent air. And he didn't change expression not even when the Vespa darted off like a rocket: he held his hands calmly clasped behind his back, as if they were handcuffed.

To the left Monte del Pecoraro, to the right the Tiburtino development at the end of the square, with the church bell ringing like crazy: everything vanished behind them. Via delle Messi d'oro vanished, with the tavern, the row of crummy oleanders along the bank, with all the procession of people, the bands of little kids, and older boys who on either side were all going in the same direction along Via Tiburtina: the Silver Cine vanished, and with it the lousy little soap factory that had just been built next door.

The Aniene reached Tiburtino, coming down from the Castelli: when it was there, it flowed under an ancient little brick bridge where there was a dredger and a little old wine-shop, a catacomb. Then it passed a few decrepit market gardens, filthy, crammed with all sorts of fruit and vegetables, on one bank, and on the other, towards the Tiburtino houses, a whole stretch of country, with reeds and stalks of clumsily-cut grain. Then it flowed below the lye factory, a pile of tanks, landings, stark terraces, that vomited a little white stream of acids into the current: it went under the arch of the Via Tiburtina bridge, disappeared beneath a tunnel of cane, and went off towards Montesacro, to empty into the Tiber.

All this stretch of flat land that Sunday had been transformed into a sea.

As far as the eye could reach, towards the Tivoli hills in one direction, and in the other towards Tiburtino, closer, there was nothing but water.

Tiburtino rose like a port, with its rows of apartments, all the same, like warehouses, with one white façade illuminated by the sun, the other, in the shadow, black.

There was no distinguishing now the fields, gardens, dykes, roads and paths. At the very end, the little gasometer and the forest of beacons and lights of the power station looked like anchored ships.

The mass of water pressed down, yellow and thick, with twisting eddies against the embankment of the Via Tiburtina, foaming: there, it stopped, angrily, falling back again into the river's usual bed and piling up in big, livid waves, then passed like a fury under the bridge: from there it spread out once again over the countryside: and the four or five farmhouses stood in the middle like so many Noah's arks.

On all that expanse of water the sun beat down, tingeing with gold a surface of thousands and thousands of waves, ripples, all yellow, and illuminating the black tree trunks, the weeds, the packing cases, the rubbish, the oil stains that floated all over that horizon of boiling water.

So the Via Tiburtina was like a dock, full of people who had come to enjoy the spectacle of the flood: it was like the night of the Last Judgment.

Then along came the 311, heading for Redibibbia: it advanced very slowly through the tight-packed crowd, and when it reached the end, at the bridge, it stopped.

Alberto and Tommaso on their Vespa, with the others who had motorcycles, followed the bus to see what would happen. Down there, in fact, about fifty yards beyond the bridge, the road was also flooded. Some of the people on the bus got out, others stayed inside and stretched their necks from the windows. Then two or three guys from Ponte Mammolo, full of themselves, took off their shoes, rolled their pants up over their calves, pirate-style, and making a fuss so everybody would look at them, began to wade across the stretch of flooded road, laughing and joking. When they reached the bridge, they ran barefoot towards Via Casal dei Pazzi, where they lived.

But those who had stayed on this side, older men, women, clerks, were gnawing their fists in impatience and anger: the conductor had sprawled back in his little seat, his hands on his belly, whistling.

Alberto, Tommaso, and a mass of little snotnoses and older kids,
all around, stood there for more than an hour, idly taking in the
whole operation: another bus had come from Montesacro on the
other side of the bridge, but didn't dare cross it: and the people,
carried across in one way or another, all glued together, took the
other bus. On the Via Tiburtina, there in the midst of the sea, there
was more traffic, a bigger jam of cars than in the centre of Rome at
the rush hour.

The only bell around there was the little one of Tiburtino. When
it started making a big racket to announce noon, the sun had already
gone.

The clouds, which had thickened and huddled at the back of the
sky, had now begun to swell again: white as cream, they had glided
overhead, massed together again, so light they looked like brides
in their wedding dresses, or dark and stripped like piles of garbage
blown by the cold wind. In the end, they had clogged up the whole
sky again, one cloud above, one below, one little, one big, one grey,
one dark, one white, and all sticky, filthy, cold. In one patch of sky
the sun was still shining, but it looked godforsaken, because a smoke
that wasn't fog and wasn't clouds ran under that scab that covered the
sky, in waves, black as a damned soul. Then one part of all that pile
of clouds, big and small, of smoke, became an even grey, towards
Rome. It was earth-coloured, and like rubbed earth it spread out,
looming, over the city: from there came a first thunder-clap that
rumbled even in your bones.

Tiburtino rose from a sea, which had spread all over the countryside, a black sea; you could tell it was water only by the vague
glistening of the ripples.

*

A storm came down, like the night before, with lightning and
hail. The people just had time to run home under the first big drops,
in a darkness like night.

Around one or one-thirty, it let up a little, but it was still raining
hard.

When he had eaten, Tommasino went down to the café below,

all dressed up as before, with his tie on, and got busy arranging the afternoon's activity.

He went to the cashier and, with a secretive manner, asked for a telephone slug: with the slug in his fingers, he chatted a bit with the owner, an old communist from Sacrofano, who had even been in jail in Mussolini's day, then he slowly headed for the phone, dialled the number, and turning towards the freshly white-washed wall, he waited. He waited a good while because he had called the family who lived downstairs, and Irene had to be summoned from a window, had to put something on, then come down the steps. When, all breathless, she said: 'Hlo!', Tommaso turned towards the interior of the bar, rested one shoulder against the wall, crossed his legs, and said: 'Hey, Irene, this is Tommaso!' Then smiling, as red as if Irene were there, he came to the point at once, the topic of the day: 'Whaddya think of this weather?' he said.

Irene, apparently, expressed her opinion on the weather from the other end of the wire, with information about some fresh lightning. 'Jeezus!' Tommaso said, in a gentlemanly tone, and then: 'Tough luck, eh? Today, of all days, when I wanted to take you into Rome, and now look what happens!' He was bitter, sincerely disappointed: and when, obviously, on the other end Irene ventured a word or two, minimizing the weather problem, Tommaso replied at once, cut to the quick: 'Can't you see how it's pouring? Irene!' and then, curtly: 'Whaddya mean, let up? It's gonna rain for a week, that's what!'

He listened for a while, then said, almost chanting, in a low voice: 'I don't have an umbrella, Irene, you know I don't!' Irene perhaps said: 'Then I'll give you one for your birthday,'; and Tommaso answered, resting his elbow abruptly against the wall: 'Well, thanks, thanks a lot!' Then obviously Irene, on the subject of birthdays and presents, told him a story about a friend, and Tommaso stood and listened, his face becoming redder and his smile slyer, saying, 'Ah' 'Um' 'Sure!' 'Who? This friend?' At the end he laughed, amiable and sweet.

As he spoke, his voice sank lower and lower, almost to a whisper, his mouth saying one thing and his eyes brightly glancing around

on their own. Finally, coming back to the subject of their date, he
concluded: 'Well, I'll hang around the bar with my friends. Maybe
I'll play a game or two, then I'll go to bed!' And he added immediately, in a louder voice, detaching his elbow from the wall again
and holding the telephone as if it were one of those trumpets that
pages blow in castles: 'Tomorrow, sure! Tomorrow, if the weather's
nice, I'll come!' Finally he huddled over, bending over the phone,
held very close, ready for the goodbyes. 'Ciao then, ciao, Irene, see
you tomorrow. Okay?' And with a final sigh, pleased and now red
as a pepper, he repeated, 'Ciao!' and hung up.

When he had done this, he passed the cashier again, buttoning his
double-breasted jacket with a little cough, and went to stand by
the glass door, looking outside. He stood there, content, his thumb
stuck absently between the buttons of his pants, observing the sky.
It had cleared a little and now it was about to stop raining.

That Sunday, at the Boston, there was *Stairway to Heaven*, and
so it was a kind of moral obligation to see it. At the INA-Case,
all those who hadn't seen it the night before were preparing to go
now.

Some groups of people, in fact, began to run by along Via
Luigi Cesana, under their umbrellas, or with their raincoats pulled
up over their heads, laughing and yelling. While he waited for the
rain to stop, Tommaso proposed a little game of cards, just for fun,
to the owner of the bar: 'Whaddya say, chief?' he said, 'How about
a game? Just friendly, though.' The old man was willing, and they
began to play on the little empty bit of marble on the cash desk,
without sitting down. When they had played one hand, they
warmed up and bet a coffee. Tommaso played, won, and drank his
coffee with the old man, and when they had finished, the rain had
almost stopped.

Tommaso stuck his nose outside, saw that there were just a few
drops still spinning in the black air, and, not going back in, he
yelled: 'See you later, chief,' and slipped into the street.

He pulled up his jacket collar, and with his hands in his pockets
he went towards the Boston. On the Via Tiburtina, the trees waved
against the sky that looked like a stormy sea; amid the confusion

of bersaglieri and people waiting for the bus, in that moment when it wasn't raining, you could hear Claudio Villa singing at the top of his lungs, over the theatre's loud-speaker. The wet air, the low clouds, Monte del Pecoraro, the few buildings among the huts seemed stunned by that voice, singing so loud it was deafening. Tommaso, happy, began to sing along with him as he went up Via di Pietralata among the other lines of people, towards the theatre. He entered the Boston, humming; it was full to bursting, and it was like going into a Turkish bath, with that stink of wet clothes, of dirty feet and sweat. The kids were yelling in the front rows, even sitting on the floor among the stripes of piss that ran down between the chairs, among the peanut shells, even under the screen.

So he forced his way into the midst of the crowd, along the peeling wall. He became excited at once, in the midst of that pile of cunts around, with their boyfriends or maybe their mothers. Tommaso stood behind a little column, and soon glimpsed a movement in the crowd, a little ponytail near by, flapping this way and that. It must have belonged to a young kid, judging by the way she had fixed her hair, and because she was short.

Let's have a look!' Tommaso thought, and got busy, trying to reach her.

He pushed through the crowd, the women complaining, furious. Behind the column there was a bit more space, because you couldn't see, and the people were on either side of it, stretching their necks. Tommaso settled there, content to see only a piece of the screen, and began the movement, with his feet and his hands, to work the girl over. She was really new to it. Jeezus, Tommaso was thinking, am I a monster or something? but he wasn't laughing, even though he made that crack at himself.

So maybe fifteen minutes went by and working steadily, Tommaso already had almost managed to get his thigh against the girl's: but then the lights came on, and there was the usual ruction inside the hall.

Some were shouting, some singing, some yelling for the peanut-seller, and on all sides you could see people climbing over the backs of the chairs.

Tommaso tried not to lose his position: but it was like being on the sea in the midst of a storm. To act casual, he took out a cigarette and lit it, slipping his hands from his pockets one at a time, in the crush; but as he looked around, pressed against the column, he saw on the opposite side of the column a person he didn't recognize, not at first, and then, when he had placed him, he had to take a good look at him to believe what he saw.

It was Zimmìo: but apart from the fact that in those past months he had got bigger and harder, he was now so elegant that he looked like anybody but himself. On his head he had one of those grey hats with a round dome and a brim a bit broad and stiff, with a white border all around it, the kind Milanese business men wear: it was brand new, and it sat on his head as if a breeze could blow it away, resting there by chance, though it came down almost to his eyebrows, covering half the pimples on his forehead. Serious as it was, that hat gave Zimmìo's face an expression of even greater slyness. Then he was wearing a nice white shirt with a bow tie, dark blue with white dots: he had on a light topcoat, grey, of the best wool, the shoulders a bit narrow, the latest style, English, and under it you could see his dark suit, almost black, with a row of white buttons, and a waistcoat of the same material. He had a leather glove on his left hand, holding the right glove: with his right hand he was smoking a cigarette stuck in a long amber holder.

So, a real high-life gentleman, he was leaning against the column. 'Hey, Zimmì!' Tommaso called. Zimmìo looked at him, raised his head slightly in greeting, laughing a bit under his moustache.

Tommaso held out his hand, and so did his friend, and they clasped fingers as if they were all sticky with glue, very polite. 'Eeeeh,' Tommaso sighed, stretching, 'goddammit!' Zimmìo looked at him, his mouth ready to laugh. 'Well, whaddya up to these days?' Tommaso inquired, amiably.

'Whaddam I doing?' Zimmìo said. 'Buggering sparrows!'

'Eh,' Tommaso sighed again, looking at the way he was dressed, 'with the money you've got!'

'Sure!' Zimmìo said, pointing his index finger like a knife against his throat, 'I'm flat. Not a lira. Bled white as a turnip!'

'Stop shitting me!' Tommaso said, incredulous.

'Can you lend me a five hundred?' Zimmìo blurted, shameless.

Tommaso looked at him, gaily, pensive: 'Jeezus,' he said 'what a sonovabitch!'

'Mamma, your boy's so happy!' Zimmìo sang.

So the lights went out and the film began again, amid the final yells and whistles of the crowd.

When they came out of the Boston, Tommaso thought he would find everything dark, because at that hour night had usually fallen. Instead it was still light. You couldn't tell where the light came from, maybe the world had been turned upside down, and up above you you could see the mouth of hell from which the flames came down. The sky was all black around the edges, but in the middle there was a kind of gap in the clouds, a bit of pale blue and from there, like the walls of a well, the clouds were illuminated by an orangey glow that spread all around. But a dark steam was passing in front of all that radiance, a vapour the sirocco drove at top speed, and it became thicker and thicker and so low it touched the tops of the six or seven big new buildings of Pietralata, going towards the Aniene, towards Prati Fiscali. Soon that black smoke became a real cloud, that filtered the light dripping like blood from the centre of the sky, and dimmed it, scattering it over Pietralata like the ashes of death.

So in no time darkness came, and it was night. After a little while it started raining again. Along Via di Pietralata you could see the people hurrying home, and others, farther off, in the light from the bar, waiting for the bus under the warm gusts of the sirocco.

Running, leaping over the puddles, with his hands in his pockets and his collar turned up, Tommasino reached the bar with Zimmìo after him, running and cursing, but to himself, with the same propriety that he used in leaping the puddles to avoid soiling his clothes.

The bar was all full, smoky and stinking of dirty, wet clothes, stifling.

They were all there, more or less, Lello, Zucabbo, Cazzitini, Hyena, Greasy, Prickhead, Pincher, Buddha, Hawk, Nazzareno,

and lots of others standing, huddled together on the wet floor, some
playing cards, some talking.

Tommasino came in and nobody saw him, as usual.

But as soon as Zimmìo entered, first Buddha, then Prickhead,
then gradually all the others of the band turned to look at him: they
examined him for a moment, dazed, then one after the other they
burst out laughing so hard they had to grab the tables to keep from
falling down, writhing and pissing themselves. Zimmìo stood
inside the door, observing them silently with a smug face, but with
laughter shining in his eyes, too. He stood there a while, watching
them, while they bust their guts in front of him, wriggling like a
bunch of loonies: then, slowly, he unbuttoned, one by one, the
buttons of his coat, opened it, stuck out his belly, and grabbing
himself below with a hand like a hod, he yelled: 'Take this and
laugh about it!' Then he passed by swiftly, as if he had an appointment, went to the bar, looked at the bartender, with a face all red,
melting like fat in the fire, laughing to himself, and said: 'Gimme
a coffee, kid!' And he cast another look around, like an old fox.
The others went on yelling haw haw haw: 'You belong to the big
time tonight, eh?' the Hyena yelled at him. And Nazzareno: 'Who
deloused you, Zimmì?' 'Zimmìo, you're the number one of
Pietralata!' Buddha said, in his syphilitic voice.

Then little by little, they calmed down, and those who were
playing cards started another hand. Tommaso went over to Lello,
who was watching Buddha, Hawk, Nazzareno, and Delli Fiorelli
playing. He slapped him on the shoulder, saying: 'How're things,
Lè?' 'Okay,' Lello said, not turning around, 'Howdya think they
are?'

There were also some older men in the place, some old crocks
drunk to the marrow. They were bunched against the counter,
there beside Zimmìo, arguing, yelling at the top of their voices,
with long rambling talk, slapping themselves on the chest, their
eyes popping out from below the dirty hair of their eyebrows.

At full speed, their noise drowned by a clap of thunder, another
three or four customers came in from Tiburtino, and among them,
Carletto with his guitar. They came in, puffing, shaking their

wet clothes, stamping their feet on the pavement, which was a swamp. 'Four rum punches!' they said to the barman, yelling. They glued themselves to the counter, Carletto took his tear-jerker from his shoulder and propped it beside him. 'Look,' Hawk said, 'the guitar!' He got up, went to the bar slowly, as if his knees were sagging with fatigue, and said to Carletto: 'You mind?', took the guitar, and began to let out:

'Strings of my guitarrr ... '

'Cut the shit ... Hawk!' the guys at the table with him yelled. Hearing Hawk sing, another guy who was playing cards also started singing, not 'Strings of my Guitar', but 'Only for You': then a third joined in, and after a while, six or seven were singing, each on his own, some one song, some another. Chestnut sang:

'Oh, wave of the sea,
so beautiful ... '

Buddha, who was already beginning to go bald, but still had a lot of fine, transparent little curls on his head, said: 'Bums!' Then he, too, started to sing:

'Gateway amid the roses,
an angel smiled at me tonight ... '

Finally Carletto took back his guitar, cleared his throat, struck a couple of chords, and knocked them all out, singing like an angel:

'How beautiful you are, nymph of Trastevere,
born in the shadow of St Peter's dome ... '

Hawk, who had gone back to the card game, looked up from his hand, glanced around, his eyeballs glistening with contentment, and said: 'What's the singing about? Is it because you're hungry?'

He took a card from his hand and slammed it on the table, then raised his eyes again, stared at Chestnut, with a glance like an old crook and repeated: 'Aòh, haven't you guys had anything to eat today?'

'Whaddya think?' Delli Fiorelli chimed in, a butt stuck in his lips, blinding him. 'When do they eat? At Easter!'

'But when do we eat, ourselves?' Buddha burst out laughing gaily.

Outside, the storm was making more and more noise.

'Sure!' Buddha said, more jolly than ever, 'if any one of us decided to challenge Burma the Fakir, we'd starve him out of business!'

He had a face on him that made it easy to believe: and the same was true of Hawk, and Delli Fiorelli and Nazzareno and all the others, their bones visible inside their taut skin, ready to be thrown to the stray dogs.

'Speaking of hunger,' Buddha said, his eyes down on the cards, 'You remember, Cazzitì, that day I ran into you on the tram, when I was with Canticchia? Jeezus, that day we really had our guts wrung out! We couldn't even remember when we ate last! Canticchia leaned on me, and I was leaning on him: we looked like the two orphans of the storm!'

He started laughing, his tongue between his lips like a piston, spattering saliva, and he went on: 'Well, like I was saying, we were going to shed our blood at the clinic in Viale Liegi. Canticchia was scared, but he was so hungry, goddammit, he had the courage of a lion! He'd have let them cut off his arm, that day!

'Then we got to the place where they take your blood: there were whole families in there: fathers, mothers, sons, daughters, grandads! All bled white! It was like being at the slaughter-house! I said to Canticchia: "Don't let it get you, Cantì! Hold on another ten minutes, and we'll be back on our feet again. Cheer up, Cantì"'

'Canticchia's eyes were watering from hunger: I couldn't look him in the face — you know what I mean! He made me cry just to see him! He looked like thin soup, when he tried to talk, he gasped ... Then, when the time came, we gave our identity cards to those sonsabitches. They took X-rays to see if we were sick ... They could of seen through us anyhow. Even my tapeworm had died of starvation! To make a long story short, they bled us! They put those little balls in our hand. Afterwards, they took us into another room, and there they gave us a little tiny roll, a slice of salami, and a little glass of marsala. We had seen that mirage, and you won't believe it, but I felt light as air, I was flying, then I felt something warm at my asshole: "Cantì, my jaws're rusty!" I said, and as I reached for the roll, the effort screwed me, and I fell on the floor!'

He looked all around fiercely, putting one hand, funnel-like, to his mouth: 'I fell on the floor!' he repeated, his mouth drooling.

'Jeezus called me up to Heaven!' he added then, laughing again. 'I woke up in the hospital, with my head all bandaged up and a glass of milk in front of me, to save me from starving!'

They all laughed, shouting at him: 'Cut the shit!' Then Cazzitini began yelling: 'Listen to this!' because he wanted to tell a story of his own, his eyes glistening with laughter.

'I hadn't eaten for three days,' he said, 'I go into the soup kitchen, and like I had a thousand lire in my pocket, I order a double portion.

'But I was so hungry I didn't know what I was doing, and I started ordering another bowl of soup, and another, another ... '

He also put his hand like a funnel around his mouth, stretching his neck: 'I got up to thirty!' he yelled. 'And after the thirtieth, I asked for another, and they brought me the empty pot and the ladle and said: "Listen, kid, you've eaten all the workmen's soup. You've starved two building gangs!" '

The friends laughed a bit, but Cazzitini hadn't finished talking when Hyena had interrupted him: 'That's a joke,' he said, 'Now I'll make you cry! Listen. Listen to this tragedy!'

'One day,' he said, looking around, 'I was so hungry I couldn't climb up on the pavement: I went to ring the church bell for half an hour and they gave me a ticket, it was good for a meal at the San Pietro Club. Goddamm them, when he gave it to me, the priest acted like he was giving me a blank cheque! I raced over to the place, scared they would run out ... In the midst of all these old bastards, these old bags ... some had a tin, some a jar, some had bowls, or hods, or a coal scuttle ... And one even had a hat, to put the broth in: "Give me a hatful of bean soup," he said. "Give me a hat's worth of broth!"

'A woman gave me a jar to put the food in: I went off to sit in a corner, I was eating all nice and happy. But, it was pot-luck, and you know what I fished out of the pot? A rubber!'

'Shit!' they said around him, holding up a thicket of hands.

'I swear!' Hyena yelled, 'those whore-cooks, doing God knows what with those bums that bring in the stuff! And then, to destroy the evidence, they dump it in the soup! The safest place was my jar! I've got a healthy appetite!'

He laughed, his little-boy eyes shining: 'Aòh, rubber soup,' he added, 'You're all nuts! Where can you find a dish like that? Not even on the Riviera! Jeezus, I was ready to throw up!'

'Aòh,' Buddha said, purplish, 'tell us the rest. Whaddidya do? Eat it or throw it out? The rubber?'

'No, I put it on my head!' Hyena yelled, laughing.

'Why? Was it Carnival time?' Cazzitini asked him, laughing, while the others all split their guts.

But, at that moment the lights suddenly went out. It was all dark, and after a while there were only the glowing butt-ends and shadows that bumped into each other and yelled. Somebody flicked a lighter, and the barman pulled two candles from under the counter and lit them, the flames trembling faintly on the wet bar.

By that light, they all went to the door to look out: it was dark but, all the same, you could tell something had happened in the street, in the neighbourhood. The lights came on again for a few moments: the street in front of the bar was a lake, at least six inches of water. And in the other streets, the lower ones in the centre of the development, you could see more water glistening, up to the cellar windows. The houses rose directly from the water, in the light of the four street-lamps: and already the junk from the yards — poles, rags, garbage — was beginning to float. Every now and then a lightning flash, followed by a faint rumble of thunder, showed the whole area, now all in water. The lights went out again, and only the two little candles were left glowing inside the bar. Everybody was piled against the door. 'Where are we? Venice?' Cazzitini said. 'Venice, your ass ... This isn't funny!' Hyena grumbled.

The old drunks, soaked to their guts, stood there swaying and yelling meaningless words. One, in the confusion, had sunk to the floor, and lay there in the water, unable to pull himself up, raving.

Four of five guys took off their shoes, rolled their pants above their knees, and ran out: the others watched them, but you couldn't see anything; a moment later they had disappeared into the darkness, plopping through the muck.

Tommaso flung himself on one of the little chairs that had remained empty, piled together at the end of the big room: he sprawled there, his hands on his belly, with a peaceful look, as if he were preparing to wait for whatever was to come, to spend the night there, if necessary. He dug out a fag and began to puff, placidly.

At that moment he saw something that looked like lights dancing and disappearing outside, under the cascades of rain.

They approached. It was some men with flashlights, rubber trenchcoats around their heads, on their shoulders. They opened the door and began to talk in loud voices.

After a little while, Tommaso went over to listen. But the men, having yelled a few words, had gone off again down towards the houses.

You could see white lights, darting here and there over patches of brown water. 'Who was that?' Tommaso then asked Lello.

'The guys from the Party, there!' Lello grumbled.

'Whaddid they say?'

'Over at Little Shanghai, the people are drowning!' Lello said.

'Whaddya mean drowning?'

'You heard me!'

'There's a flood,' Hyena said.

'The river?' Tommaso asked.

'No, my cock!'

'Shithead!' Tommaso yelled, remembering how in the days he lived there, when it rained the water often came pouring down from the hillocks around the settlement. The bank of the river was about fifteen yards high, the river couldn't have risen above it.

'Aòh, whadda we gonna do?' Zucabbo yelled. Tommaso was

thinking, his face gangrenous, like he was drugged. He didn't say anything.

'Whaddid they want?' he asked Zucabbo then. 'They wanted us to go over, to help!'

'Sure! Next Easter!' Hyena said.

'Shits,' Tommaso said with disgust, looking them in the face. 'Couldn't we help out? You guys afraid?'

'When I wanna swim, I go to Ostia ... And I hire a boat, too!' Hyena said.

Tommaso paid no attention to him. 'You're acting like a bunch of Germans here, eh? So long as it doesn't bite your ass!'

Hyena looked at him. 'Hey,' he said with curiosity, 'Is this Tommaso here?' And to Buddha: 'You recognize Tommaso?'

'You know him,' Buddha said, sweetly, 'This is Saint Tommaso, the patron of floods!'

But Tommaso was determined, hot: 'Then you don't give a shit about those poor bastards!' he blurted. 'You guys don't deserve to live!'

Hyena was beginning to get vinegary: 'Aòh, if you feel like it, go ahead,' he said, 'run along! Hurry! Who's keeping you?'

'Sure, I'm going, you shit!' Tommaso said, more disgusted than ever.

'Well, whaddya waiting for? Put on your bathing suit!' Buddha said, without even looking at him.

Struck at his weak point, Tommaso with a wild shove pushed the guys away from the door: 'Outta the way!' he said. But he had his new suit on. He stopped.

'What? Changing your mind?' Nazzareno asked.

'Fuck you,' Tommaso said curtly. He turned to the barman. 'Hey, barman,' he said smartly, 'You got a bag, something I can put on my head?'

Without a word, the barman bent over, rummaged under the counter, and pulled up a bag, already limp. Tommaso took it, removed his jacket, gave it to the barman to hold along with his shoes and socks. He rolled up his pants, put the sack on his head and shoulder, and went outside, stepping over the old drunk still stretched out on the floor, raving and grinding his teeth in anger like a dog.

'Go on, Tomà. Tomorrow they'll give you a medal!' Buddha yelled after him, as he went out under all that rain.

It was worse than being blind. The water splashed in your eyes, ran down your face: it was like walking in a sewer. After he had taken two steps, Tommaso was soaked to the bone. 'Where'm I going? Whaddam I doing?' he asked himself angrily, half silly under that deluge. When he had taken another couple of steps the water was up to his ankles, after two more, to his calves, another four, to his knees. But his eyes were beginning to get used to the dark. He turned right along Via dei Monti di Pietralata. There ahead, confused, he could see the outline of the bus, at the shelter, the water up to its runningboard: farther down he could hear voices; and, at some windows in the flooded houses he could see the light of a candle.

Then he heard a siren scream: it screamed and screamed, but seemed to stay in one place. After a while, bright headlights illuminated the street, the whole neighbourhood, which had become a lagoon under the torrents of rain. It was a fire truck coming along Via di Pietralata at a snail's pace, the siren screaming desperately. But it couldn't go any farther, and when it came up to the bus, it stopped. It was also probably heading for Little Shanghai. The headlights remained on, and illuminated a bit of road and some houses, bright as day.

There under the strip of light, a bit ahead, an explosion was heard, something collapsing: it was a manhole that had blown up, breaking a stretch of pavement.

Tommaso stopped alongside the fire truck: the firemen were arguing, under that furious rain that drowned out every other sound. They themselves didn't know what to do. Perhaps they didn't even know where those shacks on the river were located. Anyhow it was impossible to get there with a vehicle: you had to go on foot.

'Let's go!' Tommaso shouted then, catching on to the situation, 'I'll show you the way! I know it!'

'Is it far?' a guy in charge asked him, a big black-headed guy with a coil of rope over his shoulder. 'Half a mile, maybe less!' Tommaso yelled, soaked. They took what they needed and aimed their flashlights. They walked for a while with the water up to their knees, passed the zone illuminated by the headlights, and went down into all that hell.

The families who lived in the half-basements had moved in with their neighbours on the upper floors: you could hear voices everywhere, shouts of fear, kids crying. Some of the bigger kids were out with their legs in the water, to see. In some streets, sloping a little, the water ran like a mountain stream: stuff was floating on it, drawers, sticks, bits of wood, rubbish.

At the last houses the water was still higher, because it was the deepest point, between the hills on one side and the fields along the river on the other.

They had to go slowly. In fact, at the very beginning of the street's descent, where the houses ended, a little gulf had formed: the firemen gathered around it and pointed their flashlights: in the hole, water up to its roof, there was a car, the roof half torn off, over the burst sewer.

At the edge they saw a shadow coming forward, swaying: it was a little shadow, huddled up like a dog or a kid, under the volleys of rain. Every now and then it fell into the water, its hands forward, then got up, took a few steps, and fell again. At that moment it came up to a sloping cross-street, where the water was deep and ugly, like a river. A slab of corrugated iron, bouncing along on the current, came and hit the figure in the leg, and he fell full length in the water. When they pulled him up, he was half dead; the water had mixed with the saliva in his mouth, and it all drooled out, black with mud. 'Who is it? Where does he live?' the fireman asked.

'It's Muchetta! He lives here, block "G"!' Tommaso said.

They picked him up and carried him towards home: his building had water over the windows of the basements, and the people who lived there were on the stairs, some with candles in their hands. They dropped the old man there and went on towards Little Shanghai, with Tommaso in the lead.

After the last block of apartments, the road climbed up and began to emerge from the water, until, after maybe a hundred yards, it was dry. But it was two feet deep in mud: the walking there was worse than before: almost half an hour went by before they reached the clump of shacks. But the settlement, you might say, no longer existed. It took them a while to get their bearings, in the flashlight's beams: but that's how it was.

To the right, the river flowed almost level with the street, where usually there were ten yards or more of steep slope.

To the left, towards the last hills over the road, where the shacks used to stand around the clearing, here and there in disorder, now you could hardly see a thing. Only pieces of wood, pieces of walls, corrugated iron, roofs whole but overturned, planks, beams, poles lying on the ground. And on all sides, from the top of the hills through the village, slipping down over the road to the river, an avalanche of mud and water.

Only on the other side some shacks had remained standing in a higher zone, around a cavern: and a few on this side, too, at the edge of that kind of river of mire flowing down from the slope.

Luckily the rain was letting up, and there were moments when it almost stopped: you could see a bit.

Sticking with the firemen, Tommaso climbed up, sinking into the mire, grabbing the remains of the bushes, a branch, a wet tree; they almost reached the higher part, where there was a kind of open space halfway up the slope. Some people had gathered there, after escaping from the huts, dressed as they happened to be, some even in nightshirts, with babies in their arms, and little kids crying.

Slipping, black with mud, the women ran to meet the firemen: they were screaming, begging for help. 'There it is,' they shouted as if there were any need, perhaps because they couldn't take it all in. 'There, that's all there is left!'

There hadn't been much before: a few hovels, a few rusty roofs, a few rags; and now all this had been smashed, carried down by the mud towards the river. The clearing in the centre, where Tommaso had played as a little boy, was a lake, and in the midst of it were the remains of the huts, sunk in the water.

Some of these huts, here and there, were half standing: but on the side towards the hills there was so much mud by now that it had reached the window-sills and had begun to pour inside, breaking the rotten shutters. Then, from there, it broke down the front door and began to come out again, spitting forth everything in the house: chairs, boxes, shoes, basins, a broken table or two. All this stuff piled up in front, and a little at a time, bobbing on the flow of mire, it ended up towards the centre of the little village, and with the larger wreckage of the completely uprooted shacks, it piled down towards the river.

All the inhabitants, or almost all, had assembled up there around that cavern, where the shacks were still standing: only a few people were on this side, on the road towards Pietralata.

A pack of rats, big and fat as arms, fleeing from their invaded holes, had mixed with the people on the dry land and were jumping over shoes, their long black fur all glued flat.

The river's current rumbled as it rolled away, level and full of eddies; it seemed to make the land tremble all around.

The people, waving their arms and yelling, looked towards one spot: and also staring towards that spot were Passalacqua, Di Nicola, Di Santo, and the other comrades, soaked to the guts. They had been there for a while, waiting for manna from heaven, because, after all, when you came right down to it, what could they do? The situation was hopeless. Among the shacks that hadn't been smashed up, there was one in a slightly drier spot: this was the one they were all looking at. A woman, who lived there, had nailed herself in, perhaps in the hope of saving a bit of her stuff: she had collected on the floor all the stuff that the mud was carrying away, as it came through the windows.

But then the mud had gradually risen, and she had remained caught there, alone, in her hut, and she was screaming for help.

You couldn't hear her voice at all, with the noise of the rain, the wind, the river's current. The firemen had some ropes and got busy, trying to go and save her: Tommaso obstinately stood in their midst, making a big fuss, yelling to make them pay attention to him: 'You don't know the place,' he yelled, 'you don't know

the bottom! It's all full of holes, there's a fence ... Let me go, I
know the way.'

But the firemen paid no attention to him, all concerned with
preparing the rope, under the battering rain. One man tied it around
his hips and started in. But before he had taken two steps, he slipped,
because the slope was underneath, and he sank into the mud up
to his eyes. He started to pull himself up, but he couldn't make it,
so then the others dragged him back.

'I told you!' Tommaso yelled. 'I told you you can't make it!
You can't go that way. You have to circle around!'

'Send this kid here. He knows where to put his feet!' Passalacqua
intervened.

'Whaddam I supposed to do then?' Tommaso went on shouting,
ready, flushed, 'Am I gonna go or not?'

'Here,' the chief said. He took the rope and tied it around
Tommaso's waist. Without even looking back, to show how he
operated, Tommaso jumped from the edge of the road and began
to make a wide circle instead of heading straight for the hut. There
too the mud was deep: it came up over his shins; but flanking the
huts that were more or less intact, moving around the open space,
little by little he approached. The woman was still yelling for help,
sticking her neck out of a little window of her shack.

'I'm coming. Take it easy!' Tommaso yelled from the mire.

The hardest part came now, at the centre of the clearing, where
the current of water and mud flowed down from the hills.

Tommaso flung himself in, moving both arms like a puppet
to walk, because the water was up to his bellybutton, and the
current, though it didn't look it, was strong and sucked down
towards the river, booming only a few feet away.

Rooting in the muck like a hog, slopping through that stinking
mass, teeth clenched, eyes popping with strain, he came to the
woman's hovel from the other side.

Red-faced, soaked, her hands clasped to her belly, she was
waiting for him: when he got there, she went crazy all of a sudden.
She began raving and running around: 'Let me take something,'
she yelled, 'at least a mattress, a dress ... '

'Listen, I'm not a porter!' Tommaso yelled at her nastily, while she was talking like this, making no move to go. 'Come on, come on, lady. Things are getting worse here!'

'But I'm scared! How can we do it?' she said, bent forward towards all that water, trembling, white, frozen, her hair plastered to her cheeks like so many snakes.

'Come here, stick to me, grab me around the neck!' Tommaso said, dragging her. Meanwhile he had recognized her. She was a whore who worked Montesacro, on the Aniene bridge: her pimp was a friend of his. 'Some joke,' he thought, 'if I drown on account of her!'

'You can't make it!' the woman screamed in a little girl's voice, whimpering, 'Can't you see what it's like, goddammit?'

'We gotta try. Come on.'

He half lifted her on to his back: and she clung to him. As always, in her every situation, whether she laughed or got mad, whether they beat her or not, she was half afraid in earnest, and as for the the other half, it was as if none of it concerned her, she was just amazed at what was happening to her.

'Watch out, there's a ditch. You can't get by!' she warned Tommaso as he struggled in the deep mud, that was trying to drag him away. He couldn't take much more: he was worn out, half dead, and only desperation kept him from dropping.

'Keep your mouth shut!' he yelled at her, 'I know how to get by.'

'Oh, Jeezus, Jeezus, can you make it?' she moaned, trembling.

'Cut the shit!' Tommaso yelled, her hair plastered on his face. 'You want me to drop you on the ground? If you don't shut up, I'll leave you here, and you can fuck yasself!'

Clinging to the rope, he was working desperately towards the embankment, where they were waiting for him; they also drew him along slowly. All sweating, almost splitting at every breath, he reached solid ground. The woman began to act crazy and have convulsions, while the others tried to calm her down and make her sip a little cognac.

Tommaso untied the rope from his waist, sprawled in the mud exhausted, but hunched over with his head down, because he didn't

want them to see the state he was in, without even enough breath
to curse.

Meanwhile a fire department car had arrived from the other
side, from Montesacro, and most of the people were there: the
job was done now, they only had to carry those few bastards who
had remained on this side to Pietralata and put a roof over their
heads. They did it in a hurry, because they had had all the water
they wanted: the firemen and the others carried and led the women,
the kids, the ones in worst shape, while the rain started coming
down in rivers again.

They gave Tommaso two little kids, one maybe three or four
years old, and one six: he carried the smaller one piggyback, the
other he led by the hand.

They were good little kids, God knows what they had been
through already, and they had thoughtful little faces, like old men.
They were cute, all right; they looked alike, because they were
brothers, with black, curly bangs, and big black eyes: but their
faces were pale and grave.

They walked a while in silence, their shoes sinking into the muck:
then the older kid raised his face from the turned-up collar of his
old coat, tattered but still elegant, and looked at Tommaso.

'Now we don't have any house!' he said, 'Where'll they send us?'

'Eh,' Tommaso said, 'nobody's ever died of the cold around here.
Don't worry about that!'

'Was Franco's house washed away, too?' the little boy asked,
after reflecting a while.

'I don't know this Franco,' Tommaso answered, 'but if he lived
here, his house must of gone too, you can count on that!'

'Don't choke me!' he said to the little one, who was clutching
him tight.

'Our houses were down below,' the other one went on, thinking
it over, 'the ones who have high houses, the water doesn't come in!'

'Hey, kid, stop choking me, goddammit. I told you!' Tommaso
shouted.

Slowly they arrived at Pietralata, the rain blown furiously by
the wind, as if the storm were just beginning. For the moment

they carried the homeless people to Party headquarters, which was also half-flooded. The refugees could hardly fit in, sitting on benches, the women with babies in their arms: all were crying, moaning, while outside you could hear the beating of the rain and the thunder, louder than ever.

What is this? The end of the world? Tommaso thought, looking at the scene before him, inside headquarters: one man was sitting on a rolled-up mattress with a kid on his knees: another was on a stool, wringing out his socks, drying his feet; a woman was sick and was crying with people all around her, consoling her. 'What the fuck are you crying for? You think it'll make the rain stop? You're not the only one, you know!'; but she couldn't even hear them, she seemed to be out of her mind: and, like her, there were lots of other women all around, who had lost everything they owned and were now naked as worms. On the table in the bar-room they had put all the infants like a pile of kittens, there must have been thirty at least, one on top of the other, and their mothers standing around watching them, shaking with the cold.

Three or four kids, a bit bigger, had found the flag in some corner, and taking advantage of the fact that nobody was watching them, they played with it, pretending to be Indians.

'Hey, you kids, cut the shit!' Tommaso yelled, seeing them. He went over and took the flag away from them, putting it back in its place, in the corner beside the desk. 'You're think you're home?' he yelled again, furious. 'Fuckoff!'

Nothing had happened: a slum flooded by the rain, a few smashed huts where people lived who, in their lifetime, had been through even worse. But they were all crying, they felt lost, killed. Only in that old red cloth, all soaked and filthy, that Tommaso flung in the corner, in the midst of that crowd of poor bums, there seemed to shine still a bit of hope.

*

The next morning, waking up late, Tommaso felt at once that he wasn't well, that he was dead tired, his bones aching. He couldn't manage to open his eyes, or pull up his knees, to slip out of the bed.

He lay there like a block of wood for a while, thinking. It must have been eleven at least, you couldn't hear any voices or noises, and the weather must have been still lousy, because not much light came in the window. A siren was blowing far away. Come on, pull yourself together! Tommaso told himself, curious to go out into the neighbourhood and see what it looked like, what was happening.

As he made an effort to get up he had to cough, then cough again. Goddammit, he grumbled to himself, disgusted. He coughed again, and his mouth tasted as if he had touched it with a dirty hand: a taste of cold iron, of nails. Tommaso licked his mouth to get rid of that bad taste, and bent over to slip on his shoes. But, instead of going away, the taste of iron got worse, became sweeter. Whaddid I do last night? Eat snot? Tommaso asked himself, passing his tongue over his palate. But then, by chance, his eyes fell on his undershirt, and he saw that it was all covered with red spots. It was blood. In the hospital he had never spat blood. At first it was like a dream: he looked and looked again at those bloodstains, touched them with his finger: it was fresh, sticky.

'What's this?' he said. He was already trembling, already out of his mind. He quickly realized what it was: another coughing fit, worse than the others, shook him, almost laid him flat.

When it was over, he got up to go to the toilet. He was alone in the house, at that hour the others were all off working. As he moved, he realized he could hardly stand on his feet: but he went on to the toilet anyway, to look at himself in the mirror. He was all stained with blood: chin, neck, undershirt. 'Jeezus Christ!'

Swaying, he went into the kitchen, holding on to the walls. He went to the sink, took a rag, soaked it, and began to wipe his face and the undershirt: he rubbed and rubbed until he thought he had got all the spots off. But then came another coughing fit, which he couldn't stop because there was a tickling at the base of his throat, like he had a glowing iron there, and it slammed him about like a strong wind: more blood on his face and chest. Tommaso waited till he had stopped coughing, then he cleaned himself up again.

He stood still for a moment, slumped over the sink, by the open tap and the dirty dishes: the coughing didn't come back, and then, very slowly, after wringing out the rag and soaking it in clean water, he dragged himself to his room and fell again on his bed.

He lay there a long time, motionless, his face staring up, his legs outstretched, the damp cloth on the chair with his clothes. He couldn't think, he was so distraught: he was just waiting, with all his soul, for somebody to come back, his mother, somebody, to help him. But he wasn't kidding himself, he knew what was happening to him, all right. I'm gonna die, he was thinking.

For an hour or more he lay still, not lifting a finger: finally he heard the door open, and his mother came in. 'Ma,' Tommaso said, 'I'm sick. Go get the doctor!'

'Oh, my God!' Sora Maria yelled, seeing him and realizing he was really bad: she looked at him for a moment, not knowing what to say, her mouth trembling, as if she were about to burst into tears.

'Hurry up, go get the doctor, for Chrissake!' Tommaso yelled.

Sora Maria said: 'I'm going, I'm going. Don't worry!' She turned and went out again, almost running, covering her face with her hands. Tommaso lay there, still as before, for almost another hour. Meanwhile his father and brother had come home from work, starving. When they saw dinner wasn't ready and Tommaso was sick, they sat down there in his room and stayed quiet, looking at him every now and then, waiting for the doctor.

He finally arrived, examined Tommaso, touched him all over, asked questions about when he had T.B. It was serious, you could see it was nothing to joke about. Meanwhile Tommaso had another coughing fit, and he coughed and coughed, soaking the rag in his hand with blood, and then a pillow-case his mother had run and taken from the closet, not finding any clean handkerchiefs or towels.

The doctor said it was best to take him to the hospital, and right away. Sora Maria felt her knees trembling; she fell down, her hands on the bed, over her son's body. He was the third they were taking to the hospital, in a year. But there was nothing to be done:

two hours later Tommaso was already in a little bed in the General Hospital.

For two days he was so-so, coughing up blood all the time, but he went on hoping: he had been cured the first time, and he could make it the second, too. He couldn't persuade himself that they would soon be digging a hole for him. Now he knew a bit about hospitals, and he knew what he had to say and what he had to do, to make them respect him. From the first day he made sure that they didn't deprive him of anything that was coming to him. He kept his chin up, his eye alert, fighting against the tickling that came when he was about to gush blood. But, he was getting worse all the time.

On Sunday Irene came to visit him too, with her girl friend Diasira, and with Settimio. She brought him some fruit and a bottle of Marsala, waiting for a moment when his family wasn't there; she put the things on the table, in silence. The other two were quiet, like her.

Thin as a baby under the taut covers, Tommaso could only look out of the window: he didn't say a word.

Subdued as always, Irene stayed there for a while, grieved at looking at him, talking in a low voice to Diasira: then she couldn't restrain herself and, hiding her face in her arm, she began to cry and cry. And since there was nothing but silence in the ward, you could hear her loud crying all around, and everybody turned to look at her. Holding her tight, Diasira tried to calm her, but Irene couldn't control herself, though she was now crying more softly, like a kid: she knew she shouldn't be doing it, that it wasn't right, and she hid her face with one hand, more and more desperate, until they took her away.

The men from the Party came to see him, too: they had already agreed that if Tommaso died ₁they would name the Pietralata section after him because of his brave deed he had done that he was now paying for so dearly. All worn, in bad shape himself, Lello came with them too, and Zucabbo, fresh as an apple that's just fallen off the tree, fat-faced under his dyed curls.

The only news Tommaso had about the neighbourhood was that

a cabinet minister had paid it a visit, seeing the bed of dried mud that covered it. He had made the usual promises, and meanwhile, those who were homeless had been parcelled out among some convents, some schools, where there were already other people from the shacks.

When the older men had said goodbye and gone off, Lello and Zucabbo stayed on a little longer, unable to make up their minds to leave him. In the end Zucabbo pulled a few pears and two bananas from his pocket: that's why they were so embarrassed and didn't know what to say.

'You brought me some fruit?' Tommaso asked. 'You oughtta bring a wreath!'

'Cut the shit, Puzzilli!' Zucabbo said to him, putting the pears and the bananas on the bed: but he started crying, too.

'What the fuck're you crying for? If anybody's gotta cry around here, it's me,' Tommaso said. 'You're not dying, are you?'

Their eyes glistening in their crooks' faces, burned by the sun and by hunger, Lello and Zucabbo kept standing there, not moving.

'Fuckoff!' Tommaso said. 'Instead of staying here and keeping me company, go outside and screw around. It's Sunday!'

He turned his face away and didn't say any more.

But as far as dying went, he decided he was going to die in his own bed at home: and, in fact, it was easy for them to get permission to take him away now. It was a fine day, mild, late September, with the sun shining in a sky without a spot on it, and people talking, singing along the streets, in the new buildings.

When Tommaso was back in his bed, he almost felt he was a little better. After all, they still hadn't come to anoint him; for an hour or so the cough stopped, and he even asked his mother for some of that Marsala Irene had brought him. But then, when night came, he felt worse all the time: he had another fit, coughing blood, coughing, coughing, unable to catch his breath, and it was goodbye Tommaso.

Italian literature from Carcanet

Gabriel D'Annunzio
Halcyon
translated by J.G. Nichols

Natalia Ginzburg
All Our Yesterdays
translated by Angus Davidson
The Things We Used to Say
translated by Judith Woolf
Voices in the Evening
translated by D.M. Low

Giacomo Leopardi
The Canti
Moral Tales
translated by J.G. Nichols

Gabriella Maleti
Bitter Asylum
translated by Sharon Wood

Pier Paulo Pasolini
The Ragazzi
translated by Emile Capouya
Lutheran Letters
translated by Stuart Hood

Cesare Pavese
Disaffections: Complete Poems
1930–1950
a dual-language edition,
translated by Geoffrey Brock

Petrarch
Canzoniere
translated by J.G. Nichols

Leonardo Sciascia
The Council of Egypt
To Each His Own
translated by Adrienne Foulke

Giuseppe Ungaretti
Selected Poems
A dual language edition, translated by Andrew Frisardi

www.carcanet.co.uk

Film books from Carcanet

Philip French
Westerns: Aspects of a Movie Genre

Kevin Jackson (ed.)
The Humphrey Jennings Film Reader

Kevin Jackson
The Language of Cinema

Anthony Lejeune (ed.)
The C.A. Lejeune Film Reader

David Parkinson (ed.)
Mornings in the Dark: The Graham Greene Film Reader

www.carcanet.co.uk

Carcanet has produced some of the best of contemporary writing and handsome editions of classics of all ages: the titles cover a remarkable cultural and political range, and yet have a distinctive Carcanet stamp to them. Margaret Drabble

Carcanet's commitment to publishing work in translation has been matched by an admirable concern to keep lines open to writing in Ireland, Scotland, Wales and America. Seamus Heaney

Carcanet Press publishes one of the most comprehensive and diverse lists of modern and classic poetry in English and in translation, as well as fiction, criticism and film titles.

Visit **www.carcanet.co.uk** to browse a complete list of Carcanet titles, find out about forthcoming books and order books at discounted prices.

Email **info@carcanet.co.uk** to subscribe to the Carcanet e-letter for poetry news, events and a poem of the week.

CARCANET

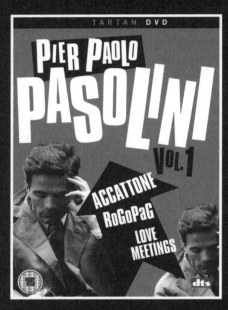
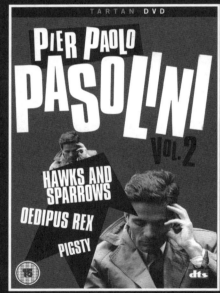